The
BISHOP'S
GRIMOIRE

MICHAEL ANSON'S

The BISHOP'S GRIMOIRE

An Apothecary Greene Procedure

PAGE D'OR
MMXXI

Page d'Or is an imprint of Prosperity Education Limited
Registered offices: 58 Sherlock Close, Cambridge CB3 0HP,
United Kingdom

First published 2021

A catalogue record for this book is available from the British Library

ISBN: 978-1-913825-53-9

Designed by Steph Thelwell
Typesetting and cover design by ORP Cambridge

For further information visit: www.pagedor.co.uk

Ad infinitum et ultra.

For Hannah, for more than words can say

Richard Greene (1716–1793): surgeon, apothecary and proprietor of a museum that attracted the notice of the antiquary and the curious of every denomination. Reproduced from Stebbing Shaw, *History and Antiquities of Staffordshire*, Vol.1 (London, 1798).

One of two surviving engravings of Richard Greene's Museum, Lichfield, published in *The Gentleman's Magazine* of 1788.

A

PARTICULAR, AND DESCRIPTIVE

CATALOGUE

OF THE

CURIOSITIES,

NATURAL AND ARTIFICIAL,

IN THE

Lichfield Museum.

COLLECTED

(IN THE SPACE OF FORTY-SIX YEARS;)

BY

RICHARD GREENE.

THE THIRD EDITION.

LICHFIELD:

PRINTED, AND SOLD, BY JOHN JACKSON.

MDCCLXXXVI.

(PRICE ONE SHILLING).

The title page of Greene's third and final catalogue. 1786. © The Samuel Johnson Birthplace Museum, Lichfield.

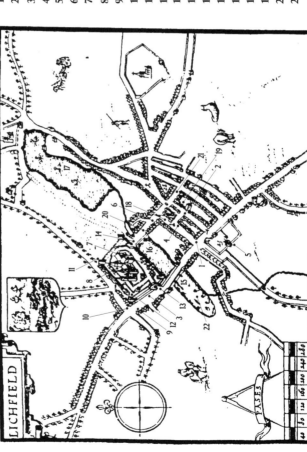

Adapted from Spede's map of Lichfield in 1610. A city virtually unchanged in the mid-18th century. Reproduced with permission from the National Monuments Record Archives.

1 Richard Greene's Apothecary
2 The Ashmole/Blomefield House
3 Erasmus Darwin's House
4 Samuel Johnson's House
5 The Friary, Michael Rawlins
6 Richard Neille's House
7 The Prebendary House
8 The Bishop's Palace
9 Doctor Milley's Hospital
10 The North-West Tower
11 The Bishop's Tower
12 Vicars Close
13 The West Gate
14 The South Gate
15 The Vivarium
16 Minster Pool
17 Stow Pool
18 The Market Place
19 The Guildhall
20 The Dam
21 Greenhill

Loyal and Ancient City

Spede's map of the City of Lichfield from the early part of the 17th century portrays an inconsiderable market town located beside a trio of large meres that separate its small quadrangle of streets from a Cathedral church set within a heavily fortified Close. It was the latter – the medieval walls, moats and two formidable gates – in addition to the singularly strategic location of the little city itself, that brought down upon it the three devastating Civil War sieges that were to utterly wreck 'this great fortress'.

By 1646 the Cathedral church was a roofless shell, its great steeple brought down by parliamentary artillery, its principal defences wrecked by the first use of explosive mines in Britain. So comprehensive was its ruin that wholesale demolition was considered by the Commonwealth parliament in the aftermath of the war. Its future was only finally guaranteed by The Restoration of Charles the Second, when Elias Ashmole – himself a native Lichfeldian, educated at the Cathedral School – led the petitioners for the resurrection of the great building at the heart of 'This Loyal and Ancient City'.

By the middle of the 18th century, its fortunes restored, and now a bustling agricultural and coaching nexus for the East Midlands, its renown as a cultural beacon had spread further still. What one of its most famous sons, the great lexicographer Doctor Samuel Johnson, described as 'a City of Philosophers' would, in fact, produce equally famous sons and a renowned daughter – from within its small ambit. Poetess Anna Seward – 'The Swan of Lichfield' – the precociously accomplished daughter of Canon

Residentiary Seward, presided over the City's formidable literary scene as hostess of her father's grace-and-favour residence, the superbly rebuilt Bishop's Palace within The Close. Her paean to Cook's *Voyages* of discovery was the first, prescient, public recognition of their historic importance.

Seward's equally formidable mentor, Doctor Erasmus Darwin, one of his era's most admired proponents of the natural sciences, provided a ready focus for the Midland's renowned Lunar Society – the intellectual power-house for the region's 'coming men' – the likes of Matthew Boulton, Josiah Wedgwood and Thomas Baskerville. Not a hundred yards from Darwin's stately house beside the ruins of The Close's West Gate was the birthplace of the celebrated actor-manager David Garrick, later the doyen of the London stage, whose reputation would bring even the great theatrical diva of her age, Mrs Sarah Siddons, to perform to rapturous audiences at the City's Guildhall.

Not least, in terms of his inestimable contribution to Lichfield's cultural and intellectual life over half a century, though most certainly the least likely to occupy a uniquely stellar role in the city's fame, was an Apothecary named Richard Greene. Awarded an honorary doctorate in Medicine from the University of St Andrews for his outstanding services to that profession, Greene was, in addition, one of the leading antiquarians and pioneering museum curators of eighteenth-century Britain. In an Age of Enlightenment characterised by a small and select number of aristocratic aesthetes and collectors whose deep pockets and Grand Tours swelled the private collections that adorned their great houses, Richard Greene's Museum, in rooms above his Apothecary shop and accommodation in Lichfield's Saddler Street, were open to all for the price of a few pence admission.

From its beginnings in 1740, when Greene and his wife Theodosia opened their new premises, until its closure on Greene's demise some 50 years later, the collections grew to the extent that several full-page illustrations in *The Gentleman's Magazine* of the

1780's feature the unique assemblage of antiquities, curiosities, arms and armour, clocks, printed ephemera and, most particularly natural history, that had drawn tens of thousands of spellbound visitors over the decades. Greene himself would become a regular and most eclectic contributor to the *Magazine*, encouraged by its sometime editor, his cousin, Samuel Johnson. That Doctor, born less than a hundred yards away from the famous stained-glass windows that would later attract myriad customers through The Apothecary doors, famously commented – admiringly if somewhat ambiguously: "Sir, I would rather have embarked upon the building of a Man-of-War, than undertake such a project."

The astonishing variety and not least, the scholarly identification of the huge collection is preserved in prized copies of the three ever-expanding guide books produced by their curator between 1746 and 1786, still to be found in Lichfield's Johnson Birthplace Museum and in the Salt Library, Stafford.

Just as Richard and Theodosia Greene provide both *The Burning Zone* and the companion volumes *The Bishop's Grimoire* and *The Ashmole Box* with their intriguing central characters, so too do the magnificently eccentric catalogue entries provide a verbatim header to each chapter of the novels.

(1)

A Knot and Crucifix in Silver, richly ornamented with Jewelry Work, fuppofed to have been worn by a Cardinal at Rome, on his Cloak or Mantle. An ancient Crucifix in Silver, fuspended by a Chain, compofed of three hollow filver Beads; the back part may be opened, in which are feperate Cells for Relics, &c.

Eccleshall Castle, Staffordshire. Spring 1766. The tour was going from bad to worse. The regrettable fact that a perennially absent bishop had, reportedly, waved a ringed hand in lordly acquiescence to the proposal that 'visitors of quality' be admitted in order to admire his rural palace was one thing, the actuality of these over-educated gawpers quite another – as a thoroughly disgruntled steward was rapidly deciding.

The realisation that he had greeted the visitors' wholly unexpected arrival with a misbuttoned waistcoat and recent egg stains on a brocaded lapel would only become apparent to him when such incidental mishaps had long paled into insignificance in the face of the day's calamities.

The first of what were to become the afternoon's legion problems was the weather: a perfect blue sky with a proper complement of fluffy clouds and the most unseasonal warmth in living memory. Warmth perfectly acceptable in and of itself, but considerably less so in conjunction with the second week of a drainage programme intended to clear a noisome, centuries-old moat and the castle's attendant marshes. The stench, even the ever loyal functionary had to admit, was so bad as to be almost visible; a miasma hanging across formal gardens, topiary and classical terrace alike; a stench that had met the day's visitors as they were confronted by the occasion's second problem: the transit of the moat's residual ooze across an alarmingly makeshift bridge erected beside its sturdy medieval counterpart. Access to the latter now being blocked by a rubble-filled cart half-emerged from the scaffolded ruin of a gatehouse apparently in the process of demolition by the dozens of labourers swarming about its ivied walls.

Instead of the anticipated rapid transit between their coach and the elegant portal of the great house itself, the passengers were forced to negotiate the alarmingly unsteady span, clinging to grimy, rope balustrades whilst attempting to avoid any downward glances at what lay beneath the rough planking.

In various degrees of disarray, the visitors regrouped on the perfect lawn, to be met by the liveried figure who hurried towards them, attempting, without success, to disguise his perplexity.

"We are expected, I believe?" said the older of two clergymen, clearly aware, already, that they were not but stepping forward from his companions with what appeared to be a folded letter extended to the nonplussed steward.

"His Lordship, your master, assured us of our welcome, today..." He glanced briefly at a pocket watch drawn from his waistcoat and continued, pleasantly, "...at two o'clock in the afternoon. This afternoon. So, here we are."

There was nothing to be done other than a mumbled assent to a visitor obviously not prepared to debate the point, so with all the dignity the steward could muster they were ushered into the cool welcome of a spacious hall, redolent of lavender, beeswax and the memories of winter logs consumed in the stately fireplace.

The smallest member of the foursome, now gazing with interest about them, was a quietly dressed, unremarkable figure obviously relieved to be free of the confining vehicle and the unexpected rite of passage, fanning himself with a slim pamphlet. While a cordial was being summoned for his fellow visitors, he left the group to examine a display of blue and white china on a pair of consoles set against the panelled wall.

Failing to notice a rug spread on the tiled floor, he was suddenly reduced to a flailing welter of arms and legs as it slipped from beneath him, and he fought desperately for balance. It was only the intervention of his nearest companion that averted disaster, though not before a foot had connected with a table edge and come within a heartbeat of dislodging a pair of lidded pots that tottered and slid towards disaster.

In a mixture of apparent solicitude and proprietorial panic the steward rushed forward, showing, the now-stable figure realised, a far greater concern for the china than for him.

"They're armorials, Sir, specially commissioned, only recently arrived from China and three years in the making," their red-faced host blurted, by way of what might have been intended as explanation, but which emerged as petulant accusation. "My Lord would've had my head if they'd been..." He seemed suddenly to remember his appointed role. "...That is, I'm sorry if..." Before he could compound his outburst, the clerical figure who had been standing beside a straight-backed, self-possessed young woman hurried forward, as if to defuse the misfortune of the moment, exclaiming: "Richard, you really must curb your enthusiasms or we shall be declared personae non-grata before we can even begin to take in the wonders of My Lord's Treasure House! I'm sure even Lionel will agree."

With a wan smile, the small man disengaged himself from the providential arm that had saved the situation and, having adjusted a comically skewed wig, turned, disarmingly, to the mortified steward.

"Thankfully, it would appear that both your head and your master's porcelain are safe for the present. I must apologise for my clumsiness, which my wife is forever remarking upon. I shall proceed with caution, be assured."

Richard Greene and the grinning figure of his companion re-joined Canon Seward and his daughter beside the hall's centrepiece, an elegant circular table displaying a large bronze of a Roman charioteer in headlong gallop. With a visible gulp of relief, the Bishop's steward embarked upon what was obviously a well-practised introduction to the tour itinerary.

"In the absence of My Lord, Bishop Cornwallis, I am instructed to welcome you on his behalf to his rural seat and to express His Lordship's regret that you find us in the throes of refurbishment and beautification of this ancient castle."

Greene couldn't help himself: "And would one be correct in assuming that an integral part of His Lordship's scheme of beautification necessitates the demolition of Bishop Langton's ancient gatehouse to his equally ancient castle?"

The steward stiffened and sniffed audibly before responding in an unsuccessful attempt to disguise his annoyance at the interruption: "I am not privy to My Lord Bishop's purposes, Sir, though I can attest to the dangerous condition of that old..."

Lionel Blomefield laid a quietly restraining hand on his companion's arm, speaking for the first time: "I believe we are interrupting your flow, as it were, my good man – though I must share Greene's disquiet at the sight that met our..."

"What we are all saying, of course," Seward interposed, expertly, "is: pray continue; we can scarcely wait to see the wonders you are about to reveal."

At least partially mollified, the steward attempted to regain his theme.

"Built in 1305, by the Bishop Walter de Langton as the rural seat of his Diocese of Lichfield..."

"Our very own," murmured Blomefield. "He also built our..." He was silenced by a sharp glance from the Canon.

"...Responsible also for the construction of the fortification of Lichfield's Cathedral Close," continued the steward stiffly, "and the great bridge across the city's Vivarium..."

"Whose draining we have resisted thus far," added Lionel Blomefield, sotto voce to a companion who tried to ignore him.

"And all these labours executed at a time when His Lordship was also Treasurer of England to King Edward," the steward continued manfully.

"Much as your master, our own dear Bishop, is burdened with The Deanery of Windsor and that of St Paul's simultaneously, in addition to the onerous responsibility of this, his own diocese," said the young woman, with smiling composure, linking arms with her parent as she spoke. "Where do these blessed men find the time and energy, one must wonder? It must surely be to do with what can only be described as little short of a genius for delegation. And, of course, the uncounted broad backs such as yours, gentlemen," – she embraced them all in a guileless gaze – "prepared to shoulder ever-greater burdens in the cause of such elevated servants of the church."

The steward knew that whatever was going on here, he didn't much care for it, so hurried on, staring hard into the middle distance.

"Bishop Langton's castle suffered such violence on behalf of the royal cause during the Great Rebellion that, fifty years on, Bishop Lloyd had little choice but to demolish most of the ruins remaining and build this fine..."

"A process that continues to this day, apparently," said Greene, to no one in particular.

"...House," the steward managed, "with the gardens as we see them today laid down by his successor, Bishop Hough."

"Gardens whose delights we shall have to forego, in the circumstances," added Canon Seward, unconsciously wrinkling his aquiline nose. "Had we been forewarned of the inconvenience to which we are putting His Lordship by such an untimely intrusion, we would have postponed a visit long anticipated."

Seeing the expression on the hopelessly wrong-footed steward, the Canon took mercy and said breezily, "But lead on, pray."

As one grand room led to another, with the party conducted through what appeared to be an ever more costly gamut of elegance ranging from baroque to rococo, from Rubens to Canaletto, the steward – now obviously at ease with his role – read from brief notes pointing out Bishop Cornwallis's additions to the collection. It became rapidly apparent, though, that any works pertaining to classical themes would be immediately claimed by an impossibly erudite young woman, determined to expound, at length, upon their mythology and everything else that sprang into an over-active mind.

Nearing the completion of the tour, now returned to a grand salon overlooking the manicured lawns, the Canon's daughter paused beside a spectacular prospect of the Roman Forum set in a gargantuan gilded frame. After a moment's contemplation of the tumbled grandeur she turned to her companions: "Confronted with even the noblest ruins of antiquity, am I alone in wondering why there appears never to be sufficient funds, or will, to look to our own?"

"Anna..." her father began, a note of reproof in his voice.

"No, Papa, dearest, forgive me, pray, but there must surely be a time when the nurture of our own dear old places, and, not least, the good folk who treasure them as much as we shall ever do, must be taken into account. Why, the Chapter House of our own Cathedral, His Lordship's own cathedral, is as sorry a wreck as the estate cottages we passed not a mile from Eccleshall's gates."

"As is my porch at St. Mary's," said Blomefield with feeling. "Why, even the swifts have fled from it."

"And apparently Eccleshall's venerable gatehouse," added Greene, with a smile of pure mischief, "though that is more in the nature of a rookery one would imagine, while it still stands."

The steward could no longer contain himself: "We are instructed on its dismantling following the unfortunate damage caused to His Lordship's coach at the time of his last visit."

"Would that have been early last year or was it in '64?"

enquired Seward mildly, "Time does so fly by."

Ignoring the implication, the steward blustered on in an injured tone: "A chunk of masonry the size of my hand fell and broke one of the coach-lamps, Sir, as my master's coach drove beneath. It could have been a grave accident."

"Indeed, it might have scratched the paintwork," added Greene helpfully. "So what alternative was left to his Lordship but to obliterate the offending monument?"

"Just so, Mr Greene, just so," came the grateful response.

"Well, on that happy note, I believe we should take our leave," Seward interposed briskly.

"We have a long and dusty road ahead of us."

As they stood in the grand doorway once more, the Canon dug into a coat pocket, producing a purse from which he extracted several coins, pressing them into the steward's ready hand.

Just as he was about to make their farewells, a rumbling crash, shouts of alarm and a bloodcurdling scream carried across the lawn from the wreckage of the gatehouse by the bridge. A complete corner of dressed stonework had collapsed, and a bloodied, half-buried figure could be discerned struggling weakly amidst the choking dust-cloud of rubble.

Greene was already running towards the scene, shouting back to the astonished steward, "Boiling water, cloth for bandages, brandy! Quickly! For pity's sake!"

Blomefield turned to the dumbstruck steward: "Mr Greene is a surgeon-apothecary. Do as he says!"

Seeming to awaken from a stupor, the steward turned wordlessly and hurried back into the house, shouting instructions.

Though moved as little as possible beyond the danger of further collapse, the injured man now lay propped against the balustrade of the terrace; head, shoulder and both hands bandaged in torn bedsheets, his breath coming in hoarse wheezes, his eyes wild with shock. With propriety cast aside, Anna Seward, careless of grass stains on her silken skirts, knelt beside him gently dabbing at the pallid skin with vinegar-dampened cloths.

He bent sideways, suddenly, gasping with pain, before vomiting onto the mown grass.

"Concussion," said the Apothecary with complete authority, turning to the concerned group gathered around them. "Does he live locally?"

"Less than a mile, Sir," a voice responded. "Us can get 'im 'ome on a barrow, like."

"Well, gently does it, if you do. Avoid jolting him. He must rest completely for several days, and drink plenty of well-boiled water."

"That'll be the day," another voice volunteered, met with relieved laughter from the assembled work-gang.

Greene turned to the hovering presence of the steward: "I would normally have my bag of tricks to hand, but not today. I suggest that your master would encourage you to send to Stafford for medical opinion once we have left. Fatalities on one's premises, whilst engaged upon one's business, do have a tendency to create much inconvenience, as I'm sure you will appreciate. I feel certain His Lordship will not begrudge the cost of comfrey balm and poultices for this poor fellow."

"No, Mr Greene; certainly, Mr Greene. I'm sure my master will be most..."

A shout interrupted him.

A dust-smeared figure, eyes bright in his filthy face, was coming towards them, stepping from the last of the strewn rubble. It held a sizeable object across spread hands.

Recognising the approaching man, the steward said: "It's Lowe, Tom Lowe." He gestured around the assembled workmen. "He's the gaffer here."

"Found this, Sir," said the dust-caked man to the steward. "Right behind where all that sh... stonework fell on our Will. In some sort of cupboard, like. Old as the 'ills, I reckon; like this." He held out the dull metal object, a box by the look of it, its surface pitted with rust and black with spiderwebs.

"Treasure, or what d'ye reckon then, Sir? Something in it for poor old Will and us lads, then?"

As if a veil dropped upon him, the steward within an instant was all haughtiness and cold authority. "Whatever might be contained within, if indeed there is anything but spiders – it is His Lordship's property and, most importantly, His Lordship's business! Send two men off with your fellow and put the rest back to work. Quickly now, His Lordship has not employed you to idle and gossip."

With barely concealed disgust, the foreman turned to his men, nodding them back to the ruin, then walked away without another word. Two remained to gingerly lift the prone figure into a barrow, before picking their way back through the broken arches.

With some care, the steward placed the box on the stone parapet before turning to the visitors: "Well, I must not detain you, gentlemen and Miss Seward. I shall..." He got no further.

"What we shall do now is to return to a degree of privacy, the better to examine the discovery," said Canon Seward with quiet authority. "As a churchman of some seniority I have not the slightest hesitation in acting *in loco Cornwallisis*, so to speak. By happy coincidence you have the double blessing of not only an excellent medical man in our Greene, but also an antiquarian of equal note. Your master would have it no other way." Before anyone could disagree, he placed the box in the steward's unresisting hands and led the way back into the Castle.

With the Roman charioteer set aside and the box now standing upon a hastily laid cloth, the Canon spread his hands, saying, "Well, Mr Museum-Keeper, what do we make of this?"

Richard Greene was already absorbed. Just as Seward had assumed command of the situation out on the lawn, now his own moment had arrived: "We shall need a blade of some sort to free the lid, and perhaps a drop of lamp-oil to loosen the hasp and the hinges – if they will shift at all, that is."

Within moments the box, now brushed clear, stood amidst

a scattering of rust-flakes and crawling things seeking another refuge. Greene peered closely at the lid, before requesting a lit candle be held for him.

"There's a faint scratch-carving, clogged-up at present; an armorial, from what one can discern. It will be better revealed with some polishing."

The lid, once freed, opened with little difficulty, and – as one – their noses caught a whiff compounded of great age, mildew and some faint, unguessable scent. None of it pleasant.

A book, its cover limp and dulled with antiquity filled the space as if made for it. Loosely knotted thongs of hide or of some sort of cloth wrapped the bindings, partially concealing a lone symbol burned, or engraved, into the stuff of its covering.

With a murmur of fascination, Seward, standing at the Apothecary's shoulder, bent forward and reached to untie them, only to be stopped, forcefully, by Greene.

Seeing the surprise in his old friend's face, Greene raised a hand in apology and said quietly: "Forgive me, but I rather think it would be better not to touch this even lightly – if at all."

"That," he pointed to the partially obscured symbol, "tells me so. If I am reading it correctly, this really is most peculiar; most peculiar indeed."

(2)

Fronting the WINDOW. An antique Painting, many years
in the poffeffion of the refpectable family of ARDEN, was
presented to the Museum, by the late Mrs Arden, relict of
Henry Arden, Esq, of Longcroft juxta Yoxal, in the County
of Stafford. It has been, undoubtedly, an Altar Piece to a
domestic Chapel or Oratory; and is fuppofed, by the attitudes
and colouring, to be more than three hundred years old.

Lichfield. April 1766. At the best of times, breakfast in the
Greene household was rarely a leisurely affair, given the many,
various and unpredictable demands made upon husband and wife.
Below what Theodosia Greene stoically described as their evermore circumscribed living accommodation, lay the Apothecary
premises from which their partnership operated, whilst above,
expanding into long-abandoned bedrooms, attics, landings,
stairways, corridors, each nook and every cranny, Richard Greene's
Lichfield Museum of Curiosities (natural and artificial) had grown
like a living thing over the twenty-six years of their joint tenure of
the property in Saddler Street.

This morning, today being her master's birthday, was fondly
supposed to have been an exception to a meal so invariably
hurried as to provide his housekeeper with daily evidence of her
employers' cavalier attitude to household proprieties and the easily
bruised sensibilities of the domestic treasure that she considered
herself to be. Margery was, thus, hurt but unsurprised, when her

employer managed little more than smoked fish, devilled kidneys, eggs and a pork collop before pecking his wife on an upturned cheek and expressing the need to hurry off to The Close in order to catch Canon Seward before his departure to officiate at a county baptism.

"As ever, your beefsteak and oyster pie looks irresistible, Margery, but resist it I must. The Canon's summons came so early as to sound most pressing. It will provide us with a supper to anticipate with relish, will it not my dear?"

"With relish," echoed Theodosia, avoiding eye-contact with the guardian deity of their household world. "Do try to be home before then, though, Richard. There are, I believe, some gifts to be unwrapped – though from whom I cannot imagine. What could possibly be given to a man who has long possessed everything his heart could desire?"

He left, grinning contentedly, to the sound from below stairs of pots and pans being banged with more than usual vehemence.

Several days of unremitting business had elapsed since the return from Eccleshall, though scarcely an hour had passed without the Apothecary's memory turning to the drab tome in its long-hidden box. The first sight of it still prickled, unaccountably, in his mind's eye as he hurried along the Dam causeway towards what little remained of the South Gate of the Cathedral Close. 'At least you managed to put up a long and brave fight for it,' he thought, gazing at the pocked stumps that remained of its towers as he passed through them, 'as opposed to being demolished simply to beautify the view!'

The experience of Eccleshall, its smug opulence and its absentee landlord, rankled even more now as he passed the refurbished walls of a great church whose salvation seemed to have been guaranteed only at the cost of ghastly cement-render on its ancient walls and the removal of most of those vestiges of antiquity that had remained after the devastation of three sieges.

Now, though, approaching the stately entrance to the Bishop's

Palace – the Seward residence these many years past – he felt strangely unsure of his emotions, feeling certain that there could be only one reason for today's summons. Anticipation? Yes, without a doubt, but also a profound disquiet, a nagging unease that had accompanied each memory of that drab book and its place of concealment. For it was here, now, in these most genteel and blameless surroundings. A thing, Greene felt with queasy certainty, that belonged in darkness – to darkness – its purposes left unspoken, its potency left untested, untouched.

Now, here he was, expected – no doubt – to explain himself and his immediate aversion to an ancient relic. More to the point, perhaps, required to explain why he had insisted so forcefully that it could not possibly remain at the place of its unhappy discovery that Seward had little option but to override the protestations of an affronted steward and insist it accompany the visiting party back to Lichfield Cathedral. With obvious reluctance the Canon – deferring to his companion – had penned a terse letter of explanation and reassurance that the discovery was now in safe hands. Once placed in the functionary's hand for transmission to his absent master, it had also served to assure the resentful servant that its safekeeping would be guaranteed. Seward's parting reassurance had been that he would be immediately forwarding his own communication to the Bishop, their master.

The return journey from Eccleshall had been as hot, dusty and tiring as anticipated – particularly following the events of that malodorous afternoon – though by tacit consent the book and its container had been wrapped and stowed away in a capacious satchel up with the coachman, rather than accompanying them in the cramped interior as they rattled and jolted homewards. By equally tacit agreement his trio of companions had refrained from pressing the Apothecary about his reaction to the discovery after he had quietly insisted that time and appropriate space were required before he could, or would, expand upon his initial reaction to what was a find of some note.

And now, here it was again, visible on a table set in the room's graceful bay, as his host welcomed the Apothecary into the library with his accustomed warmth.

"Richard, had I but thought to consult Anna before sending my ill-timed request this morning, I should not have intruded upon what I am now informed is your birthday. Do please forgive me, even if your dear wife will not!"

Greene smiled disarmingly in response, "We are of that long-wed condition where such feasts are almost always transferable, Canon. My housekeeper would disagree, but then that is her principal role in the Greene household."

He was amused to see Seward glance towards the door before replying: "You are scarcely alone in that, my dear fellow. As a tribe they can be quite terrifying when crossed."

Thankful that he alone had heard the word 'tribe', the Apothecary looked past his host to the table in the window.

"So, here we are," he said lamely, reluctant to renew his acquaintance with what lay on its polished top. "This is what you have in mind, is it not?"

"Indeed, indeed," murmured the Canon, "though it has sat untouched since our return. Your reluctance to engage with it left no small impression on any of us, Richard. You of all men are generally so avid, so endlessly curious when confronted with antiquity in all its forms that you have me quite confounded, I must admit."

Knowing now that there was little alternative, the Apothecary walked across to the bay, turning back to the cleric as he came to the table. "I suppose that it was the context of its uncovering that played a part in my reaction – a Bishop's Palace, no less." He smiled without humour. "But if my first impression is proved correct, the actuality of what this box contains will outweigh all else. You will want me to unwrap and open it, Canon." It was not a question. He was already removing a pair of kid gloves from a pocket.

"Richard, you will explain your singular reluctance, I have no doubt, though I can assure you on one point at least. The engraving upon the lid is sufficiently discernible that I have been able to identify it with certainty." He gestured towards a well-thumbed volume open on another of the room's tables. "It is a blazon belonging to Bishop Walter de Langton – of that there can be no doubt. As to its contents..."

Making no move to lift the pitted lid, Greene said quietly: "Well, Canon, that is less reassuring than you may imagine. If I am correct, we have here what once was known as a *grammaire* – that which the French began to call a Grimoire some centuries ago – a book of ritual magic. A book of instructions for the conjuration of spirits, the binding of demons; a handbook for cursing, divination and the casting of spells. And, here and now, all bound up in a bishop's box." – he gestured about him towards the surrounding Close – "Though not just any bishop, Canon. Might this be the rub?" With that he opened the box.

The small figure stood absolutely still; absorbed as he stared into the box. "You have not opened this since the castle, Canon? That is what you said, is it not?" Seward nodded, puzzled, his brow furrowing in concern as he joined Greene to peer within. The bindings that had partially obscured the symbol on the drab cover now lay to one side, unfastened, the image now revealed in full.

"The Seal of Solomon," said Greene. "I regret to say that I was correct in my first impression."

"And hence your obvious apprehension, Richard?" It was scarcely a question.

Greene stood, lost in thought, before replying.

"As we both know, Canon, the origins of so many of our most revered beliefs, our most dearly held tenets, are lost in an antiquity so distant as to be barely comprehensible to our present world in any form other than faith. Thus, it being impossible to quantify the potency of a symbol such as this – or any other ancient sigil, for that matter – we must rely on what little information survives to us of its original purpose." He pointed to the cover: "As you will be well aware, Canon, the Old Testament informs us that such was the unremitting severity of demonic attack upon the construction of Solomon's great temple in Jerusalem that he was presented with a divine gift, an intervention by Jehovah no less, of a symbol so potent it would bind the forces of darkness as nothing else could." He looked at the Canon's impassive face. "And here it is. What, to the best of my limited knowledge, has long been regarded as the most powerful safeguard an occultist can employ, whether drawn out upon a conjuror's floor to create an impassable defence against his summonings, or, as employed here, to bind whatever was believed to be contained within its pages."

Scarcely aware of his action, he closed the lid before continuing, "I should perhaps add that it is widely held as an article of faith – though I probably use that word ill-advisedly in this context – that such books have an innate power, some dark animus all their own – quite apart from whatever use they might be put to."

"The very fact that they have been invested with such perverted belief would explain their wholesale destruction at various times in history, as I recall," replied Seward, "let alone the suppression of whatever horrors they purported to contain. Uncounted souls will have been sent to the fire for possession of just such.

"And now we are confronted with what we must assume to have been Bishop de Langton's very own," responded the Apothecary. "Although we can also assume His Lordship to have been far too elevated a personage to be concerned with the grubby business of common law."

"One might reasonably suppose so," said the Canon with a tight smile, "if of a cynical persuasion, but my reading, earlier, revealed that His Lordship's extramural activities did not pass completely unnoticed."

"How so?" responded Greene, intrigued.

"There is a bald mention that whilst in Rome he was arraigned on charges of 'witchcraft and divination' in a trial that would appear to have lasted the best part of two years. There is, unfortunately, no other mention of the circumstances or their outcome, and I have exhausted my sources in the search."

"So, you already had an idea that..?"

Greene got no further, before the Canon gently interposed: "Some few years after the opening of your business here in the city, and well before I had made the pleasure of your acquaintance, my slight authorial talents produced an appropriately slight volume entitled: 'The conformity between Popery and Paganism'. It must be twenty years ago now that I think on it."

Registering his listener's surprise, he continued: "Not perhaps a title – or a subject – calculated to generate any widespread degree of dissemination, but a labour which necessitated investigation into many of the less well-trodden byways of belief and superstition, though," he smiled modestly, "scarcely a work that anyone of your cultivated tastes and discrimination could be expected to have encountered."

"And here was I, standing in your own library and pontificating on matters of arcane lore with all the authority of a pedantic schoolboy. You must think I am..."

They were interrupted by a timid knocking at the door. "Enter Janet. I had thought Cook intended us to talk ourselves hoarse."

A maidservant came in carrying a laden tray. "You'll take tea, Richard, before I have to take my leave? Just over there, thank you Janet; in the window. There's plenty of room on the table, so we'll enjoy the view."

Seward approached the elegant display of teapot, milk-jug and accompanying dishes with proprietorial relish, though stopped, nose wrinkling, to peer at the contents of the jug.

"Janet!" he called sharply, turning back to the disappearing servant who paused in the doorway.

"This is the second time today that we have been served spoiled milk. It simply will not do! You will ask Mrs Price to attend upon my daughter as soon as she may. I am leaving shortly."

The girl, obviously on the verge of tears, couldn't help herself, blurting: "But it was fresh as you like when I left the kitchen, Sir, honest it was; Cook's just making a custard."

The Canon stopped her. "Thank you, Janet, that will be all. We shall make do here. Take this with you." She scurried out without further delay.

"It's the strangest thing, Richard, just one thing after another since we got back. Anyone would think we'd been away for a month rather than a day's jaunt to Eccleshall. Even the dogs are acting up, let alone high jinks in lower places below stairs."

The Apothecary banished the thought that had sprung to mind, resolutely avoiding so much as a further glance at the box in the window.

"I really should not detain you, Canon. It's to Yoxall you're bound this afternoon, is it not?"

"Yes, you're right, Richard. We should perhaps continue our deliberation once another little soldier of Christ has been safely baptised. I shan't burden you with any suggestion that you take this," – he nodded towards the closed box – "to examine in the privacy of your museum?" He could not disguise a hopeful, questioning note to his words, before hurriedly adding: "No, of course not. I shall have to contact the Bishop with some despatch, just as his majordomo will have doubtlessly done by now. We shall see what His Lordship has to say on the matter."

Having made his farewells, Greene was leaving the paved forecourt when a figure turned in from the Cathedral Green, a pair of spaniels straining at their leads as they came towards him. Anna Seward waved a greeting as they met, restraining the dogs with some difficulty.

"I believe birthday greetings are in order, Mr Greene! Many happy returns!" Before he could respond she yanked at the straining leads: "One could only wish that one's own return was not likely to end in tears as soon as one reaches home. This pair race back to the idea of feeding only to be dragged whimpering across the threshold once arrived! I simply don't know what's got into them. They're as happy as skylarks normally, but perhaps a natural disaster is imminent. Are there active volcanoes in Staffordshire one wonders?"

With another wave, the Canon's daughter hurried on, leaving a still-speechless Apothecary with much pause for thought, not least in the half-remembered recollection of a troubled dream. A memory in which he had watched, helpless, as thongs like living things, serpents with a life all their own, had unwound themselves to free a drab volume they had bound.

It had been difficult to return to sleep.

He hurried home just as the rain began, sweeping in gusted curtains across The Close.

(3)

ITEM

An horizontal Section of the stock of the Mulberry Tree,
planted by Shakespear, at Stratford upon Avon; this curiosity
was presented to the Museum, by Mrs Gastrel. it is six inches
diameter. A Powder Flask of an uncommon make; covered
with Crimson Velvet, and decorated with gilt Metal; presented
with her own hands, by the late Countefs of Donegal.

Lichfield. 7ᵗʰ April. "For Pity's sake Richard, will you stop telling
me 'It's no more than a bad sprain!' It is my bad sprain – as I am
only too aware. Should I expect any less consideration than you
lavish upon all and sundry?"

"My dear, all I was trying..."

"Then try harder Mr Greene; there are times when 'matter-
of-fact' is not the right prescription for a wife who would happily
throw something at you if only a missile was to hand."

The bustling intervention of a housekeeper bearing a steaming
bowl provided a blessed respite to the harried Apothecary, scarcely
returned from his morning rounds to discover a wife newly fallen
from a step ladder in the stock room below.

"Nothing that my bone broth won't put right, Mistress," said
Margery briskly, before glaring at Greene. "Shouldn't have been
up ladders in the first place, if you ask me, not with able-bodied
men lolling about the shop, never there when you need..."

"Thank you, Margery," Theodosia said, "I am sure that your
treatment will be all we've come to expect." With a righteous

shrug of acknowledgement, the aproned figure swept out.

"Ah yes," said Greene breezily, when the footsteps on the stairs had faded: "Corpse Soup, just what the doctor ordered! If it were in a larger bowl you could always bathe your ankle in it."

For a moment, Theodosia Greene hovered between fury and helpless laughter. Fortunately for her husband, their shared and long-standing aversion to the foul-smelling broth carried the day with little opposition. "Oh Richard, this hurts quite enough already without putting my toenails at risk of dissolution. Make me feel better, please."

The last was said in such a small voice he thought his heart would melt. Then suddenly all business, he declared, "I shall send to Donegal House for ice, I'm sure they'll oblige. His lordship will scarcely begrudge a cold compress, even if he deigned to notice."

Once a maid had returned from the deepest cellar of the grand townhouse that sat cheek by jowl against the Guildhall, and her precious bundle transformed into a wrapped compress, Theodosia sat back in their parlour with a look of relief as the soothing chill went to work. Half an hour later, now with her inflamed ankle expertly anointed and tightly bound, she managed a tired smile at the well-loved figure kneeling beside her chair.

"You manage to appear so unperturbed when I turn into a spitting harpy, Richard, that I am forced to wonder whether it has become an all-too-regular occurrence?" She reached out a pale, long-fingered hand to lay upon his arm. He smiled up at her before clambering to his feet. "Lest the staff get the impression that I am genuflecting in contrition, my dear," he said archly, pretending to dodge away from her. Theodosia pointed to the mantelpiece.

"I have had no chance to mention it, but a letter has arrived for you, you infuriating man." He turned to claim it.

"It came with the London coach this morning."

"Ah, I know this hand," he said, smiling. "Cousin Johnson. It will doubtlessly contain a banker's draft for many hundreds of guineas in payment for my most recent article in *The Magazine!*"

"Oh, would chance not be a fine thing, husband? We should be rich beyond the dreams of avarice were you to receive proper recompense for your countless enthusiasms. I wonder at times whether you wear a sign announcing 'free-for-all' around your neck that I alone fail to see."

Grinning, he opened the folded package with a flourish, scanning its contents before announcing: "No draft, but an invitation, no less!"

" 'Less' being the operative word here, husband, though that comes as no surprise. Invitations cost nothing – which would seem entirely in character with your cousin's reputation. To what, pray, does he summon you?"

Squinting at the text through eyeglasses procured from a waistcoat pocket, the Apothecary read:

The erudition flaunted in your article on the purported relics of Shakespeare in your possession has come to the attention of The Club, members and associates of which – notably one Garrick of Lichfield notoriety – would have you attend one of our weekly confabulations. I can scarcely gainsay such an assembly of rogues, so shall you come? Our gathering on Monday next would be opportune as the said Garrick is planning a most particular thespian divertisement the following day to which he insists you will be most welcome. Their Majesties are, apparently, proposing to grace the event with their attendance and will doubtless remark upon your absence should you fail to appear. I shall attend to your decent accommodation and well-being, and remain, cousin,
Your servant, Samuel.

"Richard, since we both know you will go, do please spare me your equivocations and the to-ing and fro-ing that such situations usually bring about. It is infuriating on a good day and will test

even my sweet temper and wifely indulgence on one such as this."
She raised an admonitory finger before he could utter a word,
continuing: "During business hours I shall be installed in a chair
down below, issuing commands and the occasional word of
encouragement to our staff and the most gracious of welcomes to
our customers. No-one will even notice your absence. So, that's all
arranged, is it not, Richard? When shall you leave?"

Knowing total defeat and a back-handed compliment when
confronted by them, the Apothecary – attempting to hide his
delight – managed his best attempt at a rueful smile.

"Well, if you think you can manage, my dear?"

"Oh, we little women can sometimes struggle by when our
valiant menfolk are off slaying dragons and bringing home bacon.
I shall endeavour to be a model of pluck."

"Saturday morning's coach, then, I think," he said, with what he
hoped was less than indecent haste. "That would get me to Samuel
for late morning or early afternoon on Sunday – there being no
departures from here on the Sabbath. A Monday departure would
be too late to leave in the circumstances. A return on Wednesday
morn should get me home by early afternoon on Thursday, in good
time for whatever may be pressing and require my attention."

"There, that wasn't too difficult was it, husband? You can be a
model of brevity and resolution when I put my mind to it. Now,
about this club?"

(4)

Sixth SHELF A fine Rhinoceros Beetle, on a Pedestal of
Mahogany, covered with a Bell of Flint Glafs. A small human
Faetus, dried. A starved Swallow, both covered in Glass. Fragment of
a Rock of Granite, found in a Morafs, near the Bay of the Gulph of
Finland, by Count Carburi and brought to Ruffia for the purpofe of
erecting a Statue of the Emperor Peter the Great; length of the Rock
42 feet, breadth 27, height 21 feet, weight of the Rock, 3000000 lb.

London. 13th April. Following a night's stay at Towcester,
remarkable only for its cost and lack of home-comforts, an
indecently early start after a cursory breakfast saw the London-
bound passengers back en route by seven the next morning.
Whilst the unmitigated awfulness of the southbound roads was
nothing new to most of the bone-shaken travellers, even Greene's
unspoken oath fervently resolving to avoid all and any such
purgatorial travelling for evermore, melted at the first distant
prospect of the City's spires – bright against a Spring-blue sky –
as a frisson of anticipation and delight swept over him.

Their arrival at Holborn plunged the descending passengers
into the everyday cacophony of the capital's streets – no respecters
of Sabbath proprieties either visible or audible to the small, excited
man who pushed his way from the coaching-yard of the Horns
Inn out through the bustle and jostle to the broad street beyond.

He knew from Cousin Johnson's directions that his route
lay down the length of Shoe Lane, following its dog-leg course
towards Fleet Street and the still-distant Thames, *thus avoiding the
present stench and clamour at the foot of Ludgate Hill whilst all that*

remains of that noisome ditch so mis-called 'fleet' is decently buried.

With all too recent recollections of the putrescent crossing of Eccleshall's vestigial moat he was happy to follow this advice, recalling as he came out onto the thoroughfare of a blamelessly paved Fleet Street, lines from a wonderfully descriptive poem recalled from school on just that 'noisome ditch' – it being just the kind of thing that boys remembered when all else was lost:

Sweepings from Butchers' stalls, Dung, Guts and Blood,
Drown'd puppies, stinking Sprats, all drench'd in mud
Dead Cats and Turnip-Tops come tumbling down the Flood.

"Mmm, poor metre," he said to himself, grinning, only realising he had spoken aloud when an oncoming figure rapidly left the pavement ahead of him and crossed the road, eyes averted.

The Apothecary's previous visit to Johnson had been to the lexicographer's rather grand house in Gough Square, a home relinquished with no small regret when his cousin had been more-than-usually beset by financial adversity some seven or eight years earlier. This had necessitated removal to the smaller, less imposing house in Bolt Court, which was the weary traveller's present destination. Since what now felt uncomfortably akin to far-off days to the striding man, not only had his altogether remarkable relative's fame burgeoned to an ever-greater degree, but so too his finances. The award of an annual pension of a princely £300 per annum little more than four years previously had so transformed the life of the extended Johnson household, that their breadwinner could pursue his myriad interests and inspirations without the threat of penury that had once been such a constant and unwelcome companion to his ceaseless labours. Even the ongoing success of his great Dictionary of a decade past had failed to provide that long-sought security once all its attendant fees and costs had been settled. Despite Theodosia Greene's less than charitable sentiments towards a relative she had yet to meet, her husband knew that here was a man touched not only with greatness but one possessing an unmatched generosity of spirit.

As the Apothecary neared Bolt Court and the welcome he knew would await him, his thoughts drifted back, unbidden, to a bleak March day in Lichfield just short of thirty years earlier. There had been scant welcome in the Johnson house that day, only tears and bitter recriminations, as the very heart went out from the life of the bookseller's widow Sarah.

On a brief, unannounced visit, Richard Greene had been visiting the city of his birth that day on business for his apprentice-master, an apothecary of some standing at Shrewsbury. Intending little more than a to pay his respects to the family he had scarcely seen since he had begun his studies three years earlier, he had entered the sparsely stocked shop only to be met by sounds of mounting hysteria from beyond the closed door to the household. Rushing through from the deserted premises, he came upon a sight that remained only too vivid to this day: scuffed, down-at-heel shoes on dangling legs in urine-stained breeches: his cousin Nathaniel Johnson, the youngest son of the house, hanging, crook-necked, tongue lolling from gaping blue lips, his spindly, awkward body swaying in the stairwell as vain attempts were being made to grasp and support it; goggling, fish-eyes sightless above a clumsily tied noose.

Shouting for a ladder to be brought, unaware even of who brushed past him to fetch it; fixated upon the dreadful sight, Greene along with other hands managed to cut the pathetic burden from its rope and bear the sagging doll-like corpse through to the nearest room. The pallid, withdrawn young man, hopelessly inadequate other than in the ever-less frequent company of the elder brother he worshipped, had been driven beyond despair only hours earlier. Samuel – in company with his erstwhile student David Garrick – having made his bluff, awkward farewells to a distraught mother and brother, had hurriedly departed on their walk to London, towards an unguessable future to be faced by two young men with exactly fivepence-halfpenny between them, but a departure lent wings by a shared conviction of their respective genius.

So, in the here and now, standing before an unfamiliar front door possessing rather less gravitas than that of Gough Square perhaps – but elegant by comparison with most doors of his Lichfield acquaintance – Greene prayed quietly that in the years since they had last met face to face, his bear-like cousin had not become a prey to his own celebrity. The Apothecary was many things to many people, but long ago he had decided with a firmness few could sustain, that he would be Country Cousin to none of them – famous cousins included. He need not have concerned himself.

As he had expected, he was ushered in by the familiar figure of Francis Barber, though before the tall black man could even take his coat or bag, the large dishevelled figure of Cousin Samuel bore down upon both, squeezing past to pump the visitor's hand, the other attempting to straighten a wig being busily tugged askew by the cat on his shoulder.

"Cousin, welcome! Their Majesties will he hugely relieved!" Abandoning any attempt at restraining the cat he shrugged both it and the wig to which it was attached onto a hall settle adding, "Don't let Hodge onto your shoulder if you value your ears: he thinks they're playthings placed exclusively for his pleasure. She's as bad," he beamed, scooping up the tortoiseshell twining about their feet, "Though Lily just thinks they're there for the licking."

After a cursory tickle of the cat's stomach, he put her aside to take Greene's elbow and guide him along a narrow, panelled corridor and into a comfortably jumbled back parlour. The entirety of its surfaces was strewn with spread broadsheets, smudged pages the visitor recognised as printers' proofs, and all set off by a large piece of unfinished knitting draped over the back of a fireside chair. Gesturing towards the unguessable thing suspended between needles, Johnson exclaimed theatrically: "Will you just look at the chaos wrought by womankind the moment a man's back is turned!" words boomed out solely for the benefit of the smiling bonneted figure now advancing to meet the guest.

Greene smiled in recognition, and extended his hand in greeting: "Miss Porter, as patient as ever in the face of ingratitude and the chaos wrought by the Creative Muse!" She bobbed a slight curtsy acknowledging the graceful barb, then turned back on her stepfather, the delighted Doctor, whose huge frame rocked and twitched as the full lips, in an alarmingly pock-marked face, beamed at the riposte.

"D'you see, m'dear? Hopelessly provincial and Greene though he may be, this Cousin of mine can feint and lunge with the best of them! What did I tell you? Sabres at dawn, I can see it now, unless I can pacify the beast in him!"

"I believe dinner will be ready for five as you asked, Samuel," she responded with a gentle smile, "I shall go and check on its progress, if you gentlemen will excuse me?"

"D'you know, Richard, I miss her dear mother as much today as I ever did. It will shortly be fifteen years since I lost Tetty and I have never ceased to blame myself for her death. Dictionary, dictionary, damned dictionary was all I could think of, before it all drove her from me. No book should ever take the place of a living, breathing love, least of all one published at little profit for the benefit of scribblers and schoolmasters!"

"Whilst I would be the first to applaud your sentiments on the place of love in our lives, Cousin – in mine alone without doubt – you do yourself grave injustice as to the value of all you've wrought. Even had there been no great lexicon, your Shakespeare works of last year alone, have set a tarnished and often misread record straight. Those eight volumes will be held as the best and most insightful delving into the Bard's mind – his very genius – that I shall be ever likely to see in this lifetime. Frankly, your achievement in decoding his allusions, his ellipses and proverbs as no more and no less than being part and parcel of a common tongue, a colloquial tongue, restores his greatness to people rather than simply to dry-as-dust scholars and pedants such as me. By insisting upon a patrician mode of speech as the only acceptable form of discourse, surely, we miss all those quirks and quiddities of language to our great detriment? I believe that in their vitality they should remain as much a living part of our language today as they ever did then."

Suddenly abashed, Greene halted. "By all that's good, I do believe I have been pronouncing! Please forgive me, Samuel. I run away with myself on occasion."

Johnson waved a huge hand in good-natured dismissal: "For all that the old scribbler shall ever remain lacking in morality, careless with his plot-crafting and often vulgar in the extreme, your sentiments were prettily said and do not go unappreciated, Cousin. I remember now why I agreed to The Club's tiresome pleas for your attendance tomorrow! But this talk of 'dry-as-dust' prompts me to offer you a more tangible welcome. My men in St. James' – brothers no less – provide a half-drinkable solution to dryness of the throat, so perhaps once you are refreshed and made moderately presentable, we shall address that problem. Francis will have taken your bag to a lavishly appointed guest room to the right of the back-stairs; it will doubtless spoil you for Staffordshire."

With a spring in his step, Richard Greene managed without difficulty to find his room, after an appreciative survey of the stairs, landing and corridors. Momentarily uncertain which of two corridors would lead him towards 'the back stairs', he was pausing by an extraordinary charcoal study of his host, dimly lit by the afternoon sun, when the familiar voice boomed from the stair-head behind him: "Reynolds swears that the proper daub is not far behind, though when one is accounting for half-a-dozen sitters a day, with the evenings reserved for the aristocracy clamouring ceaselessly at one's door, you shall judge the likelihood of that for yourself! You know it was the knight himself who persuaded me into establishing this club affair for fellow reprobates?"

"Sir Joshua's genius shines forth from this, Samuel. He has caught you as few could."

"Damn good thing he wasn't a keeper, then, or we'd have had few apples and fewer strawberries in schooldays! The fond memory of Lichfield's orchards and hothouses hold a special place in this increasingly crabby old heart."

The huge figure silhouetted against the stair window pointed towards the visitor's intended destination.

"Give a thought as to how you shall occupy yourself between our evening celebrations, Cousin, for I shall have little time and less intention of shepherding you about town! There should be This and That to distract you, though; I know you like to be kept busy."

"All decided well in advance, Samuel. I have had a long-standing correspondence with the Constable of The Tower, concerning his interest in several peculiar pieces of armoury in my keeping. I intend also to pursue a long-standing invitation from Sir John Soane to 'wait upon' him, though I have had scant opportunity either so to do or, given our short notice, apprise him of my brief presence in your busy city."

"Touché, encore, mon brave," grinned Johnson, baring a phalanx of teeth that would have sent a Turcoman horde into retreat. "I intend no incivility, as you well know, you dexterous rogue. I mean only that a lifetime of distraction, of business you might say, has deprived me of manifold graces that would have eased my passage through life, and, I dare say," he smiled, wolfishly, "that of many of those unfortunates who have encountered me on one of my more distracted days."

He paused in apparent reflection: "Remind me, Cousin, who nests in the Tower these days? It strikes a chord but eludes me. Do, I entreat you, refrain from answering, 'Ravens'."

Greene smiled in response: "John, Lord Berkeley, the Fifth of that much-gifted line I believe. Have you been to the Tower – do you know him?"

"I seldom venture into places of such dark repute, lest I am not permitted to leave. So, no, I have not made his acquaintance; If by 'gifts' you refer to cash piled in dizzying spoil-heaps, then who in Town would not know of him – and his forebears – at the very least? The term filthy rich was, I feel certain, coined for that very family. The Square they named so modestly after themselves is the least of it though. To this day they boast they can ride from that murderous keep in Gloucestershire all the way to the aforesaid Square, never leaving their own land." The huge brow frowned in concentration, before the Doctor added: "This one's an Oxford man, as I recall, a few years before my time, so he can't be all bad. Mind you, Corpus Christi rather than Pembroke."

Bushy grey eyebrows were raised in mock-censure, reminding the Apothecary of an exotic species of caterpillar as pictured by the over-heated imagination of an engraver.

With a wave, Johnson turned back to the stairs, calling back over his shoulder: "We were a nest of singing birds then, Richard. It seems so long ago."

On that poignant note the visitor was left to enter his handsomely furnished room. Having kicked aside his travelling-shoes, he sank gratefully onto the quilted comfort of the high bed.

"This will spoil me for Staffordshire," he thought wryly to himself, before awakening to the sound of the dinner-gong after what seemed no more than a blink of a tired eye.

ITEM:

In the Center, below the ALTAR table. In a Glafs Case, a variety of Artificial Flowers, by Mr Coe, of Greek-ftreet, fo-Ho, London, surrounded by Filigree work, made of Spiral Paper, the Edges of which are gilded. On the Floor, a neat Model of the double Ventilator, invented by the late Rev. Doctor Hales.

London. 14th April. Standing beneath the blackened spikes of the Middle Gate portcullis, the Yeoman Warder had seemed not only surprised, but amused by the visitor's assumption that the Constable would be in residence.

"Lord bless you, no, Sir! High days and holidays are when we see His Lordship, and not always then, unless their Majesties are coming – then, there he is, in full-fig and acting as if he owns the place, no offence intended. Too fond of his up-to-date comforts to want to put up with our draughty old lodgings. Not that I'd say no to a cosy billet like that, myself!"

Unabashed, Greene realised immediately that the universal expedient of a well-greased palm would not go amiss, and soon he was being conducted around the ancient fortress and treated to a commentary as well-worn as the ancient stones that now seemed to engulf him.

By mid-afternoon, and by then a guinea lighter, the Apothecary's head was ringing with names and dates, his eyes aching from the perpetual twilight that scarcely illumined dusty, bare interiors. Gatehouse chambers, tower-rooms, dank cells and oubliettes that had once contained a nation's roll-call of treachery, of tragedy and worse; forlorn scratches of graffiti on prison walls often the sole memory of a tortured passing – memories piled one upon another like fallen leaves.

He had thought to find it fascinating, this ancient place, an irresistible lure to an antiquarian's heart, but instead found himself heaving a heartfelt sigh of relief – of release even – as he finally re-emerged into the bustle and vigour of a London day.

Apart from the endless clamour of the Royal Mint that somehow crammed itself between the inner and outer landward walls of the huge fortress, he had found the claustral stillness, the deadening silence of massive walls and looming towers more oppressive than he would have thought possible; a brooding stillness that had contained such an infinity of human misery, of hopelessness and torment as if trapped in the stones themselves.

Greene's long-anticipated visit to the Royal Armoury had revealed a vast jumble of sparsely catalogued wonders wrought in plate and mail, a martial treasure-trove apparently defying any attempt at imposing order or organisation.

It had been equally unsettling to him now hurrying away from the stained walls. There had simply been too much of everything for him to absorb, the sheer scale of century upon century of acquisition seeming, somehow, to have rendered it a monumental trophy store detached utterly from its history or purpose. It's keeper, an irascible stick of a man, was of a type that the Apothecary recognised only too well. He had been far too busily engaged in his interrupted meal to do more than wave Greene's few enquiries away, stating that the labels provided all information available without a prior appointment. What labels there were, had, in the main, faded beyond legibility.

The Apothecary found himself longing for the companionship and human warmth that the promise of The Club held for the evening ahead. He hurried out towards Tower Hill, past the stench and clamour of the Royal Menageri; admission to the Lion Tower, he noted in passing, being threepence unless bearing a dead cat or dog to feed the eponymous carnivores.

"Back by five, spruced, brushed and booted by six, chairs to The Turk's Head for seven," had been his host's stern instructions as they parted after breakfast. 'That's if they let you out, of course!'

Despite the fact of an arrival in Gerrard Street somewhat earlier than the intended seven o'clock, the cousins were, apparently, not the first arrivals at the substantial old inn; a fact registered as a tetchy growl from the Doctor when informed by the smiling landlord, "Sir Joshua and Mr Goldsmith are already upstairs." Greene suppressed a smile in the realisation that The Great Lexicographer obviously took a very proprietorial stance when it came to all matters pertaining to The Club.

As Greene climbed the wide stairs in the wake of his wheezing and puffing host, he recalled Samuel's description of the group's original founding and its most particular composition.

"It is our intention," he had announced, as if addressing a roomful of attentive listeners rather than a solitary apothecary, "that The Club shall consist of such men, that if only two of them chance to meet they shall be able to entertain each other without wanting the addition of more company to pass the evening agreeably."

From a full – and emphatically limited – complement of nine founding members, two had – this evening – sent apologies for absence, so the Doctor was informed as their top-coats were being collected: "Sir John Hawkins and Mr Charmier, Doctor Johnson."

"So, will it be just the eight of you dining with us tonight, Sir? My Smithfield man spoke so highly of the spring lamb that it is roasting as we speak."

"You've yet to disappoint us, Charles, though the same can scarcely be said of several of our members." He turned to the

Apothecary standing beside him, who was clutching a valise to his waist-coated chest as if it were in imminent danger of theft. "Hawkins is simply un-clubbable, but we shall at least be spared his tiresome wrangling with Burke. I'll not suffer much more of it."

Turning back to the landlord, the bumbling figure seemed to suddenly regain his humour, booming, "Richard, I must mind my manners! Here stands a peerless host to our little Club, a Swinden by name of Charles. My cousin Greene, down from Lichfield to learn how we do things in our Great City, eh? Enough lamb to go round, d'you think? We'll have to send him packing otherwise!"

Reassured by the smiling landlord, they were ushered upstairs across a well-waxed landing and into the first of the private rooms above the inn. Standing beside the room's small fire, two figures turned in anticipation at their entry. Later, Greene would attempt over and again to remember the detail, the words of introduction, the glowing rush of pleasure at the genial, unforced welcome he received as first Reynolds and then Oliver Goldsmith took his hand, followed – it seemed without interval – by the arrival of the remaining members – as much on cue as if they had been concealed behind the wainscoting. Edmund Burke, Christopher Nugent, Topham Beauclerk, as one face followed another, each name seeming to supplant the previous introduction as the gathering grew, Greene's capacity for putting names to faces faltered in equal measure, until the final hand to be clasped. "Yet another of our Scribblers, Cousin, may I present Bennet Langton, late of Spilsby, and Lincolnshire's finest – or so he constantly assures me!"

Greene hesitated, scarcely realising the intense stare he was directing towards the narrow features and pale grey eyes of a figure looking increasingly puzzled at the undisguised scrutiny.

"Langton, indeed" he murmured, as if to himself, "My word, what a coincidence. Unlooked for coincidence, no less."

Then, though, as if suddenly remembering his manners

the small man seemed to wake from a reverie, blinking at the bewildered face as if seeing it for the first time and blurted: "Oh, Mr Langton, what must you be thinking of me? Do please forgive my idiocy. It is simply the strangest chance that I should meet a Langton, here of all places. Are you by any chance related to..?" He got no further, for Johnson, as if sensing impending shipwreck, caught his elbow and steered him away.

"No time for research, Cousin, you can interrogate Bennet when we've all got a decent dinner put away." Amidst the badinage between old friends, the protestations of perfect punctuality laughingly pooh-pooed by Johnson now at his most expansive, Richard Greene was already revelling in this company, its men of letters, of verse, of stage, of medicine and music, its characters as wildly disparate as the jumbled contents of a child's toy-box.

Greene knew that the first of his introductions, to Samuel's founding-partner, the urbane and perfectly mannered Sir Joshua Reynolds, had been, to the realm's most fashionable and renowned portrait painter. This, an artist whose wealth was mounting at a virtually unguessable rate funded by a rumoured half-dozen sitters daily, with evenings reserved for the likes of Lord Burghersh with a hundred guineas to spare for Sir Joshua's sublime talents. In less-than-glorious contrast, the downright ill-proportioned ugliness of the youthful pock-marked Irishman – his companion – was Greene's first acquaintance with the mercurial genius that was Oliver Goldsmith.

Arrived, bedraggled and penniless in London ten years earlier his lively, graceful and, above all, supremely readable writings had rapidly brought him to the attention first, then the patronage and friendship of the Doctor. The Apothecary had been enthralled by 'The Traveller', recommended by letter from his ever-busy cousin – it being an account of happiness, in all its varying degrees, related by a restless wanderer comparing the various cultures of Northern Europe whilst yearning for his own native land.

"You, yourself, must miss Ireland sorely, Mr Goldsmith?"

ventured Greene having expressed his admiration for the work. To his consternation Goldsmith hooted with sardonic laughter in reply, shouting, "Loathe the bloody place, as much now as I ever did. Sure, I'd burn that pox-hole Trinity to the ground given half a chance!" At which he stepped back, arms akimbo, as if to reinforce his declamation, tripped, and would have fallen into the fire had it not been for Johnson's intervening bulk materialising at the critical moment.

"Control yourself, Oliver. You'll have our guest taking refuge up the chimney otherwise." He turned to the astounded figure of his cousin, "Pay the ragamuffin no heed, Richard. We love him for his Celtic lunacies, if not his social niceties."

"Oh, Mr Greene, a thousand pardons," the gaunt figure murmured, suddenly crestfallen, but then with an almost manic change of character, bellowed, "Swinden, here, Sir, this instant! We shall have champagne, a half-dozen bottles of your best – your best, mind! I'll not have it said we drove a guest from our door!" The company, all save its twin founders, joined in delighted applause as the landlord waved acknowledgement from the door.

"His extravagance will yet be the ruin of him," said Johnson sotto voce to the painter who nodded gravely, but then rejoined the light-hearted conversations that began once more around the room, as the alarming Irishman embarked upon an enumeration of his motley employments before literary fortune came his dishevelled way.

When 'apothecary's assistant' was mentioned, followed by 'physician', Greene hid his mixture of disbelief and outright hilarity by means of a rapidly produced pocket handkerchief and an equally rapid refilling of his own champagne glass.

From its solemn opening toast, 'Esto Perpetua' proposed by Reynolds, the evening proceeded through an opulent dinner, uncounted glasses downed with a seemingly endless procession of dishes set before a company whose appetites seemed never to diminish.

It was not until the port began to circulate around the strewn table that Richard Greene remembered, with only the briefest stab of consternation, why he had been summoned to this august assembly in the first place.

A glass tinkled insistently as Samuel Johnson called them into some semblance of order before formally introducing their guest speaker with characteristic wit and brevity: "For me to compare the innumerable treasures of Mr Greene's Lichfield Museum with those of a cyclopean magpie's nest would be to traduce this most excellent collector and scholar, so I shall desist immediately. You have all read, and applauded, his learned contributions to *The Magazine* over these many years, hence your insistence upon his invitation this evening.

He will enthral you as he has me, unfailingly, on my infrequent returns to our little city.

Richard, the floor is yours."

Without a second thought, the small man found his feet and, beaming about the assembled faces, lifted his valise to the table-top, as willing hands to left and right, cleared the detritus to make space. A perfect hush descended as he lifted out the first of its contents, an object wrapped in cloth.

"When we embark upon our various endeavours, whatever they may be," he looked around the circle of flushed, attentive faces before continuing, "I believe that we share, in common, one essential, irreducible, quality. That is faith." He saw flickers of scorn, of fascination, of engagement, before continuing, "Whether it be the eye of faith," – he glanced at Reynolds to his left – "the act of faith" – his gaze turned to Edmund Burke across the table – "in believing in the perfectibility – or correctability – of our fellow man, or in cementing that faith into a belief that our words, our poems, our music, can captivate – can move – our clients, our listeners – our public of every shape and form – into a joining. Into a shared experience of that ineffable, wondrous thing that is beyond any better explanation than the power of the work itself.

Without faith, we are – our endeavours are – I believe, little more than husks blowing in a careless wind. Hither, thither, who cares? Who notices?" He had them now, to a man. The fluency came from somewhere beyond him. It happened sometimes.

"My elder brother, Joseph, by happy chance, is the Headmaster of Stratford upon Avon's ancient Grammar School, its foundation dating back to Gloriana herself, the foremost of its alumni being the reason I am here to share some thoughts with you tonight." A perceptible rustle moved through the listeners at the mention of the Warwickshire town. "And it is largely through a brother's good graces – and those of his devoted parishioners," he added with a smile, "that two of the three pieces I have brought – at your request – came into my hands. Treasured exhibits less, perhaps, in themselves, in their lack of show – of bombast – but more because of my absolute conviction – my faith, if you will – that they are what they purport to be."

"Item, the first," – he unwrapped the object in his hands – "Its museum label reads thus: 'A neat oval frame carved and gilded, an exact copy in oil colour (on a piece of the mulberry tree, planted by Shakespeare) of that celebrated poet, from the original print, engraved by Martin Droeshout, prefixed to the first folio edition of his works, painted by Mr Williams of Shrewsbury'. I can add little but my knowledge of its impeccable provenance to that. It has remained in Stratford a century and a half or more until last year when its inheritor was persuaded to part with it for a not inconsiderable sum."

Uncertain applause met him, before he continued: "Please feel free to examine it yourselves. Make of it what you will, sticky fingers permitting!" He re-wrapped the base of the frame before passing it to Johnson, who was watching him through appraising, half-closed eyes, his face sunk into creases of good humour.

"Now, however, with the second of the three relics I offer for your scrutiny tonight, sticky fingers must – I entreat you – go nowhere near the page itself. It is, I truly believe, written in the hand of The Bard himself." The fixity of the company became absolute.

"Decades ago, scholars began to examine a strange, flawed and seemingly disconnected play, 'Sir Thomas More', discovered in the collection of a London bibliophile, John Murray." Several nods of recognition around the table met his statement. "The scrappy manuscript, with three pages of revision, addition or correction in a wholly different hand from the body of the text, then passed on to Edward Harley, Earl of Oxford and somewhere or other, before entering the collection of Sir Hans Sloane about six or seven years ago. This is where I first encountered it, at Montagu House, and my interest was ignited." He grinned, artlessly, at the circle of attentive faces.

"Scholars tell me that we have only the great man's Last Will and Testament and some half dozen signatures as a basis for comparison of any fragment that chance may send our way. Well, I must tell you, just one such – a fragment of a fragment was as one might describe it – came to me, once more through my generous brother. A bookbinder in the town was stripping out a damaged cover when he came across a packing – a padding-out – within it, which is what I shall show you now." The atmosphere prickled with anticipation.

"Beyond the obvious, commonplace antiquity of the find for a craftsman such as this, was what my brother, God bless him, perceived in the text of the fragment presented in the hope of remuneration. He was convinced he had read the text before, but, for the life of him, could not remember where. He could vividly recall an encounter with the lines:

...shark on you, and men like ravenous fishes
Would feed on one another...

"The reason for this eluded him until mention of Sloane's acquisition in *The Magazine*. Given his own particularly privileged position and the authority therein, he had been granted access to study the whole play whilst it was lodged in Oxford's library. What he was given, what we now have here," – he produced a vellum folder with a flourish from his valise – "is nothing less than a discarded, rejected version of a substantial part of the second page of that peculiar addendum to the play." Audible gasps met his statement. With immense gratification he continued, "My own researches – checked and checked again – have confirmed handwriting; both Shakespeare's practised scrivener's hand and a far more laboured secretary hand employed for More's speeches, both of which compare perfectly to those niceties of the Bard's palaeography of which we can be certain, added to both text and material. I have studied the exaggeration of its curves, the particular emphases of its downstrokes, its employment of an elongated 'S' character in the Italian manner." He shrugged as if in dismissal of his labours. "The detail is as tedious as it is irrefutable – that is, if you care to share my faith – rather than demand the wearisome proofs which I can, and will, furnish if pressed."

This time the ovation came from a table of standing men, faces glistening in the candlelight, expectation painted on each as the folder then made its slow transit from hand to hand around the enthralled company. The speaker, animateur and spellbinder for these fleeting, magical moments in this extraordinary company, now came to the moment that none in that candlelit assembly would ever forget.

"We began this evening with an image of The Great Bard – a copy of a copy, a likeness perhaps of a similar order of verisimilitude as whispers amongst Chinamen." Laughter, expectancy now, of a whole different order: "If, Gentlemen, I have not tried your patience and generosity to extinction, I shall conclude with what I am now wholly convinced is the sole, true likeness of William Shakespeare that can be absolutely pinpointed to his own lifetime. Not a work of fond memory, of devotion and faulty recall, but nothing less than a pen portrait made of the playwright in his glory days, translated into print by William Rogers – the finest exponent of copperplate engraving we have yet to see." He reached once more into his valise and produced a well-thumbed, aging volume which he laid reverently upon the table.

"Gerard's Herball!" he exclaimed, delighted at the mystification spreading across the assembled faces. "The bible of my profession." He paused with an almost thespian deliberation before adding, "Though not just any of its many reprints or pallid imitators; a first edition. 'Imprinted at London by John Norton 1597'." He opened the title page with a showman's flourish, spreading the large volume open with practised ease. Before continuing he tilted it this way and that in order to give all his listeners at least a glimpse of what he was about to embark upon.

"Before I share the extraordinary secret which I believe has been concealed in plain sight to all but a few since the day of this first imprint, I must plead my terror of the very real prospect that, in so doing, I shall be revealing just how dangerous a little knowledge – my little knowledge – can be. For I am quite certain that this blameless engraving, this innocent frontis, contains codes and significances far beyond my small skills to interpret; and believe me, this is no false modesty, but simple fact. He who masters this pretty puzzle in its entirety will have my vote as Genius Personified!"

About to continue, the Apothecary was completely thrown by a sudden flurry of activity and raised voices on the landing beyond their closed door – suddenly opened to reveal a redfaced, perspiring figure, half shrugged out of his coat, apparently resisting Swinden's attempts to either relieve him of it – or perhaps prevent him entering.

Johnson's initial outrage at the unseemly entrance turned to booming laughter and arms extended in welcome as the panting figure finally came in, to be greeted by smiles, laughter and waves by the seated diners.

"Davy! You laggardly rogue! And painted like a Molly! Would

you bring poor Swinden's house into disrepute?"

Greene simply gazed in bemusement at this grinning spectacle that had completely upstaged his moment of revelation. Johnson strode forward, throwing an avuncular arm over the incomer and propelling him towards Greene: "Cousin, strange though it may seem, this unlooked-for apparition is my dearest friend, indeed my erstwhile pupil – though he keeps remarkably quiet on that score in these his days of high celebrity! May I present David Garrick, arriving unannounced, apparently unfed and largely unwashed! Apparently direct from Drury Lane unless he has taken to wearing greasepaint for adventures of the night. Davy, my Cousin Greene, here as our especial guest and about to enthral us before your mistimed entry corpsed his soliloquy!"

With a smile of unaffected warmth, the renowned actor-manager strode forward, grasping Greene's hand in both of his: "One day, perhaps, you might forgive me, but all I ask tonight is to be permitted a seat at your table in the fond hope I have neither missed your revelations nor spoiled them with my clodhopping clumsiness. Your erudition precedes you in such fashion that I left the theatre within a moment of the curtain's fall in order to get here – they may still be applauding for all I know!" Good-natured groans met the grinning boast, as he disengaged himself to elbow a place at the table to sit on a mysteriously produced chair, before the landlord hurried away.

"You honour me, Mr Garrick. I had not hoped to make your acquaintance before tomorrow evening," said Greene with quiet sincerity, adding: "No forgiveness is required, Sir. In fact, these gentlemen have been given blessed moments of respite from my ramblings."

Genial protestations and more laughter met his graceful riposte, and the Apothecary found himself continuing as if there had been no interruption. In fact, now perhaps with greater inspiration than he would have thought possible, faced across the width of a dining table by the greatest living exponent of English theatre.

"I alluded to my belief that few have ever been aware of the secret presented here. One such, however, though quite who we shall never know, drew my attention to the puzzle in the first place. Here, in the margin on the bottom right of the frontis, a hand has faintly inscribed 'WS' against this image. This is what first drew my attention and led me on to consideration of the rebus inscribed on the plinth."

He bent to produce a large folded sheet from his valise, opening it to reveal an enlarged drawing of the inscription. "This will, I think, make my reasoning clearer." He laid it open at the centre of the table, as fruit and cheese were hastily cleared to one side.

"At first glance, simply 'The Sign of Four' one might surmise, with little further thought. It being one of the most frequently used printers' and booksellers' devices these centuries past." A statement met with nods of recognition around the table. "This, however, bears no actual resemblance to any of the many hundred examples I hold among my Museum references – a collection, with all due modesty, that I know to be as complete as any. So, scrutiny began: the form of the supposed Four has been wilfully distorted into more an equilateral triangle – more an arrow-head than any numeral you will encounter." Every gaze was fixed upon the enlarged design. "Yet then, I asked, why posit the numeral at all? And could find no answer until the unknowing intervention of Cousin Samuel!"

"Eh, what's this? Never seen the blessed thing before! How so, Sir?" barked the Doctor, peering suspiciously at Greene.

"Why, by answering an unrelated query some years ago, Samuel, and pointing me towards a fellow lexicographer, John Florio, a contemporary of the Bard and a scholar whose linguistic skills still leave me speechless. For it was he who pointed out to this dullard that we were not dealing with a Four in the English tongue but to one of two possible latinisms: The first possibility: 'Quater' – referring to, say, a four at cards, or used as in 'four' times, a multiplication. The second contender: 'Quat', the often-used herbalists' abbreviation for 'Quattuor' – the quantity 'four-fold' in recipes – which I must have written a thousand times."

"Now, given the absolute emphasis of the graphical design, we are being invited to append the letter 'E' to one or other. Hence: Quatere, from the verb, Quatio – to shake, or the option: the imperative of that same verb – Quate – Shake!"

"Now," – his voice rose – "we look again at that which we had supposed to be an 'arrowhead', pointed, upstanding on its shaft, and rename it 'spear' for is that any less likely?" A muted hubbub of reaction arose, most gratifyingly, around the room, but he raised a hand, grinning now, into the sea of approbation surrounding him.

"But now there are niceties, conclusions to be observed, so if you will bear with me a few moments more." The company hung upon his every word.

"In 1596, William's father, John Shakespeare, applied for, and was granted, in the face of opposition and some haughty disdain, a coat of arms. A Field of Gold crossed by a Bend of Black, a diagonal descending top left to bottom right, containing a lance or spear. That field, in all but its coloured variants being, by necessity, described by the letters OR signifying gold."

He pointed once more to the spread sheet, to the characters arranged to left and right of the spear-shaft. "On such ciphers, the Christian name of the subject usually appears at the base of the 'stalk' of the numeral; here, most intriguingly, we can discern clearly not one but possibly two intentions. One, 'W' for William – as we may well have guessed by now." Laughter and a scattering of applause followed. "But also a splay of the stem describing the form of 'A' – that quite possibly referring neatly to Arden – the gentry connection, by marriage, of our Will to his Elizabeth, forging the necessary degree of gentility that might finally persuade a reluctant Herald to grant old John's dearest wish, this being the incorporation of the Arden arms into his own, less than three years later in 1599. We even have that same 'bend', the diagonal, left to right, recalled in the top of the rebus, here."

Lifting the Herball in both hands he displayed it to the company. "Gentlemen, in good faith may I present to you the sole portrait of William Shakespeare drawn from life – in company with the great Gerard himself, there, the sometime omnipotent Lord Burghley there, and here," – he indicated the fourth figure at the top right of the frontis – 'Well, you know as much as I do – perhaps it is The Wandering Jew who has taken up horticulture."

Delighted laughter and applause swept over him as he sat down, realising, in an instant, that he probably lacked the strength ever to stand again. Utterly spent, euphoric with the compliments being showered upon him by a roomful of men seemingly determined to make some form of physical contact, he sat back and beamed, before remembering a bumper of brandy at his elbow which he lifted and drained in a couple of thirsty gulps.

The last thing he remembered was the face of David Garrick, close to his own, bending confidingly over him as he slumped, exhausted, in his chair.

"Tomorrow evening, when you do me the honour of attending my theatre, the world and his wife will celebrate the presence of their Majesties and perhaps pay some regard to a guest of note who shall also be attending as a visitor to these shores. Make no mistake, my friend, my dedication may well pay lip-service to august presences, but you, Sir, will be its true recipient. You have moved me beyond words. You have my undying gratitude for showing me the face of that genius who presides over my life."

Memories of embraces, handshakes, invitations, unstable stairs and the delicious shock of early-morning air, melded with the dazzle of swirling flambeaux and the blessed closeting of a well-borne chair faded into a perfect oblivion as the door closed upon his bedroom and he was left to float away.

(6)

A caſt in Red Wax, from the great Seal of Henry Prince of
Wales. The Seal (from whence the above impreſſion was taken)
of Henry Prince of Wales, ſon to Henry the fourth; it is of
Braſs, weight fifteen Ounces, two Inches and one quarter in
diameter, a particular account of which was publiſhed by that
ſkilful and learned Antiquarian, the Rev. Samuel Pegge, of
Whittington, in Derbyshire, in The Gentleman's Magazine.

Lichfield. 14th April. The break-in may well have gone unnoticed
until much later, had it not been for the footprints. They led from a
half-glazed door giving onto the substantial orangery and crossed
the hall flags to the door of the Canon's library. Within, on both
the dark adzed floorboards and a large Turkey carpet, the white
boot-marks described a circling of its loaded shelves, and a gradual
fading as the weave absorbed the clinging smears of lime plaster.

The intruder had forced the orangery's external door, before,
unwittingly, making his way along the brick-tiled floor and
through the spilled remnants of the lime plaster-mix being
currently employed on internal repairs to the high wall at the rear
of the large glazed structure. With what appeared to have been
well-practised skill he had then unleaded the pane nearest to the
internal handle and its key. It had been soundlessly removed, a
wrist pushed through and the key obtained.

What Canon Seward refrained from expressing by way of
visible outrage or alarm at the incursion, his daughter was busily
supplying, in alternating bouts of tears and most unladylike fury.
"Papa, I must ask once more – how can you be so unperturbed at

this attack upon us? Upon the sanctity of our very home? Could we not have been murdered in our beds? Your impassivity in the face of this, this..." The normally loquacious young woman, the most precociously literate and universally gifted young woman of anyone's acquaintance, was lost for words. Wisely, she fell back on tears and was led away for a medicinal cordial by a comforting housekeeper familiar with the highly-strung temperament of 'The Swan of Lichfield'. Her father waved her away with relief, refraining from any further repetition of: "But nothing appears to have been stolen, my dear; do try to calm yourself," an unreassuring platitude that had seemed only to result in more tears or worse still.

Lost in thought, Seward retraced the intruder's route, noting once more a silver salver bearing silver-mounted decanters, passing several small portable clocks, a mantlepiece displaying equally pocketable *objets* and mementos; none touched, nothing disturbed. As he stood in the doorway of the gracious room he murmured: "You were looking for something weren't you, you rogue, something particular? Not easily saleable valuables, that is for sure – but what, then? What could..?" He stopped, suddenly perplexed, as a thought occurred to him as he looked across to the table in the window bay, its polished top reflecting nothing more than the tulips in their delft flower-brick.

"Oh, surely not? Why that wretched thing? What could possess a thief to..?" He didn't complete his own question. Suddenly, there was no need. He had become so inexplicably ill-at-ease with the presence, the barely discernible but ever-present smell, of the battered box and its drab contents, that he had quietly removed them from the house. It had, after all, come from centuries of concealment in a tower, so where, now, more suitable for its removal, but to another one raised by the same hand?

Unobserved, the previous afternoon, he had carried the sack-wrapped bundle across to the stark ruin of The Bishop's Tower in the corner of the Palace gardens. It stood, a forlorn relic of de Langton's formidable defences, as one of the only substantial remains left by the devastation of the Civil War.

Moving aside a wheelbarrow propped against an inner wall of the roofless shell, he had revealed a weather-stained, worm-eaten cupboard door, all that had survived of the tower's furnishings. It opened with a complaining rasp of rusted hinges to a niche of rotten plaster, droppings and detritus. Without a second thought, he had dropped the box into it and closed the decaying door with a sigh of relief.

"And there you'll stay until my good friend the museum-keeper takes you off my hands." He walked back across the gathering dusk with the sense of a job well done, realising only then that he had spoken the sentiment aloud, as if to someone listening.

By mid-morning, Theodosia Greene, once again comfortably propped behind her counter, a well-bound ankle supported by a borrowed gout-stool, was contemplating the idea of a printed sign to be displayed, prominently, for the information of every literate customer that entered the Apothecary. It would read:

Mrs Greene is suffering no more – nor less than a painfully sprained ankle.

It was self-inflicted and should require no further discussion.

It will soon be better, but she thanks you for your interest and concern.

The lady was missing her husband more than she could have imagined and found herself repeatedly calculating the time of his likely reappearance through the shop's ever-opening and -closing doors. Perhaps due to her lack of mobility, it seemed to the stool-bound mistress of the flourishing premises that they had never been busier, with each new customer bent on solicitous enquiry or maddening reassurance of her condition. Hence thoughts of the sign. It was, thus, rather more than simply a call of nature that took her hobbling out to the ivied privy in their long garden. A little peace and considerably more quiet was what she craved as she inhaled the sweetness of the spring morning and rested on the remains of the medieval font that formed but one part of the ever-growing collection of sculptural salvage encroaching upon her garden.

"Oh, Richard, do for heaven's sake stop enjoying yourself and come home early. Is that too much for a wife to ask?" She found herself smiling at her own peevish thoughts, knowing her absent spouse – for all his growing celebrity and infuriating enthusiasms – to be the most selfless and self-effacing man she could have ever wished for. "Just come home," she exclaimed to the alarm of several nesting birds in the foliage above her, as she disappeared behind the wooden door, unaware of what was then occurring inside a shop normally known for its well-ordered calm.

The tall, cadaverous figure, top-coated and scarfed despite the warm morning had entered just as two previous customers were leaving, brushing imperiously past them as they sought to gain the pavement, oblivious to the affronted stares that followed him in. He was met with the well-practised courtesy of the shop-man, Tillett, but before assistance of any kind could be offered, the visitor demanded: "This museum, where is it to be found?"

"Why upstairs, as ever, Sir," replied Tillett, stiffening at the cold disdain the wrapped man exuded.

"One pays for the privilege, one must suppose?" It was as much a statement of distaste as a question, uttered as the speaker stared about him as if entirely unfamiliar with commercial premises.

"Well yes, Sir, of course. Very fine value it is too, normally, but I regret it is closed to the public during Mr Greene's temporary absence."

The figure stiffened with shock: "Closed? How can that be? I have travelled most particularly to..."

"If you will excuse me, Sir?" Tillett smiled warmly at a flame-haired girl entering the shop.

"I must..." He got no further.

With no attempt at controlling his obvious fury, the tall figure barked, "I shall not excuse you, fellow, I was addressing you in the absence of your superiors. What is the nature of this temporary absence? Does this Greene return today, tomorrow?"

"My Master will be returning in his own good time, Sir," retorted Tillett, shocked into unaccustomed annoyance. "It is his and my mistress's business alone, Sir. The museum is closed until I am given leave to open it, and there's an end to it. I have told you all I..."

Before he could finish the man spun on his heel, pushing past the alarmed incomer. As he yanked open the door, he caught its lower panel with a viciously petulant kick, leaving blank astonishment in his wake.

"What a perfectly lovely morning," came a voice from the rear door, as the oblivious Theodosia re-entered, limping back towards her eyrie. "A good day to you, Mr Simpson," she greeted a customer lurking towards the rear of the shop, "and..." she smiled at the obviously discomfited girl standing diffidently by the counter, "...to you, young lady. Are you both being..?"

She halted in obvious surprise, seeing the expressions on the trio of faces turned towards her entry. "What on earth is the matter? James? Mr Simpson? Have I missed an armed incursion?"

Tillett extracted a large handkerchief from his smock-coat, mopping his face before he could reply. Mr Simpson shrugged in bewilderment.

"The most uncivil man I've ever met, Mistress, standing there," – Tillett pointed helplessly to the space by the door – "Just barged in, demanding entry to the museum though I told him it was closed, refusing to take 'no' for an answer, demanding to know when the Master would be back."

"He kicked your door as he was leaving, hard as he could,

though Mr Tillett offered not a word of offence, Mrs Greene," added their hapless customer.

She hobbled over to where he was pointing and inspected the damage with a scowl. A white scar was scuffed into the pristine paintwork. She bent forward, running a questing finger along the damage. "This looks like chalk, or plaster. Was he wearing a working man's boots? Who exactly was this oafish creature? He'll settle for the repairs if I have anything to do with it! Did you see which way he went?" She moved awkwardly towards the handle, obviously meaning to peer out into the bustle of Saddler Street.

To her surprise, Tillett, normally the mildest and even-tempered of men, stopped her: "Even in the event of his still being in sight, Mistress, that was not a man as you'd choose to catch up with. If I never see him – or his like – again, it will be too soon. No good can come of it, Mrs Greene, please believe me."

Seeing the obvious distress in the face of her well-trusted employee, she took his arm saying, "Well, perhaps in that case you'll help this infirm lady back to her sentry-post. You'll not be treated like that again, James. Of that you can be certain." Mollified, he walked her to her stool with the utmost solicitude.

"What would we do without our Mr Tillett, I wonder, Mr Simpson? Now, whilst I attend to you, where is that boy of yours, James? There are orders to be filled and prescriptions delivered. Is he asleep in a tree? And you, young lady, what can..?"

The flame-haired girl had slipped away.

"Have you suffered injury, Mrs Greene?" enquired Simpson. "You seem to be in some distress if I may say so?" The pained look the questioner received confirmed his fears.

Little more than a few hundred yards along Saddler Street, the church of St Mary's had stood in the City's marketplace for as long as there had been a city. Its present incumbent, the Reverend Lionel Blomefield – living conveniently in its shadow, scarcely half a hundred feet away from its porch – was busily contemplating the game pie he had smelled on his departure for the morning service. Now, occupying himself with what his wife referred to as 'endless pottering with little purpose', he was tidying away the dog-eared hymnals left along the few pews that had been occupied in what he increasingly referred to as 'our increasingly godless times'. Glancing at his pocket-watch he was calculating the minimum decent interval that could be observed before his return home to pie and an afternoon busy in his potting shed. Elspeth, his wife, seemed to have increasingly strong views on the importance of a renewed commitment to his vocation, and consequently less time spent under her feet or simply in being 'spare about the house' as she had mysteriously described his presence only a week earlier to Theodosia Greene, but within his hearing.

Glancing up at the sound of his verger's footfall limping up the aisle towards him, he was both surprised and put out when informed that there was someone wanting to speak to him outside the porch – "most urgently, Reverend. Wouldn't come in, though I asked him."

Returning his watch to its pocket in the snuff-stained waistcoat, he decided that this would be a brief meeting, whatever its purpose, though one that could, at least, be held on his way home. It was only as he stepped out into the late-morning sun that the heavily coated figure turned towards him. He was met by a look of such cold indifference that he almost turned back to see if it was directed to someone or something behind him.

"You are Blomefield, I am informed." The pale, thin lips seemed scarcely to move as the figure spoke without preamble or any vestige of courtesy. "I am the Reverend Lionel Bl..."

"As I said," retorted the other. "You were recently at Eccleshall, I am informed. Is that correct?"

"Well, if it is any of your business, Sir – whosoever you may be – yes, our party was there at the express invitation of..."

"You were party," – the mouth twisted into nothing resembling a smile – "to removing that which was not yours to remove. You do not deny it." None of this was a question. "I have been instructed to see that it is returned into safekeeping. Where is the box? I shall have it."

"Oh, so our Lord Bishop has sent you to..?" The sneer that met his words was an answer in itself. "Then you are instructed by whom, may one enquire?"

"If it is any of your business," came the humourless rejoinder, "by one who commands attention and receives nothing less. By one who understands that there are matters closed forever to meddling and idle scrutiny. Ignorance of what has been removed will be no defence against its consequences. Be sure of that."

"You choose to be as gnomic as you are downright offensive. Sir. I know nothing of what you speak, and care less about its present whereabouts. Now, I have matters to attend; I wish you Good-Day."

"And I wish you nothing but ill, priest," the figure spat, turning abruptly on his heel. Pausing momentarily, he turned back, pointing a black-nailed finger at the incredulous Blomefield: "And those I wish ill do not prosper."

A hay wain lumbered past the vicar's bemused gaze, recalling him to the here-and-now of the bustling marketplace. By the time it had passed there was no sign of the gaunt visitant.

Lionel Blomefield realised he no longer had any appetite, but hurried home, nonetheless.

(7)

An Obelisk in Kilkenny Rofe Marble; on the Die a Medallion of Alexander Pope, Esq. A double Reel, in a large Vial of Flint Glafs, on wich is wound, blue and white Silk, the Stopper fecured by a Peg of Wood within the Bottle, which Peg is again prevented from being withdrawn by two others, viz one at each end.

London. 15th April. On this occasion, with Bennet Langton seated directly opposite him at a table whose sole other occupant was Cousin Johnson, Richard Greene reminded himself not to stare at the narrow, patrician features of today's host. This afternoon's invitation to a pre-theatre dinner had been made, apparently, prior to their departure from The Club in the smallest hours of this morning when the Apothecary's main preoccupation had been in remaining tolerably vertical whilst the world and his multitude of new friends shifted alarmingly around him.

This chop house and the labyrinthine inn known as 'The Queen of Bohemia' shared the decrepit antiquity of what had been the grand London home, a century earlier, of the Earl of Craven. Its gardens long ago sacrificed to a sprawl of cottage and tenement, now home to the multitude of gin-shops and brothels catering for the insatiable appetites of the crowds that thronged the narrow thoroughfare day and night.

This evening, both it and the ladies of the night already congregating outside the grimy windows were showing their age in the last, cruel hours of daylight. In thankful contrast to the less-than venerable surroundings, the renowned chops were living up to their reputation. Conversation was flagging to appreciative noises from two of the trio, and alarming whistles, exhalations and whinnying signified the complete approval of the Doctor who was busily adding to the gravy-stains already decorating the napkin tucked above a huge paunch.

Pausing to take a deep draught of his ale, followed by an appreciative belch, Johnson said: "Now's the time to continue your researches, Cousin. You have a captive at your table and need no longer commit his face to memory." Johnson turned to their dining companion: "Thought he was planning to paint you last night, Langton."

Greene grinned at both the speaker and then at their host: "Oh, Samuel must mean when I was staring at you as we were first introduced, Mr Langton – it was gauche and very rude, and I certainly owe you an apology," – this waved easily aside by the smiling listener – "but I was most taken aback by coincidence. Of your name coming up so unexpectedly after a most remarkable discovery was made, why, scarcely more than a week ago. Concerning, perhaps, an illustrious namesake?" He had their rapt attention now: "Are you by any chance related to – descended from, I should properly enquire – Lichfield's Bishop Walter de Langton, Royal Treasurer and the like to the First Edward?"

Bennet Langton seemed lost in thought for a moment before replying with a wry smile: "Had you asked that question of a certain cousin of mine – a tolerably distant cousin I am relieved to say – the answer, in the unlikely event that one should be forthcoming, would be: 'Yes, hence the retention of the prefix 'de' to one's grand and ancient name. Now go boil your head and never darken my door again or I'll set the dogs on you!'"

Both his listeners laughed at the sardonic sketch.

"You paint a most vivid picture yourself," replied the Apothecary playfully. "Is he really such an ogre?"

"Oh, he is quite unspeakable, Mr Greene. Born of an equally

appalling father, long-dead now but himself long-shunned by a generation of my Lincolnshire people. Born, though, into such wealth to believe himself godlike in his superiority to the lesser beings that constitute the human race. Both father and unlovely son were Oxford men of some distinction, though the family has long maintained that their qualifications were gained as the Varsity's means of getting shot of them both with utmost despatch!" To laughter, he continued: "They have occupied a crumbling pile somewhere in Derbyshire for centuries; an Abbey or some-such ill-gotten wreck, obtained by some jiggery-pokery at the time of the Dissolution. Mind you, they are in illustrious company on that score. I swear a good half of our so-called gentry occupy the fruits of much the same sort of sanctified plunder – not that you would guess it from their airs and graces."

"Heavens above, Bennet, you are becoming a Leveller, Sir!" boomed Johnson to the consternation of a passing serving girl who almost dropped her laden tray. "Lilburne would have been pinning rosemary on your bonnet given half a chance!"

Ignoring the jovial badinage, Langton exclaimed: "But now, Mr Greene, I declare you shall sing for your supper! We are agog to hear the nature of your intriguing interest in my often bewildering but rarely endearing forebears."

"Well," began Greene, though not before peering, unconsciously, about the crowded eating house to see they were not being overheard before continuing, "It all began as a divertisement. Canon Seward's invitation – for Lionel and me – to accompany him and the ever-scintillating Anna on a visit to Eccleshall..."

"The Bishop's castle, of course," interjected Langton. "Pray continue, we are all ears."

"*Tempus fugit*, I regret, gentlemen," interjected Johnson, squinting at a pocket watch dwarfed in his huge hand, peering over plates of congealing gravy; his cousin's account of the extraordinary discovery still resonant around them. "Garrick will have us hanged by our tripes should we miss a single word of tonight's performance." He grimaced, alarmingly, continuing, "Though, the Lord only knows, it will be precious enough to warrant such severity." He glared at Langton: "You know tonight is to be one of his very last performances, Bennet? He shelves his genius and relinquishes the greasepaint in favour of his account books and clerkery! Is it to be believed?"

To the accompaniment of much tut-tutting and the donning of coats, they rejoined the early evening bustle of the raucous lane and turned towards their destination.

They paused amidst the steady flow of theatregoers pressing past them down the passage leading into the flame-lit court before the theatre's colonnaded entrance, Johnson indicating their goal with a proprietorial wave of his arm. "Past its best, the dear old place – it must be said – but it has been keeping rascals such as the three of us off the streets for the best part of a century, since its predecessor burned down at the Restoration. Garrick is brimming with plans for its beautification, though one fears it may be a case of adding but more paint to an ancient face. Still, this old lady is the best The Lane has to offer, and no mistake, though now we'd best scurry to be in place before Their Majesties sweep in. Bad form to follow 'em."

If the streets had been noisy, the tiered and gilded interior was sheer bedlam. Once the comparative calm of the trio's plush-curtained box had been attained, a sea of whigged and bonneted heads – their owners each apparently bawling at the top of their voices – appeared to occupy every square inch of the pit that opened beneath their gaze. They were directly opposite the still vacant Royal Box.

"I swear I have never seen so many people in so small a place, Samuel," shouted Greene, staring out delightedly, fascinated in equal measure by the shielded footlights that were Garrick's famed innovation, their flickering glow adding a spectral ambience to the heavily curtained stage.

"Given half of a chance this mob would have been roosting

up there, too," shouted Johnson in response, following his guest's gaze. "Garrick almost caused civil insurrection when he denied them the stage some years back. Had to turf them off by the scruffs of their unwashed necks for weeks before they finally got the message. Kept clambering back and fighting the cast."

At that moment the musicians struck up and a flurry of gold-braid and equerries could be seen opposite as the royal party entered to the enthusiastic bellowing of 'God save great George our king' from many hundred voices. Standing beside his notably straight-backed companions during the obligatory rendition of all three verses, Greene vividly recalled the first publication of the stirring lyrics twenty years earlier. 'A new song for two voices' – by none other than the cousin beside him, then editor of *The Gentleman's Magazine*; the lyrics then being set to music by one Thomas Arne for this very theatre. The Apothecary felt the familiar frisson of an encounter with History and was suitably gratified.

As the anthem ended and the entire audience were finding their seats, he saw first Johnson and then Langton wave in recognition to another boxed party across the pit.

"David Hume, Cousin, a not inconsiderable historian for all his damned Scotchness," sniffed the Doctor, "though a sight too damn' keen on drumming up investors for the Windward slave plantations. We shall doubtless meet him later and, no doubt, that Frenchie rogue he's landed us with. 'Russo' or some such; 'philosopher' he calls himself, apparently, though what that entails remains to be seen."

The name, offered with what might have been a derisive grimace, struck a momentary chord with Greene – a name mentioned by Darwin? He had no time to think further on it before his other companion craned towards the Doctor as the hubbub began settling to low level noise. "Your esteemed Boswell is finding plenty to interest himself in, concerning the Frenchman's wife, though, if tittle-tattle is to be believed, Samuel," added Langton archly. He received no more than an ambiguous snort in response before the curtain rose to a thunderous cacophony of applause as the legendary actor-manager strode onto a stage he had made his own.

The first of the evening's two pieces, a broad comic romp penned by Garrick himself, brought howls of laughter and wild approbation from an audience happily working itself up into communal hysteria, not least one occupant of Hume's party whose delighted antics could scarcely be contained. At one stage, the same figure's demented enthusiasm brought him close to toppling over the box's low sill, to the obvious consternation not only his own companions but of a royal party now so distracted by the antics that they appeared to be paying more attention to the adjoining box than to the bravura performance being staged below them.

Following the standing ovation that marked the conclusion of the first of the night's plays, the interval was then punctuated by wine, a procession of visitors to their box and a bewildering succession of introductions made to the happily bemused Apothecary.

Christopher Nugent and Thomas Beauclerk – two of the previous night's dining companions – came by, one of them earlier described as a great-grandson of Charles the Second, the other as a specialist in the dreadful hydrophobia transmitted by rabid dogs – if Greene's hazy memory served – though for the life of him he could not remember who was which.

The evening's second play was a work by Voltaire, a performance punctuated, on this occasion, by dramatic wails and audible sobs from Hume's box as the tragedy unfolded, and the same figure visibly cowered in grief or threw wide his arms in athletic empathy as the story reached its heart-breaking conclusion.

Then it was all over, and Greene felt as if he could have glided down, light as a feather, and danced upon the departing heads of the huge audience as they followed the exit of the King and Queen.

Allowing some moments for the press below to thin, Johnson

led his companions across a rubbish-strewn floor and through a stage-side door into the maze of backstage rooms. Down seemingly endless dog-leg corridors and up and down a succession of narrow staircases, regularly populated by a cast of seventy and the permanent 'mechanicals' numbering around fifty, their sure-footed guide was met by waves of recognition.

Finally, he led them through to a shelf-stacked room with earlier arrivals already engaged in animated conversation amidst a circulation of laden trays of sliced pies and drinks, and – still awaiting the reappearance of Garrick himself – centred around the evening's other main attraction, the still-gesticulating figure beside an embarrassed David Hume.

With obvious relief, Hume politely detached himself from the circle surrounding them and came to meet the newcomers. "Samuel. Well met! Mr Langton, a pleasure as always, Sir." He turned to Greene, expectantly.

"Cousin of mine, Hume, Richard Greene by name and as damn' fine an antiquarian as y'could hope to meet."

"My pleasure, Mr Greene, we share a passion it would seem?" Appraising grey eyes met the Apothecary's, his hand taken in a firm, cool grip.

"Would that I shared the achievement of 'A History of England', Mr Hume. It is an astounding work of scholarship, even though the wait for your sixth and final volume came close to driving me to distraction. And, I regret, Millar, too; your excellent bookseller harassed over and again during those eight years by my repeated badgering as to its completion." The author of the monumental work laughed with genuine pleasure. "I am scarcely emulating Samuel's achievement of eight volumes, and all completed without the combined resources of my providential patrons."

"Oh, whilst I can imagine that the library of the Faculty of Advocates is a treasure-house for the researcher, and for the fortunate city of Edinburgh, your achievement in assembling such a great and intricate corpus of knowledge is diminished not one whit, Mr Hume."

The historian replied, "You are as generous as you are well informed, Sir, but..." Johnson cut in with booming asperity: "... yes, yes, but for all this mutual admiration, Richard has as little idea about your protégé as do I! One can imagine Their Majesties must be wondering much the same – your Man of Mystery did come close to breaking his neck and upstaging Garrick, into the bargain!"

The Scotsman gave a rueful shrug, smiling at his interlocutor. "Oh, Jean-Jacques is a man of enthusiasms to match your own, Samuel, though expressed with rather more athleticism it must be admitted." The Doctor's huge eyebrows raised in mock affront, as Hume continued: "He was simply astounded by Garrick's performance tonight and expressed it in his own inimitable fashion."

Perfectly on cue, a sudden burst of applause and cheers erupted from the room's company as Drury Lane's proprietor emerged, paint-free and fresh-faced, grinning appreciatively at the assembled well-wishers who immediately closed around him.

"Allow me to make the introductions whilst David is being lionised – that may take some time to subside! Though, it must be said that our visitor has been receiving scarcely less attention," said Hume, his voice raised above the hubbub of congratulation and adulation. Greene could not fail to see those unmissable eyebrows raised in question at the historian's statement, though Hume seemed not to notice the unspoken disbelief that they so eloquently expressed. He led them across to where the turban-headed figure was being engaged in conversation by a tall, elderly man of discreetly prosperous appearance.

Just as they were about to join the pair, however, the turbaned head turned, and a look of pure joy spread across the blue-jowled features. David Garrick had freed himself from the adoring circle about him and was pushing amiably through the throng, apparently bent on coming to meet the obviously delighted man, hand extended in welcome. Pulling his surprised companion by the sleeve of an elegantly tailored coat the Frenchman pushed forward to meet him, beginning to talk excitedly even as their hands met. Garrick stood, listening politely, expectantly, as the voluble monologue was directed through an intermediary busily attempting to disengage his sleeve from the insistent clutch of the speaker.

"Poor Davenport has got his work cut out, and no mistake," came Bennet's voice from behind Greene's shoulder. "Mind you he speaks the lingo like a native; years in Paris, wealthy as Croesus. Our man obviously has well-connected friends."

Finally, as the speaker finished with an eloquent shrug, gesturing towards his other attentive listener, Davenport turned, smiling broadly, to Garrick, saying, "Monsieur Rousseau has charged me with the most precise rendition of his words. I can only hope to deliver them with even a grain of the fluency with which you delivered your own this evening, Mr Garrick."

The actor ducked his head in appreciation of the graceful compliment as Davenport continued, "Sir, you have made me shed tears at your tragedy and smile at your comedy though I scarcely understand a word of your language. Or words much to that effect," he concluded modestly.

At this stage, the Frenchman threw his arms around the surprised Garrick, pulling him into a fierce hug. Greene heard sounds of 'magnifique' and 'incroyable' escaping the embrace before Hume and Davenport between them could coax the delighted figure to relinquish his grip and permit Garrick to compose himself.

After brief pleasantries were directed to the uncomprehending guest via Davenport once more, honour being apparently satisfied, Drury Lane's proprietor was permitted to continue his rounds of welcome and brief conversations with myriad friends and admirers. A shared, wordless smile – and perhaps a hint of comically raised eyebrows – was all that passed between Johnson and his old friend as Garrick moved away, though not before he stooped towards Greene, saying quietly, "Forgive me for being unable to engage further this evening, Mr Greene; my sentiments remain unchanged." With a parting wave he was soon lost as the crowd pressed back to engulf him. The Apothecary stood looking after him, glowing with the warmth and intimacy of the confidence he had shared

Now their turn with the evening's other celebrity had arrived, as Rousseau turned back to them, beaming as if his saturnine countenance would split in two. As the Doctor and Langton were first introduced, the Apothecary was racking his memory for the school-room French he could still recall. He took a deep breath, "Je suis très content de faire votre connaissance, Monsieur. Bienvenue en Angleterre et à Londres." The Frenchman was obviously pleased at Greene's effort and rattled off something incomprehensible to Hume and Davenport, gesturing to a small and now thoroughly embarrassed man suddenly dreading the prospect of a fraternal hug. He need not have worried as conversation via two expert interpreters moved rapidly along.

With the *sotto voce* assistance of Langton at both Samuel's and Greene's shoulder, it transpired that the Frenchman was enthusiastically accepting an offer of accommodation from Davenport, the older man busily explaining that of his various houses he would be delighted if their visitor would avail himself of somewhere called Woollaton Hall. Greene's ears pricked in recognition at the name. There, Davenport was continuing, both the Frenchman and his wife would be free of the constant attentions of admirers and the downright curious; there, as a valued guest Rousseau would be able to re-embark upon his writings without fear of the ever-present interruptions and harassment which were blighting his brief sojourn in London.

"Woollaton!" exclaimed Greene, "Of course!" Everyone turned to him in surprise. He became suddenly aware that his recognition

of the name had been said aloud. "Oh, forgive me, it's just that…
well, is that Ellastone, in Staffordshire, you're talking of, Mr
Davenport? One couldn't help but overhear," he finished lamely.

"It is, indeed, Mr Greene. Do you know of it?" replied
Davenport courteously.

"Richard is a Lichfeldian, Sir, as am I," interjected Johnson.
"The difference between us is that whereas he knows every stick,
stone, nook and cranny of Staffordshire and parts well beyond,
I could hardly get away fast enough!" He was met with polite
laughter before Davenport continued, "Might one enquire the
nature of your calling, Mr Greene? Woollaton is scarcely more
than a short ride from Lichfield."

Once more the bear-like figure intervened, "Modesty will
forbid him from blowing his own trumpet, Davenport, but I
shall not spare his blushes! Quite apart from being a surgeon-
apothecary renowned for killing far fewer patients than most, he
has somehow found both time and energy to hoard innumerable
curiosities, venerable antiquities and wonders of the natural world
beyond number and belief! I am reliably informed that he is aided
and abetted in said endeavours by a wife of saintly tolerance. She
is married to a bona fide museum keeper, for pity's sake!"

"Ah, there we have it then, Mr Greene! As our distinguished
guest will, it seems, shortly be availing himself of my poor
hospitality at Woollaton, he would – I am certain – welcome both
a neighbourly visit from your good self and even, perhaps, the
opportunity of visiting your collection? It sounds extraordinary,
and Monsieur Rousseau is a passionate botanist and student of
nature in all its forms."

Seeing the amazed gratification spreading on the small man's
face, Davenport turned back to the Frenchman, embarking on a
lengthy description of his conversation with the apothecary. It
ended with a very gallic shrug of acquiescence and a somewhat
limp handshake. "A bientôt, Monsieur. A votre service." The
conversation moved away.

"One gathers there are warrants out for him all over Europe," growled Johnson, as they began to ready themselves for departure, the gathering breaking up around them. Seeing the look of surprise on Greene's face, the Doctor punched him jovially on a shoulder, almost knocking him back into Bennet. "You are scarcely the only man to be well-informed, Cousin!" he mimicked. "It pays to know one's company, and that one has been dubbed 'The Anti-Christ' on more than one occasion!"

Before Greene could respond to his cousin's sardonic observation, Johnson's face wrinkled into one of his many grimaces as he exclaimed, "Now, to bed with you, Sir! Enough of this ceaseless round of pleasure-seeking. I'll not have you miss that coach in the morning. I'll be needing to charge you rent soon – it seems you've been here a month at least!"

To shared laughter the trio made their way back into the unrelenting bustle of Drury Lane to parting handshakes, and thence to bed.

(8)

A Mahogany Café, covered with Glafs. In a fmall Mahogany
Box, in the form of a Coffin, a piece of Flint, in the fhape of
a Child's Head, found at Exmouth, in Devonshire, given by
Mr Lister. A Chalice of Nottingham Ware, fuppofed to have
been used for religious purpofes, mounted with Silver, curiously
carved and gilded. Three Chalices of Pewter, much decayed, some
Gold Lace, and a piece of the upper leather of Shoes, found
at different periods in making Graves in Lichfield Cathedral.

Derbyshire. 14th April. It was as if the keening, bladed wind had
never dropped. Not once since the great, flat stones had been
torn from peat-black soil, sledged and dragged and toppled into
shallow pits, then left to fix the place forever on the scoured moor.
A circle it was called, 'Devil's Hoop' by others, a place for counting
days and turning seasons, a place of voices in the soughing wind
and sometimes blood. A place from whence, first west by north
then west again, the wind scythed on. Into the dales and hollow
ways, the drovers' paths cut deep by countless hooves, the broken,
cobbled tracks that marked where men had challenged all the
worst the wind could bring and often paid the price of their
presumption.

This night, heedless of the springtime greening all the soft
lands to the south, it sliced, and niggled, bent and worried grasses
browned by frost and chill that rarely seemed to lift, following

the shadows that ran ahead of a dim-red setting sun, into a place where even it was given pause. A dark, misshapen mass, a lightless pile of stone on stone, a seeming void that stood out stark against the slope of moors that rose beyond the age-stained walls, up to meet a rising moon, though one gone soon as glimpsed, blotted out by scudding clouds and falling night.

The shapes of padding dogs marked out a boundary known by them alone: half-seen, slinking forms that seemed to come and go, more shadowed than the darkness pooled around the lightless walls. A priory, built by some forgotten hands, whose dwindling brethren perished, one by one, from some contagion, nameless, deadly, brought down upon them by the tireless wind. So, when a King fell out of love and then began to count its cost, commissioners and survey-men were sent – to each place such as this; to price its worth, to burn its books, to steal its lead and auction stone. Here though, they found only what the wind – and crows – had left. A place so rank and desolate they turned about and crossed it from their lengthy lists. A place lain empty for so long that when a rich man, hunting on the moors above, looked down, he thought at first that what he saw was little more than some great tumbled cairn – a giant's work, no doubt – a place that had become at one with all the lichened rocks that lay about its empty shell.

With none who cared enough to tell him it was not his to do, he seized it in the way that money does and made it all his own. With roofs remade, with glass reset, the draughts were stopped, the leaks made good. The crumbling sag of wall and broken arch were straightened up or keyed anew, and stone-flagged floors and altar-tops all scoured until the grime of ages came away.

Then, when all was nicely done, demands all met, instructions all fulfilled with nervous care, the rich man moved his dogs and horses to this place the wind called home, his goods and chattels too – even a wife, though she was last to come and loathed it when she first set foot into its cloistered gloom. She lasted for a year, perhaps a little more, though not before she left an ailing child to mourn the comfort she alone had brought.

The years fled past and old men died, a sickly son who'd come of age now roamed the old monks' halls. He had his dogs, his horses too though this one chose to spend his hours, his weeks and months, among the books and scrolls, the weevilled dust and cobwebbed shelves, that once had been the old men's sole delight. They too – his now – were all a narrow, stunted heart desired.

Just as his sire before him – and at that parent's cold command – he had dabbled for a while amongst the costly pleasures of a fenland town where ancient learning was the thing for sale. It suited him to play its game for just so long as boredom could be kept at bay, but in the end, when its pleasures all had palled, its facile challenges all met, its examinations no more than empty rites of passage, dismissed one by tiresome one, he knew he'd shed the burden, paid the dues. Then, when the final day arrived, he'd left without a backward glance, without a word of fond farewells, his watery eyes fixed firmly on the road ahead – the road that took him back to all his crabby heart had long desired. To empty chambers, cheerless halls, to cloisters where his feet – and his alone – could pace through sunlit flickers on the broken tiles. Away from jibes, from nudges, jokes and foul-mouthed badinage, from mediocrity in all its lumpen forms.

Another might have wept with joy to see the bleached moors rising up once more before their squinting eyes, the wind a stinging lash against a cold-chapped face, the rainclouds massing to the east. He had simply gored his spurs into his tired mount's flank and hurried home.

This night, high on the moor a hare sat, rigid in the moonless dark, ears back, nose lifted to the gusting wind – and watched as light flared in a window down below. A kindled flame that settled to a glow and lit the ancient stone mullions and brought the remnants of their painted glass to sudden life. Joined now by its mate, the hares both listened to a breeze-borne sound of broken, ugly words that seemed to rise and fall; a chanting, tuneless drone that had the distant, prowling dogs first stop and then, heads down and haunches sunk, all melt back into shadow-pools of deeper black beneath the weathered walls. First one, another and then all began a moaning howl that rose and rose until it fused into an eerie chord. The light went out and silence flooded back to fill the sudden void, but not before a jagged shadow seemed to rise and caper for an instant in the flame-lit place below.

The hares ran off to tell their goddess what they had heard and what they thought they'd seen.

(9)

On the Wall, the left hand the ALTAR PIECE, in Glafs
Cafes. The Tail and Claws of the Bever. A Camelion, –
Lizard, – Leghorn Lobster, – a Crocodile, as just taken
from the Egg, – Shells of the Land Tortoife, Oftracion, or
Triangular Fifh, Rhinoceros Beetle, very large, – Sea Bat, –
Scarabeus Cervus, or Stag Beetle, – Flies from Virginia.

Lichfield. 15th April. With a wan, sheepish smile the co-
proprietor of Greene's Apothecary stood in the open doorway of
his shop, valise and travelling bag dropped at his feet, clutching
the largest bunch of daffodils that his wife had ever seen. She
sat back and surveyed the joyous sight with mock severity, ever
mindful of the sprain that was the sole reason for not damning
proprieties, crossing the floor and flinging open arms around her
husband's neck.

"What sort of time do you call this, Mr Greene?" she began.
"Was the London coach diverted via Amsterdam?" She rose,
unsteadily to peer more closely at the cornucopia of blooms. "I
declare I have never seen their like, husband. There must be a
half-dozen different varieties there. Did you wave the coach to
carry on, pick each one and walk the rest of the way home?"

"Oh, my dear, I am so sorry. As you know, I had expected to be
back hours earlier than this, but the wretched excuse for transport
shed a wheel at Bassett's Pole. We sat beside the gibbet for close
on five hours, forced to ponder on our mortality whilst trying to

pretend the ghastly thing was not there, and all-too obviously occupied!"

In the face of his woebegone apology, Theodosia relented with a delighted laugh. "All's well that ends well, Mr Greene. James, would you get the boy to take the master's bags upstairs? If you'll take my arm, husband, we shall descend to scandalise Margery. I am so weak-kneed with relief at your eventual return I simply cannot face the prospect of our stairs."

After the predicted clucks and mutters of disapproval at this invasion of her sanctum, their housekeeper settled for fussing around them until the kitchen table was laid out to her own plan of campaign, with husband and wife properly re-united over scones, cake, cheese and her largest teapot. She then busied herself with some unspecified task necessitating a prolonged sigh and a back turned resolutely away from her seated employers whilst she fiddled with an unseen task against the dresser that dominated one wall of her kitchen empire. Richard and Theodosia Greene scarcely dared look at each other as they awaited the inevitable. They were not to be disappointed.

In a voice redolent with the exhaustion, the bitter disappointment and sheer ingratitude involved in doing one's best to care for one's thoughtless employers – however little one was appreciated – Marjery finally spoke: "Not my place to say a body should or shouldn't go away and suit themselves whenever their fancy's taken by this and that, but all I can say is that when another body's too poorly to do anything at all for itself, well, who has to step up and do even more than needs doing most all of the time, anyway? Not for the likes of me to be saying, 'can't be done', but when a body works her fingers to the bone – not that she ever expects a thank you or a by your leave – it would be nice for a body to know she's not going to be left to do more of everything, all the time, with no-one but her chit of a girl to help when a body goes off and suits themselves without a thought for other bodies left behind."

They sat in well-practised, perfect silence; both – in spite of the resolutely turned back – doing their best to appear attentive and contrite, waiting for the litany to run out of steam, knowing that at any moment the speaker might turn back to monitor the effect of words addressed with such sorrow to no one in particular.

When, finally, the basilisk stare was turned on the man sitting to attention at her table, he nodded sagely, saying, "Absolutely, Margery. Straight to the point, nail hit well and truly on its head, point taken as ever. My, how I've missed your scones, light enough to float away all on their own."

With a snort of either indignation or disbelief, and eyebrows raised conspiratorially to her impassive mistress, she swept out towards the back range pausing only to glare at her employer once more to say: "You'll be telling me you've no appetite for supper, next, I suppose."

"Unfailingly caring," said Theodosia, averting her face.

"Unfailingly," added the Apothecary, waiting for the sound of a closing door. It came, and both dissolved into helpless laughter.

"There, that's telling a body, you thoughtless beast." She stared into the well-loved eyes and saw the animation and pent-up excitement dancing within. "Was it all quite wonderful?"

"Simply astonishing, my dear. I scarcely know where to begin," he said, taking a deep breath, instantly forestalled by a beaming wife: "Well, I can be of assistance on that score, Mr Greene. There are prescriptions outstanding for old Mrs Laughton, John Halliwell and that ailing son of the Padleys, out at Ridware. All three need a particularly careful hand and your best judgement with the opium dosage, Richard. So, there's as good a place to start as any! Oh, and you'll be wanting to check your surgery appointments for the morning. Six, if memory serves; all much the same as usual, but still..."

Laughing at his wife's expert intervention, Greene replied: "You'll not escape so easily this evening, Theodosia. It has been a most remarkable experience and one I know you will be most gratified to share."

"Well, that's as may be, my dear, but I shall also tell you of this morning's conversation with Elspeth Blomefield. Both they and we have, apparently, shared a most unwelcome visitor in your absence."

Seeing the apprehension cloud her husband's face, Theodosia said quickly, "Richard, what a graceless hag of a wife I am to welcome you with this on your return, it is just that…" – the Apothecary jumped to his feet in alarm as she visibly bit back tears – "…it was something to do with the museum, or with whatever you found at Eccleshall, she says. Lionel has been out of sorts ever since he was accosted, and I've been so worried that this creature might come back before you returned."

Now thoroughly alarmed he lifted his arms towards her, "Oh my dear, I never should have left you so thoughtlessly." He got no further as Theodosia, suddenly all brisk efficiency, came awkwardly to her feet and sniffed back her tears, saying, "Oh, it's nothing that won't wait, Richard. I'm just being a complete ninny – I've missed you so much."

As he moved towards her, she held up an admonitory hand and said, "Prescriptions, Mr Greene, and then all the other things you have so shamelessly neglected in your absence. Not a moment to be lost, Sir! We shall prattle to our hearts' content, but later." He knew better than to argue.

With supper finished, a score of verbal miniatures of London life sketched to a fascinated wife and an almost mollified housekeeper bade a goodnight, he had insisted on inspecting the shop's scarred door.

Returning angrily to their parlour, where Theodosia sat, foot propped, by a small fire lit against the evening's chill, he said bitterly, "I am thankful that you were spared the encounter, my dear, though it sounds as if Tillett acquitted himself admirably. Was the fellow simply deranged? He would have got short shrift from me, is all I can say! And will do if ever he has the temerity to show his wretched face again. How dare he act in such a pointlessly vicious manner?"

"Oh, he had a point, for certain, Richard, one he made all-too clear to poor Lionel. What is the nature of this..?" She was interrupted by a timid knock at the parlour door, and the equally timid face of their young maid, dressed for bed but holding a letter.

"This just came for you, Sir, from The Close," she said. "I thought I'd heard a knocking, so Aunt sent me up."

"Thank you, Maisie," said Theodosia. "That will be all. I'm sorry you were disturbed at this late hour. Off to bed with you now." With a nervous bob the maid left them.

Pulling his spectacles from a waistcoat pocket, the Apothecary squinted at the handwritten address before placing them on his nose. He broke the wax closure, opened the folded page and looked up at his waiting wife.

"Do we believe in coincidence, my dear?" he enquired, though waiting no response before scanning its contents. "This is from Canon Seward, asking that both Lionel and I attend him 'at our earliest convenience' tomorrow. He, too, has been visited it would appear. This is all most peculiar."

"And you were about to tell me just what this peculiarity is about, husband?"

(10)

An image of the Virgin Mary, finely carved in Box Wood, holding an Infant Jefus in her Arms, at her Feet, a child playing with a Lamb. A fmaller image alfo of the Virgin Mary in Box, in which the Child is feen placing a Crown upon the Head of his Mother, Thefe three figures feem to be the Work of the fame Artist and were prefented by the Right Honourable the Earl of Uxbridge.

Lichfield. Friday 16ᵗʰ April. It was late afternoon by the time that Greene and Blomefield were able to able to enjoy the sunshine of a blustery spring day as they strolled across the Dam, gazing appreciatively at the water-ruffled surface of the Minster Pool and its chattering contingent of bustling moorhens, busy amongst the profusion of greening rushes at the foot of the Close wall. The tall, gangling cleric habitually stooped when addressing the small man who was his lifelong friend, though Greene had long-ago abandoned his vain attempts to stop the infuriating practice, adding it to the lengthening list of 'Lionel's little ways' that would have driven a lesser man, a less saintly wife and a circle of less-than-devoted friends to complete distraction.

Today, the Apothecary was taking the voluble Vicar of St Mary's with grim seriousness. "You felt this, this creature actually capable of violence towards you? In the porch of your own church? In broad daylight?" Greene had stopped and, in his urgency, gripped Blomefield by his arm.

"Far worse than violence, Richard," replied Blomefield with quiet vehemence. "I shall never forget his eyes; it was like a glimpse of Perdition. By the grace of the good Lord, never before have I stared into the face of Evil incarnate. That day I did. Even the memory of it chills me to the bone. That was a man capable of anything."

"For all that she was spared first-hand experience of this vile rogue, I begin to understand Theodosia's fear of his return far better now, Lionel. Poor Tillett was deeply upset by him – and he the least perturbable of men, as you well know."

Their approach to the Palace's grand door was met by the emerging forms of Anna Seward and dogs, the bonneted figure waving gaily towards them whilst attempting also to hold down her headgear in the sudden breeze.

"Lionel, dear. Mr Greene! Papa is agog with excitement over this and that. He awaits you in the library, though might have quite worn out its carpet with his pacing. He appears so exercised that one must hope your appearance will provide the oil to his troubled waters. I have seldom known him so vexed and agitated though apparently over matters unsuited to a mere daughter's ears!"

With a smile as brittle as it was forced, she added briskly, "But I must not keep you gentlemen from your important gentlemen's business. Come, dogs!" She yanked at her leads. "Lionel, dear. Mr Greene. I bid you both Good Afternoon."

By the time that his visitors were seated, each with a glass of cordial at his elbow, the Canon had dismissed his manservant with visible impatience, before sitting himself down in what appeared to be absolute exhaustion and pointing to the carpet.

"There, Richard; there, Lionel! Do you see them? The footprints?" Each followed a pointing hand that seemed none too steady, the white marks clearly evident across the intricate pattern.

"I have left them quite deliberately for all that I abhor the memory of the intrusion." He saw the look that passed between his visitors. "We were burgled – if that is not too strong a word. Nothing was stolen to my knowledge, and I have done my level best to play the wretched business down, so as not to further distress Anna. I have forbidden any mention of it by our staff, so no word of this, this outrage, has gone beyond the Palace walls." He paused, looking almost accusingly between his listeners: "And yet, you both seem, how shall I put it? Unsurprised?"

"It suddenly appears that we all have notes to compare, Canon Seward," the Apothecary began, "though seeing these footprints left upon your floor, an account of how a not dissimilar visitation to my own premises was apparently made, should wait upon yours, I think."

They each listened avidly – and with growing concern – to the other. Blomefield's account alone, however, was what put a face – a coldly malevolent face – to the intrusions all had shared. Greene had by then explained that his shop-man, Tillett, had been unable or unwilling to describe the heavily scarfed figure in any meaningful detail, other than attempting to convey its infuriated menace.

"I regret to say that the reason for these visitations requires no imagination whatsoever, my friends," said Seward into the ensuing silence that filled the book-lined room. "Although I can ascertain neither rhyme nor reason as to how knowledge of its whereabouts or its discovery have been transmitted, de Langton's box and its regrettable contents are at the root of this."

No agreement was required.

"What I have not yet mentioned is the fortunate fact that I had removed the wretched thing prior to this." He pointed again at the carpet as if reluctant to give a name to the violation of his home. "It presently resides where few thieves would think to look."

"May one enquire..?" began Greene.

"Protected by an upturned wheelbarrow and tucked away in the most suitable place imaginable, Richard," came the bland response.

Then, though, with a dejected shake of his head, he continued with obvious reluctance: "Two further complications have emerged in the meantime, however, as if we have not been presented with upsets enough. Both within hours of that which we all experienced." His listeners stiffened with renewed attention.

Seward stood and fetched several things from the table in the bay window. Laying one, a book, on the arm of his chair, he opened the other. On stiff, monogrammed paper, a brief text, concluded with a floridly scrawled signature was held up to them. Seward balanced spectacles on his long nose before peering over them to address Greene and Blomefield: "It is a reply from our Lord Bishop to my letter concerning the Eccleshall business. It should perhaps come as no surprise that his steward's account of our visit was despatched with alacrity; self-preservation being the order of the day. It will have been couched in less than helpful terms, one imagines, doing little to reassure the recipient concerning our actions. I shall read you His Lordship's response to my own correspondence if I may, its brevity being its sole recommendation.

Your intervention in this discovery was importunate and, I am forced to say, misjudged in the extreme, usurping our servant's proper authority in the safeguarding of our best interests. Your precipitate action has invested the relic with an importance utterly disproportionate to its actuality. It is to be destroyed forthwith, along with any written record of its discovery likely to further impugn the reputation of our noted and unblemished antecedent.

"Given at Windsor, etc, etc." Seward concluded with most un-characteristic distaste.

"What a pompous buffoon!" Greene exclaimed, but then seeing the pained expression on his host's aged face, relented with a mildly apologetic shrug. "That was probably uncalled for, sitting here in yet another of His Lordship's palaces, but, Canon, could you, or anyone with even the slightest regard for history, really be expected to destroy this object?"

The Canon cut in with unexpected brusqueness: "I did say that two complications have arisen Richard; kindly permit me to finish, if you will."

Thoroughly abashed, the Apothecary sat back and waited for their agitated host to continue.

"It has been my habit for some years occasionally to assist the chaplain of St John's in his ministry, and I was making my way there on Wednesday afternoon, enjoying a walk prior to evensong, when I encountered the most unexpected – the most unsettlingly apposite – sight imaginable."

Greene and Blomefield sat motionless, transfixed by what could be coming next, each long familiar with the serried rank of great chimneys that were the distinguishing feature of The Hospital of St John's whose tranquil existence had remained undisturbed even through Civil War.

"I was about to cross to the Hospital, just past the Grammar School, when a barouche driven at breakneck speed careered from Wade Street, with utter disregard for anyone or anything that might have been making its proper way along St John Street. I was almost sent flying by the heedless fool at the reins, but not before I had glimpsed a crest on the vehicle's door, though its occupant remained screened within."

Seward reached for the book at his elbow. "That crest, I regret to say, is one with which we have all become familiar in recent weeks." He opened a book-marked page and turned its illustration towards his listeners. Both gaped in incredulity.

"Indeed, my friends, scarcely what one might have expected." The Canon laid it aside. "There can be no doubt, I must ask you to believe that. The crest and the armorial I have just shown you are identical in every respect. That coach bore the original medieval form of the de Langton arms. In the light of all that has occurred, what, pray, are we to make of that?" Seeing the bemused faces opposite, Seward added, "Please believe me, my question is far from rhetorical, gentlemen. I am utterly confounded by this turn of events."

(11)

A Peacock (cut with a pair Sciffers), by Mrs Greaves of Culcheth, Lancafhire. A beautiful reprefentation of Telemachus and Mentor arriving at the Ifland of Calypfo; it is a clofe copy, (cut like the above) from the Copper Plate Magazine, by a Spaniard, prefented by Mr Lucas Bateman of London. General Wolf, cut in Writing Paper, with a Penknife, by Thomas Hunter of Edinburgh.

Lichfield. 16ᵗʰ/17ᵗʰ/18ᵗʰ April. For once, in a life characterised by dithering and indecision, Lionel Blomefield had been implacable in his refusal to be involved in any way.

"No, I shall not stand lookout, and no, I will not provide you with some hare-brained reason for being out, trespassing, in the middle of the night. Yes, you may well be right that this folly has Seward's tacit approval, but tacit will butter no scones when it comes to Constables, Justices, or, more likely, a guard-dog with sharp teeth looking for someone to impress. It is burglary, Richard, however you choose to dress it up." The cleric had looked desperately skywards for inspiration, but finding none, returned to the hopeless task.

"Richard, you know as well as do I that every other reason for abandoning this idea pales into insignificance before the final question, 'What will Theodosia have to say about this?' About a midnight trespass into the Palace gardens – gardens now equipped with their very own guard-dog? The covert removal of what is, in all likelihood, a particularly nasty black magic book and its equally covert installation into a museum of her acquaintance? What has possessed you?"

"Forgiving you that particularly inept form of words in the circumstances, Lionel, the answer could not be simpler. We were left in no doubt that, despite his reluctance, our very proper and intensely honourable Canon believes he has no choice but to obey his bishop's instruction to destroy the book. A relic of such astonishing rarity and, dare I say? historical importance that we shall never see its like again. At risk of sounding pompous, I refuse to countenance book-burning, Lionel, least of all by a respected friend who believes that he has been afforded no other option. Why else would he have casually mentioned that this new canine sentinel of theirs will be confined to the stable block for several nights? Do we really believe that mastiffs are now to be employed as ratters?"

When Blomefield shrugged an end to his vain attempts at persuasion, Greene added, triumphantly, "And why else would he have informed us of its precise hiding-place, Lionel? 'Behind an upturned wheelbarrow and tucked away in the most suitable place possible.' – which I understand is to say: 'in de Langton's very own tower in the corner of the Palace's very own garden, no less!' I know an invitation when I hear one."

"You are on your own, Mr Greene, and there's an end to it," said the cleric dejectedly, "but mark my words, no good will come of it."

As they parted, the Apothecary was already lost in thought. "Astronomy, I think," he said to himself. "Yes, that's it. I shall be riding out to Borrowcop tomorrow night, the better to observe the transit of something or other." He looked up at the pallid perfection of a new moon, beginning its spectral ascent in the dusk. That was all decided then. He quickened his pace back to Saddler Street and supper, agreeing with himself that it would be perfectly reasonable to defer any consideration of his wife's sensitivities in certain areas of what were, after all, museum affairs, for heaven's sake.

Being a convinced believer in the virtue of coincidence, the Apothecary was relieved but unsurprised at Theodosia's reaction to what he was now describing to himself as a necessary fiction.

"I shall not be returning from Elspeth's until quite late, I imagine, Richard. Her sister's visit should provide us both with more than enough scandal and gossip from the fleshpots of York to play you at your own game, Sir! There seeming to be no end in sight regarding your anecdotes of London."

"Oh, my dear, I have no intention of..." began her crestfallen spouse.

"I am joking, Richard, quite probably," she responded slyly, delighted at his reaction. "But what I was leading up to in my interminable wifely fashion..." – she placed arms around his neck – "...is that if you are to be out into the small hours on some star-chasing ramble, I can well do without cold feet disturbing my beauty sleep on your return. I shall ask Margery to air the bed in the blue room, being certain to reassure her that our marriage is not yet coming asunder."

"Yes, my dear, an excellent idea," he replied, carefully disengaging to busy himself with the view from the breakfast-room window. "I have no wish to disturb you – or Margery, the Lord only knows."

The biting easterly wind had sprung up in the late afternoon, reminding both prudent gardeners and those of a less-well upholstered physique that the perennial contrariness of early spring weather was disregarded at peril. Fortunately for the small, well-shadowed figure now making his tentative way along the inner face of the Close wall in the direction of a low gate, both de Langton's battered enceinte and its terminal tower in the most easterly corner, were protecting him from the spite of the unremitting gusts.

The pale moonlight that intermittently pierced an aerial armada of scudding clouds failed to penetrate the deep shadows in which the Apothecary moved towards his goal.

Innumerable clamberings and measurings of the remains over many years had provided him with an intimate knowledge of the ins and outs of the warren that constituted so much of the ancient village-within-a-city surrounding the vast bulk of the cathedral church itself. Pausing to regain breath and able to raise his eyes from the careful negotiation of the broken ground, Greene marvelled – for the thousandth time – at the profile of the three spires black against the racing night. The trio, these well-loved 'Ladies of the Vale' slumbered on as he silently entered the Canon's palatial gardens, gently replacing the gate's heavy latch to its socket before skirting the perfectly mown lawns – all grey in the low light.

It was only as he reached the arched doorway of the Bishop's Tower that the Apothecary realised how cold he was, and what trepidation he felt as he peered into the pitch-black interior of the roofless ruin. A plan conceived in the genial light of day was one thing, the uncomfortable reality of executing it quite another. Glancing nervously towards the lightless Palace before checking the tinderbox and candle in a capacious pocket, he took a deep breath and stepped inside.

It would only be later that it occurred to an older and – just possibly – a wiser man, that this was the precise moment when everything began to go so wrong.

(12)

A Book bound in Ruffia Leather, 25 inches by 20, containing twenty two impreffions from Wooden Blocks, in Charo Scuro; publifhed at Venice, by J. Baptist Pasquali 1745, this noble work was executed by a J.B. Jackson, an Englishman; and entitled, "Titiani Vecelli, Pauli Caliarii, Jacobi Robufti, et Jacopo de Ponte, Opera Selectiora, a Joanne Baptista Jackson, Anglo, ligno caelata, et coloribus adumbrate." Presented to the Museum, by the Rev. Henry White, A.M. Sacrift of the Cathedral Church of Lichfield, and Vicar of Chebsey, in the County of Stafford; a most generous contributor to this Museum.

Derbyshire. 16ᵗʰ/17ᵗʰ April. Leaving in the grey light of false-dawn, the bookseller had ridden from Derby, the panniers of the mule led behind his winter-fat mare well fastened against the changeable day. He broke his fast in the late morning at the Green Dragon in Ashbourne's bustling St John's Street, thinking with less than happy anticipation of what lay ahead. But then, he sighed with resignation, guineas are guineas, and there was no shortage of coin at his destination – however little he ever wanted to retrace those lonely, windswept miles and the dank, sour place at their end. Doubtless, he would be expected to buy back, as well as sell, today – that was the usual, thankless arrangement. Once only had he attempted to renegotiate the arrangement, to be met with such implacable coldness that he wished he had never spoken. No answer had been forthcoming, by now none was expected. He simply laid out his wares – his very particular wares – for inspection, was handed the tied bundle of what he was expected to re-purchase and was told he would be summoned when a decision had been reached.

Served thin ale, sour cheese and rough bread by a mute servant almost as colourless as the surroundings, he would be left to fill his time in a drab cell beyond the cloister range. Forbidden to leave its confines, he had at times waited for hours, occasionally a day, before the business would be brusquely concluded and he was free to leave a place he had come to loathe. The only thing he could tell himself, the sole reason he made this joyless pilgrimage over and again, was that there had never been an argument concerning price. Nor the very special offerings, the unusually costly offerings, for which he was known – albeit in most discreet circles. Neither had the reimbursement he offered on the books returned ever been questioned. It was obviously assumed – quite correctly – that both transactions would be carried out to mutual satisfaction or never again. He chose never to dwell upon his queasy conviction that the volumes, the prints and fragments returned to him always had an inexplicably used quality about them; one which made him reluctant to handle them any more than was necessary. He would invariably pass them on at substantially reduced prices to be rid of them.

The barely glimpsed recipient, master of this godforsaken pile, was far from being the bookman's only customer with rarefied tastes, certainly far from alone in possessing a purse deep enough to cater to them.

This one, though, and the one who appeared to serve him, were of a different order. So removed, so frigidly detached from a world full of light, of laughter, a world of simple pleasures, that simply to be in this nameless place made him feel unclean. So, whenever the black, pin-prick pupils of those dead eyes signalled that their business for that day was done, he would feel his spirits rise as he began to count the minutes before he could breathe cold moorland air once more. This time though, was to be different.

Summoned back by a servant's mute gesture towards what must once have been the grandest of the buildings clustered close about the cloister garth, he was met and waved into a dimly lit chamber by the cadaverous figure with whom he usually dealt. For a moment he thought they were alone until a thin, sibilant voice sounded; the speaker concealed entirely by a great high-backed chair pulled close to the room's huge fireplace – this, the bookman could now see, being the only source of light.

"What you have brought is of little account but will be purchased. You will settle for the discarded pieces, as is the custom before payment is made. Today, though, one has a commission which you will undertake if you hope ever to do your business here again. You will be paid handsomely for your trouble – a substantial advance made now, the balance upon completion – the delivery, into my hands and mine alone, of what you are charged to find. Do you understand?"

"Certainly, Sir, but what if..?" It was as if he had not spoken.

"Once you have located that which is sought you will obtain it on one's behalf regardless of cost. Regardless, you understand. You will be directed towards several likely locations, and monies forwarded to you, should the necessity arise. The container that holds the object of your search will be described. That, too, must be acquired. Under no circumstances must that container be re-opened once its contents have been confirmed, or those contents disturbed. One will know if it has been disturbed in any way, and there will be a price to pay, one dearer than you can contemplate should this have occurred."

"But if this thing is not for sale?" the bookman blurted, thoroughly alarmed now at what were simply instructions.

"Then you will obtain the prize by whatever means you see fit. By any means, be clear on that account. Understand this, also, once you have accepted the payment on account..." – it sounded to the now thoroughly frightened man that the words were spoken with something that might pass as a smile – "…there will be no turning back. No refund can be offered, none will be accepted." Again, a sort of smile.

Before he could find the words to reply, to babble that he was leaving never to return, before attempting to make a run from this dreadful place, a thud, accompanied by the chink of coin, drew his eyes to the table as his side. Tossed carelessly onto it, a purse spilled out more guineas than the bookman had ever seen in one place. He simply gaped. This was an advance?

"That is settled, then. You will be expected to return by the end of the month. Leave as soon as your business is done."

A thin wrist emerged, waved a languid dismissal, a black silhouette against the fire.

(13)

A fmall Crucifix in Silver, made faft to a plate of Brafs,
intended, as suppofed, for the Prieft to prefent for the
Sick to kifs, called a Pax. A neat Bafon in Alabafter.

Lichfield. 19th April. It was well into the small hours by the time
the Apothecary had finally managed to pacify his horse with a
nosebag, a warming blanket and many soothing words breathed
into her silken ear. The agitated shivers, the wholly unaccustomed
fretting and shying calming at last in the sweet-smelling loosebox
that had been her home these many years past. Perhaps it had
simply been the tethering in an unfamiliar, shadowed corner of
The Close that had unsettled a creature of long, undemanding
habit, he told himself. When he had returned to her though,
hobbling, panting for breath, bleeding and soaked in sweat, she
had reacted as if he were a threatening stranger come to do her
harm, bucking, rearing in such fright he had thought she would
wake the sleeping Close from end to end.

Now, though, with the sound of contented munching from her
stall, he sat with a wheeze of exhaustion on the nearest of the
stable's stacked bales and began to ease his riding boot from an
agonised foot. He suppressed a groan of pain as it came away, his
hose and the lining of the boot itself soaked in blood, almost black
in the low light of his small lamp. Knowing better than to try and
remove the shard here, its jagged length glistening in the lamp's
glow, he rinsed a chamois leather and applied it, with relief and

considerable care, to the throbbing agony of his face. Unbidden, his thoughts were drawn back to the distant time before all this pain had begun. A time when he could have been sleeping blamelessly up in the tall house at the top of his garden. The words 'no good will come of it' rang, thanklessly, in his aching head.

His first step into the tower's pitch-dark interior had brought the unmistakable crack of breaking glass beneath his foot, as a razor-sharp shard penetrated boot and foot with a stab of agony. Teeth gritted in a rictus of pain, he had leant back against the lintel, fumbling for his flint and striker, sweat gathering on his brow, as he managed to light his candle-stub after several cursing attempts. Now, in the shielded glow of a small, guttering flame, the culprit was revealed: a small discarded pane, lying in crazed pieces on the rubble-strewn floor. Scarcely daring to put weight upon the injured foot, Greene knew there was no going back. He steeled himself to hobble towards the corner where the upturned wheelbarrow of the Canon's description stood propped against the crumbling stonework of the wall.

Its unexpected weight sent lancing pain through his leg and foot as he strained to manhandle the large wooden obstacle to one side. There was a cupboard, woodwork rotten with age and damp, its hinges vestigial strips of rusted iron scarcely capable of holding the fragmentary door in place. He felt suddenly chilled, though none of the night's gusts penetrated this abandoned shell.

Cold sweat trickled down his back as he pulled the resisting cover away, the box within giving back none of the flickering light that lit its place of concealment. Its weight, its frigid chill, astonished him as he hefted it out, both arms beneath a base rough with rotten plaster and the twigs of long-abandoned nests. Even by the time he fell again, tripped this time, across a hoe or some such implement, the weight of his burden seemed to have increased tenfold, each step costing a fresh stab of pain. Now though, burdened as he was, with nothing to break his fall, both nose and chin smashed violently into the metal case.

He had sat sobbing in the darkness, stars and exploding galaxies eventually subsiding in his throbbing head, too hurt to question why or how such a tool could have been discarded, abandoned, laid across a path in this garden that was a paradigm of order.

Managing finally to regain his feet, he had lost all sense of time and it was only the sheer unrelenting weight of his burden that could remind him of what he was doing here at all. Hobbling, bleeding heavily and bathed in the icy sweat of shock, he barely managed to regain the path towards Vicar's Court and his waiting horse. Even in the extremity of his pain he had stopped, not once but twice, certain that he was being followed. But he had seen no movement, nothing, in the hectic night that had engulfed him as he left the shelter of the walls.

With all hopes of a ride home dashed, all he had been able to do was to avoid the thrashing head, the kicking hooves, for long enough to shift his burden into the saddle pannier and then attempt to lead the agitated beast homeward.

With what only later he would recognize as revulsion, he considered the rusted box for what seemed an eternity, before gritting his teeth and bending to lift it from the outhouse floor where it had lain since his battered homecoming. Prepared as he was for the near intolerable burden with which he had staggered through the darkened Close, he almost fell backwards as it lifted, light as a feather, from the brick-tiled floor. It was as if it now contained nothing more than air. Unthinking, instinctively, he pushed it deep within the long-redundant bread oven that had served previous generations in the tall house, and shut the metal door. Had he intended this to be its hiding place? Why would he hide it at all?

He no longer knew or cared.

Desperate with exhaustion, limping towards his back door through the first light of dawn, all he craved was the relief he could bring to his hurts, then a blessed bed in the blessed blue bedroom. Realising, suddenly, that the perfect, noiseless calm of the city all about him indicated that this was a Sunday morning, too, he almost wept with relief.

No shop, no patients, only sleep.

Another man might have sold his soul for less.

(14)

A modern Pipe of Steel, finely polifhed, fo contrived, that by
Screws it may be feperated for the convenience of carrying
it in the pocket; a small piftol Lock is fixed to the Bole, fo
that, by the help of a bit of Tinder, fire may be procured
in the Fields or elsewhere. Purchased from Mr Richards
at the Toy Shop, Birmingham. Price fifteen Shillings.

Saddler Street. 17th April. "So, husband," concluded a beaming
Theodosia, "you agree that the arrangement presents a perfect
quid pro quo? It was wholly unexpected as you can imagine, but
Louise is such a dear, so much like Elspeth that they could be
twins rather than simply sisters, that it would be churlish to turn
her invitation down. You are sure you will be able to manage? That
you don't mind me going?"

"My dear, how could I mind, particularly in view of my own
recent gallivanting? And yes, I am quite certain that I'll stumble
along in much my usual fashion."

"Well, perhaps less stumbling would be no bad thing, Richard,"
she responded, only half in jest, as she looked at the swollen nose
and badly cut chin. "All this damage inflicted in escaping from a
single bull up on Borrowcop, you say? It must have had murder
on its mind to have you in this sorry state. How bad is your foot?
I shall bathe it and re-dress it before I go, if you will permit me."

Knowing that all traces of the tell-tale glass had been finally
removed, splinter by agonising splinter, he mustered what he

hoped would be a plucky smile and said, "Thank you, my dear, that would be most considerate. You plan to leave on Wednesday?"

"With Elspeth and Louise, yes, if you can bear it? I fear I have been of little use, anyway, with this ankle, but I am assured that any promenade around the city walls will be entirely voluntary."

"Oh, I shall envy you everything about York, Theodosia. The Minster glass is said to have no equal in the kingdom."

"Then I shall do my level best to visit it for you, and attempt to see it through your eyes, Richard," she responded fondly, "though I suspect that the city will possess charms of a different order for us more earthbound womenfolk. Its tearooms are the envy of the North from all I hear."

"Then I wish your teacups be overflowing and your cake-stands be stacked to toppling," he exclaimed, catching her joy at the prospect of this well-deserved change of scene.

As she limped happily away from their supper table, he realised – with a degree of perfectly concealed embarrassment – that he was already planning his first examination of the contents of de Langton's long-hidden box. Wednesday night it would be. Perhaps with a local clergyman of his acquaintance for company? He could of course study it on his own in the privacy of his museum upstairs but, he decided, company might be no bad thing at all.

As chance would have it, their shop-man, Tillett, had, with characteristic timidity approached them some weeks earlier, enquiring whether they might wish to consider his young niece for a junior position on the habitually over-stretched staff.

"She's fourteen, going on fifteen, and as hard-working and sweet-natured a girl you could hope to find, Mrs Greene," he had ventured. "Minds her P's and Q's and knows her manners, too. No disrespect, mistress, but what with the master being as busy as he is, a-going here, a-going there, and what with the museum and the manufactory, too – she'd be a boon to us all if you don't mind me saying."

Both husband and wife had promised to give the idea some thought, knowing that Tillett's recommendation would be as trustworthy a reference as could be found. Here, now, was a perfect opportunity to put the girl to the test during Theodosia's ten-day absence. The shopman was delighted.

"Let her start on Tuesday, James, so we can meet her before Mrs Greene leaves – to check she's not a house-breaker and that sort of thing."

"Oh, no, Sir!" Tillett had begun, horrified. "I wouldn't…" He stopped, abashed, seeing the grin on his employer's round face. Would he ever get used to that sense of humour? Probably not, but that was just one of life's many trials, he comforted himself.

When Theodosia's baggage – her staggering amount of baggage in the opinion of a diplomatically mute husband – had been carted down to the coach-yard of The George, fond farewells had been exchanged and three exceedingly well-wrapped ladies were waved off in a clatter of wheels across broken cobbles.

"I suspect that our resident enforcers will have been fully briefed as to our surveillance, Richard," commented Blomefield drily as the laden vehicle disappeared towards Beacon Street and the road north. "Elspeth intimated as much, promising me that I would be getting up to no mischief. When I had the temerity to correct her, suggesting that, surely, I should be the one making the promises, she simply said that she knew better than to expect the impossible."

"Mmm," agreed a thoughtful Apothecary, remembering, uneasily, the look of ill-disguised triumph on Margery's face when she had emerged from a lengthy tête-à tête with his wife 'concerning household matters, my dear, nothing with which to concern yourself'.

"There are, however, two things of which we can be quite certain Lionel." He lifted fingers to enumerate: "One, as far as we know, neither of our Guardian Deities has yet acquired the ability to see through closed doors, and the second, both they and their spies are invariably in bed by nine."

Grinning as they parted outside the Apothecary's kaleidoscopic windows, Lionel said: "So, about a quarter after nine, then?"

"Absolutely," the small man replied, turning to enter his premises, but then stopping as if he had remembered something: "Do you go in for holy water, Lionel, or is that a bit too High Church these days?" Seeing the blank puzzlement in his friend's angular features he added, "No matter, I just thought I'd ask," before waving and disappearing into his shop.

Even after a single day, it seemed to all concerned that Tillett's young niece, 'Emmy, short for Esmeralda, Sir', fitted the bill more than adequately. She was, as promised, bright, biddable and eager to learn. Her good looks, a freckled white face set in a nimbus of red-gold hair – a work still in progress as judged by an appraising Theodosia – had made such an impression on Tillett's boy that it became immediately apparent to her employers that the girl had already made one conquest, though, happily, she had appeared far too busy to notice. When Greene came in, the shopman was quietly differentiating the characteristic bottles and containers that crammed their many shelves. He lined up a sample on the counter for her attention, acknowledging his employer's return with a respectful nod before continuing: "And the ribbed green bottles are acids, poisons and corrosives, never to be touched without these gloves, or without express permission."

Greene passed contentedly through into his private Consulting Room and began the business of laying out his surgical instruments for cleansing in alcohol before the first business of the morning. The lancing of an infection caused by an anal fistula if he recalled. He turned to his appointment book for confirmation. The jingle of the shop bell confirmed a punctual arrival. He laid a discreet cloth over his scalpels before a knock announced the day's first patient.

As supper was being cleared away, the Apothecary had announced that he was expecting company later and would admit the visitor himself. With expertly concealed relish he watched as Margery's curiosity grow almost visibly whilst she directed the clearing and tidying with hawk-eyed scrutiny. "And will you be requiring further refreshment for Mr... the gentleman, Sir?"

"We shall see to ourselves, thank you, Margery, but you might bring up one of the crusted ports for me to decant."

"But they're for special visitors..." she began, but not quickly enough.

"Thank you for an excellent supper, Margery," Greene interjected skilfully; "The pie was perfection itself. That will be all for now, though if you'll kindly leave the port and a decanter on a tray by the museum stairs, I believe we can be trusted to take it up ourselves."

Taking elaborate care not to slam the door very loudly, she left the room, only to be heard making up for a lost opportunity below stairs.

"Round one to the male of the species, I do believe," he said to himself, unwisely.

Promptly at a quarter past nine, Greene rose to answer what he been awaiting – a discreet knock at the passage door – only to hear it being opened before he had even reached the top of the stairs.

"Was it Reverend Blomefield you were expecting, Sir?" came the sweet enquiry called from below. "Because if it was, he's here now, at the door. Or will somebody special be arriving even later?"

(15)

On the Door, on a Plate Japaned, the following infcription, in Gold Letters. Quam Mirabilis funt Opera tua, Domine! Omnia in Sapientia fecifsi: Impleta eft terra poffeffione tua. Hoc Mare Magnum et fpaciofum Manibus; illic reptilia quorum non eft numerus. Pfalm 104. Ver.25 and 26.

The Lichfield Museum. Saddler Street. 20ᵗʰ April. "You really are taking this remarkably seriously, Richard. Unsavoury as it may be, are we not investing a mite too much importance in this wretched thing, much as my ever-gracious episcopal master recently suggested?"

Blomefield reached hopefully for one of the waiting glasses on the tray, before being intercepted by the restraining hand of his host.

"Can we please first do as I suggested, Lionel? Surely it is not unreasonable to ask one's tame clergyman to kick off proceedings with a prayer? It is a rather important part of your calling as we're given to understand."

"Yes, yes," replied the cleric in exasperation, "but that's for baptisms and weddings and all that sort of thing. Aren't we just..?"

"What we are just about to do, Lionel – if I am to be reluctantly forced into some pompous sounding explanation – is to open what I suspect to be a singularly unpleasant object possessing equally unpleasant credentials. Genuinely ancient grimoires such as I absolutely believe this to be, are astonishingly rare – with mercifully few of them thought to have survived."

"'Mercifully'? Oh, please Richard, you are not normally given to such drama. Has Garrick gone entirely to your head?"

"A prayer, Lionel?" responded Greene, now thoroughly exasperated. "Surely, even you can think up something appropriate?"

Before Blomefield could even register annoyance, the Apothecary continued, "Indulge me, if for no other reason. I really do believe it to be of importance."

"Oh, very well," sighed the clergyman. "Seeing as we are apparently about to embark on a foray into the wilder realms of belief, how about something Irish?" Greene waited.

"'St Patrick's Breastplate', I believe it was called. Apparently, it worked for the man himself, at least in terms of snakes, so how about that? I think I can remember the pithy parts at least." Greene waited.

Composing himself, all flippancy gone, Blomefield sought for the words of the ancient prayer:

"God's shield to shelter me

God's host to guide me

God's way to lie before me

God's shield to shelter me God's host to secure me against the snares of demons, against the seductions of vices, against the lusts of nature, against everyone who meditates injury to me."

Christ be with me
Christ before me
Christ behind me
Christ within me
Christ beneath me
Christ above me
Christ at my right
Christ at my left
Christ all about me.

Greene thought he heard his old friend say, "Well, that's the best I can do. The original is much longer, but if that doesn't do the trick then I don't think the unabridged version would make a whole lot of difference."

As if emerging from a dream, he realised that he had been watching the speaker's mouth.

Each, and every one of his breaths had been visible. The temperature of the museum had plummeted.

"Oh," said Blomefield, as if suddenly becoming aware of it himself. "Can we open the port now? It seems to have become downright chilly all of a sudden."

Greene simply nodded mutely towards the table where the rusted metal case lay, awaiting their attention. A white crystalline film now covered it. "I do believe that's frost." he heard himself say.

They had each downed two glasses of the warming port and donned coats brought from the lobby below, before Greene was ready to put on his linen gloves and confront an unease which had grown with every minute of prevarication. Rather than touch a now frost-free lid he slid the blade of a paper knife beneath it and with some considerable effort began to lever upwards. It opened with a glutinous squelch as if it had been gummed shut, its hinges reluctantly performing with a grating squeak before the book was revealed. Its binding thongs were knotted over and again, knot on knot like worm-casts against the half-seen shape beneath them.

"Oh, would you?" Greene said quietly, addressing the tangle. "Lionel, you will find a variety of large needles in that top drawer near your elbow. That's what is needed here."

Before he allowed himself to even consider his action, he reached into the box and dragged the book free, sensing something tear, some membrane or skin ripping free before he could drop the suddenly leaden weight onto the table beside the box.

Over the course of what they would later realise was an hour or more, it took their combined efforts, at the Apothecary's terse directions, to work loose the tangle and lay the black-inked symbol bare, the bindings now gathered together and firmly held aside with a spring-clip. By now a fug of ancient mould and something rancid just below a stale, perfumed note hung all about them. They were both sweating heavily as Greene reached out the blade once more to lift the cover back. It moved, slowly, grudgingly, as if it too had been gummed shut. Then though, it was as if a naked flame flared into fierce heat beneath the probing blade. The fine linen glove delayed its searing burn just long enough for Greene to jab the cover back with a gasp of pain before dropping the blade and hugging his hand to his heaving chest. Blomefield, now lost for words, could only stare, wide-eyed, at what had been revealed, before abruptly twisting away, his bony shoulders convulsing with some violent emotion.

"Lord God, what is this appalling thing, Richard?" he whispered, not turning back. He was desperately trying to convince himself that he had only imagined the face. The squirming, writhing grotesques – the living, moving monstrosities that somehow made it up. The shifting, grinning, mockery as it saw him. He was suddenly, violently, sick.

After what might have been seconds or something more, a hollow voice he scarcely recognised spoke into his ear as a helping arm about his skeletal shoulders lifted him back to his feet. "It is a Guardian, Lionel, with power to terrify, to sicken, but no more than that."

"That's … that's more than enough to keep me away," Blomefield wheezed, wiping vomit from his chin, "but did I not just protect us, Richard?" he added plaintively. "Was my prayer just so many words – completely without strength?" he got no further.

"Lionel, make no mistake, we could both be lying dead on this floor; that, or raving with mindless terror had it not been for the protection you brought us." He avoided looking at the table before continuing: "I only sensed that this thing might possess an awful power of its own when we first came across it – some grimoires, no more than a vanishing few, are known to have been dangerous in the extreme, barely containing forces beyond understanding. Portals, God alone knows what else besides. Few people have ever had any comprehension of their origins, their survival – indeed their true purpose. Though here, 'true' is scarcely an appropriate word. What is undeniable is that whatever they were purported to contain was believed and, without doubt, acted upon. Had they then proved ineffectual – nothing more than arcane make-believe, they would have gone the way of all heretical pishery. The few were not. They were either destroyed – in recognition of the threat that they presented to everything held sacred or, mercifully, remain lost or hidden. They are black legends, Lionel; the stuff of nightmares. We, it would appear – and the damnable de Langton before us – have stumbled upon just one such."

"May God help us," murmured Blomefield, fervently wishing he were somewhere, anywhere, else.

"Indeed," echoed Greene, "but now that we've got this far, and are unlikely to want a repeat of the experience, let us endeavour to find at least a little more of what is so zealously guarded."

"You cannot be serious," hissed Blomefield, climbing to his feet. "As I remember saying all too recently, 'You are on your own, Mr Greene'. If I didn't mean it then, by the Lord God I do now. Desist, for pity's sake, while you still can. You must be utterly mad to even remain in the same room as this monstrous thing, let alone imperil your very soul by what it might – or will – contain."

Before any response could be made, both men were galvanized with shock as first one then a second window and then a third window of the museum room were struck, resoundingly, by feathered shapes smashing themselves against the glazed panes, falling, broken, to the ground below. One, a tawny owl, seemed to cling against the glass before it, too, fell lifeless away into the night.

"Close it, Richard, for the love of God!" shrieked Blomefield, "Shut that damnable book! Do you need more persuasion?"

Once more acting purely by reflex, Greene ran to the open book, avoiding so much as a glance at its open frontis as if his life depended upon it, and somehow slammed it shut.

It was as if a thunderstorm had been poised overhead, awaiting its moment.

An ear-splitting detonation shook the room just as the Apothecary managed to scoop the feather-light book into both his arms and drop it into the waiting box. When he slammed the lid it was as if time itself began again; a light rain sounded against the museum windows and a harvest moon lit a blameless interior as Lionel Blomefield sobbed like an abandoned child.

Richard Greene was desperately trying to banish the last image, a final, mocking revelation, as he had slammed the cover shut. The light had caught it for an instant, a raised nub he had thought to be a flaw in the flaccid binding-hide. He knew it then for what it was. A nipple.

(16)

An ancient piece of Sculpture in Ivory, viz. A Man and Two
Women joining hands, seemingly for dancing. Another carving,
viz, a Shepherde holding a Nofegay of flowers in her hand.

Lichfield. 30ᵗʰ April. The invitation to Woollaton Hall had arrived
four days earlier, written with an easy informality by its elderly
owner. Richard Davenport had briefly explained that he would be
staying at Ellastone for several weeks more to ensure the settling-
in of the celebrated guest and his wife, before leaving Staffordshire
and returning to his other estate in Cheshire 'in order to give the
poor fellow the peace and quiet which his muse must crave. He
was lionised until the very day of our departure from Chiswick
with a crowd of rarely less than a score of well-wishers and the
downright curious camped outside his poor hostess's door'.

Gratified that an invitation made in the hectic bustle of Drury
Lane should now have translated into actuality, the Apothecary
lost no time in calling on the imposing house, and its equally
imposing owner, beside the Cathedral's South Gate. It had been
here, on several occasions, that Greene had first encountered the
name of Woollaton's new guest.

"R…Rousseau, you s…say, Richard?" stuttered its owner,
wide-eyed with surprise and delight, "Here in b…b…bosky
Staffordshire? Who would credit it? And you're invited, you say?
Must have cut quite a dash in your London f…foray, my f…
friend, that's all I can s…say! He's been the t…talk of Europe –

the s…scandal, too, for s…some years now. House stoned in S…
Switzerland, y'know, books b…burned left right and c…centre.
Quite the F…Fireb…brand."

Erasmus Darwin, expansive with pleasure, had gone on to
enthuse upon the achievements and celebrity of this surprise
incomer to their county, but also to express his own ambivalence
concerning many of the radical propositions whose notoriety
had chased their author ceaselessly from refuge to refuge across
Europe.

Greene had completely lost track of time before he could find
the opportunity to escape a Darwin in full flow, his own head
crammed to capacity with opinions ranging from Noble Savagery,
to the Cultivation of Civic Morality.

Already flagging when confronted with the intellectual
nuances of something named Emotional Deism, the opportunity
at last came when his host had paused – not for breath, but with
a proposition: "M…might one p…p…propose oneself as a G…
Gooseberry, d'you think, Richard? C…crashing in on y…your
invitation like the shameless reprobate I am? I do b…believe that
in R…Rousseau we have both – you and I – f…found a kindred
spirit in our shared passions for B…Botany and the world of N…
Nature in all her f…fearsome g…glory."

The Apothecary would have needed a heart of stone to deflate
the almost boyish hopefulness written across the heavy features.
"Of course, Erasmus, I shall be as honoured by your company as
will be Mr Davenport and his obviously esteemed guests, without
a doubt. Your repute travels well ahead of you."

With an alarming clap of his huge hands, the Doctor boomed:
"C…Capital! That's settled then! How soon do we g…go?"

When Greene explained that in Theodosia's absence, he was
awaiting an alternative date, expecting it would be a week or so
hence, a second percussive clap resounded around the gracious
room, almost rattling the Venetian windows from their frames:

"Even b…better! We shall travel in s…style, Richard. Within

days I expect to t…take delivery of my new c…coach, the one with the D…Darwin Axle. You will recall that I explained its p… principle at some length to you and B…Boulton, when you came to m…meet Josiah."

Greene was hardly likely to have forgotten the meeting with Etruria's finest, the great potter, Wedgwood, a man busily transforming the fortunes of England's burgeoning ceramics industry – nor Matthew Boulton, another of the land's coming men; both luminaries of Darwin's Lunar Society that met, with astral regularity, sometimes in that very room.

The Doctor's invention, the latest in a long and moderately viable succession, was designed to prevent the often-fatal overturning of horse-drawn coaches and carriages, a fearful factor in the life of every traveller on the realm's appalling roads.

The Apothecary's favourite memory of that meeting, however, was that its tangible outcome had been the surprise arrival of several experimental pieces of Wedgwood's craft. Superb busts gifted to the museum by their creator. Now, though, *Time to refocus my enthusiasm*, thought Greene, seeing Darwin's expectantly raised eyebrows. "Oh, that will be as fascinating as it will be reassuring, Erasmus. The road to Ellastone will undoubtedly be as dreadful as any, particularly after the winter's snow."

"We shall take its ruts and holes in our s…stride, Mr Greene! Or rather our n…nags shall, you'll s…see, and b…bless me f… for it!"

"I shall, as ever, count my blessings, Erasmus," said Greene, seizing the cue for a speedy departure. "I will pass the date on to you as soon as I have it."

It was as he turned into Saddler Street and had paused, looking up at the tall building that housed all the loves of his life, when his thoughts were drawn back to what had occurred behind those top-floor windows now sparkling in the late morning light.

There had been no clap of thunder, no feathered carcases to

clear away, no moisture where the frost had lain across shelf, table-top and cabinet. Perhaps the cats had been quicker off the mark than the Apothecary that following morning. Perhaps the slumber of Saddler Street's inhabitants was so virtuous as to be inviolable. Perhaps the moon that would shine on them all tonight really was made of green cheese.

'But why did every clock, every watch in this house stop at five minutes past eleven?' he had asked himself over and again, receiving no answer. The vomit he had mopped from the polished boards had been real enough as well.

The Apothecary had tried to persuade himself that the obsessive enumeration of the passing days since then was no more than a measure of just how much he was missing Theodosia. Looking balefully at the calendar in his study-alcove, he knew though that the date gave him the lie. The date would brook no argument. It would have to be tonight, tomorrow night or not at all.

He could never risk the consequences of bringing the box back into a house inhabited by a wife whose vigilance – whose sheer preciousness had long ceased to amaze him. He also knew now the sum of what they might ever learn about a long-dead man. One whose armorial, cut into an iron lid, had proclaimed his pride of possession, his ownership of the vileness within.

Unsurprisingly, it had been Seward, aided by the ever-industrious Vale, Cathedral librarian these twenty years, whose researches had brought to light a previously unregarded scrap amongst innumerable other such remnants of a once great collection, ravaged over and again by war and zealotry, with most of its treasures long since destroyed or dispersed into newly covetous hands. The Canon's suggestion had been that Vale should search for anything co-eval with de Langton's life and times, with little hope for the retrieval of anything significant but, at least, a suggestion made well before the arrival of the Bishop's letter.

The librarian's discovery, presented with a degree of

embarrassment at first puzzling but then becoming rapidly apparent to the attentive Canon, was everything that an unwitting Bishop Cornwallis might have feared.

Vale had opened a shabby, well-used, folder to reveal a water-stained page fragment, its text pallid sepia at best, much of it clearly illegible even from Seward's viewpoint. The Canon had sensed Vale's unwillingness to pass it over without some explanation: "I had been expecting Latin, Sir, so it took me a while to work out that what is actually legible is in French."

"Not your strong point, one assumes?" Seward had prompted.

"No, Sir, that was the problem, I know little more than some of the often-used legal terms."

"Yes, Vale, I understand," interjected Seward, busily maintaining his patience with a man he found lugubrious at best. "Do pray continue."

"All I recognised was the name de Langton, but then I recalled that Mr Protheroe's wife was from one of the Channel Islands; Jersey, I think. He was off playing for the Song School, so I went and asked if the lady could assist." He had seemed to falter. Seward waited.

"Well, the lady was most obliging – it wasn't that she had any difficulty, Sir, it was just that what she translated was..." Rather than continue, he had extracted from the folder what was obviously a fair copy of the text, with words in a different hand penned beneath it, passing it without further explanation to the Canon.

'Registra Vaticana d'après Les Registres de Boniface VIII' was the heading of a short text. Scanning the French original, Seward rapidly gained enough of its sense to require some effort in maintaining a degree of impassivity before the librarian. The translation explained Vale's embarrassment.

"Mrs Protheroe was exposed to this, you say?" His eyes downcast, he had nodded in mute response.

"Well, then; all the damage that could be done has been done, Mr Vale," Seward said briskly. "I hold myself entirely responsible for this and shall make the necessary apologies to the good lady and, of course, her husband. Thank you, that will be all. You had better leave this with me."

Speechless with relief, the lanky form of the Librarian had bobbed out, closing the door quietly behind him. The Canon returned to a translated text penned in the most feminine of hands. "How very unfortunate," he said to himself, reaching for pen and paper, before ringing the small bell on his desk to summon a servant.

He handed a folded sheet to the waiting man. "My compliments to Mr Greene, in Saddler Street. Could he please send a response at his earliest convenience?"

That same evening the Apothecary had read then re-read both fragment and the written copies before looking over his spectacles to the impassive Cleric.

"However pointless it may now seem, wasn't Pope Boniface himself posthumously arraigned for witchcraft? Or was it one of the others?"

"No, it was Boniface I believe." – Seward gave a tired smile – "There are times, Richard, when I think we both read too much."

"I must agree," replied Greene in all seriousness, "particularly when coming across *bons mots* such as this."

This time he read out loud, "Walter de Langton was accused of a pact with the Devil. The said Bishop has been and remains publicly reputed, in the kingdom of England and elsewhere, of paying homage to the Devil and…*l'avoir baisé dans le dos*…and fornicating in the back?." He looked up, thoughtful now. "I might have translated that as 'kissing the devil's backside'. Isn't that what is called the 'osculum infame' or some-such, Canon?"

Seward simply couldn't help himself, pulling an immaculate handkerchief from a coat pocket and wiping his eyes as his narrow shoulders shook with laughter. "Oh, Mr Greene, you most certainly read too much!"

At this juncture, as if intuiting the unfinished business that hung, wraith-like, in the air between them, the Canon called for wine. Once it had been placed for the Canon to serve them both and the steward had withdrawn, Seward, now all seriousness, had simply spread his hands and enquired: "So, now more than ever, my friend, what are we to do? I am at something of a loss."

In the silence that followed, Greene sipped his wine before quietly saying, "I fear there has been another burglary, Canon."

Forestalling the look of concern that crossed the cleric's fine-boned features, he continued, "I am in possession of information that an iron box and its contents have been covertly removed from some ingenious place of concealment about the Palace or its environs. Having cached it with considerable care as to its security, you might not yet have become aware of its loss. You will forgive me that I cannot, in all conscience, reveal my source. Though whilst the act is, of course, reprehensible, it would appear to solve a certain dilemma."

Seward now seemed to take in his visitor's facial injuries and the recent memory of the Apothecary's limping entrance for the first time, before replying thoughtfully, "Not an intrusion that could have been likely undertaken, one imagines. Given a newly-arrived mastiff patrolling our perimeters; added of course, to the obstacles presented by a midnight garden."

"Very true," replied Greene with feeling, "although one can at least take comfort that in your removal of the said object to a place of concealment away from casual gaze – and adding a fearsome sentinel to the equation, there can surely be no blame attached to its unforeseen removal by some ne'er-do-well prowling the Palace, yet again, in search of opportunity."

"Indeed, indeed," intoned the Canon, staring at some point in the middle distance, "And as one cannot imagine a ready market in the Rookeries, the Thieves' Kitchens, for a grimy relic of no apparent value, it will doubtless be thrown away or, most likely, destroyed. Not that we are ever likely to know its fate."

"Mmm," replied Greene, "Neither I – nor, I feel certain, His Lordship the Bishop – could doubt that. Ultimately it will have to be destroyed, I suspect, though quite how or when I cannot imagine. The problem is, at least, no longer yours, Canon Seward."

"And for that, Richard, I am mightily grateful. It had been playing on my mind to an unhealthy degree I regret to say."

"One might say that is the very nature of the beast, Canon. Such objects were never intended to be taken lightly. It is in the false promises and predictions held out to greedy and gullible owners that madness – or worse – lies."

"Though perhaps one should add the curious to their number, Richard, for if the evil potency of such objects has not been over-estimated, then surely even the most well-meaning scholar – enquirer, into their nature – would be at the same risk?"

The Apothecary could only nod in response.

Wanting to clear his head from an encounter he had been dreading, Greene decided to take the longer way home, down through The Close, across de Langton's bridge over the Vivarium and along Bird Street to the junction with his own. He was passing the tobacconist near the George Inn, when its owner – an old acquaintance presently engaged in cleaning the panes of his shop door – waved a greeting to him.

"How's that old mare of yours, Mr Greene?" Surprised at the question the Apothecary paused, "Not as sprightly as she once was, but then neither is her owner, Mr Tierney. Why do you ask?"

"Oh, it was a week or more back, but nature had called in the small hours and I looked down" – he pointed to the windows above the shop – "and saw you passing. Thought you might have had a bit of a fall, the old girl was playing up so, and you leading her with that limp. Thought to call out and enquire, but then I reckoned that your companion was all the help you might need. Not that he seemed to be offering any, following on like that. I didn't want to seem a busybody, though."

With all the composure he could manage, Greene had made a brief farewell and moved on. A sudden leaden weight in his stomach seeming to lurch as he recalled, all too vividly, the sound of following footsteps; a memory of turning not once but twice to nothing but the empty street behind him. He had quickened his pace, suddenly desperate that the urge to look back should not betray the cold panic settling upon him like some noisome fog.

(17)

Third SHELF The sheath of a knife and Fork in Box wood; on which are most elegantly carved several historical passages recorded in the Old Testament with the following inscription in high Dutch "Weinch Wookden en die wakachtichelen onderwein end at Kedachtich Goede maniers. Ende dieki krenckt mennyghe tot groote Staeten, Anno 1598."

Saddler Street. May Day. Greene had returned from his afternoon rounds both to a shop and living accommodation freshly redolent of beeswax, blacking, metal-polish and the pervasive scent of fresh flowers. With both Theodosia and Elspeth Blomefield's return expected at much the same time the following day, the two households were a hive of domestic activity. The smell of baking and the reassuring bustle of both establishments reminding the Apothecary of how much their respective doyennes had been missed.

Lionel Blomefield had been banished from Breadmarket Street 'until we get everything just so for the mistress's return without great boots and feet everywhere, Vicar. No disrespect, but don't you go putting those on in the hall, neither. The girl's only just done polishing and we wouldn't want to spoil it, now, would we? No, not there either, if'n you please'.

To Greene's considerable relief, his old friend seemed to have slipped, if not effortlessly then at least eventually, back into his accustomed roles of harried householder and uniquely infuriating spouse once more, rather than the worryingly uncommunicative Lionel of four days ago following the events in the museum. He was even talking about shaving in honour of Elspeth's return.

The Apothecary had never seen the normally garrulous man so diminished, so obviously shaken by his experience. He knew better, now, than to give Lionel the slightest inkling of what he proposed to do behind closed museum doors that evening.

On his arrival home he had been conscious of Tillett exercising almost painful restraint as he shepherded four boys and an obviously distracted parent off the premises just before closing time, having apparently felt the need for hawk-like vigilance during their time up in the museum. Whilst the two youngest and their father had been absorbed in the extraordinary collection, the two eldest had shown little interest, and to the shopman's indignation had been found playing marbles across the polished oak floor whilst an oblivious adult had shown not the least concern, at one stage stepping over the game the better to view a mineral display.

"Honestly, Mr Greene, there are some as shouldn't be allowed out without keepers, these days. They'd had tickets bought for them too, the little beggars. Cocked a snook at me, too, when their dad wasn't looking!"

Mollified by the Apothecary's compliments on the spick and span shop, Tillett, his niece and the boy left shortly before six, leaving Greene to appreciate the perfect order that surrounded him. Emmy had proved to be worth her weight in something costly, bringing a smiling grace to the transactions, wrapping purchases with a swift dexterity that would have delighted her absent mistress. "Presentation, Richard, that's the key. Whether it be us, the shop, or the museum, as you so well know. That's what brings folk to spread the word. Mark my words."

It was only as the final phrase echoed in his memory that Greene's contentment was ruffled by the memory of other, more recent, words beginning, 'No good will come of it'. He pushed them to the back of his mind as he followed the call to supper.

He had been both pleased and more than a little perplexed by the almost genial manner of a Margery, who could not do enough for him over the past ten days. He would never know that on the night of Blomefield's ill-starred late arrival, his housekeeper, in passing, had spent several minutes listening in amazèd gratification – to the unmistakable cadence of prayers issuing from the museum above. That night she had gone to bed with a song in her much-abused heart, thanking the Almighty that at long last her ceaseless efforts and selfless striving were having some effect on an employer whose sanity and moral welfare were so frequently in doubt. Tonight, were she to be listening at the foot of those same stairs once more, she would go to bed in a transport of joy, as the words of a much quoted and well-loved psalm were spoken into a darkness lit only by one huge paschal candle. If, however, she was to gain so much as a glimmer of its purpose this evening, it would send her, the proudest of women, hysterical into Saddler Street, in her night-clothes and curling-rags.

The tall candle was used, in normal circumstances, as a theatrical prop to adorn a display of tattered and distressed religious artefacts salvaged a century before from the gutted Cathedral. Tonight, its owner hoped, it might lend more than its light to the gathering shadows.

He had decided to fall back upon several well-tried if not entirely compatible expedients. The first, the time-honoured protection of Psalm 23 from his King James Bible, the second, the supposed efficacy of cold iron in keeping at bay inimical and hostile other-worldly forces. That had been their big mistake, he had decided after much thought; the removal of the grimoire from a box meant specifically for the containment of what lay within, rather than simply something to keep it from prying eyes. Tonight, he would investigate it in situ, employing a variety of non-conducting wooden utensils to turn pages, being confident that anything untoward he might encounter would be no more real than the thunderclap of recent memory. These objects – books such as this – let alone the unnameable entities and portals they purported to contain, were tricks – tricksters, if one insisted on investing them with some form of vitality; no more nor less than illusions visited upon the impressionable and the ignorant, albeit tricks propelled by some as-yet unguessable power, now awaiting revelation by the Science of the age.

Thus, with less than complete success, he had eventually managed to convince himself on almost all points and was as ready to proceed as he would ever be. Above all else, he had decided to rely upon his common sense and a level-headedness that had served him well in his many ventures. Even as, one by one, he extinguished the candle-lamps that were the museum's usual illumination, and the great candle assumed the task, he felt his confidence falter.

By the time the dancing flicker had steadied into a graceful, inches-long plume of flame, the Apothecary was sitting, breathing deeply, preparing himself for what might lie ahead. Then he found his bookmark and opened Theodosia's family bible to the psalm he sought.

"The Lord is my shepherd; I shall not want," he began and then allowed the beautiful sonority of the ancient prayer to lead him to green pastures and still waters, to restore his soul and lead him into the paths of righteousness for that Lord's sake. "Even when I walk in the Valley of Darkness, I will fear no evil. You are with me. Your rod and your staff – they comfort me." As a table was set before him in the face of his adversaries, his head anointed with oil, his cup filled to overflowing, he asked that only goodness and kindness be permitted to accompany him, for the measure of his days, before dwelling in the house of the Lord.

He sat, then, in profound stillness, gazing at the rusty box.

"I'm ready for you now," he breathed, and lifted the lid in a single decisive movement.

The book sat, inert, as drab and flaccid as when he had first seen it in the afternoon sun on a far-off day. Its bindings lay just as they had been left, held aside by a spring-clip. Guileless. He reached for a wooden spatula and with no hesitation lifted the cover back. It opened with ease to reveal the complex pen-work of its frontis, a foliate head of leaves, berries and woven twigs. A Green Man, much like a hundred others he had seen.

Emboldened now, he turned one, another, then another of the limp pages, seeing an astral diagram, a figure splayed to reveal its pulse-points, its sex and veinous limbs, before the next page took his breath away. It was as if a window onto some paradisiacal vision lay open before his eyes. Could this be the work of a human hand? Its jewel-like detail sang from the page, its perspectives so uncanny that he seemed poised, at some great height and looking down. Down upon what he knew to be nothing less than The Temple of Solomon, vast and glowing white, perfect in every detail, baking beneath the Judaean sun, hills distant against a sky of utter blue.

He hovered on the thermals rising from a city spread below, swaying in the dust-free air, borne up by zephyrs that caressed his outspread wings. So high that all the forms seemed little more than insect mites all scurrying up the marble stairs or crowding in the sun-bleached courts. The woodsmoke of uncounted fires all drifting skyward as the offerings they claimed rose up, as one, to greet the perfect day. And then he swooped, sped down at such a speed the smoke and air both parted to his dive, and upturned faces – their mouths black o's – amazed to see this bolt, this comet's plunge, sweep down into the world of men. Then as the shadow of his outspread wings raced across the buttressed walls and towers, the portal of the sacred core stood out, beyond the topmost of the widest stairs, across a court whose priests all scattered in his wake. Then, though, just when the entrance to that inner place seemed open as a lover's arms, a blast of sound erupted from the shadow-world within, alarums from great rams' horns bellowing in the sacred gloom.

He fell, he crashed against the wall of sound and broke into a scattering of stars, black, just for an instant as they melted in the cruelty of light.

He seemed to jolt awake, a cricked neck bringing him back to painful reality. He sat up, easing from left to right, circulation restoring itself only grudgingly as the room took shape once more, around his blinking gaze. As memory flooded in, he looked down in amazement at the sepia drawing opened within the spread book. The Temple of Solomon without doubt, true to all the bible words, though what he saw now was an earthbound work, no more. Work penned with but a middling skill, a jobbing eye, devoid of colour, of significant detail, of the merest hint of vitality or veracity. So, what had he seen, where had he been? The legendary edifice, its huge courts, its massive walls and gates, destroyed before written history had properly begun, had been as real – no, more so – than anything the bemused man had ever seen. He had flown above it, godlike in the crystal sky, seen its glow and shimmer in the desert air. An image set forever in his mind's eye.

He sat in awe, in speechless gratitude for the gift – that was the only word for the transcendence he had known – his eyes never leaving the sepia lines upon a dull, stained page. And had it not all come from this poor thing, he marvelled? Overcome with an emotion he could not name, he began to ask how he could ever have shunned this marvel, called it a foul and tainted aberration, this gift that providence had delivered to his hands

Suddenly so drained of energy that he could scarcely bring himself to close the book, he managed it with careful respect, lifting the pages, now, as if they might flake away, taking their wonders with them. Then, sitting for longer than he would be able to remember, recalling the caress of air, the shrieking whistle of wind against feather.

Finally, with no idea of the time, he climbed unsteadily to his feet and crossed to the nearest window. The night was still dense across the rooftops, the three spires black against the sky beyond. It was only then that he realised the great candle had been extinguished, not by his hand that he could recall. He shrugged, mentally, dismissing it from a mind aching with wonder and exhaustion. Tea first, he decided, then his blessed bed for whatever was left of the hours of darkness.

His watch and all the museum clocks were stopped once again, he noticed without concern, treading carefully towards the armoury corridor and the head of the stairs.

The halberd that hung above the doorway had, by repute, come from the castle at Tutbury, most hated of all the Scottish queen's places of imprisonment before her last and fatal gaol at Fotheringhay. It was seven feet in length, a spiked filial at its base, a threadbare grip along the middle of its studded length, an age-blackened shaft bearing a viciously hooked axe blade that ended in a foot-long spear. It was firmly fixed, at each end of the wooden shaft, with hook and chain well above the reach of meddling hands. It had been one of the museum's fixtures for the past fifteen years, the gift of a grateful Tutbury justice discreetly treated for an amatory indiscretion. The three marbles that lay, unnoticed, unclaimed, just inside the doorway, had been in the museum a matter of hours and only since Tillett had managed to escort their erstwhile owners off the premises. The small glass orbs – one of them a fine blood alley – were just about to save Richard Greene's life.

When he had made his careful way across the unlit floor and reached the doorway, two things happened in a single crazed instant.

As its fastening seemed simply to dissolve, the razor-edged blade dropped from its place, becoming – in one lethal second – a scything tip, a pendulum now launched into a killing arc.

Just as its downward swing began, a well-shod foot connected with the playthings on the floor, its owner skidding, uncontrolled, into a tumbling flail of arms and sliding legs. The passage of the deadly blade a whistling swish above a buttoned paunch a hairsbreadth, less, below. It struck the doorway to his left, embedding blade and spike deep into the varnished frame, a great split cracking open, up its length.

In a winded daze, Greene gasped up at the sight, his bruised buttocks half in, half out of the darkened room, a shoulder feeling badly wrenched, an elbow lanced with pain. He lay there, panting with shock, trying without success to understand what had just occurred, his hurts all seeming to coalesce into one throbbing whole that set him shaking, as the bile rose in his throat.

Confused thoughts, reflexes more than anything, brought him somehow to his knees and then he saw the figure. It sat, black against the ebbing night, lolling at ease and watching as he scrambled to his feet. The sight was worse than all of what had gone before.

He heard a gasp of shock, a choking breath of formless horror that he didn't know was his – but when he'd blinked a teardrop from a streaming eye, an empty chair was all that met his clouding gaze. He passed out, somehow sliding down the nearest wall, to slump, legs spread, head down, until the dawning greyness stole across the floor and found him there.

(18)

A curious deception in a neat gilt Frame; being a Metzotint of
his Majesty King George III, which, by a touch, is instantly
changed into a resemblance of the Queen. The work of Mr Ob.
Westwood of Birmingham. A neat representation in Paper (cut
with a pair sciffers) of Mr Garrick and Miss Younge, in the
character of Tancred and Sigifmunda, by Miss Selina de Chair.

Lichfield. 2nd May. The radiant woman and her equally bright-
eyed companion, alighting from the southbound mail coach, were
agreed that nothing was going to blight a happy return from an
enjoyable holiday. Confronted by an obviously shaken husband,
his left arm supported by a linen sling, who could little more
than shrug helplessly and say "marbles" by way of explanation,
Theodosia had responded, "Yes, dear, now could you make sure our
bags are stacked securely and make sure the small one on the top
does not slip. We'll be home in a trice, and you can bring me up to
date with your stumbles then. Talking of which, where is Lionel?"

As if in comic response, a lanky figure could be seen pushing
his way through into the George's yard. With a wave he arrived,
gave his waiting wife a perfunctory peck on her cheek, and said
breathlessly: "Damnedest thing, my dear, it appears that every
clock around stopped at the same time last night. Been trying
to catch up with myself since this morning. Had a congregation
waiting that I didn't even know were there. Damnedest thing."

"Welcome back, Elspeth," said Elspeth, "It's a joy to see you returned safe and sound. Have you had a wonderful time? We have indeed, Lionel, and thank you for asking. I can imagine how much you've missed me."

"Oh, heavens, all of that, my dear, goes without saying; but honestly this clock business is most curious."

She took her husband firmly by the arm and after exchanging a single glance with her travelling companion, eyebrows raised, said, "It is so endlessly reassuring to see that nothing has changed in one's absence, husband. Shall I take you home? You must be exhausted."

After supper that evening, when the Apothecary had been regaled with accounts of the fine house in York's Whip-ma Whap-ma Gate, the elegant emporia in Stonegate, the supreme quality of chocolate and fancies served at the Assembly Rooms, a musical comedy attended and a most superior afternoon tea recital, this studiously attentive husband began to sense that his wife was leading up to something as yet held back.

"I have to tell you, Richard, that the absolute pinnacle of our visit was, in fact, a chance encounter." She then came as close to what could only be described as a simper that the Apothecary had ever known from this most matter-of-fact spouse. In an almost girlish tone, she continued, "The simple fact is, Richard, that I met the most engaging man; gallant, well-travelled and endlessly entertaining. At his insistence, his absolute refusal to hear otherwise, both Elspeth and I dined with him shortly before our departure."

The Apothecary was by now trying not to gape in incredulity as Theodosia blithely continued: "Though much the same age as you, he remains, given his charm, mysteriously unmarried. He had come in from his estate at Ripon in order to bring his young nephew into the city to be fitted for his uniform. The youngster shortly comes south, accompanied by his uncle, to join his regiment – the name of which eludes me – so I have insisted that they break their journey here. I knew you would be only too pleased. I feel that I have known him for years – a feeling that I believe is reciprocated."

She sat, surveying a husband temporarily rendered speechless, before continuing brightly, "Although I believe he handed in his papers some years ago, the gentleman in question was a military man of some standing. A lieutenant-colonel by the time of his retirement, I gather. He told me at some length how he has been much absorbed in the restoration and refurbishment of his inheritance over recent years past, much to the detriment of valued friendships and liaisons made over a lifetime's service both here and in America. He was an Officer of Engineers, apparently."

Suddenly, the Apothecary saw it; the unmistakable glint of concealed mischief, the spark of intoxicating humour bubbling behind the pale grey eyes he had loved for thirty years. As it began to dawn upon him that he was being played by a past-mistress of every game they had ever embarked upon, Theodosia's superb sang-froid began to melt.

"Oh, Richard, if only Sir Joshua could see your face! It would be a portrait to end them all! Your dismay is matched only by your outrage, my dear man. How are you containing yourself in the face of such brazen trickery?" She clapped her hands in sheer delight at the conflicting welter of emotions crossing the well-loved face, exclaiming, "The Officer of Engineers is none other than our Officer of Engineers! Harry! Harry Copeland in the flesh – and in rather more of it than when we last saw him!"

Now it was the Apothecary's turn to beam with delight. "Game, set and match, you deceitful jade! That was a terrifyingly convincing performance, though whether you shall ever be forgiven for it remains to be seen. I had pictured myself trudging off into the sunset with my few belongings tied up in a spotted kerchief and hung from a stick."

"It would need to be an exceedingly large kerchief and an even bigger stick, husband," she said, rising from her chair to fetch a small, carefully wrapped package from the sideboard. "This is where I demonstrate my contrition, and state that I have never loved another museum-keeper as I love you. Although," she added with a grin, "I must confess that the same most engaging and attentive gentleman did help me to choose this for you."

"So, Harry's put on weight has he, the self-indulgent rogue? It'll be all that good living from his two hundred acres, no doubt. Not that I ever did see the dear fellow as a country squire, it must be said. Lord, it must be four, no five years, since we last met. What a delight it will be to see him! When will they be coming?"

"On Saturday's coach, the sixth, he said. They will continue to Windsor on Monday next, but he will come back to us for several days on his return journey, once young George has been duly consigned. Harry has bought the lad's commission, so wants to see that all is in order and he's properly tucked in. Talking of which," she added, handing him his gift with a smile, "a certain party needs to be tucking *himself* in, from what I can see. Has Margery had you on extra dumplings in my absence?"

He was studiously unwrapping his gift, too busy to reply. The many discarded layers of paper finally revealed a hand-sized object which he raised to the light with a gasp of admiration and pleasure. The leaded glass lit with the glow of saturated hues, blood-red, ochre yellow and a blue that seemed to hold infinity within its depths. The head and partial wings of an angel peeped from behind the soft metal fixings that held the rough-textured glass.

"It's very old, Richard. Around the time of Henry V, the antiquary said. It is from a city church destroyed by fire, found by an ever-attentive wife in a curiosity shop in The Shambles. It was shamefully extravagant, but we both knew you would approve."

He rose and came to her, arms about her shawled shoulders. "Oh, Mrs Greene, I do. And on that appropriately marital note I do believe we should retire."

"But I have prattled on so selfishly, husband, that I have heard nothing of your stumbles."

"Little to tell and that will wait, my dear," he said, suddenly needing to maintain the evening's light-hearted conclusion. But unwittingly, he was drawn back to the memory of an agonised awakening on the museum floor not fifteen hours earlier.

(19)

ITEM:

A small knife, the Haft enamelled, on which are engraved the arms of Adrian Fortescue, Esq. Date 1584, 27th year of the reign of Queen Elizabeth, engraved in The Gentleman's Magazine. Presented by the Rev. Henry White of Lichfield Close.

Woollaton Hall, Ellastone. 3rd May. Richard Davenport found himself faced with a dilemma. To say that his distinguished guest was sulking would be an understatement of gargantuan proportions, though to alleviate the black miasma of fury and depression that seemed to suffuse the Frenchman's every waking hour, the sole remedy that his host might have suggested was laughter.

He suspected, quite rightly, that were he impetuous enough to propose such a course of action, however, it could well result in either his guests' immediate departure in high dudgeon, or even in a physical attack on the foolish proposer. Walpole's letter was the principal cause of that, there could be no doubt. The Ashbourne encounter, however, coming at much the same time, had done little to help what Davenport was coming to recognise as an alarmingly unstable temperament.

After a tedious, bone-shaking journey from London – though one through which Rousseau had managed to sleep for mile after leaden mile – at a short distance from their destination, they had enjoyed a brief watering-stop in Ashbourne's wide marketplace.

Awakening from yet another enviable slumber, the Frenchman had been looking blearily around the busy scene beyond their window, lowered now to give some fresh air to a gamey interior, when suddenly he had stiffened. With his attention now riveted by some sight outside, he sat bolt upright against his padded seat and surprised both his wife and Davenport by mouthing an audible obscenity.

"Whatever is happening, Jean-Jacques? What have you seen to disturb you?" asked Davenport in concern.

"There," the Frenchman replied, his eyes never leaving whatever he had seen. "Over by the red-painted shop, beside the coach. I know him, from Paris. You too, perhaps? Do you recognise the son of a whore? De Rais, the diabolist, part of that group of murderous filth that clustered around the lifted skirts of the Marquise de la Motte-Guyon."

Davenport had followed his pointing hand to the gaunt, heavily cloaked figure supervising a load being secured to the coach roof. "I remember her name, of course, Jean-Jacques; it is not often a noblewoman is sent to meet the headsman. Richly deserved, from what I recall. The remains of a dozen or more children were found beneath her house. At Vincennes, was it? You know that man to have been a party to such obscenity? Surely you must be mistaken. What on earth would bring him here?"

Rousseau had merely shrugged, eyes never leaving the figure that now climbed aboard his vehicle, the commerce obviously complete. "He and a score like him made the mistake of courting me in Paris at various times, stupid enough to believe all that hysterical shit about me being the Anti-Christ, the priest-hater, the heretic. I treated them with the contempt they deserved; him, most particularly. He would have killed me if he could, I saw it in his eyes. Whether it was blind arrogance, or the bad taste born of imbecility, the vain fool boasted of his descent from Gilles de Rais, the Marshal of France."

"Of course," responded Davenport. "That is where I knew the

name: the appalling creature who soldiered alongside Jeanne d'Arc. He, too, was executed for the mass-murder of children, was he not? In their hundreds, literally, if I am not mistaken."

"By his own confession," agreed the man staring fixedly after the departing coach, as it began the laboured climb up towards the high moors beyond the town. "And now this one is here, just when I arrive. He hates me, you know, Richard. Like so many others. This is not good."

The final few miles to Woollaton Hall had been travelled in moody, preoccupied silence, Madame Rousseau taking her cue from her husband; not the arrival that their host could have predicted or desired. As their coach came to a halt outside the imposing façade of the house, and the bone-weary travellers descended onto the paved forecourt, neither of the couple managed so much as a nod in acknowledgement to the staff that had hurriedly assembled at the front door to greet the owner and his distinguished guests. Pleading exhaustion, they did not descend from their rooms until the following morning, Richard Davenport having dined in solitary splendour, wondering, perhaps, on both the wisdom of invitations extended in the haste of enthusiasm and, also, on the nature of the English sense of humour.

The mail that had preceded them was presented to Woollaton's owner on his arrival. He was now bitterly regretting the fact that Monsieur Rousseau had been made privy to one of those letters – or rather to an inclusion within it, addressed to the Frenchman. Davenport had come upon it, before reading the words addressed to him, and without thinking had simply despatched it upstairs to the visitors' rooms. It was only when he digested the text intended for his eyes, that he realised the extent of his mistake. What David Hume had written was part-explanation, part-apology, for the bombshell he had delivered. The bombshell to which he himself had been an amused – if now chastened – party.

Without his knowledge, Rousseau had just been mercilessly

parodied in a fictitious, but already published letter, concocted by Walpole and his company of London wits; a letter purporting to be from the Frenchman's erstwhile – now disaffected – patron, Frederick the Great of Prussia.

David Hume, in an excess of penitential zeal, was now communicating not only the content, but his own guilty involvement in the heavy-handed joke, desperate for forgiveness. Now, though, reading an extract from that malicious text, Davenport felt his spirits plummet, trying hard not to imagine how its intended recipient, upstairs, was presently receiving a parody that reflected all too accurately the frailty of the Frenchman's self-regard and his legion fears. For a moment, Davenport felt certain that he could hear the distant sound of breaking china.

'if you persist in racking your brains to find new misfortunes, choose such as you may desire; I am king and can procure any to suit your wishes and – what surely will never happen to you among your enemies – I shall cease to persecute you when you cease to find your glory in being persecuted.'

"Company! That will be the ticket!" Davenport decided. "A kindred spirit or two, welcoming distractions until the poor fellow regains his equilibrium. Now where is the address for our museum friend? Johnson's 'Natural History man'?"

Some days later, another letter, this from the hand of a Derby bookseller, was also delivered at Saddler Street, its counterparts arriving at much the same time on the breakfast table of both Canon Residentiary Seward and that of the Reverend Lionel Blomefield in Breadmarket Street. Decently penned on nicely headed stock, they announced that its sender – one Spencer Philbrigge – 'Specialist in Incunabula and fine printed works of Particular Interests' – would be in Lichfield over the 9th and 10th of May and requested the privilege of both displaying a small selection of his finest volumes and of perusing any such that he might be offered, for purchase, assuring '…the utmost discretion and most advantageous rates'.

In the small parlour above Greene's Apothecary, the letter had been quickly scanned then left among others on the mantlepiece, by a proprietor who had never willingly parted with a book in his entire life but was now wondering how to do just that. His decision, if such it was, had been prompted by Theodosia's uncanny discovery of the whereabouts of a particular linen cloth. They had been about to dine on the evening following her return, when his wife had enquired, "Why has Aunt May's cloth found its way into the museum, Richard? You know I like it for our small table by the stairs?"

When she saw the look of paralysed discomfiture cross her husband's face she said intuitively, "It has to do with your still-un-explained stumble has it not, Richard? You know we shall have to talk about it eventually, so why not now? When Margery has cleared away anything that could be construed as a potential weapon."

She did not add, not yet, what had been revealed on lifting the pressed linen; a precise rectangle burned into the polished top of the Pembroke table. Hence the abuse of Aunt May's cloth; hence the explanation she now awaited.

"It all began that day at Eccleshall," he said quietly, suddenly sounding as weary as she had ever known him in the thirty years of a far from placid marriage. "I sensed it then, but, by heaven, I know it now. I really must start to trust my instincts, Theodosia. They could not have sent me on a stranger, more worrying path than that upon which I now find myself."

"It is here? Still in this house?" she asked, finally, in a measured, enquiring voice. "But Richard, if it is as..?"

"There is no if about it, Theodosia," he replied, "Though it pains me to say so, it is more dangerous than I, or anyone, could ever have imagined. The thing has a power – an imperative – not only to seduce and to enchant, but," – he seemed to be having difficulty – "to taunt, to hurt whomsoever it can reach. To presume it can be controlled would require a lunatic. It is of an order beyond our comprehension, my dear. Words I can scarcely believe I am uttering. Here and now? At such a time, in such a place? This mocks our every belief, our certainties, in a way I could not have believed possible; reducing them to nonsense. Within the space of an hour it transported me to such a vision as I shall never forget, one that I shall never cease to crave, and then very nearly succeeded in killing me."

He reached out both hands to grip her own. "Do you think I am mad to say so?"

"I have seen the door-frame, that dreadful axe-thing, the table-top, but, most importantly, I saw you, Richard; the state of you, on our return. I require no further persuasion. But are we safe, even as we speak?"

"Oh, yes," he responded, an uncharacteristically sardonic smile playing on the face she loved so well. "Apparently, cold iron can protect us where Science, Reason and Intellect fear to tread. We really have not emerged very far from the caves, on balance, have we, my dear? Not the most reassuring of thoughts."

"So," began Theodosia at what her husband intuited would be her most succinct, "You have solved the Canon's dilemma by the simple expedients of burgling him and assuming his burden as your own, that same burden apparently having the power to terrify poor Lionel out of his few remaining wits and endanger rather more than just your life? If I am I correct so far this could be described as selflessness bordering on the preposterous could it not, Richard?"

"Well, yes, to an extent, Theodosia, but I'm not sure about the 'more than just your life' part."

Her anger stopped him short. "If you insist that I embark upon portentous expressions such as 'imperilling your immortal soul', Richard, I shall do so! Have you actually not listened to a word you, yourself, have been saying: your conviction that from the outset something was utterly wrong about this ghastly thing?"

He looked down, shamefacedly, "Forgive me, my dear, it is just that I no longer seem... I cannot quite..." He shrugged, helplessly. "To quote the Canon: 'I am at a loss to know how to proceed'. I genuinely dread the prospect of ever seeing that thing again, even though at present it is at least tucked away outside, beyond casual intervention."

"Then might this missive from the blue provide a solution, perhaps?" she responded, crossing to the mantlepiece and retrieving the letter from Derby. Holding her spectacles in one hand, she squinted at its contents. "I gather this fellow is a bookseller even if I fail to understand what incunabula means. Could this be a providential intervention?"

"I might have agreed just that earlier today, my dear, but since a brief visit from Lionel, I am no longer at all certain."

"How so, Richard?" she responded, sharply. "I can scarcely bear to enquire, but what bad advice has your oldest friend been giving you now?"

"Scarcely bad advice, Theodosia," he replied quietly. "Lionel slipped in to propose just what you have done. He too received an enquiry from a bookseller in Derby. If by some strange coincidence the Canon has also been sent one, that will make a full set. I shall need to find out, my dear. You will appreciate that."

"What are you saying, Richard? That this man's proposed visit has something to do with this?"

"I fear it could have everything to do with it, my dear. As did the earlier visits to the three of us from that boorish creature you avoided so fortuitously. The book is being sought, make no mistake about it. Though by whom, and to what end, I shudder to imagine. It is an utter aberration, Theodosia, but one which should surely be kept from those who seek to use it, to profit from it? Even to touch it is to feel tainted. For all its great antiquity, its merciful rarity, it will have to be destroyed, of that there can be no doubt.

But quite how and by whom I honestly do not know. The idea that it could ever be sold or simply passed on is unthinkable. Why, even its cover is..." He instantly regretted the words, but they were out.

"The cover is what, Richard?" He knew he had to reply but did so with leaden reluctance.

"It bears a symbol: 'The Seal of Solomon', so called; intended, so the bible assures us, to bind demons, part-drawn, part-burned into the... what I had thought of as hide, some form of animal. Oh, Theodosia, it is bound in human skin, of that I am now convinced. Tattooed skin that still bears a nipple." He shuddered with revulsion at the memory of its touch. The cool softness, the moist feel.

His wife sprang to her feet and hurried from the table, turning, white-faced, for an instant: "Oh, Richard, what have you brought down upon us?"

(20)

In two **DRAWERS** on the Right Hand. A
collection of Moths and Butterflies.

Lichfield. 4ᵗʰ May. Emmy Tillett had never been happier. Each
morning she left the family's neat cottage in Farewell and walked
the length of Cross-in-Hand Lane towards the spires rising
above the greening hedgerows, a song in her heart. Since she had
become aware of such adult concerns she had known that her
Uncle James occupied a respected and indeed enviable position
of responsibility in one of the city's finest business, and now here
she was on a fine sunlit morning with that self-same door opened
for her. She could scarcely believe her good fortune as she crossed
the Rugeley road and made her way between the market gardens,
hurrying towards Saddler Street.

If she had been at all apprehensive of the return of the
Apothecary's mistress, those concerns were rapidly banished by
the lady herself. Theodosia Greene had warmed to the quick-
witted girl at their first meeting, and had come back to universally
approving reports, even from a housekeeper whose approval was
hard-won if ever won at all: "Knows her place, that one, and works
well enough to earn it, Mrs Greene," she had said tartly. "We could
have done a sight worse if'n you're asking me." Theodosia had not
been, but thanked Margery for her valued opinion, thinking wryly
that Emmy Tillett would never know the scale of her conquest.

Today, the girl had finished hanging out the cloths and
wash-leathers employed on a scale that at first she had found hard

to believe, but then had rapidly learned that impeccably cleaned floors, counter-tops, innumerable shelves, a half-dozen related rooms and a myriad nooks and crannies, required not only the contents of the yards-long line, but also a strenuous degree of what her Uncle James – Mr Tillett here at work – referred to as the elbow-wax to wield them.

As the girl turned from the sagging arc of the clothesline with her empty basket, the morning light seemed to pick out the small, cottagelike building with its tall, rather crooked, brick chimney and its lichened roof-tiles. Of all the single-storied ramble of outbuildings that seemed to have grown haphazardly out into the back garden of the tall house, this – apart from the stable and tack room that gave onto Bore Street at the rear – was the furthest from it. It had an air of disuse about it, its single window opaque with dust and grime. Her curiosity overcame her.

During the past two weeks she had familiarised herself with most of the dispersed activities of the bustling shop, the toothpaste manufactory, the wrapping and bottling room that was little more than a walk-in cupboard, the stillroom, the glassware scullery, and the herbarium with its infinity of nose-tickling scents, its walls and ceiling festooned with the dried bundles that were a staple of the Apothecary's commerce. This, though, with its low door was still an unvisited place of mystery. Leaving her basket on the ground, she ducked beneath the low lintel as the old, sun-bleached door grated open across its crumbling brick threshold.

The papery rustle of a lone butterfly fluttering desperately against the cobwebbed window met her as she stooped into the dry must of the interior. To her right, ancient brick stillage gathered the dust of ages, a variety of grimed bottles abandoned beneath its shallow arches. Some fragments of carved stone were stacked haphazardly against the wall to her left, its vestigial whitewash peeling in leprous flakes onto the pile – bits and pieces off all that other old stuff out in the garden, she decided. Then she saw the oven door set into the chimney breast. She'd once seen inside a bakery where a friend of her mother had worked – like that there, she reckoned. Must have been for baking too, not too high, not too low, just like she'd heard. Then she knew she had to look inside.

A smell of over-wintered apples, waxy, wrapped in paper-scraps, flooded the dim interior, and then the scent of toffee made for Christmastide, of simmered pots of everything that perfumed her fondest memories, of treats and birthday sweetmeats, ginger-bread and butter spread on fresh-baked scones. The sounds of bees, of building rooks, of choruses at dawn filled her ears, her spirits soaring with delight as she reached for the box that seemed to be the source of all her joy. It came to her hands as if it slid on oil or freshly fallen snow, an old and treasured friend leaning in to share a warm embrace.

"Emmy, Emmy? Are you in there? I'm not coming in looking for you – don't want me hair full o'spiders. Are you there? Mistress wants you, sharpish." Then she was flinching back from the stink of a rusty box, her hands coated in muck, pushing it back in revulsion, back into the dank oven-space, slamming the pitted iron door. She hurried back into the daylight where the boy was waiting.

"Pokin' about in there were you? I won't tell, honest."

"Don't care if you do," she replied coquettishly, grinning as the blush spread up the pimply face. "You can carry the basket in if you like."

He grabbed it up and hurried after her leggy stride. He'd never seen her swing her hips like that.

Canon Seward had carefully poured a bowl of tea for his visitor before responding to Greene's enquiry, "Having also received prior indication of this bookselling fellow's visit next week, I am quite certain you are correct, Richard. I know of no other recipients. That wretched book is being most actively sought, as you have suggested. One can only thank Providence for its disappearance

– just as, in fact, one has been engaged in communicating to our Lord Bishop."

"With little or no gratitude likely from that quarter, one imagines," added Greene.

"Well, that's as may be, my friend," the cleric responded evenly, "though, from a purely selfish point of view, one is forced to admit that a situation which could only be described as 'self-inflicted' has been mitigated. I was indeed precipitate in removing the wretched thing from Eccleshall, but, to my shame, took little pleasure in being so forcefully reminded of the fact."

"Yes, but surely motive must be judged alongside bare fact, Canon. You, we, acted from the best of intentions."

"Perhaps, Richard, but might one be uncomfortably reminded of the old saw concerning the paving on the road to Hell? How, one wonders, is the book's current possessor finding such a path? Unless, of course the thing has already been destroyed as one might hope."

"Easier to say than to do, Canon," said Greene, then hurriedly continuing, "From what little I have been able to learn. I mean that such works – the rare, the singular books – have a reputation for defending themselves against such attempts. There are several Arabic references, texts of exceptional antiquity found in Toledo, that detail grisly fatalities involved when such action was embarked upon without the requisite protections, safeguards, in place."

"Heavens above, Richard, you are sounding as if you give credence to the excesses of all that necromantic pishery. You'll be having us believe that djinns – or worse – will be hovering ready to pounce to the thing's defence? Come now, my friend. It is, or should I say was, a most unpleasant memento of an age mercifully long past, but no more nor less than that, however repugnant one may personally have found it or whatever its deluded seekers may still choose to believe."

The Apothecary had remained unresponsive to the Canon's rebuttal, as if his mind was elsewhere, but then said, thoughtfully,

"Their identities, his identity, might well be determined – or, in fact, confirmed. I for one would wish to know for certain who directed the intimidating creature that intruded upon us all. Who it was that attempted to burgle this very house, Canon? If my suspicions are justified, then this Philbrigge of Derby will have been despatched by the same hand and, if so, I have no intention of his leaving Lichfield without sharing that intelligence with us. Your own sighting of that escutcheoned coach points towards an identity that might have strained credulity had I not heard the same name mentioned quite fortuitously, only days before. A week ago, I wrote employing my cousin Johnson's good offices in passing on an enquiry to Bennet Langton. It was he who described the pretensions and the hostile eccentricity of his de Langton relation. How many could there be with such very particular credentials, I have asked myself? I await a reply, and, I trust, the precise whereabouts of his singularly unpleasant kinsman."

"As our removal of the book from Eccleshall, and hence the supposition of our continuing possession of it appear to be common knowledge - in a certain quarter at least - then I shall make no bones over its disappearance, Richard, should the opportunity present itself. In that fashion I would expect to remove unwanted attention from us all."

In different company Greene might have responded with the expression 'a pious hope', though not here, not today. Listening to the Canon's bland assumptions, he was chilled anew by the realisation of what he now knew to be at stake here; the sheer blood-curdling potency of the thing he had chosen to bring into his life, his home.

"Indeed, Canon, that is fervently to be hoped for," he agreed.

(21)

Under the CASE, in a Drawer on the left Hand. A Mifcellaneous
collection of Coins & Medals in Silver and Copper, viz. Late
Lord Anfon, by Pingo; Reverse, Saunders, Brett, Dennis, Campbel,
Keppel, Saumarez; the Officers, who accompanied him in his
Voyage around the World. Alexander Pope, 1741, (Copper). General
Wafhington, (Copper). William Pitt, Esq, (Copper). King James
2d, Coronation Medal (Silver). Mary his Queen, do. &c.

Saddler Street. Saturday 6th May. In a scene all too reminiscent
of the worst excesses of popular theatre, the arrival of Harry
Copeland and his nephew at the Apothecary was punctuated by
voices raised in outrage, hysterical tears, cringing embarrassment
and barely controlled fury. All this late on a busy Saturday morning
and mostly in full view of the weekend's regular customers. The
Officer of Engineers (retired) had been no stranger to mayhem
in its every form – not least in this city, this house, twenty years
earlier – but to a wide-eyed, open-mouthed George Copeland it
seemed that they had entered a madhouse.

Richard Greene had met them from the southbound coach,
arms spread wide to embrace his oldest friend, as the solid, grey-
wigged figure climbed stiffly down to the cobbled yard. Laughing
with pleasure, he had looked up into the lined, weather-beaten
face, "Theodosia was right, Harry! 'Fat of the land' was mentioned
and now I can see why!" With accustomed impassivity, the soldier
turned to the young man who had joined them. "You see, George,
I did not exaggerate. May I present Surgeon-Apothecary Greene

who thinks he knows most things about everything and – more's the pity – is often correct! Richard, this is my nephew, Mr George Copeland, soon to be Ensign Copeland in His Majesty's Forty-Second Regiment of Foot."

"Your servant, Mr Greene. Uncle Harry has told me so much about you, I have long anticipated this meeting – and your museum, too."

"Well said, young man, well said," beamed the Apothecary, "Your uncle has obviously primed you with his accustomed efficiency. Let's get some food and drink inside you both before His Majesty can accuse me of neglecting you."

The soldier had paused, momentarily, as they turned into Saddler Street, looking up to the tall house that rose on his right. "It's good to be back, old friend. It has been far too long." Sentiments he might have had cause to regret short moments later.

As Greene held open the door to his guests, they were met with a hysterical shriek from within and greeted by the sight of a dishevelled, semi-clothed young woman, clawing away from the grip of an equally unkempt but fully clothed housekeeper, mob-cap awry, grey hair straggling from beneath it.

"Emmy! What in God's name?" Greene shouted, only to see James Tillett following behind, dragging a blubbing shop-boy by the elbow, the red blazon of an open-handed slap all too apparent on the youngster's chalk-white face. With features set in grim fury, Theodosia pushed past the males, to grab the wild-eyed Emmy and propel her back into the Consulting Room, slamming its door with a percussive bang. Greene, realising that he had to do something in the face of a half-dozen astounded customers nervously backed against the multi-coloured windows, blurted, "A most unfortunate accident outside in the garden, ladies and gentlemen. All most upsetting, especially for the youngsters, but no serious hurts taken, thank heavens! Our most sincere apologies for this upset – if your business is of an urgent or personal nature, I shall endeavour to see to you straight away, otherwise may we crave your indulgence to return when we have all had time to draw our breath? Exceptionally, we shall close for an hour to reopen at two o'clock. Thank you for your understanding." To a man they left.

Ushering his guests to the foot of the stairs, he said breathlessly: "Harry, Mr Copeland, a thousand pardons, but will you ascend and make yourselves at home? Harry, you know the way. I shall try to work out what on earth has been going on, if I can get a word of sense from anyone." He got no further before Margery, now a galleon under full sail, loomed between them.

"Debauchery, Mr Greene, the only word for it!" she wailed, in genuine distress. "Out in the old bakehouse, her – that wanton little chit with legs a-flaunt – and that halfwit boy, with his ... at it like a ... Oh, Mr Greene, what have we come to? A bawdy house in our own garden." She pulled her apron over her face, tears of fury and distress streaming down her lined cheeks. "It shouldn't be allowed, Mr Greene, it just shouldn't be allowed."

Less than an hour earlier, Emmy had been called into the stillroom, supposedly briefly, to take over the stirring of the copper cauldron as it steamed just below a boil. The heady fumes of the celebrated elixir first seemed to clear her sinuses, then to impart a glow of well-being as she inhaled the intoxicating fumes of alcohol and the Greene's patent and highly secret ingredients steeped prior to overnight cooling and then bottling. When the maidservant eventually came back from the garden privy, she pointedly inspected the seething liquid before taking back the ladle from the red-cheeked girl.

"At least you didn't let it boil," she said, gracelessly, before donning a fine cambric face mask and returning to her task.

"And thank you so much for doing my job for me," said Emmy with a haughty smile before seeking some fresh air.

She looked down the long garden, her eyes drawn to the cottage-like bakehouse slumbering in the early afternoon sun.

It was then that the ebbing glow within her seemed to intensify, spreading deliciously along her arms and legs, across a budding chest, across her taut, flat stomach, down between her thighs into a private place. She moaned aloud with pleasure and when, once again, all the sounds she'd loved came back to fill her ears with the music of memory, she'd slipped under the low lintel into the dusty gloom.

He had seen her as he came up from the stable where the big carboys were stored, straw from their padding spread across his chest where he'd manhandled them into the rearrangement he'd been shown. Poking about again was she? Well, this time he'd see what was what, wouldn't he?

Left ajar by several inches, the sight that met him when he peered in past the weather-beaten door to the dim interior would stay with him for the rest of his life. Emmy, head thrown back, lost in ecstasy, was frantically rubbing beneath her lifted skirts, her other hand kneading and squeezing a little exposed breast. She saw him then, but scarcely faltered, hissing, "Quick, in here! Pull the door, be quick!" He needed no second invitation.

Only moments later, Margery had found them, after almost dropping her laden laundry basket in alarm when she heard a crescendo of moans coming from behind the bakehouse door. Wrenching it open her fleshy jaw dropped in shock and dismay at what was revealed. Then furious outrage flooded through her and she launched herself at the boy, turning now in horror, his hands still clasping the girl's heaving buttocks. Tillett heard the housekeeper's bellow of fury from the stillroom's open window, and rushed out into the garden, just in time to see the boy propelled from the bakehouse door before tripping in the breeches tangled about his ankles and falling flat. As the shopman reached the prone figure struggling to regain its feet, his niece was dragged out by an incandescent Margery.

"Bringing this little wanton here! I said no good would come of it!" she spat. "Look at them, Mr Tillett, just look at what the filthy little…" She struggled for the words. As full realisation dawned on the gaping man, the boy – now hopping about on the sparse lawn – was trying to rebutton his breeches. Without thinking, Tillett stepped up to him and slapped the terrified face with all his might, sending him tumbling back to the ground. "You little animal," he shouted, "Defiling my Emmy, my own little…"

"It was 'er, Mr Tillett! Honest to God it was," the boy wailed, tears streaming down his thin face. "Called me in, couldn't stop 'er." As Tillett lunged forward, the boy cringed back, both only coming to a sudden halt as Theodosia's furious voice sounded from the back door, where she stood, aghast, at the tableau now frozen before her unbelieving gaze.

Summoned, in extremis, to help, Elspeth Blomefield's assistance had been a godsend for what was left of an exceptionally busy afternoon. It was only when the last customer had been waved off through the door that she turned to Theodosia saying, "Being busy is one thing, my dear, but being busy without Lionel constantly under one's feet is a rare pleasure. If only Richard could pass on some hint of his ability to circumnavigate you and your staff, life – in the form of one's husband – would present rather fewer obstacles in my house. The dear man has an absolute genius for being in the wrong place at the wrong time."

"Much like two youngsters rather too close to this house, Elspeth," she said. "I have no idea how we shall cope without them – and just when it all seemed to be going so well."

"They will both have to go, then?" Elspeth responded, seeing the concern etched into her friend's pale features.

"Oh, without a doubt. I mean how could one contemplate any repeat of today's homespun disaster. Frankly, it is beyond comprehension. It was as if the girl, Emmy, was possessed. She was out of control, almost demented, until I could calm her behind closed doors. Then, when she did seem to return to some sort of sanity, it was if she had woken from a dream – one of which she had no memory."

"A dissembler, at that tender age?" replied Elspeth Blomefield.

"We shall not go into the 'tender' part of that, but," she paused, lost in recollection for a moment, "no, surprising though it may seem, I really do not believe there was pretence involved, but then everything about this wretched business is a mystery to me."

She looked up at the large tavern clock above the door. "My dear, I am eternally grateful for your assistance this afternoon, but you must not think me rude if I turf you out. Harry Copeland and his nephew arrived on today's coach and I have been able to offer them nothing but apologies thus far. They will shortly be returning from an enforced trudge around the Cathedral and I really must make myself at least half-presentable before their return. Perhaps you and Lionel will take tea with us tomorrow afternoon? Harry will be delighted to see you once more."

"I shall relish the opportunity of relinquishing my role as chaperone, my dear," replied Elspeth mischievously. "Until tomorrow then, Mrs Greene."

(22)

Under the CASE, in a Drawer on the Left Hand. A
collection of Roman Coins, (in five sliders), in Copper,
Brafs, and Silver,in Number about 1779. Another Drawer,
in which are 78 Roman Coins. A collection of Town and
Traders Tokens, or Halfpence, mostly dated 1664.

Lichfield. Sunday 7th May. As had been their habit for many years,
and regardless of the size of the Sunday congregation, Richard
and Theodosia Greene occupied their accustomed place in a pew
at the rear of St Mary's pillared nave. Given the unpredictability
of the Reverend Blomefield's sermons – both in their content and
duration – the couple had long ago decided that discreet access
to the exit was an imperative. There had been occasions, all-too
memorable occasions, when the cleric had become so enraptured
by his topic – if not by the sound of his own voice, as had been
unkindly asserted more than once – that he had been known
to preach for more than two hours, completely oblivious to the
snores and furtive departures of his congregation. Today, the
couple had been joined by their guests, young George Copeland
in his pristine uniform, and his uncle in elegant charcoal-grey
broadcloth. Whilst the barely concealed glances and inaudible
comments directed towards their party might have been construed
as no more than curiosity for the newcomers, the Apothecary and
his wife knew their fellow citizens well enough to be certain that
news of yesterday's debacle would have spread like one of the city's
all too regular fires. They nodded and smiled at each of the turned

faces as if they had not a care in the world, but as is so often the case in such displays of public equanimity, the reality was at odds with appearances.

Husband and wife had sat up in bed conversing in urgent whispers into the small hours, after bidding their guests a good night shortly before midnight. By tacit agreement the embarrassments and upsets of the day had been avoided through a long and convivial evening, not least by a housekeeper whose earliest memory of tonight's senior guest had been of him stripped naked in her kitchen, blue with cold and exhaustion. Just as the semiconscious master of the house, bleeding, half-drowned, had himself been stripped bare, before both men could be wrapped in blankets and revived over the course of several desperate hours.

For the Officer of Engineers, tonight, sitting at his ease with a bumper of brandy in hand, what they had witnessed on their arrival, today, would have simply paled into the realms of domestic trivia – light relief by comparison – had he not been able to detect the gravity of its impact upon these well-loved old friends. All was not well, he knew it in his bones, but, equally, knew that until his host decided to unburden himself, in his own good time, he would remain none the wiser.

"What can you mean, the girl was not to blame, Richard? She played that poor boy, enticed him like a seasoned whore, a hot little strumpet! How can you doubt the evidence? He would no more have forced himself upon her than he would have flown round the great steeple. We both know he is biddable to a fault. There is not a bad bone in that body or a bad thought in that vacant head. He will never reach what we think of as maturity, husband, you know that, but he is a dear, simple youngster, incapable of the vicious assault that poor Tillett assumes. To be rid of him would be a condemnation so public, so damning, it will ruin his life. You know I am right."

"I cannot disagree with any of your sentiments concerning

him, my dear; he is little more than a guileless child and will ever remain so. It is the outright condemnation of Emmy that I cannot condone. No, let me speak now," he said urgently seeing that she was about to interrupt. "As Elspeth was about to leave, I chanced to hear the end of your conversation as I was crossing the landing. You used the word 'possessed', my dear, and I greatly fear you were correct. The book is hidden where I foolishly believed it would be safest. Out there, in the oven, behind an iron door. She found it somehow – was drawn to it, I have not the slightest doubt. It was a vile, corrupting power at work out there today, Theodosia, not the simple itch of a horny lad and the awakening, for want of a better word, of that sweet young thing. I have experienced that dreadful power, not once but twice; I know with absolute certainty that this is what occurred. I had to steel myself to replace that damnable box back into the oven. She had removed it; was, I think, seated on it as..." He faltered and stopped, wretched in their candle's flickering light.

Whilst, on another occasion and from a degree of experience, she might well have taken issue with the evaluation of this – or any – fourteen-year-old girl as simply 'a sweet young thing', Theodosia could not argue with the fierce certainty of her husband's assertion. Had she not tried to hold her, contain her, as the girl wriggled and fought? Blank, wild eyes, huge in a stranger's face, until she had suddenly seemed to deflate like a pricked bladder, a lanced boil, the toxin draining from her. Leaving a spent, sobbing child to face the consequences of actions she could not, would not, remember.

"Then what in the name of Heaven are we to do about it, about them, Richard? I am at a loss."

"Let us begin by sleeping on it," he had said with finality, leaning to snuff out the light.

Conscious, possibly, of his social obligations later that day, Lionel Blomefield kept the morning's sermon to a decent minimum, allowing the Greene party to remain, with moderate attentiveness, before they and the rest of the congregation could regain the sunlight of the marketplace and the usual after-service greetings and conversations. Given the perfect clemency of the day, the Apothecary proposed a walk around the reed-fringed banks of Stowe Pool. They were joined by Elspeth Blomefield in her Sunday best and by a grateful husband presented with the opportunity of removing ecclesiastical garb and escaping the further attentions of persistent parishioners.

"One gathers you had a spot of bother yesterday," was his opening gambit as they set off, only to be silenced by two voices in perfect unison saying: "Not now, Lionel." Greene and Elspeth shared a small smile of complicity.

As they strolled towards the landmark of Michael Johnson's windmill, its sails sabbath-still in a breeze that was sending wavelets scudding across the wide expanse of water, they arrived at the humble profile of St Chad's church.

"Might this be same Chad as our Cedd at Lastingham?" enquired the young man.

"Close, Mr Copeland, close," replied a smiling Greene. "They were brothers. Ours, it is said with some authority, had his cell right here, and if the legend is to be believed, spent much of his time up to his neck in that," – he pointed to a well-like structure close to the church – "praying for divine inspiration. Hence," he continued, with a theatrical flourish towards the spires rising against the westerly skies, "our wonderful Cathedral, a thousand years on."

As the party gazed back across the ruffled pool, if either the Apothecary or Harry Copeland were thinking back twenty years to the frozen night when the soldier had dragged a halfdead Greene from an icy death, then neither revealed a flicker of that, or any other recollection from that awful time.

"And there, Mr Copeland," said Theodosia pointing towards the new building that rose as a complete anachronism from the eastern wall of the Cathedral's medieval defences, "is what will forever be called 'Spite House' whether its malicious builder likes it or not."

"You are looking, Sir, at a house positioned solely to spoil the view of our cathedral that Stowe House," – she pointed once more, to the opposite end of the mere, close to where they stood – "was built to enjoy. What breath-taking small-mindedness our species can achieve when it has a mind to."

"A properly philosophical note for a Sunday afternoon, my dear," laughed her husband.

"Did not Cousin Samuel describe us as 'a city of philosophers'?"

The afternoon had continued in that timeless ease that old friends share, until, with tea finished and just as sherry was proposed, Elspeth Blomefield announced that it was time for them to go home and allow the Greene household and its guests a peaceful evening. Casting a wistful eye at the decanters, Lionel followed her to the door.

"We shall need to talk about the buying and selling of books, Richard. I presume you have a strategy in that direction?" Greene could only shrug helplessly in response, holding open the door to their departure, and saying, "It is only one of a number of things on my mind at present, Lionel."

Leaving Theodosia and their guests at ease, after explaining the pressing need to resolve the staff problems they had witnessed on their arrival the previous day, the Apothecary hurried out. Promising to be back for a late supper he set off towards Farewell and a meeting he was dreading. He was not to know that at least one of the problems had already been taken out of their hands. His arrival at the cottage door was met with an odd mixture of deference, defensiveness and annoyance by Emmy's mother, the widowed sister-in-law of James Tillett. Their shopman himself was there, looking wan and exhausted, greeting his employer with unaccustomed awkwardness as Greene entered the small parlour.

Emmy was nowhere to be seen. Once seated, the Apothecary spread his hands, exclaiming: "Well, what a to-do, Mrs Tillett, James. I have come in the hope of righting an unfortunate occurrence for which I accept complete responsibility." Before he could continue, James Tillett said, "How so, Mr Greene? It wasn't you out there acting like a..."

"Please, please, hear me out," interjected Greene, "Allow me to explain my culpability in this." Neither responded so he continued, "James, you are well-versed in all our preparations, our processes, at the shop, and as such are aware that we employ many of our ingredients – our tinctures, our drugs – with great care; knowing both their efficacy and their potential for harm if abused, or treated with insufficient care?"

His listener nodded, respectfully. "Well, of course, Mr Greene."

"Good, so you will also be aware that on Saturday our usual batch of elixir was being prepared, overseen by one of Margery's girls..." – Tillett nodded – "...and that our mixture, our most confidential recipe, contains the precise addition of both poppy-syrup and Egyptian hashish to the raw alcohol, along with the other herbs and spices. The maximum quantity, in fact, of both drugs that I judge to be a prudent dosage when employed exactly as directed."

The shopman was looking puzzled, obviously not understanding where this might be leading. "But, James, neither you, nor I, nor my wife, were aware that young Mabel took a lengthy leave of absence, out in the privy – with one of her chap-books I suspect, taking shameless advantage of a newly arrived trainee and leaving Emmy to watch the preparation. To watch it, knowing nothing of its potency if inhaled – because no one had thought to mention it. Leaving her without one of the masks we all wear in contact with the process." Greene spread his hands once more, and then carried on: "Your daughter, Mrs Tillett, your niece, James, left her unwonted station in a state of complete intoxication, having been exposed for some time to the narcotic fumes. I hold myself completely responsible for what then ensued. Emmy was simply not herself; she was drugged to the eyeballs, not to put too fine a point upon it."

He took a deep breath before continuing, "If I may speak plainly in the circumstances, of what we all know to be acutely sensitive and highly embarrassing for all concerned – what then occurred – but what I am assured was interrupted in short order – was the regrettable but all too understandable combination of intoxication and youthful desire. Both parties entirely innocent – in their own way – of any artful assignation, any guilty forethought whatever. To be absolutely blunt, Mrs Tillett, an inadequate, almost child-like boy took advantage of an invitation made by a young girl in command of neither her reason nor common sense."

"But what about common decency, Mr Greene?" the woman said angrily: "My Emmy's ruined, spoiled for life. What's to do about that, when all's said and done?"

The Apothecary resisted the temptation to shrug, before answering, "Who knows the truth of what happened, Mrs Tillett? Who knows what even occurred out in the seclusion of my garden? It was interrupted, Mrs Tillett, in the most meaningful way; must I spell that out? Howsoever much we may regret it, or condemn it, what has occurred is no more, no less, than what has been going on behind every hayrick, in every hidey-hole, at every naughty opportunity, since the beginning of time. I have already ensured that not one word of this indiscretion has gone beyond my immediate house. I can give you my firm assurance that my staff will hold their tongues at cost of their continuing employment, as will my wife and I for obvious reasons. That leaves you and your daughter, Mrs Tillett. Might it perhaps be wise to speak to Emmy now?"

"She's gone, Mr Greene," the shopman sighed. "Emmy's not here. I took her to our people in Ashbourne yesterday afternoon. I've only just returned. A fresh start, like? Didn't see that there was any choice. Not with the sort of prattle a body can expect around here. Didn't know you were going to come and explain it all, like. It's done now, probably for the best."

Mrs Tillett broke into tears. "It's all very well saying what you said, Sir, but when all's said and done you've got it all haven't you? Emmy's all I've got – all I had – now my Tom's gone."

The Apothecary stood to leave. "I'm so sorry, but what more can I say, or do? I came to make the best of a bad job, to help Emmy to feel better about herself." He turned to the silent man. "Perhaps you'll take a day off tomorrow, James. You look exhausted. We shall see you on Tuesday as usual."

"Not if that boy is there, you won't, Mr Greene."

"Do you know, James, I do believe we shall." retorted Greene, a new edge of authority to his voice, "You are an intelligent man, a valued man and an old friend. You of all people know that there is neither wickedness nor guile in that poor, simple head. Are we about to ruin a defenceless wight out of anger or a misplaced desire for revenge? No, we are not. And there's an end to it! Life goes on, either with us or without us."

"Good night, Mrs Tillett. I shall see that any outstanding wages are honoured, and, in addition, a week in lieu of notice. I trust that will be acceptable."

No answer was forthcoming. As he left, drained but guiltily relieved at the turn of events, he knew that Emmy's departure had a certain inevitability about it, however unjust or hurtful it would seem. Now though, a second call had to be made. He felt suddenly inadequate, bone-weary, but knew there was no alternative. He was not prepared for what he found.

Although the Apothecary had never had cause to visit the small farm out beyond St Michael's church on Greenhill, he knew that the boy, Timmy, was cared for, after a rough and ready fashion, by the family who worked the arable pastures out towards the Burton road. He had been abandoned shortly after his birth by an unknown parent, left at the door of the church in whose shadow he had now lived for the past fifteen years. As Greene nudged his mare into the stable yard in the amber dusk of a fine evening, he saw a curtain drawn back at the sound of his hooves on the pamments close to the low door of the farmhouse. To his surprise the door opened before he could even dismount at the block by the porch, spilling light out into the darkening yard.

"It's Mr Greene isn't it? The Apothecary?" called the emerging figure of a stocky, thick-set man Greene recognised as the boy's de facto guardian. Waving acknowledgement, the small man dismounted gracelessly but before he could speak the other continued, "You're a welcome sight, and no mistake, Mr Greene, but how did you know to come? We've had no chance to send word – been too busy reviving the daft lummox."

The Apothecary's stomach seemed to lurch at the words – a terrible certainty flared in his chest. "Revive, Mr Handley? How so? What's happened here?" The farmer looked nervously from left to right, as if checking they were alone in the twilight. "You'd best come straight in, Mr Greene. This to-do isn't for prying eyes or nosey parkers. Beats me, all this shite. Can't think what got into that daft noddle of his."

Now the Apothecary knew with intuitive certainty and he felt sick with it as he ducked into the low, beamed kitchen where a small, plump women stood, wringing her apron in wordless agitation. "We'd not have known ought were going on, if the ninny hadn't knocked over an empty churn and a stool wi' basins stacked on 'im, when 'e fell."

"Fell from what?" blurted Greene urgently.

"From that, Mr Greene," said Handley morosely, pointing through the open door to the byre that adjoined the house, a palliasse on the earthen floor just visible in the far corner, roughhewn roof timbers stretched above it in the gloom. "Halter broke, and down the daft loon tumbled; saved him though. E'd 've strangled for sure if'n it'd 'eld. But what it's all about, The Lord only knows, Mr Greene. What could've driven the lad to it?"

Before the shocked visitor could respond, the farmer continued, in an aggrieved tone, "Nothin' fancy 'ere, that's for sure and certain, but 'e's allus had a roof over 'is daft 'ead and food in 'is belly – and 'e goes and does this, Mr Greene. What's it all come to?"

"I must see him, Handley. Quickly, where is he?" exclaimed Greene impatiently. "He must be helped."

The farmer, annoyed at the visitor's brusque tone responded hotly, "What d'you think us did, Mr Greene? Stood and watched the lummox choke?" He jerked a thumb over his shoulder towards the front of the house. "'E's in the parlour, where 'e's got no leave to be. Stretched out on a decent rug and makin' the place look untidy. Missus didn't want 'im moved again 'til 'e'd got some colour back. Mollycoddling if you ask me."

Greene pushed past him to gaze down at the thin youth stretched out on a rag rug, with a coarse blanket covering a chest that rose and fell with an untroubled regularity of sleep, hugely reassuring to the peering Apothecary,. He noted a livid burn around the throat where the halter had gripped for a few deadly instants, and kneeling beside him, with infinite gentleness brushed coarse, sweat-matted hair from a brow pitted with acne scars. The boy's eyes flickered open at his touch, a welter of emotions darting through them, only calming as he saw, and recognised, the round, smiling face above him.

"Now then, Timmy, what's to do, old lad?" said Greene quietly. "You're safe and sound thanks to these good folk." He indicated the watching figures in the doorway behind him "but you've given us all a turn, and no mistake. If we prop you up a bit, do you think you can tell me about it?" Greene saw the boy's eyes dart to the silent couple and then, imploringly, back to his employer. The Apothecary understood.

"I'm certain Mr and Mrs Handley won't mind giving me a spot of peace and quiet whilst I examine my patient," – he looked meaningfully at them – "but perhaps Mrs Handley could manage a bolster or some cushions first?"

Some minutes later, after Handley had closed the parlour door with less than good grace, Greene had pulled up a chair beside the propped figure who was by now breathing hoarsely and waiting with obvious trepidation.

"There was no need for this, you know, Timmy. You were foolish, and wrong, to give in to Emmy, there's no denying that, but I'm not so old that I can't remember just how hard it would have been for me to say, 'No, thank you', if I'd been in your place. Did she call you in?"

"No, Sir," the boy croaked, before Greene handed him an earthenware mug from which he drank greedily before continuing: "Us'd seen 'er pokin' about in there earlier and wondered what she were up to. Just followed 'er in, s'pose, curious like, and there she were, a-rubbin' and a fingerin' and she just says, 'Come on then, quick', like she'd been espectin' us." Tears had sprung into the glaucous eyes by now.

"But when ol' Margey-Bargey banged in," – Greene grimly suppressed a smile – "and then Mr Tillett, like, us didn't even know where us were, what was goin' on, like; just that it were feelin' really good an' all. Then Mr Tillett, 'e 'it us 'ard and everyone was shoutin' an' all. Only later, after us 'ad been sent 'ome and knew us'd lost us job and been really really bad and let everybody down, like, I couldn't get over it, not knowin' ow us'd tell 'em." He pointed limply towards the closed door. "Wouldn't be able to give 'em any money for us keep an' that." He stopped, sobbing.

"Right, now let's get one thing straight," said the Apothecary earnestly: "You have not lost your job. Emmy won't be coming back, and I've just come from having a quiet word with our Mr Tillett. I think you'll find that when you come back to work on Tuesday – yes, Tuesday – after you've both had a day to get over things, that the less said about all this, then the sooner it will be mended. Mr Tillett might well be annoyed with you for a while, but that's no more than you deserve for your foolishness."

Greene looked down into a face of pathetic gratitude. "Do you understand? We're all going to put this behind us, and no-one will be any the wiser about the upset we've had." As the boy nodded his speechless gratitude and relief, Greene added, "I'll see that Mr and Mrs Handley say no more about it."

Then, as the Apothecary stood to leave, the pallid boy looked up and spoke words that pierced Greene like spikes of ice, "But what about 'im? T'other one? 'Im what sat there laughing, like, when us'd climbed up an' 'ad the leather all tight 'round us neck and was going to jump, like? Dunno where 'e'd come from – just there all of a sudden 'e were – but 'e'll tell, for sure. Whoever 'e were. Lovin' it, 'e were. Nasty, 'im."

The Apothecary swayed and almost fell, numb, winded, gaping down at a boy who had no concept of what he had just guilelessly described. "Imagination, Timmy, that's all it was," he somehow managed. "You were so very upset you will just have been seeing what wasn't really there. Trust me and have no more fear on that score," he finished lamely. "We shall see you, fit and well, on Tuesday." He turned and hurried out to the waiting couple, searching for inspiration.

"Know what us seed," murmured the boy to the closing door. "Nasty, 'im."

(23)

Within the Table, in the middle of the ROOM. Two breadths
of Crimſon Silk, much faded, embroidered with Silver, being
part of a Garment worn by Queen Elizabeth. A piece of Muſlin,
ſpriged with Flowers, in various coloured Silk; the work of
Lady Raleigh in the Tower of London, during the impriſonment
of her huſband Sir Walter. A Ribband of Orange coloured,
watered Tabby, worn by the Prince of Orange, afterwards
King William 3d. A blue Ribband, worn by Queen Ann.

Monday. 8ᵗʰ May. The Copelands had departed, as planned,
on the morning coach. Having read the exhaustion etched
into his old friend's face, Henry Copeland had known that any
explanation of what lay beneath it would have to wait his return.
Late on the soldier had decided to extend his southerly sojourn to
include several days in London, rather than the direct return from
Windsor originally intended. Copeland's decision had come as
something of a relief to Greene, in view not only of the impending
visit from the mysterious bookseller later in the week, but also that
this morning's mail had brought the awaited re-scheduling of the
Woollaton invitation from Richard Davenport for the following
Saturday. It was accompanied by an explanation that due to
pressure upon him to return to his Cheshire estate, little more
than two weeks remained before Davenport would be leaving
Ellastone – and his guests – in the hands of his long-standing
staff. He was, he wrote, hoping to have created a small, carefully

chosen circle of acquaintance for his guests before his departure.

Davenport had also expressed his delight – and that of Rousseau – that the celebrated Erasmus Darwin would be a part of it, emphasising the welcome that awaited both at Woollaton.

Much gratified and replying by return of mail, after a hurried confirmation of Darwin's availability on that date, the Apothecary had thought to include a copy of the Lichfield museum catalogue for the advance perusal of both their host-to-be and his illustrious guest. Whist Davenport's schedule might well not permit him to accompany the Frenchman on his promised visit to view the collection, he could at least prime him with any necessary translations that might whet the visitor's anticipation for what lay ahead.

Bowing to the inevitable, a neatly penned announcement, prominently displayed against the multi-coloured glass lozenges of the Apothecary's door, explained that with regret and sincere apologies to valued customers, the shop would only be open for business between the hours of 11am and 2pm, due to unforeseen staff indispositions. It would reopen, as usual, on Tuesday. Sharp at a quarter to nine in the morning.

Elspeth had, once more, happily agreed to assist Theodosia for the three hours of business, though her oldest and closest friend could well have done without Mrs Blomefield's light-hearted admission that she loved playing shop.

At much the same time that Richard Greene was embarking upon his afternoon rounds of the bedridden, the infirm and those patients with exaggerated self-esteem and a depth of pocket to match, Richard Davenport's coach was entering Ashbourne's Market Place. Descending with a degree of hauteur, handed down by an ever-gracious host, Madame Thérèse Rousseau gazed disconsolately around the bustling rusticity of the scene around them.

"The milliner's we seek is, I believe, to be found just around the corner there and opposite the inn named 'Green Dragon'," said Davenport, lifting his cane to indicate a bow-fronted premises off to their left. "And the druggist, as I recall, is closer still,"

"If you will permit me." He took the Frenchwoman's arm and began to lead her through the stalls of the market.

Scarcely fifteen minutes earlier, the gaunt figure of the man called de Rais, had left the stableyard of The Green Dragon, making his way with single-minded purpose towards the druggist's shop in the Market Place. Despatched upon a regular errand, one tolerated exclusively for his own purposes rather than those of his employer, he gazed neither left nor right, taking no interest in the simple pleasures and amenities of the small town.

Entering the familiar premises to the sound of its jangling doorbell, he was immediately approached by the diffident figure the druggist's assistant.

"Mr Ray, Sir; will it be your usual order?"

The heavily scarfed figure nodded curtly in response.

"Then I'm afraid there will be a delay, Sir." He saw the anger flash behind the piercing black eyes and hurriedly continued, "Oh, only a very brief delay, I do assure you, Mr Ray. Perhaps ten minutes, no more. Mr Tomlin was called out to attend to an elderly lady as took a tumble over there," – he pointed out across the square – "and he will want to serve you personally of course." Looking nervously at the obviously annoyed customer he added, "May I suggest you take a seat through in the Consulting Room. Mr Tomlin will attend to you immediately upon his return."

With a disdainful shrug de Rais pushed past him and took a seat in the small windowless room. He consulted a pocket-watch and then sat, apparently lost in thought, awaiting the druggist's return. He was alerted by the door-bell minutes later, but on realising this had sounded for the entry of customers, sank back into his reverie until suddenly galvanised by the realisation that their conversation was in French. He stood and leaned towards the open door to the short passage beyond, the better to overhear.

"Being a mere man and an unmarried one at that," he heard the man's voice say in almost impeccable French, "I would not normally presume to accompany a lady into either her milliner's, her haberdashery or, peril of perils, her dress shop. So, Madame Rousseau, you will, I trust, forgive my presence here today so that I can serve as interpreter for your requirements, if not as an arbiter of all things feminine?"

The listener, now rigid with a fierce intensity, heard the woman as she laughed at this heavy-handed courtesy, replying, "Your presence will be as welcome as is your kind hospitality, Mr Davenport. London was proving to be too much for my poor Jean-Jacques. Whilst he does love the attentions of his admirers and acolytes, I sometimes think that he fears them in equal measure. As to my simple needs, I shall do my utmost to spare your blushes."

De Rais could scarcely believe what he was hearing. Rousseau, that jumped-up, sanctimonious, pig-bastard was here? In England? In this one-horse town in the middle of nowhere? The same great Jean-Jacques Rousseau who had spat in his face and made him a laughingstock in front of his jumped-up pig-bastard worshippers? De Rais silently clasped skeletal hands to his breast in a parody of prayer, the humourless rictus of a grin splitting thin, bloodless lips. How sweet revenge could be when tasted cold.

As he heard the woman's few requirements being first translated and then, catered to by an assistant obviously bent on pleasing these well-heeled customers, the listener noted all and everything that could be used to his advantage. A peppermint elixir for the treatment of a husband's dyspeptic stomach, James's powders, a styptic balm and items of womanly needs, culminating in the man's instruction that this bill and anything else his guests might be requiring in the weeks and months to come, should be addressed to Woollaton Hall where the account would be settled on the Englishman's usual monthly basis.

Just as they were about to leave, Thérèse Rousseau gave a small exclamation of annoyance. "Forgive me, please, but I had forgotten a particular request from Jean-Jacques. Can you please ask if this man has any raw sugar cane? My husband so loves to chew it while he writes, so like the child he can sometimes be." She laughed, fondly.

"Ah, of course, said Davenport, "The reed that produces honey without bees, as the Greeks would have it. I do believe the government of your country thought so highly of its delights that they exchanged your snowy possessions in North America for the return of your Sugar Isles – Martinique and so on." Thérèse simply shrugged in response as if her country's affairs were of little interest.

When her request was transmitted, the assistant expressed his regret at its lack of immediate availability, promising that a supply could shortly be arranged to arrive with his master's next order from Bristol. "Two weeks, no more, I do assure you."

De Rais memorised the information with fierce relish. He had waited so long for an opportunity to avenge himself, never imagining how and when it might present itself.

Shortly after they had departed to the sound of the bell, the druggist returned, breathless and perspiring from his labours. After a few brief whispered words with his assistant, Tomlin appeared in the Consulting Room, thin, stoop-shouldered and smiling his transparently false smile of welcome.

"Mr Ray, Sir! A pleasure as always! A thousand pardons for the delay."

He got no further. De Rais, standing now, looked down at the fawning man and rasped, "My order, as usual. I have no more time to waste."

"Of course, of course, it is being seen to even as we speak, though you will understand, Sir, that such quantities of narcotic intoxicants must be regulated with the utmost probity and could not be dispensed without my presence."

De Rais silenced the voluble shopkeeper with a single finger raised to blue-tinged lips, the pin-prick pupils seeming to bore into him as a purse was opened and coins counted into the waiting palm.

"And this, of course, will be for more of your principal's experimentation?"

"Of course," came the hoarse reply, "Should you actually believe his purposes to be any of your concern."

"No, no, absolutely not. I had no wish to pry, it is simply that the quantities involved..."

"Are paid for in full. That is all you need to know, shop-keeper – for are there not many more such as you..?"

There was an accent there, the distracted druggist decided, a hint of something foreign that would explain everything about this appalling man's lack of even the most basic civilities.

With the transaction complete and a wax-sealed package delivered into the bony hands, de Rais paused as he was about to leave. The druggist's spirits sank.

"If I should require something of singular potency for the elimination of rats, you will be able to provide it?"

"Why, yes of course, Mr Ray. We look forward to being of service to you."

When the door had closed upon his unwelcome customer, the druggist turned to his assistant with a sigh of relief. "For all that his coin is as good as any," he said, stiffening, " I find it hard to stomach that man. Each month enough raw opium to kill a dozen horses; what must they do with it?" Shrugging, he concluded, "We shall increase our Bristol order to keep up with our stock. Make note."

As his employer went about business in the rear of the premises, the assistant stared after the dwindling figure across the Market Place. "It's his rats I feel sorry for," he murmured to himself.

Around the corner and out of his sight, further small purchases were concluded by a handsome woman and her most patrician companion. An uncle? A protector? wondered the milliner, as she absently served a regular customer, intrigued by the interpreter's easy facility as he passed on his companion's instructions to the inexpert girl who was serving beside her.

When the well-to-do couple had left the millinery, the owner turned to her new shop-girl. "It's just as well you made a half-decent fist of your wrapping, my girl; the ribbon you cut for the lady looked as if you'd done it with a knife and fork. It won't do, Esmeralda, it won't do at all. If you're to repay my generosity you'll do it in short order, d'you hear me, girl? There's no place here for shirkers or lally-gaggers, you mind my words."

Emmy Tillett burst into tears and ran into the back, hating her aunt, her shop and everything else in this hateful town. She just wanted to die.

ITEM:

Returning from the Inner Museum; On the right hand, a large Medal in Copper, gilded, of Dr. Stukely; Reverse, a reprefentation of Stone Henge on Salisbury Plain. Linneus and Thomas Pennant Efq; of Dowming in Flintshire, in Plaifter of Paris coloured. Two Indian Lances.

Lichfield. Thursday 11ᵗʰ May. "Should we appear seated a little less like a Tribunal, do you think?" enquired the Apothecary, looking to left and right at his companions arranged around the museum's largest table.

"No, absolutely not, Richard," replied Blomefield with uncharacteristic conviction. "If this fellow has the slightest connection with that blackguard who accosted me, he will richly deserve all the intimidation we can manage. Do you not agree, Seward?"

"At risk of sharing a most unchristian sentiment, I must agree, Lionel," replied the Canon. "Albeit that we may about to be faced with a blameless tradesman, I concur that we should occupy the strategic high ground from the outset. At worst, we might make the odd purchase if the fellow turns out to be nothing more nor less than what he says. At best we might discover who is behind the unhealthy interest being shown in us. He will doubtless have been alerted by our decision to receive him all together, but then, gentlemen, we have nothing to hide, do we?"

The Apothecary managed to avoid eye contact with the Canon by cupping a hand to his ear as the sound of a laboured ascent of the steep stairs to the museum reached them. "Enter Bookseller, Stage Left," he murmured.

A perspiring figure, fighting for breath and dragging several panniers behind him appeared from the Armoury Corridor. They rose as one to meet him.

Gulping for breath, the newcomer sagged against the newly split doorframe. "Mr Greene, I presume. Forgive my disarray, but those stairs..."

Greene went forward, hand outstretched: "Mr Philbrigge, encumbered with Incunabula it would appear! Shall we give you a hand?"

Before the wheezing figure could object, his bags had been lifted to the waiting table and a chair procured for their owner. He surveyed the assembled trio with a wan smile of gratitude.

"We thought to spare you the necessity of a three-pronged assault upon our purses, Mr Philbrigge," said Seward with every appearance of geniality, indicating the company, "unless, of course, we were mistaken, and you had approached more Lichfeldians than just us three?"

"No, Sir, your assumption was absolutely correct," replied Philbrigge, now visibly recovering from his exertions. "You will appreciate, gentlemen, that in my line of, shall we say specialised, business, intelligence regarding discriminating collectors and their particular fields of interest is what I can best describe as being my stock-in-trade, quite literally. It is only by a gaining and sharing of such knowledge that we few engaged in specialist dealing can thrive. To the benefit of all concerned, I assure you, gentlemen. Both as sellers and in some most advantageous circumstances as purchasers, too."

"To business, then," declared the Apothecary. "Any items of our own that we may be considering for sale will be dealt with by us individually in the privacy of our own homes; but for now, show us your wares, pray."

Within minutes an array of books and ephemera had been laid

out for their inspection on the wide tabletop. The display ranged from more than a dozen superbly crafted bindings, through scuffed and dog-eared volumes, to pegged bundles of salvaged leaves, a couple of magnificent hand-coloured vellum plates broken from some lost masterpiece, and several rolled scrolls.

"Without wishing to sound presumptuous, unless my intelligence is faultier than usual, I believe there should be something of particular interest for each of you, gentlemen." All three were already busily inspecting whatever had attracted their attention, each already absorbed in a world of their own.

"Canon Seward, Sir, if I might draw your attention to this first edition of Tradescant? Mr Greene, you may be interested in the earliest guide I have ever come across. I believe it predates Leland's *Itineraries*. And you, Reverend Blomefield, ah, I see you have already spotted the fly-fishing work, Sir. It contains the most comprehensive..."

An hour had sped past by the time Philbrigge was replacing stock into his capacious panniers, and each of them had assembled a variety of pieces for the negotiations that would supposedly follow. Having cleared the final volumes away, the bookseller regained his seat and said, "Might I suggest that as each of you gentlemen has indicated that there are items you may wish to sell, you might first welcome the opportunity to peruse the choices you have made here in the privacy of your own homes, where I shall call upon you, individually, tomorrow morning at a time to suit your convenience, should you so wish?"

"You're good," thought Greene. "Now, though, shall we see just how good?"

Indicating the choices each had made, now laid out in front of them on the cleared tabletop, he said, conversationally: "That which you refer to as your 'intelligence' is obviously of a high order, Mr Philbrigge: you, or whoever sent you, have read us to a nicety." He watched the gratified smile falter and disappear as he continued: "But does this intelligence usually encompass breaking and entering, attempted burglary and aggressive intimidation? We are all ears, are we not, gentlemen?"

Philbrigge gaped, speechless, as the atmosphere of shared geniality in the museum room froze. Looking at the face slack with shock, Greene was reminded of a gaffed fish.

"I don't... I have never..." the bookseller began, spluttering, wide-eyed, suddenly looking as if he were praying for the ground to open beneath him. He came to his feet, his chair toppling beside him as he made to retrieve his bags. The Apothecary strode past his fumbling efforts to reach the door, closing it with a decisive slam before appearing to turn a key in the lock.

"You, Sir, are going nowhere before we receive some answers," he said quietly.

"You don't understand," Philbrigge shouted, face ashen with fear. "I have been sworn to silence, told my very life depends upon it. I know nothing about house-breaking, burglary, as God is my witness! I am just a bookseller sent to..."

"Locate something we are believed to possess? To buy it? To steal it? Speak up while you have the chance, man," interposed Seward, his voice cold and authoritative. "Or do you choose to be sentenced as willing accessory to attempted theft and violent extortion? The hangman will make little choice between them, believe me."

They watched, with every appearance of impassivity, as Philbrigge seemed to collapse into himself, tears springing to his eyes as he stood, swaying, looking desperately about him, seeking some means of escape. Greene stood once more, retrieved the bookseller's fallen chair and said: "Sit."

Regaining his place at the table, Greene looked at the picture of misery now facing them and said: "We await an explanation. Begin at the beginning."

Head bowed, Philbrigge strove to control himself, hands clasped, knuckles white with the intensity of his grip. It was several moments before he managed to begin, "I have built up a number of particular customers over many years, dealing with those like me in France, in Spain, the Low Countries. Suppliers of supposed arcana, hermetic texts, occult nonsense of every complexion, erotica for more tastes than you would believe possible. I have dealt, bought and sold, with little or no thought for the content, always for the profit. In recent years there has been a growing taste for magic, diabolism, whatever you wish to call it. I have become known for accessing the genuinely old, the original, in what has become a welter of fakery, of pallid concoctions and downright gibberish newly penned for posturing lunatics. It is why I have been charged with obtaining a certain object that is known to have come into your possession, by…" – he hesitated, visibly – "…a principal who has bought extensively from me over recent years. All works of magic, of conjuration and the like. All old, all costly and rare."

Philbrigge paused, extracting a kerchief from a pocket and wiping a moist, pallid face. Shrugging, he continued: "I am not proud of myself, being a greedy, needy man, gentlemen, not a brave one. For my sins, though, I have become increasingly frightened of commerce with both him and his creature. A Frenchman, I believe. They are driven, relentless men – men whom I now believe to be capable of anything to gain their ends. I have come to realise that this principal has but a single objective. He is obsessed with the goal of achieving the degree of Ipsissimus – that which is believed by some – by him, indubitably – to be the pinnacle of a Magus's power. Deluded madness you might well say, but their ready coin always took me back to their door."

"Which is where, exactly" enquired Greene.

The bookseller appeared not to have heard, continuing, "On my last visit to them, a most significant sum of money was unexpectedly pressed upon me to accept a certain commission. In my greed I accepted that which can never be returned, before even being aware of what is so avidly sought."

"And your understanding of that is?" said Seward quietly.

"That it is a most ancient book of power, a grimoire as the French call It. From its description – given that I should recognise what I was charged to find – I believe it to be one of the rarest in existence, most probably the source of many copies – and even they are great rarities. I am empowered to offer whatever price is put upon it and I wish to God in Heaven that I had never heard of the damnable thing or agreed to seek it. It is believed by some to have once been the property of a bishop, an adept himself, and that it was stolen by him, or on his orders, from safekeeping in the Vatican. For centuries its continued existence has become little more than a myth, a black legend. It was known either as The Clavicule or The Book of Solomon."

"Hence the Seal on its cover," murmured Blomefield, as images of god-like flight flashed in Greene's head.

Philbrigge stopped in the stunned silence that followed before gasping, "So, it is true? You have seen it?" He looked from one to the other. "Please," he begged, "please, tell me you have not opened it, meddled with it in any way?" Only silence met his horrified query.

"But it will be guarded," he shouted, "guarded like no other! What kind of blind, ignorant fools are you? Once opened without protections it will be a threat beyond all hope."

He turned helplessly to Seward. "Canon, I implore you to divulge its whereabouts. You cannot comprehend the awful potency of this thing. It claims dominion over angels, over demons, will have been used for the conjuration of spirits." He paused for breath, looking beseechingly at the impassive cleric before rushing on. "I have been provided with a safeguard, a form of words, of protection, to employ in the event of obtaining it. It must not be handled – and never opened."

"In the light of what you say, I have no regret that the object in question is no longer in my keeping," replied Seward. "It disappeared from a place of safe concealment, as I believed. I have no idea of its present whereabouts."

"Oh, Sweet Jesu," whispered Philbrigge, looking wildly about him. "Then I am a dead man."

Before anyone could react, he had leapt to his feet and hurled himself at a door which opened effortlessly to his scrabbling hands. Then he was through it to the top landing. With a sudden shriek he seemed to trip, losing his footing and pitching forward to tumble, headlong, down the steep stairs.

For a frozen instant they remained seated, staring, transfixed, at the void beyond the open door. "But you locked it," whispered Blomefield. "I saw you do it."

Then, as one they rushed to the head of the stairs. Below, Philbrigge's body, head grotesquely skewed, lay sprawled on the narrow landing. Sounds of alarm and raised voices sounded from the shop, footsteps clattering up towards them.

"May God rest his covetous soul," said Seward with infinite sadness.

"Though leaving us none the wiser," added Blomefield, sublimely unaware of the looks his companions turned upon him. "So, what should we do about the books?"

(25)

Over the Door, on a SHELF. A Mahogany Glass Café, in which,
is the Face and Neck of a certain Countefs, modelled in Wax
as large as the life, by Mrs Wright; fhe was ninety years of Age,
and without a wrinkle. Prefented by Mr Willerton of London.

Woollaton Hall. Saturday 16ᵗʰ May. Realising that disaster, or,
better, the avoidance of it – would be the only means of confirming
Darwin's elaborate claims for his innovatory coach axle, Greene
steeled himself for a journey involving proximity with its ever-
voluble inventor, now fairly bubbling with excitement at the
prospect of their coming encounter.

From the moment that the Doctor's elegantly painted vehicle
had embarked towards their destination, he too had embarked
upon what the Apothecary knew would prove to be a monologue,
concerning the extraordinary polymath they were shortly to meet.
Today, though, the Apothecary was more than prepared to let
Darwin's enthusiasms wash over him, as he sank back into the
plush upholstery; a blessed relief from Philbrigge's starkly tragic
death and its repercussions.

Had the Doctor been paying attention to anything other than
the sound of his own voice, he might, at one stage, have noticed
his passenger giving a violent shake of his head, as if attempting
to dislodge some irksome memory. A memory, an all too vivid
image, of staring into bulbous eyes frozen by violent death as he
went through the bookseller's pockets behind the closed door of
his Consulting Room.

He had lost all sense of time as he had sat, later, turning the pages of a well-thumbed notebook drawn from a deep pocket in the dead man's coat. Page after page listed abbreviated titles – few of which he could interpret; each of which were annotated with the cryptic initials of what he supposed were purchasers or sellers. By the time he had checked, and rechecked the neatly penned entries, he had discerned close on thirty of them initialled DL with prices – some, eye-wateringly high – and dates recorded against each. A time period covering, in the main, the previous five years. Their sheer obscurity meant that most of the listings were impenetrable, but those few that the Apothecary could discern – 'The Booke of Honorius Of Thebes', 'Le Petit Albert', 'The Book of Simic The Magician', had been exclusively occult works.

The other discovery from the corpse, its waxen seal broken, was a folded sheet of costly laid paper upon which what Greene assumed to be three kaballistic symbols had been carefully penned, a phonetic translation beneath them. The desperate urgency of Philbrigge's words returned to haunt him yet again: 'I have been provided with a safeguard, a form of words, of protection, to employ in the event of obtaining it. It must not be handled – and never opened.'

He jolted awake from his painful reverie as Darwin tapped him briskly upon a knee to reinforce a point. "C…consigning one's own four young to a F…Foundling Hospital played all t…too readily into Burke and V…Voltaire's hands when it c…came to demeaning Rousseau's works , but the attacks are little m…more than argumentum *ad hominem* – based on their d…distaste for the f…fellow himself rather than any informed c…criticism. Shabby s…stuff, Richard, sh…shabby stuff."

Their departure from the house by the West Gate had been made shortly after dawn on this bright, fresh morning, with the intention of arriving at their destination well before noon; a reasonable proposition as it proved, the miles slipping away behind the well-appointed coach as it negotiated the pocked and rutted roads. They crossed the pretty meander of the river Dove, and after Sudbury, following Davenport's directions, they left the route that led west to Uttoxeter and on to Stoke upon Trent, turning North towards their goal.

Greene gazed admiringly out at the grey-timbered splendour of Somersal Herbert as they rattled past the ancient house, a sight far closer to his heart than Darwin's avid recounting of Rousseau's high-handed refusal of a pension for life from the King of France. This, a monarch so enthralled by the precocious musical talents – displayed in both libretto and music for Rousseau's work entitled 'The Village Soothsayer' – that he was reportedly mortified by the perverse refusal. "He is f...forever turning down offers here, f... favours there. Says he won't be b...bought!"

By the time that the final bone-jarring miles were almost covered, Greene had become less than certain of the reception that awaited them. He need not have been concerned.

As they turned in between the grand gate-pillars that announced the drive leading to Woollaton Hall, an imposing example of what Darwin rather pompously pronounced as 'gentry classicism' was revealed. Well-drilled staff were assembled, ready to meet the visitors, even before their coach had arrived at the broad terrace surrounding the Hall itself.

The familiar figure of Richard Davenport, a sprightly man Greene had judged to be in his late fifties, hurried down the broad steps to greet them, a smile of pleasure creasing his aquiline features as he extended a long-fingered hand in greeting: "Mr Greene! Doctor Darwin! welcome to Woollaton, gentlemen! Mr Greene, you present me with double the pleasure I had anticipated when we first met in London. Doctor Darwin, you honour us with your presence, Sir. I am so pleased that you have come – as is Jean-Jacques. Come in, come in."

The Frenchman's pleasure at their arrival remained an anticipation, however, neither he nor his wife materialising as the visitors were ushered into the grand entrance hall. "Our philosopher is presently toiling at his labours down below," said their host cryptically, pointing down at the superb marble flooring on which they stood and smiling at the polite question on his guests' faces. "He is not, however, you will be glad to hear, engaged in the preparation of our repast." He went on to explain that his guest required total solitude for his writing, a facility that Woollaton could provide in the form of a grotto beneath the broad terrace on which the house stood.

"He can retire each morning, solitary as an anchorite, but a sight more comfortable than one of those wretched hermits so beloved of our more eccentric landowners. His appetites are well supplied from the kitchen, his inspiration from the craggy walls of his refuge. Jean Jacques is altogether remarkable, gentlemen, as you will shortly discover. We shall be dining with the man who scolded Frederick the Great on a regular basis and still retained his love."

"Walpole's fabrication was a c...cruel joke," agreed Darwin, breaking an unusually thoughtful silence, "Although it m...must be s...said that your remarkable g...guest does seem to arouse incendiary emotions with c...consummate ease."

Davenport smiled, ruefully. "Jean-Jacques is blessed – cursed, some would, and do, say – with the volatility of true genius."

"Quite so, q...quite so," interposed Darwin, to Greene's alarm, continuing, "One's muse c...can, at times, f...flit about m...most alarmingly."

Mercifully, before either of his listeners could reflect on the import of the Doctor's words, a turbaned figure with a handsome, dark-haired woman on his arm, made his entrance.

As introductions commenced, the Apothecary chanced his linguistic arm once more, shaking the Frenchman's notably limp hand, saying: "We met at the theatre, some weeks ago."

"Oh, really?" replied Rousseau, without a flicker of recognition, until their host skilfully intervened: "Mr Greene is our museum keeper, Jean-Jacques. You were most impressed with his catalogue, as was I." A light dawned in the saturnine features. "Oh, of course! Forgive me, Sir, what must appear as my lack of courtesy is no more than a poor mind grappling with all the new faces and impressions which have surrounded us in past weeks. Your museum sounds truly remarkable in its breadth and diversity. Both my wife and I look forward to our visit with relish."

As Davenport interpreted this skilful recovery, and then moved on to a fulsome introduction of Darwin to a visibly more engaged Rousseau, Greene, for all his gratification, was becoming aware that here was a man whose attention was engaged either in full or not at all. A day-to-day existence engaged in entrancing the crowned heads, nobility and patrons of his ever-shifting places of comfortable refuge across Europe would surely demonstrate that this philosopher was possessed of a surfeit of mental dexterity to be employed as required.

As Darwin responded to their introduction by plunging into a torrent of execrable French – though, oddly, with notably few stutters – Davenport turned back to the Apothecary: "Thank you for your forethought in providing us with a catalogue of your marvels. It makes enthralling reading. Jean-Jacques is genuinely excited by the prospect of a visit, especially, as I fear he may already be discovering a paucity of intellectual stimulus in Staffordshire. Whilst he can be difficult to read at times, the true constant, the lodestone of his life and work, is his passion for the natural world."

"One which he and Erasmus would appear to be sharing already," smiled Greene, indicating the pair deep in conversation at the nearby window; Thérèse Rousseau in dutiful, if mute, attendance.

Following the Apothecary's glance, Davenport said intuitively, "I regret your wife was unable to accompany you today, Mr Greene: I am sure Thérèse would have welcomed some female company."

"Simply one of the occupational hazards of our business life together, Mr Davenport, though I know how much she would have enjoyed meeting you all and, of course, visiting your lovely home."

The meal was announced, and the company settled into the politely formulaic interactions demanded by such occasions, interrupted only by Darwin's repeated appeals to their host when his random linguistic forays failed him entirely. Abandoning his own attempts, Greene, too, employed their host's easy fluency to engage Thérèse Rousseau.

"I think that when your visit to Lichfield can be arranged, both you and your husband might enjoy my wife's botanical paintings. Although modesty would forbid her from agreeing, they are of a high order – though perhaps more a celebration of nature on a domestic level than the grand sweep of M. Rousseau's vision."

"Oh, I see nothing contemptible in that, Mr Greene," she said. "One can sometimes regret that there have been few occasions to establish – or maintain – the simpler pleasures of house and home. There have been times when we have scarcely shaken the dust of travel from our feet when the unwelcome attentions of Jean-Jacques's persecutors have forced us to move once more."

She bestowed a glowing smile upon their host, adding, "We hope to redress that balance here, though, thanks to this kind friend's generosity. Jean-Jacques is embarking upon a huge project and this opportunity to write in peace and solitude is the greatest blessing that could be bestowed upon us both." Davenport smiled wryly as he interpreted her gracious sentiment, before announcing that he had something 'of note' that he wished to show Greene before their departure.

"Our philosopher shall shortly be retiring to rest, as is his habit, before continuing with labours that will carry him well into the night, so we shall, I regret, be shortly deprived of his company." As if this was his cue, the Frenchman courteously took his leave, and with Thérèse on his arm, left the table.

"If we might consult our diaries shortly, gentlemen, I shall make the necessary arrangements for my guests' Lichfield visit before I leave for Cheshire," adding with a smile, "practicalities of that nature not being Jean-Jacques's forte."

"Well, Richard, I do d…declare we'll all d…dine together chez m…moi," Darwin's gross features contorted into an endearing grin of self-mockery, "…I …d…do believe I'll offer these good p…people bed as w…well as b…b…board rather than they should have to f…face the long haul home after enduring your m…museum and my t…table! Polly will be delighted. She might even have popped by then!"

Davenport's evident puzzlement was only partially addressed when it was explained that the Doctor's wife was imminently due to give birth to a son. A boy to be christened Robert Waring Darwin upon delivery.

"May one enquire into the grounds of your certainty, Doctor?" he enquired. "Oh, f…feel it in my w…water, Sir! Rarely f…fails!"

Saturday 30th May was agreed as the optimum date for all concerned, with Davenport expressing his regret at missing the excursion.

"Whilst I shall endeavour to take up both your generous invitations when next in Staffordshire, gentlemen, I can now share a small treasure of my own with you both." He led the way into a library looking out over the summer landscape beyond the terrace.

Opening a leather portfolio laid upon a central table, Davenport indicated three tissue wrapped objects. "I propose to frame these pieces together – as the companions you will perceive them to be. Having only recently acquired them, I have had, as yet, little opportunity so to do." Carefully unwrapping each revealed a stained and dog-eared sheet of parchment, a torn fragment of much the same and a small, faded embroidery. "Any clues, gentlemen?" he enquired, playfully. They leaned forward.

"May I?" enquired Greene, indicating the first, a faint sepia diagram.

"Perhaps with these?" suggested their host, handing a pair of linen gloves to the Apothecary, who beamed appreciatively, saying, "Very proper, Sir, one cannot be too careful." He stopped, all attention now on the sheet in his gloved hands. "Oh, this is Tutbury Castle, a plan, though far more complete than the sorry wreck we see today. Fascinating, quite." He paused, looking to their host: "You said 'companions', though, Mr Davenport? Could these possibly be..?"

"Bravo, Mr Greene, I do believe you have placed them already! They all pertain to the imprisonment of the Scottish Queen, Mary, in that horrid place. These two, though," – he pointed reverently to the scrap of what appeared to be an abandoned letter and to the embroidery – "are both by that poor lady's own hand. See, there, just barely discernible beneath the scratchings-out, the signature and the date on the fragment.

"And this, the fleur de lys, a recurrent theme in Mary's embroideries. Perhaps you have seen their beautiful counterparts preserved at Cowdray Park, Mr Greene?"

"Only as engravings in *The Magazine*, I regret," replied the enthralled Apothecary. "What treasures, indeed. May one enquire how you came upon them?"

"If it will not strain your credulity, I shall explain, my friends," laughed Davenport. "I was investigating a haunting."

(26)

Third SHELF An Amulet or Charm, being a ring of
Brass, found on the Field of Battle; near Bosworth.

Woollaton Hall. Saturday 16ᵗʰ May. It was more than an hour
later, with a depleted decanter between them, that Davenport had
concluded his telling of a remarkable, if inconclusive, story to his
guests. The Apothecary had at first been surprised by Darwin's
obvious enthusiasm for their host's tantalising statement.

"A haunting, you say, Sir? What? Of the G…Grey Lady and
B…Bumps in the Night species, D…Davenport?"

"You have the idea, Doctor," he had replied.

"Do tell," responded Darwin with relish, "Though perhaps if
spirits are to be involved, might we perhaps..?"

Sitting at ease with his guests, the master of Woollaton
had begun to describe his acquisition of the fine house and his
subsequent fascination with the landscape, the curiosities and the
antiquities of a new home county.

"I had high hopes of settling with wife and family at my knee
in those far-off days," he recalled, somewhat wistfully, "but that
was not to be."

"I must confess that the frissons offered by the diplomatic life,
in Paris most particularly, do take some beating. And for a younger,
unattached man, such as I was..." He shrugged expressively.

"However, in recent years, with greater leisure to pursue tastes
of a more mature nature," – he gestured, smilingly, to the many
hundred fine bindings that filled his shelves – "I have followed

byways, tangents and blind-alleys to my heart's content – not least in my fascination with the other-worldly which, I believe, we pooh-pooh to our detriment. For many years I have collected what might be called arcana," – he gestured to the shelves about them – "otherwise referred to as stuff-and-nonsense by most scholars of repute, though the oddities and quiddities of man's beliefs – and his fears – have long fascinated me. Hence, what I think of as the Tutbury business. A thoroughly nasty footnote in a less than glorious history – referred to, by repute only at that stage, in this sad scrap of Mary's letter that has finally come into my possession. In the full text, which I once had the opportunity to view, Mary writes of her anguish when a Jesuit priest was hanged in full view of her prison window. Executed as a taunt, gentlemen. What a regrettable species we can be. It occurred just there, in fact, on this plan." He pointed to a structure built against the outer wall, projecting into the castle enclosure; its interior shown subdivided into compartmentalised spaces. He continued, "It was drawn perhaps fifteen or twenty years after the event, by an unknown hand, though one familiar with the castle that had remained virtually untouched, unloved, since Mary's transfer to Fotheringhay and her death. The existence of this and the other pieces, only became known to me after repeated hearsay had reached me, concerning a spectral figure seen hanging just as in the actuality of this awful account, and on repeated occasions around the date of the original execution. A figure reputedly watched by a silent woman, visible in that window there." His listeners were enthralled.

"And s…so, you decided to see f…for yourself?" said Darwin in obvious anticipation.

"Just so," nodded Davenport, "just so. Though I shall not bore you with the details of what was, for the most part, a crude and tasteless hoax."

"A hoax? How so?" enquired Greene. "And you say 'for the most part'. You have us entirely hooked, Sir."

"Most appropriately," their host began, "it was a night of little or no moon, and very low cloud. Fog shrouded the higher levels of the ruin. I had gone in company with a Tutbury justice of my acquaintance and two friends, fierce sceptics, though courteous enough to affect open-mindedness, together with another of your calling, Mr Greene. Tomlin. The Ashbourne druggist?"

Greene nodded. "I know him slightly; our paths have crossed several times. Not a friend, though, by any stretch of the imagination."

"Of mine, neither, Mr Greene, particularly in the light of his utter credulity. He was simply introduced as one who had experienced the phenomenon some years earlier and would guide us in our vigil."

"And d...did you..?" began Darwin in almost childlike impatience.

"Oh yes," replied Davenport, gravely. "Around midnight, up above the curtain wall, a crook-necked figure could be seen, hanging as if some spectral gallows bore its weight. We saw it in the mist, all five of us, Tomlin whimpering like a lost girl beside me."

"And then?" whispered Darwin.

"And then, whichever cack-handed boy was charged with hoisting our phantom aloft, must have just lost his grip and, from the sounds of all too mortal anguish soon coming from the bramble scrub outside, tumbled down the hefty drop along with the dummy that he'd held with more thumbs than fingers."

Darwin hissed his disappointment like a punctured bladder. "A jape, then, nothing more," he growled. "How very disappointing." He glared at his empty glass as if in recrimination. "Not entirely," rejoined Davenport, with the quiet skill of a born raconteur. "For, as we left, I happened to glance up for a moment, as the mist gave way to the merest tug of breeze, and saw – as clearly as I see you now – a shrouded woman's form, up in the window, there, that looked upon the tasteless prank that had gone so far awry. Her head was bowed as if she wept. Then she was gone, as the mist flowed back; gone from that window in a tower that is no longer floored. It stands open to the rooks that are its sole denizens these days."

"Oh, c…capital, Davenport! You had us in the p…palm of your hand, Sir!" boomed Darwin, reanimated and suddenly boisterous, clapping huge hands together in his appreciation.

"You really saw the lady, then? How very intriguing," added Greene in quiet appreciation. "I do not doubt you for a moment, Mr Davenport. Thank you for sharing that experience with us: it was most apposite."

The elderly man glanced keenly at Greene, obviously struck by his choice of words, "And you, Mr Greene? Perhaps you share my fascination?" The Apothecary, becoming suddenly aware of Darwin's attention, replied hastily, "Oh, only in my bookish way, Mr Davenport, though you may have noticed a number of items in my catalogue that will be of interest to you, no doubt. The Egyptian amulets, the scrying stone, the witch tokens and so on."

"The entire gamut of your collection astounds me, Mr Greene, as it will our French friends, I have no doubt."

Sensing a certain note of finality, their host appearing suddenly tired and perhaps distracted by the potency of his memory, Darwin and Greene took their leave.

As they were seated in the waiting vehicle, Davenport looked up to the open window, saying, "I shall take up both your generous invitations with alacrity on my return, gentlemen. I have greatly enjoyed your company. God Speed."

Darwin was fast asleep within a mile of Ellastone, giving Greene much pause for thought as the rising crescendo of his companion's snores settled into the rumble of distant thunder. Only good manners had prevented him from prowling around the contents of Woollaton's loaded bookshelves, especially in the knowledge of their being stacked with what Davenport had described as 'arcana'.

If only he had not been in company with the ever-attentive

doctor, he might have seized the opportunity of unburdening himself to their host on that very subject, though in the circumstances he had instinctively restrained the impulse, knowing that there were certain unspoken limits to his and Darwin's long association which, for all their shared enthusiasms, neither transgressed.

As they left the Derby Road at Sudbury, ahead of the long climb up the valley escarpment at Draycott in the Clay, Greene's eye was drawn inexorably to the gaunt outline of Tutbury's ill-favoured castle against the clouding sky. The relics of its erstwhile prisoner were extraordinary, purchased for an unguessable sum, and after much prevarication from that same Tutbury justice whose largesse to the museum – in the form of a halberd – had almost cost its keeper his life.

The life that had been lost, scarcely days earlier, at the foot of the museum stairs, had been the cause of much soul-searching and recrimination on the part of at least two of the three participants in the bookseller's demise. Informed, post-haste, of the accident, Philbrigge's brother and sole next-of-kin had travelled from Derby and arrived in Lichfield barely in time to arrange a perfunctory burial service at St Michael's. Shaken by the bereavement and the unwonted pressures his brother's death had placed upon him, he professed himself at a complete loss as to what should be done with the stock, both here and in the Derby premises.

"We were never close, Spencer and me. He went his way and I went mine," the brother had said.

"Which was to where, if one might enquire?" Blomefield was gazing pensively at the tableful of books.

"Buttons," had come the reply. "Gents', ladies', military, you name it. Quality guaranteed, quantity no object."

He had then proposed a job-lot sale of all the books his brother had brought, "For whatever you gentlemen think they might be worth – just a load of unwanted weight for me to shift back and dispose of. What do you say?" Whilst Greene and Seward had simultaneously demurred, with all due courtesy, Lionel Blomefield had said plaintively, "I really was rather taken by the fly-fishing book," only to become aware of the expression on his companions' faces. "Ah, no, of course; not proper at all, in the circumstances, taking advantage of, er... no, certainly not, thank you."

Alone in the gravity of the situation that had played out to near tragedy in the Apothecary's bakehouse and now doubly upset by a tragic fatality on her premises, Theodosia had reluctantly accepted her husband's makeshift solution: the stoutest padlock that Lichfield's locksmith could provide, and a complete embargo on any discussion concerning it. Spilt poison, from a carelessly discarded bottle, disturbed from its long-forgotten concealment beneath the stillage had been the hastily contrived explanation that emphatically closed the subject. What remained out of sight – though never out of mind - had been concealed once more, though now behind an iron door sealed up with putty and would stay untouched until they could determine a final solution.

As the miles went by to the unabated snorts, whistles and mumblings of his sleeping companion, Greene fell to wondering how long it might take for word of an agent's demise – an agent's complete failure – to reach his erstwhile principal; how long it might take for that dark hand to find the means of reaching out once more. The shiver that ran through him had little to do with the fast-approaching dusk as they rattled and bumped through Yoxall towards the distant spires.

To the north, then west up to the wind-wracked moors that hid the darkening pile, shadows deeper than the tendrils of descending night were scarcely pierced, as candle upon candle flared into the claustral gloom.

"The pendulum, de Rais, go fetch it, quickly, now," the thin voice croaked. "I must know."

Then, when the map was spread, its corners weighed with anything that lay to hand, a skeletal finger – its unkempt nail like yellow horn – tapped briskly on the place marked Derby. "There, just at the edge. He must be there, if he is not yet here. He will not dare be elsewhere if he has it safe."

The gaunt figure, cheeks sunk into blackened pits beneath the flicker of the candles' light, squeezed a single drop of blood from the finger he had pricked. He smeared it on the tip of the metal plumb that dangled from its chain; a rosary, bereft of cross, wound all about the veinous hand. He bent over the map and loosed the plumb to dangle from its beaded line.

"Now, just there, just where I show you, he is bound to be."

Both watched as the pendulum hung, inert, motionless above the diagram below.

"He is not there."

"Then that, his bill of sale, quickly, place it there."

The pendulum hung above the neatly penned signature on Philbrigge's last account. Inert, motionless.

"He is dead, there is no doubt." stated de Rais, flatly. "This does not ever fail me."

He paid no attention to the sound of breaking glass, as a decanter was hurled to the stone-flagged floor.

"The book then, tell me where."

"You must say the words. Take care though if you do, or they will return to wound you once again." He looked without a flicker of pity at the ruined man slumped in the high-backed chair. "Are you strong enough, or will you need the pipe?"

"The pipe, yes, the pipe." The figure twitched uncontrollably in the shadow of the enveloping wings that shielded him from light, nails clicking a staccato rhythm on its arms.

"Quickly now, the pipe."

Then, when the smoke hung like a spectral pall above them, quivering hands enclosed the metal plumb and stick-like arms lifted them to cup around thin lips, as words – harsh, broken sounds – were breathed upon it in the acrid haze.

The pendulum was released with a shuddering gasp and tumbled to the tabletop. Without another word, the Frenchman lifted it once more and held it over the map. This time it swung straight at the place marked Lichfield. He moved his hand above the ink-drawn shape and now the plumb's swing became a focused twirl, an ever-faster vortex blurring the name beneath. Then it broke, scattering the beads like bullets out across the ancient room, de Rais snatching back a hand as if it had been burned or stung.

"It is with the one called Greene. Protected, but I saw the place. I know it now."

The lolling head could only nod, exhausted, drool shining in the amber glow. Then it whispered, "Fetch it. Find a way."

(27)

On the right Hand the Shell Cafe Part of a Copper Boiler, found in a Subterranean Kitchen at Herculaneum, preſented by Doctor Solander; the other part in the B. Museum; near 3000 years Old

Saddler Street. Wednesday 20ᵗʰ May. Emerging from his Consulting Room following a morning spent on much the usual minor surgical procedures, the Apothecary was met by a housekeeper brandishing a pair of letters. The first long-awaited, the second a most welcome surprise. The latter, bearing a discreetly embossed armorial had obviously persuaded the lady that prompt and efficient delivery should ensue.

After a moment spent hovering in suspended anticipation, she turned away with a haughty sniff on realising that her employer had no intention of opening either in her presence. "Unfailingly caring," he murmured to her retreating back.

Intrigued by the object of Margery's curiosity, and not recognising the crested seal, it opened to reveal the source as Woollaton, its writer Richard Davenport.

Dear Mr Greene,
having both greatly enjoyed your visit and expressed my regret
at being unable to accompany my guests on their planned visit
to Lichfield, I now am the bearer of what I can only hope to be
glad tidings.
The tiresome legal matter which was compelling my early return

*to Cheshire has, unexpectedly but most happily, been resolved
in my absence. News of this reached me only by Monday's mail
from my man at law, so I now write in the hope that your
earlier invitation to accompany Jean-Jacques and his charming
wife remains open in these changed circumstances.
I look forward to renewing a most stimulating acquaintance,
and am, Sir, your most obdt. servant.
Richard Davenport*

"Oh, capital!" exclaimed Greene, and then turned his attention to
the letter written in Cousin Johnson's unmistakable hand. Even
before reading its contents he realised that its almost indecent
brevity – its sheer terseness – would be construed as downright
rudeness from any correspondent other than this most over-
worked and much put-upon relative. He might have grinned at its
masterly economy had it not been for its content:

*Cousin, Apropos enq. to BL. – his response delayed by frivolous
absence. Location of unsavoury kin: Malbecq Priory, near
nowhere, somewhere n.w. of Ashbourne. Derbysh. Avoid all
contact, repeat all, says L. Both location and owner perilously
unstable. Come again but not too soon, regards in haste, Samuel.*

It was at this stage, with both letters open on the cluttered writing-
table in the museum niche he thought of as his office, that Greene
realised the extent to which he had been impressed by Woollaton's
owner.

His easy cordiality, the breadth of his travels, his cultivation,
all had transformed what the Apothecary had feared might
have been a day of polite social niceties into one of genuine
enjoyment. And perhaps, just possibly, in the light of Davenport's
enthusiasms, a providential meeting of minds at a time when
Greene was feeling exposed and isolated in the face of what lay
behind nothing more than a stout padlock.

With Bennet Langton's information – setting aside his unequivocal warning against using it – Greene was now in possession of not only a location – however hazy – but also what he believed to be absolute confirmation of the dark obsessions of its owner.

The simple fact that Greene's intuitive leap of faith would have been instantly dismissed as 'circumstantial' and thrown out by any court in the land, mattered not one jot to him. He was now convinced, beyond any reasonable doubt, that the apparently bottomless purse behind the years long purchase of dozens of occult titles and the denizen of Malbecq Priory were one and the same – and de Langton by name.

It was only then that he began to wonder whether the squire of Woollaton might not also have been a customer of a certain departed bookseller of Derby. Oh, how he would have relished the opportunity of perusing Davenport's laden shelves.

His reverie was interrupted by the announcement that 'a boy with a boil that just won't burst' had been brought in by a concerned parent, and could Mr Greene please come down to see him straightaway?

In Ashbourne, a series of small coincidences – for want of a better word – was taking place at the same time as a Lichfield boy with a bandaged neck was being rewarded with a candystick for his bravery.

Emmy Tillett had fled her aunt's shop in tears after what had become a daily recitation of her shortcomings. These included daydreaming, her uppity manner, her apparent inability to cut a straight line and anything else that a thoroughly bad-tempered, middle-aged woman could dream up in between hot flushes and ever-present reminders of her own lost youth and looks. Had it not involved a return to her stuffy room above the hated shop, Emmy had almost reached the point of packing her few belongings and beginning the long walk home, when the druggist's assistant had his nasty fall. It was about to occur only yards away from the miserable young woman sitting on a horse-trough and staring dejectedly at ants busily at work between the paving stones at her feet.

She had scarcely registered the sight of the gangling youth emerging from the covered passageway beside the shop, a long ladder manoeuvred with some difficulty to rest above the bow-fronted windows. Its foot was propped in front of the spiked iron railings that guarded the drops to each side of the shop's doorway – well below street level – to the window-lights of the druggist's basement.

With a bucket hooked over one arm, a mop protruding precariously from it, and a variety of cloths draped over a skinny shoulder, he began his awkward ascent.

He had reached the top and begun to edge himself to the right, to begin mopping the protruding shop sign and the painted legend above the windows, when a sudden gust caught the large, hinged sign of a stoppered jar. It swung far enough and unexpectedly enough to dislodge the already straining figure so that he lurched back to compensate his imbalance. The base of the ladder, inadequately propped against the raised lip of the pavement flags, slipped sideways sending a shrieking assistant, bucket and all, down into the railed well, but not before a flailing leg had been impaled upon an iron spike to leave him hanging, head down, his screams amplified by the void beneath.

Emmy leapt to her feet and was the first to reach him. Realising instantly that she couldn't raise the agonised youth, she stood back as several men rushed to the railings and began the appallingly difficult task of trying to reach over, reach through, to gain enough of a grip upon the screaming youth to haul him up and off the spike that was spearing him. His agony seemed to redouble as they began to lift him, and without a second thought Emmy ducked beneath the outstretched arms of the nearest and pushed at the impaled limb with all her might. With the gasping lifters managing to bear his weight, the leg came free in a sudden gout of blood and the girl fell back from them. Collecting herself in an instant, she began frantically ripping at her petticoats to tear off strip after ragged strip.

The pair at the rail managed to stagger free with a now mercifully unconscious burden. Aided, then, by a third passer-by, they laid the deathly white figure on the ground, blood already pooling around the ruined leg. Emmy darted forward calling, "Lift up his leg, gentle though, quick!" With deft movements she bound the terrible wound tightly as the leg was raised by unseen hands behind her. Even as she bound, the blood blossomed through the layered bandaging. "A belt, now! Who's got a belt? He must have a turn-key higher up or nothing'll stop him bleeding."

Willing hands now took over, as someone bent over her to thread a broad leather belt beneath the blood-soaked thigh and then to wrench it tight, an action that seemed to rouse the victim from his stupor, to howl with renewed anguish as the belt did its life-saving job. The growing crowd was joined, belatedly, by the druggist Tomlin, bursting from his shop to stare in dumbstruck horror at what met his gaze.

Lost for words, his eyes ranged frantically from left to right, as if attempting to make some sense of what he was seeing. Before he managed to say a word, a voice called, "Saved 'im, likely, that lass! Look, the bleedin's stopped!" One of the rescuers, kneeling at the stricken figure's head looked up at Emmy, "He's right enough, lass. All our heavin' and puffin' would've been for nought had you not staunched him. Proper little angel, and no mistake."

Surrounded now by smiling faces, the girl, white-faced and trembling, burst into tears.

A little later, sitting on a chair habitually reserved for customers, in the sunlight from the druggist's window-bay, with a second reviving glass of elderflower cordial in her hand, an idea began to form in a quick-witted young head. When Tomlin finally emerged from the Consulting Room to the rear, into which his barely conscious assistant had been carried half an hour earlier, he beamed at the seated figure.

"Well, my dear, there was no word of exaggeration in what was said of you out there." He nodded towards the marketplace. "Your quick-thinking undoubtedly saved poor Barnett's life. He has sustained a terrible wound, only exacerbated by the weight it bore for those few dreadful minutes. He may never properly regain the full use of his leg. He is sleeping peacefully now, following my stitching and sedation, but tell me – where did you gain your skill, your knowledge of a tourniquet? I am intrigued."

"I worked for a short while at Greene's Apothecary in Lichfield, Sir, and was really happy there." Tomlin sat with eyebrows raised in expectation for a fuller account. "But family business made me cut that short, Sir, and I had to come here to my Aunt May, at the Haberdashery, Sir."

"Ah, family, of course. Who can resist those tender demands?" he said tritely, as if that closed the matter. He was astonished by what followed.

"I hate it, Sir, I really do! Don't know why I had to come. She doesn't like me, not one bit, Sir. Says I can't do anything right. Day in day out, it's just getting worse, Sir, honest it is, however hard I try. And I do try, Sir. It's just that I was learning a proper trade at Greene's, something I could've been good at, something that let me use the brain the Good Lord gave me and not just a stiff old pair of scissors for a stiff old woman."

Once more, Emmy burst into tears, and sat, shoulders hunched, shaking with sobs.

"Oh, come now, my dear, this will never do! You have shown yourself to be a young woman of pluck and resourcefulness today, and I won't hear otherwise! Nor, I can assure you – will poor Barnett when he has recovered sufficiently to thank you. It is no small thing to save a life, so together we shall pay a call upon your dear aunt and I shall apprise her of your bravery."

"She'll hate me the more for it, Sir, I know she will. Just me being there annoys her, Sir. And I can't bear more of it, honest I can't. I'm just going to collect my bits and pieces from that stuffy old room over the shop and leave it to the mice, then I'll walk home, Sir. It's all that's left for me."

Passing the distraught girl a large pocket-handkerchief to forestall a new round of the tears he could see brimming in the big brown eyes, Tomlin said, "Now, let's not do something in haste that will be repented at leisure, my dear. You say you had some aptitude for the work at Greene's Apothecary – it is a well-respected name even as far away as these parts – what would you say if I were to approach the good lady myself and have a word in her ear?"

"Sorry, Sir? What word? About what?" Emmy asked, big eyes lifted in apparent puzzlement towards the druggist.

"Why, about the fact that I am now – for the foreseeable future – without the services of an assistant. An assistant that I must somehow replace as a matter of urgency, my dear. Do you begin at all to follow my drift?"

"D'you mean..? Are you saying..?" she began, a lower lip beginning to quiver.

"Yes, precisely, my dear, if you are agreeable and you can provide some kind of recommendation – however informal – from Greene's, then I think we might get along famously, don't you? We can discuss a wage – limited though it will be during a period of training – and I am sure accommodation can be provided with…" he permitted himself a smile, "…fewer mice than you may have become used to. What do you say?"

If he had expected more tears, he was to be surprised. A suddenly self-possessed young woman looked up at him and said brightly, "Oh, yes, Sir. That all sounds most agreeable. You won't regret it, I promise. I'm sure Mrs Greene will say a word on my behalf; she was very kind. When would you like me to start? I could pick up my things as soon as is convenient. My aunt won't mind a bit."

That evening, Tomlin raised a large glass of amontillado to congratulate himself on his acumen in seizing the opportunity presented to him by a generous fate. In his glow of accomplishment, he had little difficulty in dismissing the simple fact that he had been unaware even of the young woman's name until her aunt had repeated it within several less than flattering admonitions concerning the abuse of her generosity and all-round good nature. She had, as promised, been only too pleased to agree that Esmeralda would be far better suited to the druggist's employ, and the very proper accommodation being offered by that worthy tradesman's widowed sister.

The relieved haberdasher had also agreed, at Tomlin's prompting, to communicate her own acquiescence to her niece's changed circumstances in a letter to the young woman's mother in Lichfield. His announcement that he, too, would be writing to request a reference for his new assistant from Greene's Apothecary was met by no more than a supercilious sniff intended to convey a world of scepticism. One, though, which singularly failed to hit its intended target.

"Splendid, splendid!" was the response from a delighted druggist: "That's all settled to everyone's satisfaction, then." He watched as the flame-haired girl hurried past her aunt and disappeared up the pinch-beck stairs to collect her belongings.

(28)

Within the Table, in the middle of the ROOM. A pair of Buck-
fkin Gloves, worn at the Battel of Dettingen, by King George
2d. A Gentleman's Cap, very ancient, neatly worked in Silk,
with Flowers; and ornamented with Gold and Silver Spangles.
Another, worked with Gold Thread, laced and fpangled, worn
by Burghleigh, Lord Treafurer; Presented by Mifs Astley of
Tamhorn, now Mrs Dyott, of Freeford, near Lichfield.

Saddler Street. Saturday 23ʳᵈ May. Harry Copeland's scheduled
return on this morning's London coach was little short of
providential in its timing.

Theodosia Greene had found herself watching her busy
husband with growing but concealed concern as the day of
Lichfield's annual descent into mayhem and genial anarchy drew
ever closer. It would be Greenhill Bower Day on Monday – an
occasion for licence of a generally non-injurious kind for many,
leisure for all but the increasingly harried organisers of the huge
event, though now a day of a very different complexion for a few
at least, Richard and Theodosia Greene chief among them.

Twenty-one years earlier, amidst the wild festivities, a close
friend had died in what was, to this day, accepted as no more than
a tragic accident; the bullet between his eyes believed to have been
a ricochet from any of the scores of firearms mindlessly discharged
during the day's vast mêlée. The fact that this was but one of a series
of appalling murders had never been made public by a husband
and wife who had only barely escaped with their own lives.

It was not an anniversary that could ever be forgotten. All about them, the city's frenzied descent into thoughtless jollity only exacerbated memories of loss and the jeopardy which had haunted their lives through that terrible time.

Now though, heaven be praised, she thought, Harry would be here to lift their spirits and provide the fondest of reminders of the time, back then, when he had done not only that but so much more. He too, a rock-solid presence at their side, had come close to losing his life to the demented evil they had jointly overcome. It was not a friendship that could ever be underestimated.

With the annual onset of one of the several occasions of what the Apothecary would wryly describe as 'siege mentality' – a widespread panic concerning the shop's single day of closure – both husband and wife were too busy to meet the soldier as he stepped down from a coach little more than two hours late – something of a record in itself – to survey the purposeful bustle of the little city he had come to know and like so well.

It was worlds apart from the vast, malodorous capital he had recently quit with such relief, and the rolling, windswept landscape of his adopted Yorkshire home. He was now on holiday, he decided, determined to renew acquaintances, ranging from Burton's strong ales to Richard's rambling anecdotes and proud acquisitions, often to be enjoyed in tandem.

Margery's pies had also been known to tickle his fancy, he recalled.

He turned back to where a huge spotted dog sat licking its haunch, unconcerned by the jostling and clattering of the carriage-team's unharnessing all around it. With a grin of pure affection, he crossed to it. As the large head was raised to his approach, a yap of recognition sounding as he stooped to fondle the soft ears. "Time for a rest, for both of us, eh boy?"

"He's a fine one," said an appreciative voice from behind him. "Walked all the way, has he?" He turned to recognise the aproned landlord of The George. "Why, Colonel Copeland, Sir, didn't expect to be seeing you here. It's a fair number of years since we had the pleasure of your company, if I'm not mistaken, Sir?"

"It is indeed, though he and I," – he jerked a thumb at the attentive Dalmatian – "shall not, I fear, be availing ourselves of your excellent hospitality on this occasion. We're bound for Richard Greene's first and then home to Yorkshire. But yes, to answer your question. This fine old fellow steps it out as well as any horse, in amongst the hooves with never a paw put wrong." He bent once more to ruffle the dog's neck. "They're not called carriage dogs for nothing."

"Well, I'll be," said the stout man admiringly, "I've come across them now and then trotting about with the local gentry, but this fellow's the first I've seen a-coming all the way from London. More than most folks round here could manage, let alone their hounds."

"We've only known each other a week, haven't we, boy?" said Copeland. "So, yes, he's stepped it out like a champion, just like I was told he would. Now, I'd best get on or our Mr Greene will think we've gone astray."

"No disrespect, Colonel, but I'm surprised he's got the room to squeeze you in at Saddler Street. That museum of his seems to grow every time we visit. It'll be filling the Apothecary one of these days."

Waving off the garrulous innkeeper with a smile, Copeland accepted the fine leather gun-case handed down with care from the coach's luggage rack, its canvas carrying sack dusty from the roads. Here was an exhibit to match anything that Mr Museum-Keeper Greene was likely to muster, he thought, a grin cracking deeply lined and weather-beaten features. How he had missed playing Richard at his own game. The man and his dog set off at a good pace towards their destination, followed by a perspiring porter.

That evening, with the day's business concluded and two days of uninterrupted holiday stretching before them, Copeland's host and hostess appeared to be on good form, aided and abetted by a housekeeper so close to geniality as to provoke unease in most other circumstances.

"Now don't you go a-scraping of the pattern off my best service, Colonel," she had said approvingly, watching as the last vestige of her casserole disappeared from the soldier's plate. "There's more of the beef and oysters for those who appreciate a poor woman's best efforts."

Several hours later, leaving a table littered with nutshells, cheese rinds, biscuit crumbs and the remains of a spectacular fruit trifle, Theodosia climbed wearily to her feet. As both men struggled to emulate her, with varying degrees of success, she shooed them back to their seats. "I shall refrain from saying anything as pointless as 'don't be too late' to either of you, but do try not to wake a crotchety old lady with raucous laughter or sounds of breaking crockery." She bent to peck Henry Copeland on his upturned brow. "It's a delight to see you here once more, Harry. We miss you so." He reached up to take her pale hand in his.

When Theodosia had waved her departure for bed, Greene had silently pointed to the ceiling and stood to collect a decanter and glasses.

"I need to collect something from my room to show you, Richard," said the soldier. "I'll follow you up."

"Just so long as it's not more animal-life secreted in your luggage, Harry. The cats are terrified as it is." A distant bark sounded from below, perfectly on cue, as both stood. "He is a prince, I must admit – I even caught you-know-who slipping him a bone, and that is a lady not generally keen on most members of her own species, let alone large dogs suddenly wished upon her."

"I simply couldn't leave him behind, Richard. He came along with what I am about to show you upstairs. I think he would simply have been turned out to starve had I not agreed to take him. We do get along famously, it must be said. First dog I've had since I was a youngster. Didn't know how much I missed 'em till

Jack came along. He adopted me, though, if truth be told."

By the time Copeland had refreshed himself and climbed the steep stairs to reach the museum above, Greene had lit several candle-lamps to further brighten the first of the moonlit rooms. "By God, this takes me back, Richard. Was it really twenty years ago?"

"Twenty-one, actually," replied the small man. "Still as pedantic as ever, you'll note."

"I expect nothing less, my friend, but now," – he lifted the leather gun-case with a theatrical flourish – "I shall show you what detained me in Town; something you'll not be expecting. Try to contain your excitement while I just..." He fumbled at stiff buckles to unfasten the polished leather straps.

The case opened to reveal a magnificently fitted interior, with bullet mould, powder flask and a variety of glistening tools and accoutrements nestling in green baize and surrounding the finest firearm the Apothecary had ever seen. He sat and whistled in admiration.

"Have you taken up burglary, Harry? This must be worth a king's ransom."

"A dusky potentate's, at least," he agreed, smiling artfully. "Wait till you see it assembled." Copeland removed a superbly chased octagonal barrel and firelock from perfectly fitted nests. "Hold this for a moment. Drop it and it will be your last act." He reached back to remove an elaborately carved and polished stock, while Greene examined the metalwork with open-mouthed admiration.

"Was this potentate called Midas by any chance? I have never seen its equal, Harry."

"It is really quite old, Richard, from about the turn of the century, I believe. When I caught a whisper of it, I simply had to try to track it down."

Greene spread eloquent palms, waiting for the explanation his friend was aching to impart.

"The original gun-maker, Sepp Herrlich of Augsburg, has been a legend for well more than a century. He and one or two others, all Germans, were the first to perfect the technique of rifling a barrel."

"For spin, for accuracy and all that?" interjected his excited listener.

"Just so, Mr Greene. Now sit up, don't fidget and I'll tell you the rest of the story," continued Copeland, relishing the moment. "This, sadly not by the master himself, but by his grandson of that name, is known as 'The Bubble Gun'."

"Come now, you jest," said Greene, grinning.

"I assuredly do not," replied Copeland, "Pay attention. It was originally purchased for an eye-watering sum by one Everard de Quincey, as he rode the rising surge of the South Sea Trading Company."

"Until 1720," said Greene, unable to help himself.

"Until 1720," replied Copeland patiently, "when said de Quincey lost his all; his shirt, his wits – the lot, when 'The Bubble' burst and half the greedy gentry of England suddenly wished they had listened to their strict old nannies preaching about avarice and quick profits."

"So?" said Greene, "The suspense at this time of night is giving me indigestion."

"So, The Bubble Gun, along with everything a de Quincey in Queer Street could dispose of was snapped up by those of the ravening pack who still had the wherewithal to profit from their fellows' misfortune. It then passed through a series of hands though, somehow losing much of its cachet in the process; becoming, if you wish, a first-rate, tradeable commodity amongst gentry – or money-men – who had little or no idea of its extraordinary rarity or importance. It remained desirable, certainly, but truly appreciated by only a vanishing few who knew – and understood – its provenance."

"And so, you..?"

"And so, last week, I happened to hear over dinner at my club that amongst the effects of a recently deceased young hothead killed in a duel at Hounslow was 'a damn' fine gun by some cabbage-eater with a name like Hairlick. The lad's poor Ma's in such a bate she wants to be rid of everything that reminds her of 'a wasted life'."

"Something prompted me to follow it up. Frankly, Richard, I could have bought the thing for a tenth of its worth but ended up by giving the lady twice what she was asking. Having met her – one of those icy, disdainful matriarchs that are the bane of society – I could fully understand why her poor son had gone off the rails, but at least salved a part of my conscience by letting her think I was a well-heeled nincompoop."

"So, Mr Greene, I give you The Bubble Gun." He fitted stock to lock and barrel with a scarcely audible click. "Arguably one of the finest rifles ever produced. I took the opportunity of testing it up on Hampstead Hill. I killed two pigeons on the wing with two shots. Its accuracy is simply uncanny."

"May I?" Greene reached out to take it, hefting it between his hands. "The balance is extraordinary – even a mere civilian such as me can appreciate that – and for a barrel of this length it is exceptionally light, Harry."

He sat back for several minutes of companionable silence, examining the craftsmanship of the superb piece, then looked up, saying: "So, country estate, dog and gun – you've become the Compleat Squire, my friend. You'll be evicting tenants and claiming Jus Primae Noctis before we know it!" Once their laughter had subsided, Copeland looked across at his host busily refilling their glasses.

"Without wishing to cast a pall over a delightful evening, I cannot help but recall a dark night long ago, sitting much as we are now, when you first shared a terrible confidence with me, Richard. Could one hazard a guess that another unburdening might now be called for?" Greene looked up sharply, the decanter poised.

"Am I really so transparent, Harry? I shall have to give up playing cards." The attempt at levity fell entirely flat. Copeland sat, waiting.

The Apothecary thought for what seemed several minutes before he could find the words to begin. "Imagine, if you will," he said, "some equivalent to a situation in which however one might wish to begin an explanation – an unburdening, in your words – one must first enquire of a professional soldier – a man of wide and often deadly experience – whether he believes in fairies."

Copeland stared at him in genuine bewilderment. "Forgive me, Richard. Does that actually require an answer?"

Greene sighed. "After a fashion, yes, it does – in that the soldier in my example may begin to comprehend the questioner's dilemma in having no option other than spouting what is likely to sound like demented drivel to most listeners."

"Richard, you have known me long enough to be certain that I shall take you at your word however outlandish that word may sound. Now, try me, for God's sake, before we both perish from old age."

"Very well; you have been warned, Harry." He took a large swallow from his glass, followed by a deep breath. "It all begins with one Walter de Langton, a late-thirteenth, early-fourteenth century Bishop of Lichfield, a man of huge political power. An intimate of Edward the First, in fact later to be appointed that monarch's executor; of immense wealth, universally loathed and with a singularly unpleasant fascination with diabolism and sodomy. I see I have your attention."

The night was ebbing into the pallid grey of false dawn, when Copeland, bleary with tiredness asked, "The appalling thing is still here, Richard? Why in the name of Heaven have you continued to put yourself in such jeopardy? You must be rid of it!"

With infinite weariness Greene replied, "Perhaps your answer is, in part, contained in your own question, Harry. My quandary centres upon a conviction that this awful thing presents such an unthinkable threat to everything I hold sacred, that it has become a responsibility I cannot shrug off, for fear of consequences beyond our imagination. If this is, as I dread to acknowledge, the so-called Book of Solomon – the stuff of black legend since its theft, first, and then its disappearance close on five hundred years ago – then I bear a burden whose weight I can scarcely contemplate. It has the power to kill, Harry. Look at that door-frame once more if you can still doubt it. It can seduce, it can enchant, it can burn, it can freeze – and, Lord help me, I have witnessed just these few of its tricks. But worse, far, far worse, its ultimate purpose is to provide a portal for conjuration. The means to summon the unspeakable into our world, Harry. For this and this alone it is somehow protected – as surely as the sun rises in the east. It will not only resist any attempt to tamper with it but will strike back in its own defence. My presumption, my sheer blighted arrogance in seeking to gain possession of it has left me open in a way I cannot begin to explain or understand. It is a monstrous perversion and it has come to terrify me. It must, of course, be destroyed, but I am at an utter loss to know how to proceed. From my own bitter experience, I know it to be dangerous beyond belief, but I must thank you for your indulgence – your trust – Harry, in hearing me out. Most would have me consigned to Bedlam by now."

"No, not that but bed, Mr Greene, bed," said the soldier, tottering stiffly to his feet as he added: "I cannot believe we have spent the night in traversing such an unimaginable realm. Though I fear it will still be there in the cold light of day, perhaps a few hours of sleep will mitigate its chill."

Each went off to seek what comfort they could find.

(29)

In a lofty Glafs Case, on the left hand the entrance to the Inner Museum, are the following articles brought from Otaheita, O-why-ye, New Caledonia, Easter Island, and other Iflands in the South Seas, viz. A Syrinx, or Musical Instrument, compofed of ten Reeds of different lengths, of the kind wherewith the God Pan is usually depicted, A broad Sword, of brown, hard Wood, neatly made, called Pah-oh-wah. New Caledonia. Two forts of platted Aprons, of open Work, worn by the Women of Otaheite. The Tatowing Instrument.

Lichfield. Greenhill Bower. Monday 26th May. Whilst the martial Array of olden days had long-since dwindled into an annual excuse for uniformed posturing amongst that coterie of Civic society with a tendency to take themselves and their status over-seriously, what had once been a muster and review of a Lichfield Militia numbering several hundred was now enacted as a hasty prelude to the day's festivities. Since dawn, the lanes and roads converging on the city were busier by far than even the mighty influx seen for the celebrated Race Days out at Whittington.

The principal components of the huge parade – the great dray-horses that would draw the huge floats and their elaborations of automata and invention – were assembling wherever space and tolerance could be found, whilst the Guilds, the Club-Men, the Societies, the bands and whosoever could dream up a costumed reason for joining in, milled and surged like tidal entities as attempts at imposing order and coherence went unheard or were genially ignored. Out on the road from the market-place the whole of Greenhill was already thronged with the hundreds that would shortly become thousands jostling for vantage points and the vast quantities of food and drink laid out all around the leafy construct that formed the Bower itself; fuel for what would become not just one, but – reprehensibly, in many disapproving eyes – a second day spill-over of public drunkenness and debauchery.

By tacit agreement, Richard and Theodosia Greene's long-standing ambit avoided the worst of the crush and the ever-present dangers presented by a massive procession rarely under any semblance of proper control. More to the point, perhaps, was their avoidance of one of Greenhill's grander houses, that of the Honourable Mrs Seppel. It had been whilst sitting outside its porch, a guest of the lady herself, that Michael Rawlins had been murdered those many years before. It was neither a place nor an occasion that the Apothecary would willingly revisit.

Today, they would join the Blomefields and a small group of other close friends on a balcony well above crowd-level, to sedately enjoy the early prospect of a parade that would generally disintegrate into hilarious disarray the further it progressed towards its Greenhill destination. Joining them would be Henry Copeland, though unaccompanied by Jack the Dalmatian.

"Animals get terrified by the din, the gunshots, the whole raucous mish-mash," Greene had explained, "which explains why so many of the parade-horses run amok. So how about we give him the run of the garden, more or less? A lead long enough for him to prowl about to his heart's content, but that keeps him clear of the stable and the side-gates?"

Copeland had gazed with amusement around the growing collection of ancient architectural fragments that now populated the long garden. "Are they all self-seeded or did you plant them yourself?" he asked his host, hoping to distract his friend's attention from a large spotted dog cocking a leg against a battered marble font.

"They are all of the threatened genus 'Relic' that no longer flourishes in our Age of Improvement," replied Greene with every appearance of seriousness, adding, "Don't worry about the font, Harry, it has suffered far worse at the hands of those who should have known better."

Even faced with the prospect of a day that promised perfect weather, he had wrapped the folds of scarf around the livid scars on his neck, concealing the rope-burns that would forever indicate the fate he had escaped those many years ago. That and vocal cords so damaged that the grating rasp was all that remained of a voice that could once so persuasively charm the objects of his desires.

He rode from the sepulchral gloom of the Priory out into the sweetness of a day he failed to notice, intent solely upon the purpose of the ride that lay ahead. This 'Bower-Day', he knew, would be a time of empty houses, closed shops, holidaying servants – all off to wallow in their imbecile pleasures. De Rais knew that he would never be presented with a better opportunity. An image of the place that had been revealed to him, with its crooked chimney, its padlocked door, was fixed in his mind. It was only a matter of time now.

He chose to draw no attention to himself – not that he ever attracted small-talk or more than a hasty glance – and by late morning was content to let his tired horse amble along amidst the generality as they approached the city outskirts. On his earlier visit, he had partially made up for an otherwise fruitless journey by a careful reconnaissance of the various means of access to – and escape from – the three locations that had been the original targets of his search. That myriad possibilities had ever been narrowed to such a degree had been an exhausting drain upon his powers and those of the fading creature he nominally served. Had it not been for the stygian aura of the book itself, they might never have managed to focus a search. But now he knew, and it would know of his coming. He checked, once more, the reassuring weight of the oil-clothed roll at his saddlebow that contained his tools. His knives and pocket-pistols were closer to hand.

Margery and her girls had all left as soon as an early breakfast had been cleared away, off to join whatever company they had chosen for the big day, whilst their employers and houseguest spent some time in preparation for one of the year's dressier occasions. As ever, eagle-eyed wifely scrutiny sent an initially resigned husband off for several changes of ensemble before finally pronouncing herself satisfied and him presentable. Copeland managed to keep a non-provocative profile while this occurred, knowing that the slightest snigger – or worse – the merest hint of sympathy for his increasingly harried friend would not be well-received.

When all had been arranged to Theodosia's satisfaction, with Jack properly tethered and well-provided with water and a large mutton-bone, all windows securely fastened and gates bolted, the party headed out into the affable chaos engulfing Saddler Street.

Around one in the afternoon, with the mounting cacophony shifting away from the centre, a heavily scarfed figure appeared, picking a careful way down across the heavy slates of the stable roof, aided by one of the longer overhanging branches of the beech tree that marked the garden boundary with Bore Street to the rear. The thump of his heavy-footed descent awoke the large dog, slumbering in the dappled shadows beside the ivy-covered privy. It watched, motionless, blinking across the short, sunlit grass, as the intruder stopped and appeared to listen for any sign that his arrival had been noticed, eyes checking, rechecking, the shuttered windows to the rear of the tall house. The sound of Jack's growl, deep within his chest, was lost entirely in the din that came and went with a rising breeze. He watched the cautious approach to the small outhouse opposite his place of concealment in the shadows. He hadn't liked it over there. The smell had driven him away. He didn't like the look, the smell of this one, either. Not one bit.

He saw the man stoop to place on the ground a bundle which he unwrapped before sliding a metal crowbar from it. As the dog watched, a handle was attached, doubling its length. Then a smaller bundle of what looked like spikes or thin blades was unlaced, and the man held the heavy padlock in one hand as he tried several of them in the keyhole. After several more were employed and rejected, Jack heard a hissed curse before the bundle was rewrapped and stowed away. Removing an outer riding coat, the man now inserted the crowbar's spiked tip into the fitting-plate bolted to the old oak lintel, and began to work all his weight against it. As he heard the first complaining split sound from it, the dog arrived at a conclusion. The smell was bad, the shadow all around this man was flickering and changing, flashing with angry colours; what was being done was hurting this place he liked. He would stop it for his friends.

The dalmatian came lithely to his full height, tensing with what was to come. He began slowly padding across the grass, soundless, focused on the oblivious, straining back. He stopped within feet of the man, easing back on heavily muscled haunches, ready to spring.

In that instant, some second sense prompted de Rais to swing around, suddenly aware of the threat, instantly alert and grabbing for a pocket.

With a full-throated snarl, the dog sprang at the shocked man, razor-claws lacerating one side of the gaunt face raised towards his attack.

De Rais toppled from the sheer impact of the spring, shrieking in pain as teeth sank into his unprotected shoulder, ripping cloth, flesh and sinew in a single agonising bite. As he fell, blood gouting from the awful wound, his hand closed upon the bone-handle of one of his knives. With strength born of desperation he tugged it free of the clinging fabric and slashed wildly as the sprung blade flicked open in his frantic scrabbling grip. A howl of agony met his first vicious cut, as the crimson claws and muzzle rolled away from his own writhing body. He cut and cut again, blinded by blood, deafened by the dying wails of the huge dog that now lay, thrashing in its death-throes, across his legs.

To heave the dead-weight off him – with one arm and shoulder immobilised by the throbbing wound – took more effort than he could have believed possible. He came to his knees, gasping, nauseous, knowing he must staunch the bleeding. It was only as a fluttering movement caught his eye that he saw cloths left out to dry on a previously unremarked line beside the stable wall. He came to his feet, already light-headed from the loss of blood, and crossed, unsteadily, to rip them from their pegs. He folded each of the half-dozen into a wad and then, with agonised difficulty, held them in place against the bite as he struggled back into his riding coat. Stooping to a half-filled bird bath, he scooped and scooped again to sluice the blood as best as he could from his face and hands, before hastily gathering up his bundled tools. Trembling with pain and impotence, he stared for one last moment of frustrated rage at the padlocked door, pausing only long enough to deliver a single vicious kick to the dog's corpse before hurrying to unbolt the rear gate.

Regaining his tethered horse, he somehow hauled himself up into the saddle, bathed in a sour, stinking sweat of pain and exhaustion, knowing that he must find the resolve to stay mounted for the long ride back to the moors.

He had survived worse, infinitely worse, he told himself, goring metal-shod heels into the unresisting flanks.

(30)

In a lofty Glafs Case, on the left hand the entrance to the Inner
Museum, are the following articles brought from Sandwich, Friendly,
King George's, New Amsterdam and other Iflands in the South
Seas, viz. A Formee or Military Gorget, worn by the Warriors,
compofed of Feathers of the Tropic Bird, Teeth of the Shark,
and fringed with Hair of the White Dog, in a curious manner.

Saddler Street. Thursday 29th May. Preparations for the
Woollaton party's much-anticipated arrival were well in hand,
both at Saddler Street and in the Darwin household, though any
similarities between the mood in the respective houses ended
there. Whilst all could be loosely described in terms of 'business
as usual' in the Doctor's hectic family domain, much-centred upon
the imminent arrival of a confidently predicted son, business –
in its literal sense – and the excuses it provided for staying busy,
was about all that was making life remotely tolerable at The
Apothecary.

The brutal horror of the discovery that had met their carefree
return from a rare day out, had plunged the entire household into
despondent gloom. Above stairs, into outrage and profound shock
at the violation of their home, whilst below, Margery had retreated
into an impenetrable sulk, blaming everything and everyone for
Jack's death: "Outside my own kitchen door, Mistress. Shall we all
be murdered in our beds next? Not that some around here would
so much as notice if'n we were."

For all that Copeland had been a military man of thirty

years standing, he had been cut to the quick not simply by the dalmatian's death, but the utter brutality of it.

"The poor old fellow must have been slashed a dozen times, Richard, even before his head was smashed." Unshed tears glinted in the pale blue eyes. "By God, if ever I can lay my hands on the fucker responsible for this, he'll not walk away in one piece. He was after your wretched book, you think?"

"What else? Why else?" replied the Apothecary with a miserable shrug. "We always knew he'd be back. It is a measure of my thoughtlessness that I failed to see Bower Day as a prime opportunity." He reached out a consoling hand to Copeland's shoulder. "I'm desperately sorry, my friend. I am single-handedly responsible for all this. I know how much you'd come to care for Jack; it just breaks my heart."

"Has it occurred to you, Richard," said the soldier quietly, his eyes never leaving the small, morose man, "that had it been any one of us – Margery, one of the girls, Tillett, the boy Timmy – who had come upon this vicious bastard, then it would most certainly have been a matter of cold-blooded murder – rather than the death of a dog? We are dealing with obsession here – violent insanity. In search of a book? Unless you can find the means of getting shot of the damnable thing, there can be but one effective defence against it, my friend: kill the bastard before he can kill you. You do realise that by now, don't you?"

The Apothecary raised both hands in helpless surrender. "Oh, Christ, Harry," he whispered, "What am I to do?"

"Well, the first thing is to show me this bloody book – I can't begin to help you unless I've at least had sight of what I'm supposed to be dealing with. You must see that."

"You are not alone in that sentiment, Harry," said a quiet voice from the doorway. Theodosia, her own eyes red from sharing the soldier's grief and fury, came to sit beside them. "We can no longer lock doors and turn away from what has been brought into our lives, Richard." She raised a pale hand to forestall his reply:

"We all know that your motives, your intentions in this ugly matter are honourable, if, with the sorry benefit of hindsight, wrong-headed and sorely misjudged." He could only nod miserably in agreement. "So," she continued, "whilst some sort of practical solution must be found and found soon, I too insist on at least a sight of this horrid thing that you have brought into our lives."

He knew that there could be no prevarication now. He had been dreading this moment.

"At risk of sounding over-dramatic, I can only agree to this if you will trust me. I had hoped to possibly enlist Richard Davenport's help – or at least sound him out – this coming weekend." He looked at the determination written across the faces of both his listeners, "but I understand now that this will not wait for his arrival. We shall all attend Lionel's place of business in the morning having arranged to take communion, and, in the meantime, I must try to understand the efficacy of a further means of protection, shall we say, that has come into my hands. I will not go near that thing again unless I can feel prepared. Do you both agree?"

They had joined the small congregation at St Mary's for the morning service, much to its vicar's mystification. "It's not your birthday or something I've missed, is it?" Lionel Blomefield enquired as they were about to leave. "Elspeth is usually au fait with that kind of thing."

After reassuring him on that point at least, they took their leave, though not before the clergyman had been struck by their obvious preoccupation. I might just drop in later, he thought.

Just as they had been about to open for business on this Tuesday morning following the events of Bower Day, both husband and wife had been surprised but pleased when James Tillett announced that he had taken the opportunity of the long weekend to visit his niece in Ashbourne. In explaining her change of circumstances, the shopman revealed a glimpse into a private life that was normally a closed book.

"Both me and her mother had hoped Emmy would settle with her aunt, but it was probably a lot to expect. May's not been the same since she lost her husband, can't seem to take pleasure in anything – let alone a bright young thing like Emmy about the place, anyhow." He'd gone on to explain Tomlin's offer and both the girl's and the aunt's grateful acceptance, and then, the nub of the account was reached, "Emmy was hoping, like, that you might be prepared to do her a kindness in saying the odd word on her behalf to Mr Tomlin. About the work, like. How she seemed to take to it?"

Seeing the entreaty in Tillett's pale eyes, Theodosia said brightly, "Why, certainly James. We were sorry to lose her, as you know. I shall jot down a line or two when I have a moment. Shall you be returning to Ashbourne any time soon, so that I can send a letter with you?"

"Happy to, Mistress, next weekend, if I might be allowed to take the afternoon off on the Saturday. It's a fair old step."

Theodosia was about to agree when she remembered Saturday's singularly pressing engagement. "Oh, James, you know I would normally agree most happily, but with the arrival of our Woollaton visitors both Mr Greene and I are invited to dine at the Darwins' on that same afternoon following their visit to the museum. I suggest you take Monday morning instead, if that will suit, returning straight to work from your journey back. Shall you be able to cope with that?"

He had happily agreed and, between serving and his other duties, returned to supervising the boy's unceasing labours: deep cleaning every nook, each dusty cranny of all but one of the Apothecary workrooms and outbuildings. He hadn't enquired into the damaged doorframe or the freshly dug dog's grave out in the garden. He too could keep his counsel.

Returned now to something approaching the even tenor of a normal working week, Tillett would have been grievously tried had he known what had confronted his niece only hours after his departure from Ashbourne and a congenial meeting with Emmy's new employer.

After only four days at the busy druggist's, the young woman had already been introduced to the bare bones of a business that fascinated her, but even had she been there four months would still have been ill-prepared for the last customer of Monday afternoon. He arrived as most shops in Ashbourne's marketplace had already closed for the day, and while she, in fact, had been sweeping up prior to hanging the closed sign on the door as she had been instructed. It had only been due to several late-running customers that Tomlin was still open at all when the door crashed open and the skeletal, bloodstained figure had lurched into the shop.

"Tomlin, where is he? I must…" croaked the apparition to the terrified girl, before collapsing into the chair in the bow-window. His close-cropped head lolling as he attempted to focus on his surroundings, the dried blood on his facial lacerations looking like some grotesque, half-painted clown mask. The druggist emerged at Emmy's urgent call, looking every bit as shocked as his new assistant by the sight that confronted him.

"Why, Mr Ray, Sir, whatever has happened? Have you been set upon?" Seeing no reply was immediately forthcoming from the stricken man, he turned urgently to the young woman and said, "Quickly, put a kettle on to boil and set out towels, bandage and brandy. The decanter above my desk. Quickly now!"

She needed no second bidding. She had instantly recognised the wounded man and was now praying silently that he had not recognised her. With a feeling of revulsion that she dared not show, she had now been called upon to help the barely mobile, rank-smelling figure onto a low bench in Tomlin's Consulting Room.

"One will, of course, attend immediately to what lies within one's powers, Mr Ray, but I really must call for medical assistance of a more experienced nature. My facilities are limited at best."

"No!" croaked de Rais, rallying. "No doctors! It was a dog.

Clean this." He raised a filth-caked hand to his cheek. "And the bite on my shoulder. Clean both now. No doctors, you understand? And her, out, now." He sank back exhausted.

She turned, uncertain, but Tomlin hissed: "His coat, I cannot manage it alone. Help me first then you can go."

"Her, out, now!" De Rais snarled. "She does not touch me. Do your job, man."

"Well, actually Mr Ray, it's not..." began Tomlin but stopped at the look of feral ferocity in the black eyes. "You had better leave, my dear, I'll finish up here."

The eventual removal of the topcoat and the wadded cloths beneath revealed the extent of the wound. In a town served by four doctors, the druggist's limited surgical skills had rarely been called upon, other than in unforeseen emergencies. This, he sternly admonished himself, should be regarded as just one such and any feelings of distaste for the individual in question, or horror at the savagery of the wound, must be sublimated in the interests of good business if nothing else.

Whilst not entirely inexperienced in minor surgery, the cleaning alone turned Tomlin's stomach – not least after the patient had gripped his wrist in a vicious hold as he reached to remove the tightly wrapped neck-scarf that was impeding access to the mauled shoulder. "Touch that once more and you will regret it. It stays. My shoulder, not my neck is hurt. Have you no eyes?"

Tomlin had delayed the final closing of the gaping tear for as long as he could, but with the final abrading of the torn skin around its edges, knew he could postpone it no longer. "I shall have to stitch you now, Mr Ray. It will be most painful, I'm afraid. I suggest a large glass of brandy before I begin." The suffering man nodded his agreement and gracelessly accepted a brimming glass. He consumed it in several deep gulps. "Do it, quickly." Wishing he had taken a glass for himself, Tomlin threaded a large needle with squinting deliberation. At his first puncture of the livid flesh, a foul-smelling sweat sprang from the grey features, thin lips gritted in a rictus of pain. Then with a second and a third, Tomlin began to draw the ragged wound together. De Rais gave a shuddering gasp and fainted, his stubbled head lolling like a broken puppet. As it did, the neck-scarf slipped to reveal the deep-ridged scar tissue beneath. Tomlin jerked back in shock and disgust. *No wonder you keep that covered up. You, Sir, are a dead man walking*. He knew all-too-well what had left those indelible tokens. Looking down at the raw-boned intruder he prayed he had not spoken his thought aloud. He finished a dozen or more coarse stitches with grim determination. De Rais came around as Tomlin was washing his hands in a bowl of tepid water.

"You have finished?" the voice croaked, hooded eyes regarding him without a flicker of gratitude or emotion. A bony hand rose to test the dressing on his cheek. "I shall stay in Ashbourne tonight." Perhaps he saw the fear in Tomlin's eyes, "At the Green Dragon. You can send your man up to Malbecq at first light." It was neither a question nor a request. "I will give directions. It is not sign-posted. A coach will be sent for me, and your bill will be settled then. Tonight, I shall require your Egyptian hashish to sleep." He felt, carefully, to the heavy dressing around his shoulder. "What did you use for your stitching? A blunt stick?"

Smarting at the gratuitous insult, Tomlin took quiet pleasure in replying, "I regret I have no man to send, Mr Ray. He fell victim to a bad accident himself and will not be returning to my service for the foreseeable future."

"The girl, then; send her. Who is she? I have seen her before but not here."

"That will be neither possible nor practical, Mr Ray. I need her here and would not send a young woman off, riding alone, under any circumstances." With a certain satisfaction he added, "Emmy has only just joined me, Mr Ray; from Lichfield, in fact. Greene's noted Apothecary no less."

Without a word of acknowledgement, de Rais struggled to his feet.

"The hashish, then, and Jesuit bark." He swayed with exhaustion. "Quickly."

He remembered her now, the red-headed presence as he put the imbecile shopman in his place. In his mind's eye, undimmed by pain or exhaustion, he could even see a resemblance between them. He remembered her now.

(31)

A figure in Bisket or unglazed China, of our Saviour crowned
with Thorns, his Hands bound with a cord, a loofe mantle thrown
over him, which reaches to the Ground; this Statue was made at
the China Manufactory at Derby, & moft exquifitely finifhed, is
twelve inches high, and is covered with a Bell of Flint Glafs.

Saddler Street. The night of Thursday 29ᵗʰ May. Richard Greene
would not have admitted the fact, but it had taken a large bumper
of old Scotch whisky before he could steel himself to return once
more to the stuffy bakehouse, unseal the oven-door, lift the iron
box from its place of supposed concealment and to carry it up to
the innermost of the museum rooms on the top floor of the tall
house. This evening, the question of how a would-be thief had
known to seek it behind a padlocked outhouse door was only one
of many things that the Apothecary was striving to order in a
fretful mind.

During an hour of thoughtful deliberation and repeated forays
into the furthest depths of his stacked and shelved reference
materials – jumbled to an extent that would appear to the
uninformed eye to be indiscriminate chaos – he had retrieved a
small, ragged volume. Missing its front board, its tattered frontis
announcing it had been printed in Amsterdam some one hundred
years earlier, but written, unaccountably, in something approaching
English. It was titled 'Kabbalah'. Beneath the smudged characters

of the title, a subheading in mis-set type announced:

Etz HaChayim. The 10 Sephirot and the 22 Paths.
Mystikal Wisdom of The Antient Jew.

From his pocketbook, the Apothecary withdrew the folded sheet
he had removed from Philbrigge's body and spread it beside the
small book, though carefully covering the phonetic translation of
the three symbols with another sheet. He had no intention even
of mouthing those words without the reassurance he now sought.

"Now let us see what we can find," he said to himself, beginning
to leaf through the small volume, referring repeatedly to the three
symbols so carefully inked on the bookseller's sheet. *I have been
provided with a safeguard, a form of words, of protection, to employ in
the event of obtaining it. It must not be handled – and never opened.*

On various occasions over many years Greene had returned to
the ancient mysteries of this most intriguing – and impenetrable
– work, with its graphic portrayal of a Tree of Life from which
all wisdom and knowledge were said to have proceeded, and its
dark and impure hermetic counterpart, Qlippoth – an abstract
portrayal of what was also referred to as Sitra Ahra – The Realm
of Evil.

Amongst the bewildering complexity of page upon page of
diagrams and aramaic letterforms, he had found what he sought
to confirm – if not understand. The three inked symbols, though
here not in the conjunction he now possessed, were powerful
evocations concerned with Light, Purity and Spiritual Strength.
That was all he needed to know, he had decided, closing the little
book with some relief.

They assembled in the museum after a tense supper, conducive
to no-one's digestion, and were now seated in a trio of chairs
arranged in front of the burned table.

"Unnecessary though it may be to say this," Greene began,

looking intently at each of his companions in turn, "under no circumstances touch the box, or – least of all – the book itself. When we are prepared, I shall open the box to examine the present state of the binding-thongs around the book. If they have been re-knotted it will be an indication that, once more, the task of opening it is being frustrated from the outset. This will, I think, indicate the danger of proceeding. It took Lionel and me more than an hour to untangle, and that was before he was scared witless by the frontis – nothing more. Once open, if that proves possible, I shall avoid physical contact and intend to lift pages with this," – he held up a wooden spatula in his gloved hand – "it being non-conductive to the extremes of temperature this thing has generated. I consider it highly likely that the pages themselves have been impregnated with some form of hallucinatory agent that must be avoided at all costs. Hence, at risk of looking far sillier than usual, I shall wear this mask over my mouth, to avoid the possibility of inhalation. I believe we should begin with the Lord's Prayer and anything else that might come to mind in the form of a spiritual buckler – for want of a better word. I shall also employ a Hebrew charm which poor Philbrigge was given in the name of 'protection' – this by a principal who knew to take this thing every bit as seriously as we must now. Are we all ready?"

As time-honoured words were spoken with quiet reverence, the distant sound of the striking hour rang across the Minster Pool from the Jesus Tower of the great Cathedral. Even before its final chime the buzzing had become apparent.

At first, each of them glanced about, seeking its source only to simultaneously realise that its source lay on the scarred tabletop. It grew louder and more persistent, the dirty iron box vibrating ever more, the table legs beneath it now beginning to match the shaking above.

Greene, with grim deliberation, opened the folded sheet, laid it beside the box which now appeared to be moving with an inner life of its own, and carefully enunciated the three words over it.

Total silence descended. The buzzing, the frenetic vibration, ceased in a second of the utterance of the final syllable of the unfamiliar sounds. He sat back with an exhalation of breath. "I believe it will be safe to open now."

With the handle of his spatula he pushed back a lid which now appeared to lift with perfectly oiled precision. The smell that rose with it was nauseating.

Flinching back from its miasmic stench, Greene gasped, "Flies. Hundreds, all dead; covering the book entirely." Copeland, gripping a handkerchief against his face, leaned forward, the better to peer into the open lid. "Corpse-flies, hence the reek. Dear God, they revolt me even now and I've seen more than my share."

"Calliphoridae," agreed the Apothecary, unnecessarily. "Blowflies to most." He turned to his determinedly silent wife and said, "There was not even a maggot to be found in there, my dear. I would have spared you this."

"A little late for that sentiment, do you not think, husband? Shall we just get on with opening the wretched thing."

Gingerly, Greene scraped the myriad blue-black corpses away from the book cover, revealing it to be unbound though now surrounded by such a depth of dead insects it appeared to float within a glistening, stinking sea.

"If anything appears to move, to flicker, look away if you can," he said, inserting the wooden blade beneath the greasy cover, its incised symbol scarcely visible in the dying light.

The elaborate frontis was revealed, an intertwined patchwork of leaf and twig looking like nothing more than any of the Green Men that populated a thousand country churches. The anti-climax began here and ended after more than a score of limp, inert pages had been painstakingly turned, their arcane contents little more than the artlessly recorded diagrams of some unmourned, lost science. No visions of Jerusalem, no snarling bestiary, nothing but the tired, inexpert scrawlings of some diseased and long-forgotten obsession.

"I really do believe we have seen enough," said Theodosia, sounding as tired and unimpressed as both her companions. "It is obviously of great age but, frankly, its attraction," – she looked sharply at her puzzled husband – "if ever there was any, must surely begin and end with that. I find it distasteful in the extreme, Richard, and I beg you now to be done with it."

"Amen, to that, Theodosia," said Copeland heavily. "It reminds me of nothing more than the grisly trophies to be found in some shaman's tent, filled with inexplicable rubbish all tainted with death. If you are still unsure as to the means of its removal, its destruction, then I'm your man, Richard."

Greene appeared lost in thought for several minutes before he responded. "To say I am disappointed with this," – he gestured lost for words – "would be absurd. I am relieved more than I can tell you that nothing untoward has happened, but after all that has occurred, I am puzzled in equal measure. You must both think me an utter fantasist. In your place I would, without doubt."

"There are more things in Heaven and Earth, Horatio," boomed the soldier, intent on breaking the dismal mood and clapping the small man on his shoulder as he stood. "Now leave the damned thing where it is and let us all go downstairs and forget about it until tomorrow. What we all need is a stiff drink, and quite probably another after that!"

The Apothecary could only agree.

Copeland had the soldier's knack of sleeping wherever and whenever the opportunity presented itself, though with that innate sense of ever-present wariness that accompanies it. The slightest noise, the least change in atmosphere could bring him out of the deepest sleep in an instant.

He thought he came awake to the first sound made by the intruder – no more than the lightest tread upon old uneven boards. No more than a blade of moonlight escaping the heavy curtains at his window; that, though, was enough. A body, naked, oiled and glistening in the eldritch radiance, tattoos black against the pallor of its muscularity, slid towards him through the gloom. He tried to move, to shout, to raise at least an arm to hold the gliding horror back. An Iroquois! His blood froze in his veins.

He knew too well that half-shaved skull, the filed-down fangs for teeth set in a blue-lipped grin, the twining snakes that inked the thighs and arms, the hooked blade of the tomahawk rising for its single downward slash.

Theodosia struggled out of clinging folds of fog and half-formed dreams, into a twilight world she recognised too well. Bound, hand and foot, gagged so tightly that she fought for every stinging breath. The reek of ether clinging to her smarting face, the once homely tang of lamp-oil rising from her soaked shawl and dress. Paralysing dread swamped her very being as the struck match flared behind her.

At last he found his voice and bellowed out in terror as the axeblade swung down towards his face.

An inhuman howl burst from her heaving chest, her pinioned head, as searing flame engulfed the very air itself.

Richard Greene jolted awake in blind, bewildered panic as his wife's demented shriek of agony, of terror, was joined in frenzied discord from the room next door. Theodosia, bolt upright in their marriage bed, eyes unseeing, wide with dread, was frantically brushing at her arms as if to extinguish fire. From Copeland's room the sound of a heavy body hitting the floor and a door wrenched open, joined with the formless, gibbering wail from the woman beside him. Greene threw his arms about her, pulling her into a fierce embrace just as their bedroom door flew open and the wildly dishevelled soldier stood swaying in the doorway, grasping the frame for support.

"Oh, Sweet Jesu, her too?" he managed, gasping, breathless. Below them the sound of banging doors and feet upon the stairs.

(32)

Within the Table in the middle of the ROOM Gloves worn by King Charles, 1st, given by Mr Kemble, father to Mrs Siddons.

Saddler Street. Saturday 31st May. The previous day it had taken all the Apothecary's powers of invention and diplomacy to restore some measure of the shattered calm that had awoken staff, alarmed close neighbours and continued to haunt both his wife and his old friend.

Neither Copeland nor Theodosia could be persuaded back into bed until after they had spoken at length about the malignant aberration that had possessed them both, simultaneously, leaving them shaken and diminished in its wake.

"You do understand that there can be no question of coincidence involved here?" Greene had said quietly. "You have both been the victims of attacks born of your deepest fears, your worst memories. This is the essence of the vileness I was attempting to protect you from. Its utter unpredictability makes it virtually impossible to defend against. Thwart it one way and it will strike from wherever it is least expected." He had paused then, as if not knowing how to continue, but finally seemed to arrive at a conclusion.

"The worst of this situation you do not, I fear, fully appreciate."

Both listened in horrified fascination, as he continued: "As if the mental images, the nightmares, visited upon you were not real enough, there was also a physical dimension to the attacks." He paused to take Theodosia's still-trembling hand. "I can still detect the odours of both oil and ether in our room, my dear, whilst in yours, Harry, I came upon these." With elaborate care Greene unwrapped a cloth to reveal a pair of crudely fashioned fishhooks, their barbed points coated black.

"These were on the floor by your bed Harry, right where you could be expected to place your feet."

"Oh Christ, no, not those," gasped Copeland in horror.

"The very same," replied Greene, solemnly. Theodosia raised hands to her mouth, "You cannot mean that these were the hooks that were used to kill Pomlett? The poison that reduced him to..?" She could not continue. The memory of the librarian's unspeakable death; the vision of the suppurating monstrosity that had once been a man: however much she had tried to banish the vile imprint from her mind, it had ever left her in all the time since that appalling murder.

"They have been behind glass upstairs for twenty years, along with the other Iroquois artefacts with which you are familiar, Harry. The cabinet remains locked, the key has never left my person, and yet..."

"But Richard, why now? Why me?" began the soldier, realisation dawning on the open features even as he spoke. "I threatened it, did I not? Told you I was your man if it was to be destroyed?"

"And I did, too," added the pale woman, tonelessly. "What presumptuous fools we all are." She reached across to take hold of her husband's hand. "What on earth are we to do, Richard? I cannot endure another..." She could not continue.

"I am fervently hoping that Davenport may hold the key to this – or that at least may be able to point towards a solution. Thank the Lord he is coming tomorrow." Gently disengaging, he stood, and with leaden reluctance said, "But first, something must be put back outside."

On the appearance of a smiling and excited Anne Protheroe shortly before the expected arrival of the Woollaton party, the

Apothecary congratulated himself on a piece of cunning and inventive quick-thinking. Knowing the lady to be of Channel Island extraction and, hence, fluently bilingual, Greene had reasoned that her attendance would have a twofold purpose. First, to provide Madame Rousseau with a companionable French-speaking guide to those aspects of the huge collection most likely to be of interest to a visitor of the female persuasion and, secondly, to perhaps create at least a small window of opportunity for the Apothecary to discreetly engage with Woollaton's master.

Given the distance involved and the state of holed and rutted roads, Davenport's coach arrived with enviable punctuality to be met by a delighted Apothecary and his welcoming wife. A certain Officer of Engineers, retired, had absented himself from the occasion, having expressed his less than flattering opinion of the French nation in general and firebrand Radicals in particular: "Had it not been for Johnny Frenchman and his garlic-crunching compatriots, the Seven Tribes would have dealt with us man-to-man; not whipped up into being the murderous bastards they have become," he had said with authority. "Frankly, Richard, I say, damn the French and all their works."

There was no arguing with that.

Introductions having been made, and even before the party were shown upstairs, Thérèse Rousseau was expressing her delight at the bountifully stocked Apothecary with its consummate range of cosmetics and ladies' particularities. Her husband seemed equally drawn to the superbly displayed range of leaves, powders, granules, unguents, twigs, fungi, liquids and nameless varieties, all ranked in their decorated jars, multi-hued vials, gilt-lettered bottles and straw-wrapped carboys.

"A veritable lexicon of Pharmacopaeia if ever I saw one," said Davenport, admiringly. "I made quite certain that Jean-Jacques brought his pocket-book," he added with a knowing smile as they awaited their absorbed female companions. "I rather expected this.

They have both been greatly looking forward to today. What a splendid thought to provide Mrs Protheroe, though, Mr Greene. I shall be spared the exercise of my wholly inadequate talent for all things feminine."

"As we are both Richard, shall we keep it simple?" suggested the Apothecary with a smile.

"Indeed. Just as I had intended," agreed the visitor, extending his hand once more.

After they had taken a cordial in the parlour upstairs, with Rousseau expressing his admiration for Theodosia's botanical paintings displayed there, Greene led the way up the steep stairs to the museum.

Once inside the first of its rooms, their curator paused to allow his visitors time to enter from the narrow Armoury Corridor. He turned to watch their expressions as the first vista of the extraordinary collection revealed itself. This was always his favourite part.

With a perfect Gallic shrug, Jean-Jacques turned to Davenport, saying, "But this is incredible! I was expecting nothing like it. The work of a lifetime is it not?"

The Apothecary had been well briefed by Darwin, and being now forewarned concerning the Frenchman's passions and prejudices, was completely unsurprised by either the wild enthusiasms and haughty dismissals expressed as display after display were introduced to them all.

Within minutes, they had largely separated, the ladies busily enthusing over the textiles, relics, jewellery, paintings and elaborate curiosities, Rousseau's frenetic enthusiasms leading his fellows from natural wonder to natural wonder. He clapped, shouted his delight and, at one stage, confronted with magnificent shells and pressed and dried ferns and plants from Cook's voyages, jumped up and down with the pure delight of a small boy.

"Such great adventures have coloured my whole life," he

exclaimed, "to an extent that neither reflection nor experience have ever cured me of what are called my bizarre and romantic notions concerning our human life. In our uncorrupted state we are the perfect miracle that will never be improved upon!"

In a never-to-be repeated attempt to engage his volatile visitor with a display of the tribal artefacts from those same voyages, they were dismissed with little more than a disdainful sniff. Seeing the disappointment that Greene failed to disguise, Davenport explained: "Jean-Jacques insists that all expressions of what we call art – and decoration in virtually its every form – however beautiful some may find them, are transgressive. Whilst prepared to accept the workaday value of the artisan's output, he insists that any move towards the creation of art – applauded or collected by the rich – is a debasement of that noble perfection found in so-called primitives, it being, he believes, a pointless embellishment of a nature that in its perfection requires none."

"Then we shall agree to differ," the curator replied with a somewhat strained smile. "Perhaps you would like to point out to our guest that I am counted amongst those benighted souls who believe art to be the highest expression of our humanity. A need expressed in tangible form since the beginning of time. With it, in it, surely, we express that purity of spirit, of inspiration, that he extols."

"Well said, my friend, but I shall perhaps forego that particular translation lest we get blood on your fine carpets. Our friend is known for a certain fixity of opinion on that and much else."

It was then, providentially, that Thérèse broke from her company to insist on leading her reluctant husband across to join Theodosia and Anne Protheroe around the extraordinary clock that towered above the displays in the inner room. Greene seized the moment.

"Richard, not to put too fine a point upon it, I have been anticipating your coming with some degree of urgency. I am confronted with a most challenging problem that is proving well beyond my small resources to deal with. Knowing of your interest, your studies of what you described as the 'other-worldly'. I wonder whether you will be prepared to assist me?"

"If I can, I most assuredly shall," came Davenport's quiet response. "What does this problem concern?"

Greene found himself looking nervously about him before he replied, *sotto voce*, "A grimoire, Sir. One so ancient, and – I greatly fear – so infamous that I am at a loss to know how to rid myself of it. It is believed by some at least to be a work known once as 'The Clavicule of Solomon' – perhaps you have heard of it? It is genuinely terrifying and more dangerous than I could have ever believed possible. It is a hateful thing."

Davenport's patrician features underwent a brief transformation as he gaped in sheer incredulity at his host

"Heard of it? My dear man, you are talking about one of the black legends of history – known only through poor copies, incomplete fragments. Why, its very existence has come to be increasingly doubted in the five hundred years since its disappearance. How..? When..?"

"May I ask you a couple of questions before I answer yours?" said Greene. "They are apposite to the explanation I shall then be happy to provide."

"Of course, my dear fellow. Please." responded Davenport eagerly.

"Have you ever had dealings with a Derby bookseller named Philbrigge?"

"I have indeed. He is one of a vanishingly small number of specialists in hermetic texts. His prices are high, but his connections must be extensive, given the sheer volume of material that he has had on offer over the ten years I have had dealings with him. May one enquire..?"

"One more question, if you will indulge me," insisted Greene: "Are you familiar with the name de Langton?"

Davenport failed to disguise the wrinkle of distaste with which he met the query. "That is not a name I expected to hear today, in these most pleasant surroundings, Richard. But yes, I am all too familiar both with that name and its most unpleasant associations. Not only has the apparently bottomless purse of the present bearer of it deprived me of certain objects I should dearly love to have owned, but to my certain knowledge has allowed him to acquire what I can only describe as obscenities whenever they have been offered. Vile works that I was offered and shunned, as would any collector of moral discrimination. They were concerned with the ritual corruption and abuse of children, with bestiality and other topics I shall not even name. He is a pariah, Richard, but of an ilk that attracts similarly debased company. To be avoided at all costs."

It was as he finished that Davenport appeared to have been struck by a sudden thought, but before either he or Greene could pick up on it, the Frenchman re-joined them with a grin of relief.

"We must continue this as soon as may be," said Greene, before smiling at his other guest once more.

"In this case we have one hundred and twenty-six specimens of wood, Monsieur Rousseau, including, I am proud to say, a sample of mulberry planted by our great poet William Shakespeare, whilst above it there is the horn of a narwhale, or sea unicorn."

So great had been the party's absorption in the endless cornucopia of exhibits, that the visit had, at last, to be curtailed as the dinner-hour at Erasmus Darwin's home grew ever nearer. With bilingual felicitations, exclamations of regret and repeated thanks, the visitors from Woollaton took their reluctant leave of the museum. Deciding they would enjoy the clemency of the day and accompanied by Anne Protheroe to direct them, they elected to walk the short distance to their next appointment, followed by their coach and overnight baggage.

Richard and Theodosia Greene promised to meet them there within the hour, and waved the happy group off before hurrying back upstairs for what the Apothecary insisted on calling 'a spot of spit-and-polish.'

"I have promised Thérèse the opportunity of making some private purchases in the morning, Richard, particularly as the excellent Mr Protheroe has extended an invitation to our Frenchman to attend the final rehearsal for a choral extravaganza in the Song School. Did you know of Jean-Jacques's 'Village Soothsayer' composition? – words and music, I am informed by a proud wife. Apparently, Louis the Fifteenth was so taken with it he offered our visitor a pension for life."

"Which he, of course refused, effortlessly turning royal favour into right-royal sulk," grinned her husband in response.

"How on earth did you know that?"

"I didn't, I simply guessed." said Greene. "Our visitor is as well known for his sheer perversity as he is for his inflammatory tendencies." He continued: "I am looking forward to dinner, particularly should Erasmus take issue with just about anything that Rousseau holds dear. It has been some time since we've had a firework display to enjoy."

"Talking of which," Theodosia said, "have you had the opportunity of broaching a certain matter with Richard Davenport? I saw you both in conversation upstairs."

"I did indeed, though we were interrupted before anything of substance could be discussed. He will help me, of that there's no doubt. Though how, or when, remains to be seen. If Jean-Jacques is otherwise engaged tomorrow morning, it will provide the perfect opportunity to continue where we left off."

"I pray that it does, Richard. This wretched business will not wait."

Although Polly Darwin had gone into the first stage of labour barely an hour before his guests' arrival, Erasmus Darwin was in no way distracted from the business of being their most genial and welcoming host.

"R…Robert Waring may be j…j…joining us for breakfast," he announced in explanation for his wife's absence, "so, p…pray do

not be d…disturbed by any d…distant shrieks. I would not w…
want you to th…th…think I have a madwoman c…confined t…
to the attic." With these words of reassurance he led the way to
dinner, prompting a degree of unspoken trepidation from those
guests shortly due to be spending the night beneath the same roof,
Davenport having translated their host's words with some alacrity.

The continuing company of Anne Protheroe, joined now by her
husband at the huge table, had been readily agreed by Darwin as
"encouraging d…dialogue on the d…distaff s…side and letting us
m…men g…get on with it.'"

Armed with his execrable if enthusiastic misuse of the French
language, he and Rousseau were soon doing just that, with Darwin
loudly extolling the little-known virtues of one James Burnett,
Lord Monboddo, to his guest. Greene watched with genuine
admiration as their host plunged into a description of Burnett's
ideas on evolutionary linguistics and the dilemma faced by any
spoken language in leaving not a trace of empirical evidence.
Rousseau appeared engrossed in the bombastic monologue,
nodding continually in what the Apothecary could only hope
was not an indication of approaching catatonia. Reassured
then by Davenport's active engagement, Greene happily joined
a conversation on the ubiquity of man's objects of desire: lust,
hunger and security.

By the time that a spectacular syllabub had been served and
many glasses of excellent wines consumed, even the hypothesis
of an ever-evolving human species, rather than as the one-off
creation of an all-powerful God, had ceased to scandalise those
of the company still functioning on a critical level. Even when
the ribald proposition of 'air-Baths' was floated by a more-than-
usually mischievous Darwin, every appearance of civilised debate
ensued concerning the regrettable incidence of disease resulting
from man's removal from a naturally unclothed primal state and
the deleterious effects of his lack of exposure to the extremes of
climate swing.

"Talking of which," announced Greene, after catching Theodosia's eye across the strewn table, "though fully clothed, you will be relieved to hear, we shall brave the extremes to take our leave, if you will forgive us, Erasmus. You may have a busy night ahead."

"As n…neither mm…midwife nor w…wet-nurse, Richard, my c…contribution shall be limited to b…billing and c…cooing at the appropriate m…moment. Namely, b…breakfast t…time."

As he waved them off from the gracious hall, he briefly took Theodosia's hand and said: "You have been the p…perfect ornament to a t…table of fascinating f…friends, my dear. Thank you so m…much for your delightful c…company."

"Why, Mrs Greene, I do believe you are blushing like a little maid from school," her husband teased, as they descended the gracious steps.

"The paying of compliments is an art, Richard," she replied tartly. "Perhaps you should take it up."

(33)

ITEM:

A Roman Bodkin in Glafs, greatly decompounded by
time; found at Wroxeter (Uriconium) in the County of
Salop. An ancient piece of Sculpture in Ivory, being a
reprefentation of a Man on the back of an Eagle.

Saddler Street. Sunday 1st June. Davenport arrived in the
company of Thérèse Rousseau, shortly after eleven o'clock, with
Richard Greene wishing he felt as clear-eyed and buoyant as did
his visitors. Within moments the Frenchwoman was immersed
in an esoteric world of cosmetics and particularities, conducted
by an Apothecary's wife confident that in the absence of Anne
Protheroe's translational skills the lingua franca of femininity
would suffice. Before retreating up into the museum realm,
Davenport had assured both ladies that he would be within hailing
distance should any insuperable linguistic problems emerge.

With considerable reluctance, his host had once again fetched
the iron box from its garden concealment, displaying it again on
the table it had scarred so irreparably. Due to its presence in the
innermost of the museum rooms, Henry Copeland now awaited
introduction in the outermost, the Apothecary having insisted
that the two men should meet, and that the soldier be privy to all
that was discussed or decided this morning. Once the formalities
were accomplished and Greene had described his old friend's all-
too recent experience after the viewing of the book and its box,
they went together through into the furthest room.

"It did that?" breathed Davenport as the damaged table was pointed out.

"Oh, that was amongst the least of its little tricks," replied Greene quietly. He pointed to the scarred doorframe. "That was where it was at its most spectacular. It came within a hairsbreadth of killing me."

"Please, start from the beginning, my friend. It already has the sound of a long and dark path you have chosen to tread."

"Chosen? No, not really. The truth is that I was foolish enough to believe that I had no choice. The attacks, the subterfuges of which this thing is capable are not restricted to the physical, Richard – that is what makes it so damnably dangerous. I was persuaded, one way or another, that unless I acted to save it, an invaluable antiquity was at immediate risk of destruction." He laughed mirthlessly. "If only I had known then what I realise now." Greene spread his hands, helplessly, "So, here is how it all began. You will recall that I asked if you knew the name de Langton, yesterday? Well..."

"And those Indian fish-hooks would actually have killed Colonel Copeland? You believe that?"

"The merest prick from them would have resulted in an infection so virulent that Theodosia can still scarcely bring herself to speak of its effects twenty years on."

"I can also attest to their dreadful lethality, Mr Davenport," said Copeland evenly, continuing. "Amongst the terrible deaths that I have seen inflicted by the tribes of the Iroquois – all of them cruel beyond reason – the effects of that specie of poison are like nothing imaginable."

"And the cabinet from whence they came..?" Greene pointed back into the other room. "Locked then as it is now. I have the sole key."

He pointed once more, to the long halberd restored to its position above the door. "Just as with that. Its fastenings, chain and hook, were untouched and yet it fell as if they had never existed."

Greene paused, then, as if momentarily unsure or unwilling to continue. He stretched out a hand to place lightly on Copeland's shoulder before continuing "Simultaneous with the visitation upon Harry, Theodosia too was attacked, made to revisit the worst and almost the last moment of her life – enacted when she was bound and utterly helpless in that room through there and on the verge of immolation."

Davenport stared in consternation as his host resumed his narration.

"In what could otherwise be dismissed as nothing more than a dreadful nightmare, a long-buried memory reawakened by recent events – there, too, was a physical element to it. Twenty years ago, with this good man at our sides, we three stood against a monstrous evil. Its perpetrator, stopped only by the grace of God, had first drugged my wife with ether before soaking her in lamp oil. For several hours after Theodosia's experience last week, the smell of both those substances hung in our bedroom air." Copeland nodded in wordless agreement.

"Allow me then to make a proposal," said the elderly man. "If you are prepared to show me what the box holds, given the form of protection you obtained from poor Philbrigge." He could not help but glance through the museum towards the distant landing. "Then I shall neither interfere with it, nor – given your earlier warning – speak of any course of action I might suggest. It should be removed and returned to wherever you have it in safe keeping before any discussion takes place. Are you agreeable to that?"

Greene nodded. With a sigh he removed the folded sheet from his pocketbook once more. "I had rather hoped never to be doing this again – but, of course, you must have sight of it, at least."

He pulled his chair forward, leaned in over the iron box and carefully enunciated the words of Aramaic. With the wooden blade inserted, the lid again opened effortlessly. No stench. No flies – not a single blue-black corpse within. The leather binding thongs were looped casually together across the half-concealed symbol of the seal.

"Dear Lord, Richard, you were right. That is a nipple. This is human skin," Davenport murmured. He reached for the spatula, but the Apothecary shocked them both by snatching it back. "No! You must not..."

He stopped, eyes wide, blinking, "Oh, forgive me, I don't know what..." Before he could continue, the iron lid lifted of its own accord and then slammed shut with such an incredibly percussive bang that they were both thrown violently back in their chairs, Greene's toppling backwards only stopped by his feet hitting the table edge.

They sat, frozen, gasping in incredulity. "That could have been my hand," Davenport said in a whisper, "taken off at the wrist."

Coming unsteadily to their feet they backed away. "Say nothing," said Green urgently. "Not yet."

He was certain that he caught the sound of buzzing, rising even as he spoke. "Downstairs; I shall lock the door below. Say nothing till we're safe below."

Once they had reached the parlour, the Apothecary poured them each a brandy with a shaking hand. He looked at the pale, drawn features of the visitor and simply shrugged with both hands eloquently spread. Copeland sat, impassive, studying their visitor.

"No, you did not exaggerate, my friends," said Davenport, responding to the unspoken question.

"In the netherworld of the occult there are as many forgeries, frauds and shameless fakers as there are stars in the night sky. It is a place of shadows and half-heard whispers that permit every form of charlatan, trickster and outright lunatic to claim that they alone possess the key of access to a hermetic sphere whose very existence is thought of as the stuff of legend and fairy-tale – to be scorned by any intelligent, right-thinking, God-fearing man. Amongst it all though, beneath the dross there exist fragments of scarcely believable antiquity, of untainted record and belief. That,"

– he pointed to the floor above – "astonishing though it may seem, can only be what you claimed."

"What I feared, Richard; not what I claimed. I wish to God I had not been proved correct." said Greene miserably.

"There is, I regret to say, more to this than one might suppose – however vivid an imagination that might require," said Davenport, grimly. "I am now convinced that you are under attack, in the most literal sense. It is not simply a matter of that," – he pointed upstairs – "manifesting a guardian in order to protect itself. There is an external force – I believe a demonic force – being summoned and despatched against you – or, I suspect, against whomsoever might now find themselves in possession of the object."

He continued, thoughtfully, "It might, however, explain a most unexpected and unwelcome sighting made by Jean-Jacques whilst in my company in Ashbourne some weeks ago. It might also explain what you described as the intrusion of a singularly unpleasant visitor into both your home and those of your clergy friends and the most recent attempt at burglary here."

The Apothecary leaned forward in rapt attention, a strained smile of puzzlement on his face. "In Ashbourne, you say?"

"Yes, unlikely though that may sound. Amongst his many other skills Jean-Jacques has an encyclopaedic memory, not least for faces, and he pointed out a tall, hard-faced man he swore he knew from Paris. Though I had never come across the fellow myself, the moment he mentioned the name, I too remembered both it and the foul circumstances of its notoriety. He calls himself de Rais – I see from your expression you recognise the name of the monster from whom he claims descent."

Greene nodded, silently, allowing his visitor to continue, "He and a dozen or more like him were self-proclaimed diabolists, enjoying - as they fondly believed – the favours and protection of a tranche of French nobility whose immersion in every form of perversion and debauchery has become a byword for all that is corrupt both in the royal court and in the so-called beau monde."

"Until that appalling affair of the child-murders came to light?" said Greene.

"Indeed, until their depravity could no longer be ignored or tolerated. Their éminence grise, a diseased creature of immense wealth called the Marquise de la Motte-Guyon lost her raddled head to the axe, while most of her circle – her coven – either fled into obscurity or were caught and hanged."

"Until that day with Jean-Jacques, I had believed that this de Rais was among the latter. I am certain I recall an account of his capture and execution in Nantes." He spread long-fingered hands. "I was mistaken in supposing him dead."

"But surely Jean-Jacques could not have been involved with such filth?" Greene asked in puzzlement, "So how..?"

"Oh, he has been courted by all and sundry in his peregrinations about Europe, Richard. All too often by just such as de Rais, credulous enough to believe the crazed accusations levelled at Rousseau's ideas, his questioning of so very much that is fundamental to religions of every complexion and the nature of our own humanity. They invariably get short shrift from him, but still seek him out like the carrion they are – forever prowling to sniff out some new dark star to feed upon. Fortunately, for as far as we know, de Rais is unaware of Jean Jacques' presence in Staffordshire, as, in fact, are most. My guest is not given to broadcasting his whereabouts, as you can imagine. Our friend believes that de Rais would kill him given the chance. With such a creature his utter humiliation at Jean-Jacques' hands would call for nothing less."

"So, you believe..?"

"From your own account, from de Rais' sighting and its proximity to that ghastly pile called Malbecq – added to what I know of its addled master – I am certain that this revenant has found new employment, Richard. He is not only a Satanist but a condemned murderer."

"And I thought things could not get any worse," said Greene

in little more than a whisper. Davenport, now visibly recovered, drained his brandy and managed a bright if not entirely convincing smile, "But, we shall now endeavour to improve them, my friend. Here is what I propose."

(34)

In the fore part of this Shelf, a neat piece of Carving in Box Wood, reprefenting the judgement of Paris. A Terminus, being the buft of a Lady in Bifket China. A Terminus of Heraclitus, in Terra Cotta, by the ingenious Mr Wedgwood of Etruria.

Saddler Street. Monday 2nd June. Returning from his afternoon rounds, Greene was surprised to be met at the door of the Apothecary by a most concerned-looking wife who hurried him through the busy shop and into his Consulting Room to the rear.

"James has returned from Ashbourne with news that you really must hear – particularly as it was first recounted in Harry's hearing. I have had the devil's own job in restraining him since then."

Before he could begin to question Theodosia, she continued, "I shall send him straight through to you, Richard, but I must attend to business in his absence. We've not drawn breath since you left and there was only the boy to help me until James returned."

It was only when Tillett entered some moments later that Greene remembered they had agreed to the shopman's late return from his visit to Ashbourne. He himself had been too busy with his Monday morning surgery to notice the absence. An ever-efficient wife had handed him his filled prescriptions and all the regular requirements of his home visits. He had then hurried out after a hasty lunch of cold pie brought to his desk by a disapproving Margery. Now, as closing time approached, it became immediately apparent that the long-serving James was not his usual, diffident self.

"It was him again, Mr Greene, I'll stake life upon it! Emmy described him to the life – there's no mistaking it!" Seeing the complete bewilderment on his employer's face, he took a deep breath and said, "I'm getting ahead of myself; it's that creature who came in here threatening us, Mr Greene. Him who went on to the Reverend Blomefield, and did the same, like."

The Apothecary only just stopped himself from asking how Tillett had known any of what had occurred between Lionel and the viciously aggressive intruder. Instead, with quiet urgency, he said, "You must explain what you are talking about, James. Kindly slow down and begin at the beginning. This is about Emmy? Your visit to her at Ashbourne?"

Tillett gulped, obviously marshalling his thoughts and trying to control his agitation. "It was late last Monday, Mr Greene, our Bower Day, just before Tomlin's was about to close – later than usual though, it was. In he comes, covered in blood, great scratches down his ugly face, she said, and him nursing a right bad wound under his coat. Wouldn't let her near him, not that she wanted to you understand, but when Mr Tomlin wanted Emmy to help with him, nearly had his head bitten off. Sent her packing before she could see what was up."

Greene just managed to contain himself, knowing he would have to let this come out at Tillett's speed and in his leaden fashion, or not at all.

"So it's only the next day as Mr Tomlin tells her that it took an hour of cleaning out and more than a dozen stitches – which Mr Tomlin didn't want to have to do in the first place, saying it was a proper doctor's job and not his – that she finds out it was a dog bite. A big dog's bite an' all, what with the damage it had done. Could have lost the use of his arm, Mr Tomlin reckoned, it was that bad, and still could if it didn't get looked after properly, like." He paused, suddenly awkward, before nodding in the direction of the garden and blurting: "And what with whatever happened out there to the Colonel's poor beast."

"So, what happened then?" pleaded the Apothecary, having no intention of permitting any form of discussion about the unmarked grave down by the stable.

"Fellow's not fit to ride on, he says so himself. Put up in the town overnight, saying he'd send on for a coach to collect him and pay Tomlin's bill for the treatment and the drugs and all. Came late next day. Settled in cash by the coachman, no sight of his nibs at all. Must've been taken off home then."

"To where? Did Tomlin know?" Greene demanded, a new urgency in his question.

"Oh, right enough, Mr Greene. I wrote it down, from Emmy, like. She found it in the accounts and orders, like." He reached into a pocket and withdrew a folded slip. "Has a monthly order for enough raw opium to kill a..."

"The address, James, if you will," Greene cut in tersely, biting his tongue as to the professional proprieties of any medical man being free and easy with a patient's – any patient's – confidential matters.

"'Marlbeck', or something like that. Old ruin of a place up on the moors. Middle of nowhere, Mr Tomlin reckons. Wouldn't send her up there when this fellow Ray wanted his coach asummoning. Must have thought they'd all jump to it, but Mr Tomlin wouldn't on account of..."

"This place you mentioned? The fellow is the owner?"

"Oh, no; owned by a Mr Langdon or some-such, Mr Greene. Not that he's ever seen out, apparently. Not for years, Mr Tomlin reckons. A right hermit, like his father before him, Mr Tomlin says."

"Thank you, James; I get the picture," said the Apothecary as the shop doorbell rang yet again. "You'd best get back to business.

It sounds as if you'll be missed out there. Thank you for all you've told me." As Tillett left, Greene called after him, "And Emmy, James? How is she?"

"Well and happy, Sir, and thank you. Mr Tomlin was made up

to get the Mistress's kind words, now that Emmy's settled into place."

"Indeed," thought Greene, "and one way and another Harry and I shall drop in for a word with your Mr Tomlin – about finding another place."

It was as if the thought had summoned the soldier. Entering, after a cursory knock, Copeland sat down heavily in the newly vacated seat.

"So, it sounds like we've got the black-hearted bastard, Richard. It's only a pity that poor old Jack couldn't have finished the job himself. Now, what I propose to do is…"

"Whoah, Harry!" exclaimed Greene in alarm, "I hope you are not contemplating what I think you are? 'An eye for an eye' is one thing, but should that thing involve a dog, then I'd feel on safer ground with, 'vengeance is mine saith the Lord.' You can't just take the law into your own hands."

"Richard, you heard Davenport, only yesterday, talking about the aberration that is calling itself de Rais. He is a dead man walking. I shall do anything in my power to end the walking part. I learned a long time ago that there are creatures on this earth that are no more than husks masquerading as men. Without exception they have forfeited the right to life by the vileness of what they carry within them. So, spare me the homilies, my friend, you of all men know how disease must be fought and eradicated; it is not a matter of choice."

"No, Harry," Greene replied hotly. "There is choice and it must involve who shall carry out that treatment, that eradication! Otherwise who shall not set himself up as judge, jury and executioner? Who, or what, gives you or me that right, however aggrieved or sinned-against we may be? That way lies barbarism and I shall be no party to it."

"What gives that right, Richard, is natural justice. There are occasions – rare occasions, I grant you – when it must be accepted as the supreme power, of that neither you nor I can have the slightest doubt. Surely to God you must see that after what we have endured together?"

It was as if the Apothecary deflated suddenly. He gave a shudder of resignation, of bone-weariness, before saying: "All I know at this moment, Harry, is that I am desperate to be rid of that godforsaken thing out there. If you are still prepared to accept Davenport's offer of his coach on Friday, and accompany me in its safe delivery to him, the cup will be passed. He feels completely confident of both the security that will await its arrival, and of his course of action when the time arrives. I had very much hoped we might see this through together, but if you are fixed upon going after de Rais..." He tailed off, helplessly.

"Oh, for the love of God, Richard, do you really believe I would leave you to finish this alone? Yes, I shall pursue that excrescence and, one way or another, see that he receives the worst I can visit upon him, but not at the price of our friendship. And – if we are going to wax biblical about the situation: Could you have doubted that, Oh ye of little faith?"

"Very well, Harry," said an Apothecary hiding his embarrassment with sudden briskness and renewed purpose. "We're agreed then that we shall travel to Woollaton with horses in tow, unburden ourselves at the first possible opportunity and accept lunch. I then propose we ride on, put up at Ashbourne's Green Dragon for the night, having elicited what added information we can from the druggist Tomlin. Davenport assured me he is not made of stern stuff and will be unlikely to resist a frontal assault concerning Malbecq and its denizens – even though a certain young woman in his employ reckons her master lives in fear of de Rais' visits, if not his coin."

"In that case, said Copeland, once returned here, I shall intend to take the Monday coach for the North, spend several weeks repairing my neglected fences, evicting tenants and claiming my rights upon their hapless daughters. I shall then return in time to join you for our return to Woollaton for the twenty-fourth, as

Davenport so eloquently persuaded us, before concluding other business as I see fit."

"Every inch the squire, if I may say so, Harry. You will raise the tone of our venture."

His unspoken gratitude knew no bounds. The Summer solstice, with its Midsummer Fire to celebrate the annual triumph of light would see an end to the blight that lay upon them.

It had been Davenport's idea – his inspiration – and Greene gave thanks for it.

Unspoken thanks.

ITEM:

In large DRAWERS, marked with Numeral Letters. IX. A large
and fine Collection of Lythophites, or impreffions of Plants in
Iron Ore. Presented by Mrs Darby of Coalbrookdale in the
County of Salop. X. Nautilus, Ludus Helmontii, Pectenites,
Centroniae. Auftracites, with a variety of Shells and Petrifactions.

Woollaton Hall. Friday 6ᵗʰ June. On the Thursday evening, prior
to their departure, an invitation for the Apothecary and Copeland
to 'a bachelor supper' had been delivered by Elspeth Blomefield.
Sensing a momentary hesitation in Greene's open features, she
said, "Though he would never admit such a thing, Richard, Lionel
has been missing you." Chiding gently, she added, "You and Harry
seem to have been much taken up over the past couple of weeks, a
fact made all too apparent by the amount of time the dear man has
been spending under my feet. You would do us both a service if
you can find the time when Theodosia and I are at the Box Club."

Smiling at this, one of their oldest and dearest friends, he
replied, "Of course, nothing would give me more pleasure, Elspeth.
As is too often the case I have become overly preoccupied with
day-to-day demands to the detriment of the things – and the
people – I value most."

"Well, be he thing or person, and sometimes I am less than
certain on that score, Lionel will be delighted," she replied,
pecking him lightly upon the cheek. "I do hope he has not been

so more than usually volatile, that you have felt the need to keep him at arm's length whilst you draw breath, Richard. He does so treasure your friendship – in his own peculiar way."

"Have no fear on that score, my dear," said Greene, praying that his guilt was not apparent to this visitor's prescient grey eyes. "We shall continue leading each other astray, much as always, especially now that my thoughtless negligence has been pointed out. It should not have been necessary, but thank you for it."

It was only as he went about his business that he admitted to himself that in the redoubtable company of Harry Copeland over the past week, Lionel Blomefield's volatility had, indeed, ruled him out of the increasingly grim preoccupations that had come to dominate the Apothecary's days and nights. Yet another pressing reason for tomorrow's ride, he told himself, as if he needed one.

For all that this vehicle lacked the ponderous dependability of Erasmus Darwin's innovatory axle system, the superbly sprung chassis of Woollaton's best made for that rarest of experiences – a comfortable journey wherein the twenty-five miles to Davenport's grand house slipped away with the minimum of heart-stopping lurches and stomach-churning bumps through the summer country-side.

Strapped to the rear, swaddled in old blankets and packed tightly within a battered travelling trunk, the iron box and its contents had been hurried from the garden gate onto Bore Street where the coach awaited, then stowed securely aboard to the heartfelt relief of all who knew the contents. Amongst them, Lionel Blomefield watched the removal with none of his usual insouciance, his lips moving in what might even have been a prayer.

Becoming aware of his old friend's raised eyebrows, he responded to the wordless query with, "Can't be too careful, Richard. Just bear that in mind. God speed." He waved a hand and quietly walked away.

As they had drawn up in front of the pillared portico of

Woollaton Hall, Davenport climbed aboard to join them while the coach was driven to the rear of the large house, past the commodious outbuildings and then along an unmade track that led to a rocky knoll set amongst a stand of oaks. Here they dismounted, watched as the heavy trunk was unfastened and lowered to the ground, and waited until the coach was being driven cautiously back along the rutted track towards the house.

"Whilst I may yet face revolt on the kitchen front over the next couple of weeks, it has been impressed upon my staff that the icehouse is beyond the pale and must not be opened for any reason. As far as all and sundry are concerned, we are conducting a scientific experiment regarding snakes, their habitat and their diet. Woollaton has more than its fair share of adders, so it is just the kind of behaviour to be expected from a wealthy squire with too much time on his hands."

"Are you taking notes, Harry?" enquired Greene, already feeling the crushing weight of responsibility slipping away. Copeland grinned in response, picking up on the tangible relief at seeing an end approaching to his friend's dark road.

Between them, he and the Apothecary lifted the weighty trunk and waited as Davenport ducked in through the low, iron-strapped door. They paused as he lit a torch from a canvas-wrapped bundle stacked in a large niche behind the jamb, before beckoning them in. A ground-level antechamber gave way to a steeply sloping cobbled passageway that brought them to a cavernous crypt fashioned deep beneath the knoll, the temperature plunging the further their echoing steps took them down.

The eerie dance of flame upon rock walls seemed to have led them to another world, a place untouched by light, by warmth, by life itself. It suddenly seemed more appropriate than anything the two bearers could have imagined. Lit by Davenport's torch, an altar-like stone slab stood amidst the stacked ice-blocks.

"There, I believe," said Davenport, his voice flattened in the sepulchral gloom. They laid their burden down and stood back for a moment of strange solemnity before following the light-bearer back up into the world of summer. With a reassuring crash the heavy door swung closed behind them and they stood, blinking against the brightness of the day.

"Lunch, I think, gentleman, and a glass raised to a job well done."

They walked back towards the terrace on which the grand house sat, as Greene tried to banish thoughts of premature congratulations. This, surely, was a day to savour. He must strive to regain the habit, he reminded himself.

To Greene's relief, their host announced that Jean-Jacques could not be disturbed from his labours and that Thérèse was indisposed. Whilst he had found the former utterly fascinating in his driven convictions, his passionate originality, and his wife a charming if somewhat detached presence, he was glad that he would not be forced to patrol a social situation wherein the soldier's well-tried patience would be severely put to the test. Not least, he relished the prospect of his first opportunity to glimpse at least some of the contents of Davenport's library.

They dined most convivially on Dove salmon and a dessert creation that would not – could not – be recreated without benefit of an icehouse; a fact tactfully passed over when the compliments to their unseen chef were paid. Copeland and Davenport regaled each other with self-deprecating tales of gaffes and social blunders made with the acquisition of their respective estates, the Apothecary an appreciative audience for speakers entirely devoid of pretensions, both sharing an intense love of the English countryside.

Laughingly, their host declared, "Here at Woollaton I suspect that I am perceived as little more than a parvenu by the crustier relics of Derbyshire and Staffordshire society, having been so unspeakably vulgar as to actually purchase the estate."

"Whilst stooping to share your table with trade would be

the final nail in one's coffin, would it not?" added Greene with a mischievous smile on his round face.

"Oh, social death, without doubt," responded Davenport, obviously delighted by Greene's sally. "Such relics as you describe are alive and well in my little city, Richard. You must come again so that we may avoid them together."

Davenport went on to describe a Cheshire family that had the decency to date back to one Orme de Dauneporte in 1086. "We became Davenports with the gaining of the hereditary title of Magistrate Serjeants of Macclesfield Forest around the middle of the fourteenth century – powers of life and death now long since relinquished I am relieved to say."

Greene avoided the soldier's eye.

Copeland responded with accounts of life on his beloved moors and what he declared to be the most impassive country-folk on the face of the earth.

"My most immediate neighbours are two brothers surviving from a trio that had farmed their dale for longer than anyone can remember; both must now be in their late eighties, as much a part of the landscape as the trees. These are folk who brought their deceased sibling on a bier to the manse, expecting the vicar, poor long-suffering man, to leave his table to bury him so they could get straight back to the harvest. "'But a grave will have to be dug', protested the hapless man, 'the sexton summoned'.'Did that earlier when our oud lad first got took queer', came the response. 'Bugger's waiting on us, your sup'll keep'."

The listeners roared with laughter, encouraging Copeland to finish by saying, "I swear that if they were to be confronted with The Second Coming and The Heavenly Host their response would be, 'Appen'."

To Greene's well-concealed consternation, the hours ticked convivially past until he could contain himself no longer. "Richard, will you think me an absolute boor if I ask to examine your library before we take our leave. We were to be in Ashbourne before closing time, but our errand will have wait until the morning now, by the look of it."

"May one enquire as to its nature? I had not intended to delay you, but if there is something I can do?"

As soon as their purpose was explained, Davenport exclaimed, "I shall not tolerate the thought of your spending a night in some flea-pit hostelry when I have an indecently large home at your disposal. You, Mr Greene, can gorge on my shelves to your heart's content whilst you, Colonel Copeland shall continue to enthral me with your exploits!"

Before his two visitors could respond he clapped elegantly manicured hands together and exclaimed: "Capital! That's decided then. Now, Richard you know the way to your heart's desire, though be warned, much of what might catch your eye is the work of charlatans and self-deceiving fools, collected for their sheer inanity if nothing else. For each of the few real gems you might discern, you'll find a dozen born of blind, benighted ignorance dressed up with signs and symbols to bedazzle fools. So, my friend, enjoy your ramble through my magical domain whilst Harry and I shall endeavour to entertain each other as old bores do. We shall leave all discussion of a certain pile up on the moors – and its godforsaken residents – till late enough that we do not spoil a splendid day."

(36)

In a Closet near the Fire Place A large collection of Foffils
and Marine productions, viz. A Cornu Ammonis, fourteen
inches in diameter – a large and perfect Brain Stone – A
Nautilus, fplit open and polifhed – several plates of foffil Shells,
Spars, Corals, Stalactites, Sea Fern, Sea Weeds, & etc.

Ashbourne. Saturday 7ᵗʰ June. Even before their mid-morning
arrival in the bustling streets of the small town, Greene and
Copeland travelled with the disheartening knowledge that
the object of their enquiries was well beyond the reach of law.
Candlelit conversation with their host into the small hours had
served only to confirm that no evidence remained of the Palace
break-in, no crime – other than repugnant discourtesy – had been
committed in either the Apothecary or St Mary's, no bookseller
remained to speak of coercion, no witnesses could attest to the
identity of the dog-killer, the would-be burglar of Saddler Street
garden premises. The fact that that his identity, his principal and
their motive had become transparently obvious to the flagging
talkers failed to alter the unpalatable truth. Whilst de Rais and
his employer remained an ever-present threat in every real sense,
no solid grounds for judicial action existed. None present in the
warm glow of Woollaton's security could know how soon this
would change.

"Neither the fact of that creature de Rais' sentence of death
– nor the unguessable means by which he survived the French

hangman – could hold sway in an English court, whilst every other fact, if they can even be so named, will be judged as being entirely circumstantial in the eyes of the law."

"Hence, 'Blind Justice', one supposes," the Apothecary had added morosely. "So, essentially, nothing legal can be done before our enemies – and that is the only term for them – are good and ready to act against us, once more. This time by directing their malign attentions to one of us rather than to a hapless dog. Can any one of us doubt what that revenant is capable of? Why, oh, why must we wait on the book's destruction, Richard? Can we not have done and put an end to this in the morning?"

Woollaton's master had been at his most persuasive: "We three take no convincing about the potential lethality of that object out there," – he nodded towards the parkland beyond the well-shuttered windows of the grand house – "which is why I so firmly believe that we must invoke the invincible power of light against it. At no time in our year is that more potent than at the Summer solstice – I had thought we were in complete agreement on this?"

"Oh, I suppose we are, Richard, it's just…" he gave up, wanly. "All I am fit for is bed, but I know I shall not sleep easily until we have destroyed it."

Greene climbed wearily to his feet. "Please do not think me the worst kind of ingrate, Richard; both your hospitality and the solution you have proposed are more welcome than I can say. I am just not fit for anything more."

His companions watched him take his leave before they, too, admitted defeat. "I have had many occasions to wonder how great a heart can beat within so small a frame, Richard," said the soldier. "Our Apothecary should never be underestimated."

Davenport had insisted they take advantage of his coach once more, it being despatched on a variety of errands to the market town. "You'll have a long-enough ride home as it is," their host had insisted. They had readily agreed. Their arrival at Tomlin's shop, however, was to a confounded druggist attempting to cope unaided with a day's busy trade.

"It was only a telling-off, Mr Greene – you know how it can be with these youngsters. Need a bit of putting in their place now and then, and at the end of the day it was the dratted girl's fault anyway. Anyone would think it were mine! Still learning the ropes, but thinks she knows it all, already. High-handed, I call it, frankly, but I'm being made to take the blame."

Tomlin spread stubby-fingered hands in an appeal for understanding from his impassive visitors.

"So, what exactly happened? Again, if you please, Mr Tomlin? I fear you lost me along the way."

Now that they had the small, well-ordered premises to themselves for the moment, the druggist took a deep breath and began again: "Some weeks back, I took an order from the French lady staying with our Mr Davenport..." – only moments earlier he had watched the two men alight from the immediately recognisable Woollaton coach scarcely yards from his door – "... who is of course a most excellent customer of mine – for sugar-cane, it was. Raw cane for her husband. The French gentleman." They waited patiently. "Likes to chew it as he writes, apparently. No accounting for taste, but these foreign gentlemen," He paused, eyebrows raised, but gaining no response continued: "Well, anyway, it went onto my regular Bristol order, which, in fact, arrived last Thursday. So, I should have been able to hand it over to your coachman, just now, like he was expecting me to, but couldn't because Emmy had already sold it all, the whole blessed box! And not just that –without a by-your-leave, but rat-poison, too. Something that only I ever handle myself, as you can imagine, Mr Greene.

"And the little minx came straight out with it. 'But you weren't here, Sir', she said, 'and I know that Mr Langdon, from Malbeck, is one of our regular customers, so what's the harm, Mr Tomlin? The coachman paid us there and then. I knew where to look for the prices in that red ledger, like you showed me'. Then she burst into tears when I told her off and she just ran out. That was yesterday and I've not seen her today. What's to do Mr Greene? I'd thought she could be trusted."

"She can be trusted to return, of that I'm sure, Mr Tomlin," replied Greene with hard-won diplomacy in the face of the druggist's petulance, "but had an order for sugar cane been placed by Malbecq? How else would they have known you stocked it? It is a rarely requested item, even in Lichfield."

"I've been just too busy to wonder," replied Tomlin with some asperity, but even as he spoke, a thought seemed to occur to him, a frown creasing his plump features: "Oh, that's it of course! That man Ray was in my Consulting Room when I came back and began serving Mr Davenport and Mrs Rousseau, the French lady. I didn't even know he was there until they had gone. He'll have heard the order being placed, for billing to Woollaton Hall, the cheeky devil."

"And he'll have heard the lady's name too, no doubt," thought the Apothecary, grimly. "The name of a man who'd publicly humiliated him. A man he'd surely kill if he could."

"And the rat poison? Is that a regular purchase?" interposed the soldier.

"First time for that particular gent," said the druggist tartly. "He enquired of its availability as he was leaving on that same occasion. Business I could well do without, to be honest, gentlemen. Quite possibly the rudest man I've had the misfortune to serve, but from what I've heard, when you live in a godforsaken ruin like that old place, I'm surprised they're not ordering it by the cart-load."

"About his injuries, Tomlin? James Tillett explained that you had taken him, us, into your professional confidence."

Tomlin puffed visibly with self-importance, rising to Greene's prompt.

"We medical men cannot be too careful of course, Mr Greene, but there was something most untoward in his refusal to allow

Emmy to assist, or for me to call in a surgeon such as yourself. Not that I couldn't manage..."

"His injuries?" repeated the Apothecary with fraying patience.

"Dog bites. Clawed badly too, Mr Greene. Must have been a real brute, huge jaws to inflict the wound I treated. It took a dozen stitches."

The Apothecary resolutely refused to look at his silent companion, as Tomlin continued: "That old ruin is teeming with them, great mastiffs, from what folk say. One of them, it'll have been, 'as turned on him. Must be one of the reasons that the place is avoided. You'll not find an Ashbourne trader who'll deliver there."

"But if one wanted to find the house? It appears on no maps we know of."

"Well, why would it? Crumbling great ruin, they say, all alone in its dale. No village, nothing. I can draw some sort of a map, though, if that's what you're asking. Only general at the end, you understand, but from here up to the Stones and then a few miles further I can help. Though, why?"

"The Stones? Would they be what's called Arbor Low? It's many years since I visited them but have passed them many times on my way over to Bakewell."

"The same, Mr Greene. Lord knows there are precious few landmarks up there. I'm guessing that Malbeck would be about five miles north by west, deeper into the moor, as the crow flies."

"Then if you'll oblige us with what directions you can offer, we'll take up no more of your time. Does the Malbecq coach visit the town with any regularity?"

"Fridays, regular as clockwork, Mr Greene – though fortunately only once a month or so with that particular gentleman aboard."

"He comes for the regular drug order that you told Tillett about? The opium?"

"And hashish, too, Mr Greene. For scientific experimentation, he said, when once I enquired. For his principal, Mr Langdon."

"I do believe that the only experimentation going on there is with the boundaries of their sanity, Mr Tomlin. Do you think it prudent to continue aiding and abetting such long-term abuse?"

Tomlin bridled at that. "It is scarcely my responsibility to enquire into the use or abuse of my merchandise, Mr Greene. I am running a business here."

"Of course," replied Greene, smiling blandly. "And business is business after all, Mr Tomlin. We medical men must stick together, must we not?"

"Indeed, we must, Mr Greene, indeed we must."

"Well, thank you for your assistance," said the Apothecary, folding the sketch-map into a capacious pocket. "I feel sure that Emmy will shortly reappear, full of contrition. The young seeking to please us by showing their initiative can be so trying."

"Indeed, Mr Greene, indeed."

As Copeland and Greene crossed to where Woollaton's coachman had tethered their horses, they had no way of knowing that fifteen hours earlier and less than a hundred yards from where they mounted, that same young woman, furious with the unfairness of life, freckled face still wet with tears, had been recognised and discreetly followed.

Some five minutes later, as she made her way down the broad street towards the parish church and her lodgings close by, a coach had pulled in beside the raised pavement and a door swung open in tacit invitation. Even before her better judgement could be invoked, or the half-glimpsed figure of the coachman at her side registered, a choking, gaseous reek swamped her nose, her eyes and gasping mouth. As numbing terror flooded her senses, her last thought was, 'Sweet oil of vitriol. Never inhale this'. Tomlin's words of wisdom were lost as the darkness crashed in.

De Rais had never been a man drawn to country life or to the healthful benefits of fresh air and the pleasures of nature, but earlier that morning had seized the opportunity of the coach's regular outing down to the small town. Even stiff with pain, anything to escape the sick-room fetor, the claustral gloom of the Priory; worse, by far, the constant needs and pawings of its raddled owner. De Langton's patronage – even in his ceaseless pain, he smirked at the thought – and his ever-accessible purse had provided a welcome bolthole when most needed. That time though, was fast coming to its end.

The skeletal husk now so utterly dependent on his pipe and his pathetic belief in de Rais' affections and loyalty, was fading day by day, sustained solely by his demented obsession with the acquisition of a book. A book he claimed as his, and his alone, brought forth from darkness by the power of fate, a book to remake all his bitter, thwarted life, make good his wasted, child-like limbs and dwindled lust.

And suddenly, right here and now, in the chance sighting of a freckled girl, looking as if she bore the troubles of the world on her small shoulders, striding out alone along the barely peopled street, appeared the means towards a longed-for end. The wretched book for its wretched would-be master, and release from the half-life up on those wretched moors where winds seemed like assassins sent to prey upon the endless nights, on this victim trapped within the age-stained walls. He would be done with it all – he saw it clearly now, and laughed his ruined, rasping laugh.

She lay there like a crumpled doll, her red-gold hair spilling out across the cushioned seat, a blindfold knotted, grubby against her milk-white skin, slim wrists pinioned in her lap.

"Drive on."

(37)

In a deep set gilded frame, two ancient martial figures,
sleeping, nicely carved of Nottingham alabaster, still in
their paint. Doubtless remnants of a larger figure group
broken from an Easter Sepulchre by zealots.

Saddler Street. Wednesday 11ᵗʰ June. It was as if a cloud had
passed, a dark foreboding to which none could put a name, gone
just like the padlock on the bake-house door.

The knowledge shared between husband and wife that a blight
had been removed from their lives seemed to add a zest, the thrill
of new beginnings, to the daily round. Both found themselves
revelling in the simple normalities of shop and home, even with
the departure of the man who, once again, had come to seem a
part of all they valued most. He would be back, he'd said, in good
time for the return to Woollaton and all that it entailed. It was on
that evening, though, the day of their old friend's departure, that
the dreams began.

To begin with, they seemed entirely natural, the perfectly
explicable result of a chance encountered scrap. John Jackson,
printer and bookbinder of Saddler Street, the fount of all inky
wisdom in their long acquaintance, whose press had produced
each and every printed sheet to do with catalogues, notices,
announcements and invitations for the museum over the previous
twenty-six years, had presented himself shortly before closing-
time, fairly seething with uncharacteristic excitement.

Viewing this normally most unflappable of tradesmen fidgeting for the Apothecary's attention as her husband served the day's final customer, Theodosia said brightly: "John, may I be of assistance? Richard may be some minutes yet."

"Something to show him, Mrs Greene. Something a bit special, could be..."

"Oh, I've seen inky fingers before, though probably not as un-scrubbable as those," came her husband's voice, as he waved off the departing shopper. Grinning, the Apothecary came over to them. "What's to do, John? Ants in your pants?"

The badinage ended just as soon as Greene could extract spectacles from a waistcoat pocket and peer, frowning with attention, at the wrinkled scrap held out on the printer's hand.

"Mmm, thought you might be interested. Found it used as packing in a binding I'm remaking. Old as the hills if you ask me. Tell me what you think it is, then I'll tell you."

Just by the feel of the laid paper the Apothecary could immediately sense its age, but as he deciphered the convoluted gothic script of a torn heading, the remaining half of an illustration beneath it and a single complete paragraph above a torn, largely indecipherable line, he gasped with delight, "Oh, John, what have you found?"

"That's what I'm asking you, Mr Museum-Keeper," came the smug response. "I reckon I know what it is, but do you?"

A mouthful of bad teeth grinned at the Apothecary's absorption.

"I believe I do," said the small man triumphantly: "It's by Wynkyn de Worde, isn't it? Malory's 'Le Morte D'Arthur'? Printed with Caxton! Oh, this is simply wonderful!" He tested the texture of the paper once more. "And this is William Tate's paper, too! The first ever English papermaker, can you credit it? Late fifteenth century if it's a day! I can make out that the header, complete, should read, 'The Seconde Boke' and under what is left of the illustration is clear, 'Here foloweth the seconde boke of that noble prynce king Arthur'. The rest is scarcely preserved. I think it says, 'of a damoysell which came', and here it says, 'sworde'. And at least part of the illustration, too. It must be Arthur, drawing that sword from the scabbard held by the lady at his side. That's the lot, but by heaven, John, what a find! Rare as a red hen's teeth!"

The printer grinned his alarming grin once more, "Suppose you'd better put it upstairs then, along with all the other bits and pieces. You wouldn't want me lighting the fire with it, would you?"

So, when the first dream was still a hazy memory that following morning, the fact that it had involved a sword, a stone, and various fast-disappearing knightly images, came as no surprise to a museum-keeper relishing his latest acquisition.

It was only after another night, another half-remembered dream of a sword, followed by a third, this one involving repeated visits to a lake, a sword, and an inexplicable sense of loss, of apprehension, as he awoke, that the image began to play on his mind, like it or not, during the busy waking hours that followed. He could scarcely have imagined the significance it was about to acquire.

Shortly before noon, as he was washing his hands following the departure of the morning's last patient from his Consulting Room, he became aware of a voice raised in alarm from the shop, and the sound of rapidly approaching footsteps down the pamment-tiled corridor to his door.

"You can't just…" he heard the shopman exclaim, but before he could finish, a voice he immediately recognised as Tomlin's shouted, "Out of my way, Tillett. You of all people must hear this, too! Greene! Mr Greene! I must speak with you."

In annoyance that instantly became consternation at the sight of the wild-eyed, dishevelled druggist, Greene ushered both men into the room, firmly closing the door behind them. "What on earth is going on, Tomlin? James?"

"Dammit, Sir, that is what I should be asking you!" shouted Tomlin, throwing down a crumpled wrapping onto the table between them. "What do you make of this?"

The Apothecary opened it to reveal several locks of red-gold hair. Unmistakable locks of red-gold hair. Tillet gave a gasping moan at the sight of them, shrinking back into his chair. Now, tears springing into his bulbous eyes, Tomlin drew a folded sheet from his coat and threw it down to join the sight that was transfixing both his listeners.

"This came with it. So, tell me Sir, just what is going on? Is it some frightful jape at my expense?"

Scrabbling for his spectacles, Greene grabbed up the paper and read the scrawled contents with mounting horror. "Oh, Sweet Jesu, no." he breathed.

> *Tomlin*
> *If you or anyone who cares for her hope to see the girl again you*
> *will take this to Greene in Lichfield and be certain he reads it.*
> *He must retrieve that which is sought and bring it to you*
> *within twenty-four hours.*
> *You will be contacted with instruction of where and when it is*
> *to be delivered to me by you and you alone.*
> *She will be free when I have it.*
> *If you disobey me or seek out help I shall know.*
> *She will die but not quickly.*

Tillett gaped in incomprehension, as the Apothecary repeated the message as if to convince himself of its contents. "But how on earth could he or anyone know where..?" he began, speaking to himself, but got no further, seeing the expressions of shock and outrage on the face of his listeners.

Before either of them could speak, Greene said, "James, this is the work of that foul boor who accosted you, here, those few weeks ago, seeking to gain access to the museum. Mr Tomlin, you know him as the brute whom you call Ray. I have only recently discovered more about this vile creature but had no reason, then, to share it with you. I shall not insult your intelligence by making light of this, James, of the terrible danger Emmy has been unwittingly placed in. This man will stop at nothing to acquire a book of great value that only recently passed through my hands. He has somehow learned of the connection between that dear girl and me, us, here in Lichfield, although he seems aware the object is no longer in my possession."

"She was in the shop, our Emmy, when he came in and made such a scene. He must have spotted her that day and then recognised her at yours, Mr Tomlin," Tillett blurted, looking beseechingly between his listeners. "But she'll be all right, won't she, Mr Greene? You'll make sure of that, won't you? Just get him what he wants and then he'll…" – he stopped as the horror of realisation dawned on him – "…But if she knows who he is, then…" He crumpled in his seat as the first convulsive sob shook his narrow shoulders.

"I shall do immediately what is required, James, have no fear on that score. The blackguard will never know it, but we shall not be without assistance. Of that I promise you." He turned to the ashen-faced druggist, "The object will be brought to you, just as he has ordered, Mr Tomlin. I shall leave as soon as may be, to collect it. We shall, no doubt, be watched, so follow the instructions to the letter; speak of this to no-one, and we shall then see what is to be done. James, you must trust me completely in this," he added, attempting reassurance where he felt nothing more than sickening uncertainty. "Mrs Greene will be depending completely on you in my absence. It will be best that no word of this reaches Emmy's mother. She would be worried to distraction to little point. Your girl will be restored to you, to you all." He took in the attentive druggist as he spoke. "I give you my solemn word. This has all gone too far by half."

"Mr Tomlin, it will be best you return to Ashbourne and I shall join you at the earliest possible moment. James, on my wife's return will you explain that I have been called urgently away and am unlikely to return until sometime tomorrow." He looked at the trembling man and gripped his shoulders firmly. "We, you and

I, must be strong for Emmy now, you understand? No word of this to Mrs Greene; you agree?" He knew the miserable nod of assent was the best he was going to get. "Good man, we'll see this through together."

He was hurrying upstairs when he remembered the gun: Copeland's superb rifle. The soldier had opted to leave it until his return, on Davenport's promise of a fine day's shooting at Woollaton once their business was done. He collected it from the cupboard in the guest bedroom, momentarily heartened by its heft and balance. It was only then that the thought struck him – the dreams remembered when least expected – the veil torn aside – a terrible clarity that seemed to freeze his blood. The force of it was such that he sank down onto the freshly made bed, breathless with understanding, "Excalibur, oh Sweet Lord, how could I have missed it?" The knight, Bedivere, charged with the destruction of the magical sword. The wounded, dying king, Arthur, unable to move, despatching his most trusted knight to carry out the task that he could not; to destroy the sword that had won him his kingdom, to hurl it down into the fathomless depths of Dozmary Pool. Not once, not twice the knight fails in his task, incapable of destroying what he knows to be a blade unlike any that the world had ever seen. Not once, but twice, returning to the fading king to say it had been done. Sent back, each time, told not to fail, told not to let the blade's magic overcome his reason. Until – at last – he somehow finds the strength to withstand its lure – its fatal glamour – to carry out the final act. Only then is Excalibur drawn down into the haunted depths and lost forever to the greedy sight of man.

The Apothecary saw it now, with eerie clarity. Davenport, the bibliophile, collector par excellence of 'otherworldly texts', persuaded by a siren voice, a whisper borne upon the wind, 'just one brief peep, one careful glance at what this ill-famed book contains, at what this icon of black legend might hold'. How could he not, now it had come into his hands?

Why should he not, just once, before it was too late. Before it was too late. No, a short walk, a well-oiled lock, a candle's light. Who'd know? Who'd care? Was it not his own icehouse, his land, all in his care? Was he not master of his will?"

"Oh, Richard, what have you done? It's how they know that the book is no longer here: *he must retrieve that which is sought.* You have not been able to resist it, have you? Not one of us was, so why should you have been, poor foolish man? And by opening it, a black beacon lit, a summoning begun, the re-awakening of what lurks within." Only then did he realise he had been speaking aloud to the empty room.

The Apothecary hurried down through the garden to the stable door, a bag and gun-case in his hands, praying that he would not be too late. If his business was going to hell in a handcart, he feared he might arrive there first.

ITEM:

In Eighteen fmall DRAWERS. No.1 A fine collection of Dudley
Fossils, in a variety of attitudes; called Pediculi Marini. 2. Marine
Shells, of the Cockle kind; found near the center of the Kingdom
in the Chalk Pits, at the depth of forty, or fifty yards. 3. Other
Shells from the fame Pits, viz. The Echinus Marinus, vel Centronia,
Centroniae with variolated papillae, Shark's Teeth, Spines of
the Echinus, &c. some filled with Flint, others with chalk

Malbecq Priory/Woollaton Hall. Wednesday 11ᵗʰ June. She had
exhausted every means of freeing herself from the bleak stone cell,
every tear that could be summoned from red-rimmed eyes, but still
one saving grace remained. She was alive, and being kept so – fed,
watered, with a blanket for the straw-filled palliasse that was her
only comfort – but alive, and for some purpose too. Unguessable
though that was, it joined her utter bewilderment of where she
was being held and by whom.

When first she'd begun to struggle awake in the jolting coach,
it had been no more than a bleary, unfocussed moment before that
stifling wad had been pressed against her mouth and nose once
more, and with it came another tidal wave of choking blackness
drowning out the air and light.

She'd lost all track of time since then, waking sometimes to the
sound of feet and a trencher pushed in through a barely opened
door, a coarse clay pitcher filled with water brought in while she
slept, a stinking bucket taken out. She knew now that her food
was drugged but wolfed it down, not knowing when the next

might come, then welcomed sleep although her dreams were filled with sights and sounds beyond the realms of anything she'd ever known. At first, she'd called out, tried to speak to whoever stood behind the barely opened door and screamed until her throat could scream no more. To no avail.

Then, when she thought she'd never hear a voice again, it came in what she believed at first to be another dream. A figure, black against the darkness of the open door.

"Tomorrow," the voice said, "you will be freed if I am brought what I desire. Greene and Tomlin have the power to deliver you. If you have a god, then pray they use it well." She knew better than to reply – she'd recognised that awful throaty rasp, and with that knowledge came despair.

From the moment that the mirror-black door of Woollaton Hall was opened by the liveried servant, Greene knew that all within the grand house was far from well. He could hear the sound of a woman's voice, Thérèse Rousseau's well-remembered voice, now hoarse with agitation, rapidly approaching, "C'est lui? C'est enfin le médecin?"

As the door was opened fully, the alarmingly pale woman was revealed, fear and worry writ large across her face. As she recognised the visitor, hope and disappointment fought in her expressive features as a torrent of explanation poured forth. "Oh, Mr Greene, it is you. Forgive me, J'attends le médecin. On l'a appelé ce matin, mais personne n'est encore arrivé. Mon mari ne va pas bien du tout et ça ne s'améliore pas. Et on ne peut pas réveiller Monsieur Davenport. La porte de sa chambre reste fermée à clé depuis plusieurs jours et il ne répond pas."

Seeing the woman's desperation and attempting with all his might to understand the torrent of words, he took her, reassuringly, by her shawled shoulders, saying: "Gently, my dear lady, gently – and more slowly – if you please. You have been awaiting the arrival of a doctor, summoned some hours ago, but no-one has yet arrived?" She nodded, eyes bright with unshed tears, so he continued, "Your husband has been very ill and is getting worse, you believe?" Once more a fearful nod. "No-one has been able to summon Richard Davenport who is behind locked doors and refuses to answer?" Suddenly her face seemed to crumple, and he knew that she had reached the point of extremity; he caught her as she fell.

"Quickly! Fetch help for this lady and take her somewhere close by where she can lie down. I shall return to her shortly, but she is not to be left alone." Servants and a pair of maids had suddenly appeared as if they had been waiting in the wings for their cue.

"Now, quickly, where is the French gentleman? Take me to him."

As the door to the Rousseaus' apartment was opened, the Apothecary reeled back, momentarily, from the choking fetor. A miasmic stench of vomit and faeces clogged the shuttered twilight of the rooms. Greene had to propel a footman across the reeking bedroom to heave open the shuttered windows, admitting a breezy gust of clean air and daylight into the squalid chaos that was revealed.

The Frenchman was on all fours, twitching, spasming uncontrollably, beside a ruined bed. As Greene approached, Rousseau's back arched, jerked violently as if in a parody of puppetry, before he collapsed, sprawled face down upon the fouled floor. At first, as the Apothecary bent over the motionless form, handkerchief pressed tight against his face, he feared Jean-Jacques was dead, but as he took a closer look, a muffled groan came from beneath the turbaned head.

"Quickly! he must be turned! How could he have been left like this? There will be hell to pay for such neglect." He turned furiously to see the hovering figures edging for the door.

"Now, damnit!" he rasped. "Must I drag you to your duty? Both of you, now! I'll not tell you again."

Within thirty minutes, the sickroom had been transformed. Clean bedding replaced irreparably fouled sheets tangled about the barely conscious figure, light and air filled the rooms where most of the household staff now laboured assiduously at their allotted tasks. They were overseen by the sharp tongue and eagle-eye of the small but ferocious man who was galvanising the paralysed house whilst ministering to the waxen-faced patient now blanket-wrapped and seated in a large wing-backed chair.

"Before I attend to your master, listen carefully to my instructions," said the Apothecary briskly, addressing what he judged to be the two most responsible and capable of the milling servants, "Mr Rousseau must be given freshly-boiled water only, every five minutes whether he likes it or not, even if he can manage no more than sips. Dehydration alone could have killed him. He must also be persuaded to swallow these little charcoal pills, like so." He placed the tiny black pills on a spoon, placed his hand on the stubbled cheeks and opened the unresponsive mouth between fingers and thumb before sliding the spoon between the full lips. "Now, hold the patient's nose like so, and follow them with water. Do it correctly, firmly but gently, and he will have little option but to swallow. Like this. Do you understand? They will begin to absorb the toxic humours in his stomach and prevent both vomiting and the rest. I shall return as soon as I have been able to attend upon your master, and we shall proceed with Mr Rousseau's treatment then."

Nervous nods and bobs of assent were made as he hurried away after pointing, "Two strong men, now. You and you, follow me."

Even after repeated hammering upon the master-bedroom's door, and appeals shouted over and again had failed to elicit any response, neither the men nor the crowbars he had summoned as a last resort turned out to be practical. Following a squinted examination of a large keyhole visibly blocked by the locking key within, they were faced with the certainty of irreparably damaging the superbly joined oak door in attempting to force it, even if that were to prove possible given the sterling quality of its furniture.

Only one alternative remained to the increasingly apprehensive Greene.

"Bring a long ladder, two if they can be found, around to the terrace beneath your master's windows. Sharpish, now, there's no time to delay."

Once outside in the increasingly blustery late afternoon, Greene looked enquiringly up at the large sash windows in the wisteria-clad wall. "Which windows belong to your master's rooms?" Of the five pointed out by the leader of the ladder-bearers – Richard Davenport's personal servant, a well-built man called Peters – the furthermost pair were for the Squire's piano nobile salon, the next pair for his bedroom, all shuttered. The last, though, a dressing-room with a bathroom beyond, was only lightly curtained as far as could be seen. Intuition warned the Apothecary that he and he alone should be the first to discover what lay behind the locked door above.

"The dressing-room then, both ladders, side by side and as quick as you like. Break the pane next the catch and together lift it up for me. It is a big window, but one each side should do the trick. Do not attempt to enter, but once I'm inside return to the landing and await my instructions there. You understand?"

His terse instructions followed to the letter, within five minutes a perspiring Apothecary had scrambled gracelessly across the broad sill, brushing broken glass aside with a gloved hand and wriggled down onto the carpeted floor. Coming unsteadily to his feet he stood and listened. Nothing but the sound of distant rooks out in the parkland carried to his ears, so cautiously he turned the large brass handle of the bedroom door.

If the stench of Rousseau's room had been bad, what met him here was unspeakable. He reeled back, retching uncontrollably as it seemed to coat him like some foul living thing, allowing no more than a single glimpse of the cowering, naked figure, huddled against the farthest corner of the room. Alone, this time, he somehow steeled himself to gulp down what breath he could, and then plunge back into the hellish gloom, staggering across the garment-littered floor to wrench the shutters open and to heave the stiff old windows up before his reeling senses could shut him down. With both open he bent across a broad wooden sill, gasping, gulping in each breath, thanking providence that there were no longer watchers on the terrace below, witnesses to his distress. Then he turned back to where the master of Woollaton crouched, quivering, a pallid spectre in the early evening sunlight that now flooded the fouled bedchamber.

Greene ran to his side, as Davenport looked up, eyes crazed with sleeplessness, spittle crusted around his bloodless lips. As recognition dawned, he raised a trembling hand, and Greene just stopped himself from flinching back, away from the stinking mix of urine, semen and rancid sweat that rose like vapour from the shrunken man, whose hoarse voice managed just one word, but one that brought a gasp of horror from the stooping man, "Lammia." Then he passed out, his stubbled, wigless head lolling like a doll cast aside.

"Oh, my poor, dear, foolish friend," Greene whispered, knowing in that dreadful instant what had beset the broken man. He reached for his hip flask and gently tilted brandy between slack lips. Gradually, animation seemed to flicker back into the crumpled form, and with panting effort Greene hoisted him up onto a stool set back against the chimney piece.

He chafed the ice-cold hands, then bathed the filth-sheened, corpse-like face, tilting more spirit into Davenport's mouth and only stopping when the shoulders heaved with racking coughs.

"I'm so sorry, I only meant to…" whispered the shivering man.

"Shush now, there will be time to talk, but not now. I shall call for your man Peters, and tell your staff that you were struck down by a virulent ague – much like your…" He managed to stop himself, realising that this was no time to be the bearer of bad news – least of all, news that one's celebrated guest might well be dying from poison.

"You are to be bathed, wrapped warmly, fed with beef-broth and perhaps a little steak. You must begin to regain your strength, so perhaps a glass of red wine, too. I shall not leave you tonight." He could not fail to see the child-like gratitude in the other's face. "You will be quite safe and can sleep in the certain knowledge that you will not be visited. One thing before I leave you, though. I must have the key."

He offered no further explanation, knowing none was needed, and waited for a nod and the weakly murmured response, "Up there, behind the clock." The fine-boned finger shook as it pointed to the mantlepiece above them where they sat.

"I shall be back well before dark, by which time you will be settled; feeling more yourself. The chapel out there remains unlocked?" He nodded towards the rising ground beyond the house.

"As always," came the whispered response.

Knowing that his time was limited the Apothecary stood and collected the heavy iron key, ice-cold in his hand, and hurried away, praying that he had spoken the truth on both counts. He felt as if he was exchanging one realm of mythic nightmare for another, though the knowledge of what he faced was far, far worse.

(39)

An American Pipe, the Bole of brown baked Earth, the
Tube, a flender piece of Wood,covered with the Bark
of a Tree, 5 feet, 2 inches long, the Mouth piece Agate
and Amber. fmall DRAWERS Presented by the Rev. Mr
Seward, Canon Residentiary of Lichfield Cathedral.

Woollaton Hall. Wednesday 11ᵗʰ June. He stood in the marble
hall collecting himself for several minutes before embarking on
the purpose of his mission. He called over to a housemaid espied
as she peeped around the green baize door behind the grand
staircase. "You will go to your housekeeper," he said, "and tell her
that whatever salt can be found in the kitchens is to be taken up
to your master's rooms to await my imminent return. Hurry now."

As one of the male servants appeared at the head of the
stairs, Greene called brusquely, "You! Outside now and find a
wheelbarrow. Bring it immediately to me on the rear terrace by
the steps." The liveried figure scurried past the small, commanding
visitor, making no attempt to hide his utter bewilderment, but
knowing better than to question his orders.

Some fifteen minutes later, leaving behind him a Hall a-buzz
with urgent purpose, wild speculation and mystification in equal
measure, the Apothecary stood in front of the rocky knoll that
concealed the subterranean Icehouse. Panting from his exertions
after pushing the large, iron-wheeled barrow out along the rutted
track, he paused at the threshold, gazing at a heavy metal-bound
portal that had somehow assumed a new, baleful significance.

Knowing he must not hesitate, he thrust the frigid key into it and, as soon as the dark hallway was revealed, followed Davenport's example, finding the oily torch and tinder cached behind the open door. As he descended the sloping tunnel, the beat of his heart seemed to grow louder with each muffled step, the smoky flame dancing wildly on the rough-hewn walls. Nearing the cave below, he at first sensed rather than saw the water ahead of him, until the opaque blackness that stretched before his feet gave back a glimmer of the flame. The ice, block upon block, hacked out, stacked high in winter's depths, had melted. Not a trace remained. Just a black pool where it had been. Then he saw it, what he sought and feared: angular, blacker still than what had risen, inch by inch, to engulf the rock-cut plinth on which the iron box still sat. Little but its top remained above the icemelt's reach.

It was as he realised with mounting dread that to wade across remained his only choice, the mirrored surface of the pool was cut with a flash of movement, a darting shape revealed for just an instant, scales picked out in the baleful light. Another, then another joined it then until the surface seemed to boil around the hidden plinth. An awful groan rang out, echoed by the brutal walls. To his dismay Greene knew it as his own.

As cold sweat seemed to wrap him, head to toe, he found the strength somehow to speak out loud, "By the grace of God I know this for the vile falsehood that it is. There are no eels – there is only my fear." Without another thought he plunged ahead, waded down into the icy murk, groaning with revulsion as dreadful, unseen shapes wriggled and slid about his legs and thighs. Then he had reached the sunken pillar at the centre of the hellish pool and grabbed up a box so light it felt like feathers in his sodden arms. He turned and fought against the water's tug to struggle back, up onto the cobbled ramp that led back to the realm of light.

He lurched out of the low doorway into the golden radiance of the setting sun, lacking only an angelic chorus for it to seem like heaven on earth to the sodden, gasping man. With exaggerated care he laid his burden onto the waiting barrow, before collapsing against the doorframe with a wheeze of profound gratitude. He took several minutes to gather his wits, but then with renewed purpose, slammed and locked the icehouse door once more, before taking hold of the barrow handles and beginning the long plod up towards the ancient chapel on the greensward slope above the Hall. Rabbits, curious at first, ears pricked, nostrils twitching at the scent of his approach, turned and scurried back into their warrens as ever-wearier footsteps clambered past.

Leaving the barrow at the sandstone porch, Greene ducked beneath the zigzag chevrons of the inner doorway and entered the little nave. A dozen grey-bleached pews were all that furnished a sparse interior whose lime-white walls and hacked, disfigured stones told the same old dreary tale repeated in a thousand once-loved places such as this. There the similarity ended though, much to the Apothecary's unspoken relief; for here, thanks to a landowner untouched by cant and sanctimony, a single candle flickered in a ruby glass upon an altar where a shrouded tabernacle stood alone. Greene stood for some time savouring the simple sanctity, the still air of eventide among the ancient stones, full of gratitude for the generous heart that had thought to provide such rare solace to any one that cared to find his way across the fields to seek it out.

He returned to the barrow and, steeling himself, stooped to lift a box that now seemed made of solid lead, vibrating dully to his touch as he struggled back into the nave intoning words he knew by heart. He carried it with failing strength behind the altar to an empty niche-like space that once had held the relics of a long-forbidden faith, and laid it down among the cobwebs and the gritty dust.

Just as he reached the round-arched door, a stooped figure hobbling on a crook-like stick stopped in surprise, registering the sodden figure still dripping on the stone-flagged floor, then raised a hand in welcome, "Good evening to you, friend. It being dusk I am about to lock up for the night if you've quite done."

"I have indeed, and thank you, friend. At what time will you return tomorrow morn?"

"At dawn, friend, much as ever. God give you a good night."

"I pray he will," replied the Apothecary fervently, "and good night to you."

Once readmitted to the Hall, its front door answered this time with respectful alacrity, Greene was struck by the transformation of the household's atmosphere. Gone the dulleyed torpor, the fearful inertia that had met his earlier arrival, as now both the visible staff busily engaged on returning normality to the huge house and the dark-haired woman coming to meet him gave out a renewed energy and vitality.

"Monsieur Greene, mon cher époux a déjà l'air d'aller beaucoup mieux. Il est loin d'être guéri mais il est dans un état que je trouve bien préférable à celui où je l'ai trouvé ce matin."

"No, of course Jean-Jacques is not yet fully recovered, dear lady, but I am mightily relieved you find him so much better than he was." Thérèse Rousseau's tired smile gave way to evident puzzlement as she continued, "Je ne comprends absolument pas ce qui aurait pu causer ce malaise. Tous les deux, on a mangé les mêmes plats depuis notre arrivée."

"So, you have shared everything, all your food, your drink, these weeks past? I can understand your perplexity. There has been nothing else that could have caused it?" He had hardly finished his question when a faint smile reappeared to light her expressive features. "La seule exception c'est le sucre de canne; mais ça ne peut pas être ça – c'est un vrai don de la Nature, n'est-ce pas? Et il adore grignoter cela lorsqu'il travaille."

"The sugarcane, oh dear Lord, of course!" Greene smacked himself on the forehead much to the surprise of his companion. "You describe it as a gift of nature, quite rightly, Madame, but how did this gift arrive here? When did it arrive?"

Blank incomprehension met his urgent question. He tried again, "Who brought it here? When did it arrive?"

She simply shrugged in response as if such domestic trivialities were beneath her, but then said, "Il le grignote depuis deux ou trois jours. Je lui dis toujours que ce n'est pas bon pour les dents. Mais il ne m'écoute jamais."

"Well, he will listen to me if I have anything to do with it, Madame; though far more than his teeth and his appetite are at risk here, let me tell you. Will you kindly show me where Jean-Jacques has been writing? It is a grotto, I believe; outside?"

This question at least was understood. "It is a grotto, yes, but we shall not need to go outside. If you will follow me?"

Mystified, Greene allowed Thérèse Rousseau to lead him through the green-baize door and down into the maze of corridors beneath the Hall. When he thought they must have passed beyond the extent of the house above, she indicated a door at the end of the passage. As they entered the cavernous space, she said, "Normally, no one – least of all me – is permitted to disturb my husband at his writing, but there, look, over by his chair, is that perhaps what you seek?"

"We are privileged indeed, then, Madame, if not even you are permitted to enter while Jean-Jacques works. I could appreciate much the same myself." He followed her pointing hand into the low light of the cave-like space that opened before them, roofed in part by the terrace above, the natural rock tamed into supporting walls with a large window fitted into what had evidently once been a natural fissure. Thérèse was indicating the box in which the sugar cane had been delivered; it stood against a chair drawn up to a paper-strewn table.

The Apothecary hurried across to it, noting several splintered, well-chewed pieces of cane lying where they had been carelessly tossed onto one of the large rugs spread across the rock floor. Opening the wooden lid, he could see immediately that only a single cane of the tightly packed dozen-or-so remaining had been consumed. There was hope in that small mercy.

"This must be destroyed, Madame," he said, lifting the box, and indicating they should leave. "It will be the cause of your husband's sickness without doubt." He did not add that his first task would be to discover who had delivered it.

The dispiriting, if predictable response to that arrived shortly after their return to the kitchens through which they had passed, "Just left propped outside, against the scullery door, first thing Tuesday, Sir. No cause to remark on it: simply an early delivery from Ashbourne. There's usually somebody about to take it in, but it must have come extra early, Sir. That's all I can say."

Thérèse accompanied him to their rooms upstairs, where in the freshly aired and newly spotless bedchamber her husband, still cocooned in his wing chair, managed a wan smile of welcome whilst trying, weakly, to ward off a hovering spoon.

After administering a large sachet of powdered Jesuit-bark diluted in water to the grimacing patient, he left them to their rest, departing with instructions conveyed in the universal language of a wagging finger, a stern expression and a water carafe waved emphatically in front of them both. "As much as you can drink, it is most important."

Once in the master-suite the Apothecary found that patient also much restored, and straightaway dismissed the servants before grimly addressing the most pressing of his priorities. "Before we speak, Richard, you will permit me to establish a very basic, but – I trust – a very effective defence." It was not a request. "I have no idea whether it may prove even necessary, in fact I pray it will not to be, but nonetheless." Going from room to room, the Apothecary poured coarse-grained salt along each of the windowsills before closing and fastening the shutters of the two principal rooms, moving through into the dressing room where he repeated the painstaking procedure. Then, retracing his steps from the bathroom door, he laid an unbroken ribbon of the glistening crystals carefully across each of the thresholds before closing each of the doors to test that the salt remained beneath. Satisfied, he finally rejoined the newly bathed and shaved master of Woollaton, sitting, ill at ease, beside the salon's small fire, the evening's chill growing about them. Gesturing weakly towards the tantalus that had been left between them, Davenport murmured, "Perhaps you will be so kind?"

Greene poured them both a large whisky before looking intently at his erstwhile host. "Before you offer any more apologies, my friend, understand, please, that they are not necessary. You have been suborned, just as I was, into the mistaken belief that that appalling thing can be controlled. It cannot, that is now abundantly clear, though I greatly fear that the remedy you proposed in all good faith cannot now be acted upon – shortly I shall explain why." He forestalled the look of anxiety growing in his listener's face.

"First, let us establish what resulted from your curiosity – the same irresistible impulse that lured us both to imperil far more than just our lives. It has been sending a succubus to you, has it not? A lammia as you chose to call it?"

Davenport assented with a barely perceptible nod, whispering, "My appetite for her, or it when first it came, fills me with a disgust that I fear will never leave me, Richard. Whilst never a rakehell or a womaniser – like so many I could name – I had thought myself a man of the world until this, until what first I thought of as a frenzied dream became more real than night or day. It came again and again, each time I tried to sleep, to close my eyes, to rest. It made me … I wanted … I was crazed with a lust that could not be satisfied whatever or however… Oh, Christ, Richard, can I ever find forgiveness for the things it made me do? The things I wanted, needed, more than life itself."

"Truly, my friend, there can be no guilt in this, not once you became entranced. Since legends began, since myths were made, these foul excrescences have been known, and feared. Desired, sought after, even summoned by the damned. They are as real as fear, as lust, embodiments beyond our power to imagine. They are corruption made briefly flesh. You are truly blessed to be alive, Richard, make no mistake about it. These incarnate evils have the power to drain a soul. I believe that now it will not come again – or if it should – will not prevail."

"I see the salt, but what else? How have you..?" He simply could not find the words.

Greene told him of what he'd found, and of the box's temporary resting place.

"I shall reclaim it, as I must, when your custodian unlocks the chapel up above."

Ignoring the look of puzzlement that, for some reason, flickered briefly in the patrician features, Greene hurried on, knowing what he must explain. "As if we were not already over-stretched and harried to extremity by every aspect of this wretched affair, I must tell you that the object that is our bane now threatens to exact an even higher price. That of a blameless child's life, unless it is surrendered to the fiend that holds her. Tomlin's shop-girl, our own just only weeks ago, has been seized. She will certainly perish if this bastard fails to get the book. He has promised as much. I endanger her just by betraying this confidence. It must leave with me at first light."

"But who..?" Davenport began. With infinite weariness Greene interposed: "The very same man who has attempted to poison your renowned guest, during your indisposition, my friend." He saw a new shock of horror join the exhaustion in Davenport's features. "He might well have succeeded had not this chain of events brought me back to your door. A supreme and blessed irony that one day we may celebrate, but only when the revenant is dead."

"De Rais, you mean? That foul..?"

"The very same, Richard, but thus far at least, fate has scotched his vicious game."

"He has tried to murder Rousseau under my own roof?" hissed

Davenport, fever-spots of colour burning on his pallid cheeks. "By God, he'll pay for this, but tell me how."

"I shall, but then if you have the strength, we might discuss quite how we'll make the bastard pay," said Greene, distracted, momentarily, by half-heard sounds beyond the shuttered window-panes.

A freshening wind rustling through wisteria twigs that scratched insistently against the glass? The far-off, keening howl of fighting cats? Perhaps.

(40)

ITEM:

A Chinese Pagod, fomewhat in the fhape of a Lion; a fire
place and grate within the Head, for burning fweet fcented
Woods, Gums, & etc with a communicating aperture in
the Noftrils and Mouth, for emitting Smoke and Flame;
it is placed on a Pedeftal oppofite the Tartarian Image.

Woollaton Hall/Ashbourne. Thursday 12th June. Was there anything odder and less predictable than these educated gentlemen?
the stableman asked himself, having been roused well before dawn
and told by this one – the one who'd had the whole house topsy
turvy since the moment he arrived – that four good horse-shoes,
each the same size, were to be delivered to the back door, sharpish.

With a large canvas bag slung across his narrow shoulder and
a small sack containing what remained of Woollaton's supply of
salt clutched in his hand, the Apothecary reached the little porch
as the morning sun began its ascent over the Hall below, his own
ascent of the long incline to the church leaving him a sight more
breathless than he cared to admit to himself. His horse, saddled
and ready for his return, grazed contentedly on the lush grass of
the parkland verge below.

As he expected, the ancient door swung open to his hand, and
once again he ducked into the timeless world of dust-motes and
the scents of age-old wood and candlewax.

It was only now, approaching the altar, lit as ever by its tiny
ruby flame, that he realised he had come here yesterday as if he'd
always known this place, had known to find the niche, had sensed

this was the refuge, the concealment that he sought. Silently, he gave thanks for that, knowing better than to question the sense of rightness that he felt here, knowing too that both it – and he – were about to be tested yet again.

He knelt behind the broad stone table raised up on its tiled steps and, once more, reached into the deep recess to draw the iron box into the light. Setting it aside on the gritty floor, he emptied out the contents of the salt-sack and spread the crystals evenly across the stone shelf within. Then, mouthing the words that were second nature to him now, lifted up the unresisting lid, took out the book with two gloved hands and laid it, face down, upon the salt, its bindings wrapped about it like a tight cocoon.

Immediately, he sensed the air begin to change, a prickling, stirring wrongness rising like a gust of smoke from a damply kindled grate. With single-minded urgency he brought out the iron shoes from his bag, and, one by one, laid them down upon the stained drabness of the back cover to form the four limbs of a cross fleury. The air became air once more, the menace passed like the fleeting wind-blown shadow of a cloud. He stood and with a small groan, bent stiffly down and picked up the empty box.

Carrying it to the pew nearest the door, he opened it again, before lifting out a cloth-wrapped volume from his bag. Yes, he'd guessed it right – the size was perfect as he tested it against the metal void. When he'd seen it first, amongst the costly contents of one of many shelves, he'd felt impelled to lift it down. It was only then, seeing that self-same seal incised upon the scuffed and grubby binding, that the spark of an idea might – unknown to him – have begun to smoulder into life.

Now, as he unwrapped the book, Davenport's words came back: "For each of the few real gems you might discern, you'll find a dozen born of blind benighted ignorance, dressed up with signs and symbols to bedazzle fools."

With all his heart, the Apothecary prayed that this would serve just that purpose: the bedazzling of a calculating, vicious foe who was no fool. That much, if little else, was certain. With the iron box filled once more, Greene hurried down the slope to reach his horse. He stowed his burden carefully into a saddle-pannier, fastening its buckled straps with care. Without a backward glance he rode away. Had he turned back, the Apothecary might just have seen a stooped old man, hobbling from the porch above, an iron key clasped in his hand, who watched the horse and rider dwindle in the morning haze.

"I won't do it, Mr Greene! I can't, God help me, I just can't! None of this is of my making." Tomlin was a shambolic shadow of his former self. A twitching, sobbing wreck, pacing up and down in his shop premises, pausing only to glance nervously past the 'Closed' sign hanging in his shop door, out across the busy marketplace. Moaning anew each time a would-be customer approached his door, only to turn away frowning or mouthing their annoyance. "I shall have no business left at this rate. And all because I..."

A small boy, clutching a folded paper, knocked at the door. When the druggist moved to wave him away, Greene stopped him brusquely, saying, "Had you not better open up and see what message he brings. This could be what we are awaiting, could it not?"

As Tomlin cringed away from the possibility, Greene pulled open the door himself, and took the note. Before the child could turn away, he asked, "Who gave you this?"

The boy just shrugged his bony shoulders. "Just a man, gave us a farthing, tight bugger. Never seen 'im afore."

Unsurprised, Greene watched him as he turned and hurried off. Opening it he knew the scrawl on sight:

midday exact tomorrow – leave horse at road and walk
to the circle stones up on the high moor
leave it in the middle – you will see the girl up on the hill
come alone or she dies – you will be watched

"These must be the stones we talked about; Arbor Low off the Bakewell Road."

A renewed wail of protest rose from Tomlin: "That must be the best part of a two or three-hour ride! I cannot do this, Mr Greene – I am still exhausted from being obliged to rush to you in Lichfield. Who is to say I wouldn't be struck down as soon as I have delivered this damnable thing?"

"It is the price of this young woman's life, Tomlin. Surely you can understand that?"

"No, Mr Greene, it is you who fail to understand!" came the petulant response: "I am a druggist, not some merchant adventurer, but I see from your expression that you believe I should be what I am not! I cannot believe that any one in their right mind would measure the life of young Emmy against some wretched book or other. I mean no disrespect, but I believe you are caught up in some terrible fantasy of your own imagining. This is Derbyshire in the year 1766, not some wild romance from a dusty volume on your museum shelves."

"I wish to God Almighty that you were correct, Tomlin," said Greene quietly, "and I can understand how you might judge this matter as you do. You should never have been involved." With that he picked up the saddlebag and turned to leave, knowing with numbing certainty that this was how it was always going to end. He had deluded himself to believe better of this ineffectual man.

Glancing at his pocket-watch, he knew there was not a moment to lose and regained his saddle with a bleak sense of foreboding. His destination was as remote as could be contrived. He prayed that the odds of recovering a terrified girl in exchange for a largely worthless book would be better.

(41)

A Mahogany Case, covered in Glass. Contains two Ribs of
King Richard 2d. Part of the Coffin, &c of Humphrey Duke
of Gloucester; from St. Albans, – Queen Catharine, she was
the Daughter to Charles 4th of France, and Consort to Henry,
5th, of England; after whofe Death fhe married Owen Tudor, she
died Anno 1437, at the Monastery of Bermondfey in Southwark
and was buried in Westminster Abbey; but being taken up in
the Reign of Henry 7th, remains unburied near the tomb of
her first husband, Henry 5th, from whence a piece of her dried
Flesh was taken in August 1746, being 309 years after her
Decease. Part of the Shroud of Edward the Confessor, &c.

Malbecq Priory. Derbyshire. Friday 13th June. It might as well
have been a drear winter's day for all the impact that the flawless
summer morning was having on the sombre twilight within the
Priory. De Rais had packed with care, gathering the monies and
the various portable objects that he had assiduously assembled
over the interminable months of his employment. Langton was
by now so far gone that the Frenchman could have removed the
household's furniture unnoticed, just so long as his next pipe was
in view, the rags of his towering ego massaged on an hourly basis,
and his tiresome fumblings and fawnings grimly tolerated. De
Rais had become de facto master of Malbecq exactly as he had
intended. Now though, he would be done with the owl-haunted
shit-heap in a few short hours. He smiled a smile of mirthless
satisfaction, savouring the perfect simplicity of a plan that would

leave a fitting token of his departure with the ruined husk of a man he had come to loathe.

Beyond its undoubted currency value – for he recognised that the book he was shortly to acquire was of such an order that would open many well-concealed doors for its bearer – he cared less than nothing for its antiquity, its provenance or its supposed powers. A precarious, predatory lifetime spent in the liminal shadows of Europe's netherworld had fostered in him a detached contempt for its credulous, hag-ridden habitués, but a profound respect for the depths of their purses.

As he finished his preparations, he reviewed the sequence of the morning's events with as much care and attention to detail as any tactician. The girl had already been drugged with precision. She would be capable – just – of playing her part at noon. He would carry her to the carriage himself, having instructed the driver that he was not required.

His saddle horse would be led behind until the destination was in sight. The coach would be abandoned. He curtly dismissed the idea of quick escape once his purpose was achieved. His departure would be as unhurried as he chose to make it, with whomsoever might be left behind powerless to prevent it. He would ride cross-country to begin with, thus confounding any attempt at pursuit, however unlikely, then choose his road to the East Coast and thence to the Low Countries in his own good time.

Over the past months the Frenchman had come to know the ancient warren of Malbecq with a sour familiarity, although as de Langton's addiction and growing frailty progressed, the daily ambit of their shared life had become ever more limited. Now, the nominal master of the Priory rarely, if ever, left the east cloister, with his bedchamber in the monks' Warming Parlour, his place of study and of his works, the Chapter House, beside it. The Priory's few servants were permitted access only at strictly regulated times, the various claustral doors to the virtually derelict monastic offices kept locked as a matter of course. To de Langton control was paramount, even if now its exercise was little more than a matter of irascible habit and petulance. De Rais savoured the sweetness of the moment as he carefully selected the appropriate keys for what would be his final moments in the crumbling pile.

He had carried the insensate girl from her cell to the waiting carriage, filled his saddlebags, and now turned back towards the chamber beside the dark entry and the night stairs where the mastiffs were kennelled. For the previous three days and nights he had instructed the mystified kennelman that they were neither to be fed nor let out for their accustomed guard-duty. Not until now, when everything was in place.

De Langton had awoken – to the extent that he ever did, these days – as excited as a child on a birthday morning, knowing that today he would become the master of the book. The book whose rediscovery, whose power to fulfil his every blighted hope and twisted dream, had occupied his days and fevered nights for months. He had explained to the barely attentive Frenchman that he would spend the hours until its arrival, and de Rais' return, preparing the Great Pentacle, its herbs, its salts, its incense and its paraphernalia made ready for the conjuration that would be the apogee of all his studies, his life.

De Rais could confidently predict that in childlike anticipation of what was to come that night, de Langton would don age-old priestly vestments that had been ritually defiled, then cannibalised to make up his ceremonial robes.

Tonight, the portal would be opened to his command and he would achieve Ipsissimus.

De Rais knew that the feverishly obsessed man would never notice the contents of the deep pockets in the magisterial finery, let alone imagine their purpose.

He pushed strips of raw meat deep into each. One by one, he unlocked the doors leading through to the Chapter House, before slipping the bolt on the kennel's inside door and stepping out smartly through the wicket gate which he locked behind him. It would be just a matter of time.

With a light flick of his whip the carriage pair trotted off towards the High Moor.

(42)

A figure in Bisket or unglazed China, of our Saviour crowned with Thorns, his Hands bound with a cord, a loofe mantle thrown over him, which reaches to the Ground; this Statue was made at the China Manufactory at Derby, & moft exquifitely finifhed, is twelve inches high, and is covered with a Bell of Flint Glafs.

Arbor Low. Derbyshire. Thursday 12th/Friday 13th June. Convinced of the time-honoured adage 'knowledge is power', Richard Greene had employed the tedious hours of his enforced wait as best he could. Leaving the querulous Tomlin with a mix of relief and trepidation, Greene had left the bustling town in the early afternoon and having led his mare up the steep hill that rose from Ashbourne's marketplace, embarked on the sparsely travelled road to his destination several hours ride away. From a visit a dozen years earlier, he recalled that the ancient site gave little away in terms of a silhouette against the wind-scoured skies of the high moors, nestling within its eroded earthworks of ditch and bank; its stones – a score or more – radiating about the central sanctuary. Embedded in the sparse moorland soil, they lay flat rather than standing like so many stone fingers, much, the Apothecary had come to believe, as they had been intended. The only landmark, if such it could be called, was a much-eroded tumulus, an ancient barrow named Gib Hill, that must be the hill of de Rais' instructions. In all it was a timeless, desolate place, rarely visited and barely seen from the road below. Hence its choice.

He would at least provide himself with what small advantage he could, knowing that Copeland's gun – his very long gun – whilst an invaluable and reassuring asset, could not be carried unobtrusively when he approached at the appointed hour. He could not afford to be seen arriving so obviously armed, so had determined that this reconnaissance, some twenty hours early, was the only solution.

He had not the slightest doubt that de Rais would be armed, unpredictable and untrustworthy. He could only pray that by concealing his own weapon and regaining at least a nodding acquaintance with the barren terrain of the coming encounter, that neither he nor the hapless Emmy would be completely at the mercy of a calculating evil.

The sole habitation visible for miles around was a decrepit, seemingly long-abandoned farmhouse whose equally ramshackle byres and outbuildings straddled the rough track leading from the road up to the stones. Today he left his horse tethered there, but, on the morrow, he knew he would have to obey his instructions and leave her down below, visible on the road.

Rabbits scurried from his path as he entered the shallow causeway that breached the encircling earthworks and bridged the huge ditch between them. Scents of bracken and heather wafted on the light breeze within the henge, and he walked its circumference before finding a viable place of concealment for the soldier's prized firearm.

A narrow, fern-shaded declivity beside one of the larger stones provided as good a hiding place as he could find – one close enough to the central sanctuary stones for rapid access once he had seen that the girl had been brought, alive, to honour the malign bargain. Securing its canvas wrapping after checking the rifle's load and, priming and wrapping the lock in a large 'kerchief, he laid it below ground-level, shrouded in fern, where only a determined search would come across it. Leaving the encircling berm, he trudged up to the gibbet hill, for that was what it had become over recent centuries – a vile marker, visible for miles around, from which the tattered rags of caged cadavers swung in warning on the gusts of ceaseless winds. The weather-bleached pole, mercifully bare today, leaned crookedly askew, stark against the sky. This was where Emmy would be brought and, he prayed, collected by him on the morrow.

Over to his right a sparse copse rose below the skyline. Looking around, the Apothecary concluded that this would be the Frenchman's vantagepoint: he would be able to see any arrivals on the road down below, the clear approach of anyone climbing to the henge, and, most importantly, the sanctuary stones where the book was to be left.

In his mind's eye, Greene saw the girl being sent down to mount the barrow mound once he had been seen to leave the book, whilst de Rais rode up and around to approach from the rear to claim his prize, as a would-be rescuer ran up to claim the girl. Though the timing would be crucial, he knew that once she was in view and seen to be alone, there would be nothing to lose in revealing the gun.

There was no more he could accomplish now, and with weary resignation he rode on towards the moorland village of Monyash. He recalled there being a charmless inn, close to the church. He would seek whatever accommodation could be provided for what promised to be a long and sleepless night.

Chafing with impatience, light-headed with sleeplessness and covered in the bed-bug bites that had spoiled what little chance he had had to rest, the Apothecary made good his escape from the dreary inn shortly after dawn. Intuition insisted that he should not be seen approaching from the North, when expected from the South, so he had come to a compromise with himself by gaining directions to the hamlet of Pilsbury – scarcely more than a couple of miles west of his destination – thence further southwards to Heathcote and the Ashbourne road. He would thus be seen approaching both where and when expected.

With profound gratitude he broke his fast at a cottage bake-house, wolfing down a trencherbread stacked with salty bacon and a mustard-laden piccalilli that took his breath away. Washed down with an earthen mug of tepid cider, he had seldom enjoyed a breakfast more.

Once back at the junction with yesterday's road, and now retracing his steady trot up across the empty, rolling landscape, he came to his destination around a quarter of an hour ahead of his instructions. After tethering his mare to roadside gorse, the Apothecary unbuckled his saddle-pannier, and with it slung over his shoulder began the trudge up towards his barely visible destination. He knew, with a tingle of dread, that from here on his every step and move was being watched.

Had he not known otherwise, it was as if he was alone in an empty, windblown universe, inhabited only by the wheeling crows that circled far above. He crossed the rank-grassed causeway, seeking any signs of footsteps made before, saw none and crossed to where the inner core of stones lay prone. Haphazard to a passing, casual gaze, their lichened, weatherworn assemblage was focused now, razor-sharp, a place of endings. He unfastened the buckles of the leather bag, withdrew the cloth-wrapped bundle stowed within and with elaborate care unwrapped it and set down the iron box upon the nearest of the stones, before he turned and scanned the skyline, left to right.

For minutes that stretched frayed nerves close to extremity there was no sign, no movement that would indicate he was not, indeed, alone. Then in a heart-stopping instant she appeared, her flame-red hair rising like a morning sun above the barrow-top. The slight figure tottered up the rearward slope to stand, unsteadily, on the low summit, arms bound behind her back, a gagging scarf bound around her head and across her chalk-white face.

Greene grabbed the gun from its concealment and with a bellow of greeting, fear, fury, ran towards the swaying girl, his heart beating a wild tattoo as he jumped and clambered over broken ground towards the gibbet hill.

As he clambered up the last few yards, towards the eyes that blazed with terror and helpless supplication above the brutal gag, she crumpled and fell, twisting as she toppled down. It was then he saw the blood. A trail that marked her stumbling passage from the trees. Above the coarse rope that bound her, both of Emmy's wrists had been slashed. With a blinding, incandescent fury born of horror and desperation, Greene cast aside the gun as he fell to his knees, ripped the gag away from the bloodless lips, the ashen face and with frantic skill bound it around one of the dreadful pulsing wounds. Panting, he pulled open his coat and waistcoat, hauled out his broadcloth shirt tails and ripped a seam with all his strength to tear off as long a strip as he could. He bound up the second wound as tightly as he dared, before staggering to his feet and pulling out his belt and ripping off another length of shirting. Stooping to the barely conscious girl sprawled on her side at his feet, he bound them both as tourniquets above her freckled elbows, praying as he had never prayed before that he had been in time. It was only then that he could begin to saw through her bonds, wound over and again then knotted with vicious precision. He turned her, then raised her with loving care. Cradling the slight, unresisting form in his arms, he fished a hipflask from a top-coat pocket and tipped a little of the brandy between her slack lips.

Her beautiful blue eyes flickered open as she coughed and choked down a few drops of the fiery tonic. "Thank you," was all she could she whisper before sinking deeper into his arms and lapsing into unconsciousness, her breath shallow and rapid.

"Breath, nonetheless," murmured the Apothecary before offering up his silent thanks. It was only then that he remembered the gun, lying a few feet away, thrown aside in his haste. Only now did he turn to look across the windblown curls of red-gold hair pressed into his shoulder and see the horse and rider cantering away. Uphill, across country, though even now not beyond the rifle's range. A tiny moan, a little shudder running through the wounded girl made up his mind.

He might, perhaps, have recalled the words, 'Vengeance is mine, saith the Lord', but gave no indication, simply redoubling his embrace of the youngster whose very life lay in his arms. He sat staring out across a sunlit afternoon that was newly imbued with wonder, scarcely aware of the familiar coach now halted beside his tethered mare on the road below. He felt strangely reluctant when, some little time later, he had to relinquish hold of his precious burden into others' helping hands, and to be helped, himself, down to where Woollaton's coach now stood, drawn up among the ancient stones.

"Tomlin said we would find you both here," said a familiar, if weakened, voice, as he was handed up to sit beside the barely conscious, blanket-wrapped girl propped against piled cushions. The Apothecary gave a small smile of acknowledgement to Richard Davenport, managing to explain to him and the coach's other occupant that tourniquets had to be periodically loosened, before he passed out like a snuffed candle.

"We shall probably manage that between us, Doctor, don't you think?" enquired Davenport of his companion.

"I dare say," responded his companion, attempting a degree of gravitas not helped by his boyish features; a formally dressed young man still wondering how he had allowed himself to be plucked from his newly established Consulting Room in Ashbourne.

Doctor Matthew Parr was, in fact, newly established in every sense. With ink barely dry upon his certificate of Qualification, he had arrived in the small town with the joint recommendations of affordability and, hence, biddability – rapidly becoming a sought-after addition to the small coterie of local medical men.

"Your Mr Greene does seem to have a modicum of professional skill."

"Oh, he does," replied Davenport with heartfelt relish. "He does indeed."

(43)

ITEM:

An image of the Virgin Mary, finely carved in Box Wood, holding an Infant Jefus in her Arms, at her Feet, a child playing with a Lamb. A fmaller image alfo of the Virgin Mary in Box, in which the Child is feen placing a Crown upon the Head of his Mother, Thefe three figures feem to be the Work of the fame Artist and were prefented bythe Right Honourable the Earl of Uxbridge.

Holymoorside. Derbyshire. Friday 13ᵗʰ June. His intention was to reach Chesterfield before night fell, and once past the riverside town of Bakewell, de Rais had felt sufficiently at ease to rejoin the road after some hours of rough riding away from the stones. What he had left behind him would have guaranteed that whoever had brought the book – it had not been the fool Tomlin, that much was certain – would have been nicely distracted. His gaunt features cracked into a rictus grin at the memory. It was regrettable that he had not seized the further opportunity presented to him.

He was distracted, momentarily, but not for the first time – sensing that there was someone on the road behind him. Swivelling in his saddle, he glanced back along the empty road. He was tired; it had been a busy time. He grinned again, thinking back to the despised ruin he had so recently left, picturing lean, prowling shapes following an irresistible scent.

Reaching down, he patted the reassuring shape of the iron box within its canvas saddle pannier. Once dismounted amongst the stones he had immediately seen the incised armorial on its rusted lid and gained a brief – annoyingly brief – glimpse of its contents.

The seal had been there, just as promised, but the sight of the long gun that had suddenly appeared in the hands of the running man had dissuaded him from verifying it with his pendulum. Unfailing as that would have been, he knew the range of long-barrelled guns, having used just such with relish, firing from concealment at distant, fleeing men. Happy days indeed, but the pendulum would have to wait until Chesterfield, he had told himself, since remaining as an exposed target on these desolate moors would have been plain stupidity. No shadow of a doubt remained of course; why should it? This had all been planned so well.

It was as the landscape all about took on a golden, evening hue, that once again he felt the prickle, the trusted itch, that warned him of pursuit, of being watched if nothing more. He reached casually down, unfastening the holster flap of the heavy horse-pistol at his knee, gripping its butt before he swivelled back towards the setting sun.

This time his senses had not failed him. There was a walking figure, somehow close behind him on the dusty road. At first it was a figure, stooped and old, bent upon a walking staff, a blackened silhouette against a blood-red, sinking orb. De Rais straightened in relief, his hand leaving the pistol grip, about to spur his tired mount away.

It was, as he turned, that from the corner of his eye the figure seemed to change, and as it did a spike of dread drove through the mounted man. What only seconds earlier had been a shadow, black against the setting sun, now stood only feet behind his horse's tail, straightening, growing in the unbelieving eyes now transfixed by what they saw. The sunlight now shone through the presence on the empty road as it raised its staff towards him. "Get down," it said.

Two words seemed to come from deep within the horseman's head, to fill it with such numbing desolation that it all but froze his blood. He knew the figure now.

In blind terror, the Frenchman turned back to seize his reins, only to find his horse had bowed its head down to the road, as if submitting to the awful voice, standing still as stone, unmoving in the gathering dusk.

De Rais swung down from his saddle, desperate now to run, to hide, to...

No ground remained beneath his boots.

No voice was left to shriek.

No air to fill collapsing lungs.

No hold to halt his endless fall.

Only darkness, ebon, winter black.

Swarming in to claim its own.

(44)

A CABINET on the right Hand the Fire-place. On the top,
a Grotto form'd of Ores, Spars and other Minerals, mostly
found in Derbyſhire, covered with a large Glaſs Bell.

Saddler Street. Friday 20ᵗʰ June. "So basically, it all went well?"
Lionel Blomefield opined, his eyes following the path of a dying
wasp up the window frame.

"Oh, absolutely," responded Greene, thanking Providence that
his many shared years with this, one of Nature's genuine curiosities
and coincidentally his oldest friend, obviated the need for physical
assault, "with the possible exceptions of a brutalised young woman
spared from death only by the grace of God, a murdering, revenant
diabolist poisoner escaped to spread his foulness where he will, his
erstwhile principal's gnawed bones found in the smoking ruins of
his home and an object, vile beyond comprehension, remaining to
be destroyed before it can blight yet more lives."

"So, all's well, then," responded Blomefield, debating whether,
or not, he should feel satisfaction as the wasp became ever more
tangled in an ancient web whose weaver could now be seen
advancing from a mildewed corner.

As if called back to reality by some unheard voice, he turned
to Greene and said, "We are all invited, did I tell you? Seward,
the thrice-favoured Anna, the Darwins, Elspeth and of course, as
you will well know, you and Theodosia – first and foremost – to
Davenport's Midsummer Extravaganza. Quite pushing the boat
out, from what we hear, determined to put himself and his grand

house about a bit, so we gather. It sounds to me like being a 'Life is too short not to share it with one's own kind of folk', sort of thing. Something of a Road to Damascus experience one suspects. He was only a whisker away from being a recluse, one hears – though a damn' wealthy one, apparently."

Blithely unaware of the rapidly glazing eyes now regarding him, the cleric continued, "One gathers his Frenchy guests are less than enchanted by the volte face and are about to up-sticks and return where there be dragons, so Darwin has heard. Claims the staff have tried to poison him, or some such hysterical Frenchiness. Bit of a mixed blessing, by all accounts, but it's the bonfire that's the big attraction. The staff have been building it these two weeks past, by all accounts. Topping idea, don't you think? A champagne breakfast at Midsummer's dawn to welcome the season in? We're all invited to stay the night before, naturally – as you well know – so I gather the ladies are planning some financially injurious shopping on the strength of it. Richard, have you been listening to a word I've said?" Blomefield added in an injured tone.

"Oh, Lionel, how could I not have been?" the Apothecary responded, hauling himself back into the moment with adamantine resolve, "There have been just so many of them."

"Oh, well," responded a now prickly cleric, "Harry Copeland's imminent return will doubtless curb my garrulous proclivities, that is if our paths even cross." Greene's response was to stand, abruptly, reach for a water-jug on his table and empty the contents over the Reverend Blomefield's bewigged head. For an instant, the Rector of Saint Mary's simply gaped in spluttering outrage at the Apothecary, before reading the expression in his face and pulling out a grubby pocket-handkerchief from somewhere deep within a sodden coat, his anger dissolving as rapidly as it had flared.

"Point taken. Was I being particularly stuffy, Richard? Elspeth tells me I'm getting worse."

"Particularly, Lionel," Greene agreed. "But not to the extent that I shall be forced to forgo our dinner with Harry at The

George tomorrow night. For some unknown reason he has invited us both. I received his letter on Wednesday. One can only assume his intention is to give our respective spouses a little light relief. It will be a most exclusive affair involving just the three of us."

The wet man brightened visibly, before striding across to the window and making as if to wipe himself down with the heavy, crewel-work curtains.

"Do so much as touch those and Theodosia will first break both your wrists before removing your hands with a blunt knife and having you consigned to the worst of the Guildhall cells for Elspeth to collect – or not – on the way to Davenport's. You really do believe in living dangerously, Lionel."

"Pot calling the kettle precisely what, Mr Greene?" replied Blomefield with regained asperity. He stopped then, frozen in almost theatrical immobility, a thought process creasing his brow, "This bonfire, Richard, surely it will not contain..? Davenport can't actually be meaning to...? Is that why it has been timed for..?"

Greene nodded in an uneasy response: "Yes, I fear, to all your questions, however tardy the enlightenment which prompted them. Did you think the guest-list was drawn up from whimsy? Our friend apparently believes in the old saw of safety in numbers, though I might have hoped his recent experience to have persuaded him otherwise. I would have felt very different about entrusting the safe-keeping and final destruction of a certain item into his hands had I realised it would be turned into a public spectacle. I simply don't understand him."

"Well, hardly public, Richard, but what's all this about his recent experience? You've been tight as a mollusc when it came down to the actualities of what went on up there? Theodosia has been heard complaining of just that to my own dear wife. Expressions like 'explanations economic in the extreme', and 'his infuriating brevity', have been bandied about in our parlour, not to mention, 'Far too old for derring-do.' A bit unkind that last bit, I thought, but one doesn't wish to be controversial," Blomefield added, beaming at his dangerously impassive listener.

"Oh, Lionel, if only your memory was a long as your sermons, you might recall your own recent experience, upstairs, in the museum?"

"Oh, merciful Heaven, that kind of experience was it?" replied Blomefield, with a new gravity. "I had no idea there had been more of that frightful jiggery-pokery going on, Richard. Thought we had seen the back of it, what with you going to..." The long face fell anew. "So, what you're saying is that all that's been happening is still connected to that appalling thing? I see now why you are so unlike your usual self."

"It is simply that I do not normally have a water-jug to hand; so, I beg you, do not ever underestimate your power to drive me to distraction, Lionel; but, yes, that is what I am saying. None of us who have been touched by it can ever again rest easy until it can be destroyed. I have come to believe that it has the power to leave a lasting taint, as if those unfortunates who have been exposed to it have been somehow collected – as part of some ineradicable memory. The sheer rottenness, the depravity that it has unleashed would be simply beyond belief had we not experienced it first-hand."

"Yes, but surely, as far as you and I are concerned, all that immediate nastiness is a thing of the past now that it's been whisked away? And once a flame has been lit under it, that's it."

"'Once' being the operative word here, Lionel. We must hope and pray that it can be accomplished as swiftly and easily as it can be said."

(45)

In the Drawer marked R. Peacock Coal, Lancashire. Toad
Stones, in part filled with Spar, Lava, Derbyshire. Opake,
calcareous Spar. Mafs of fmall Crystals. Inflameable Earth, Exeter,
Devonshire. A fprig of Virgin Silver on a bed of Spar, from
Christianburgh, Norway. Crystal Spar, called Briftol Diamonds.

Woollaton Hall. Saturday 21ˢᵗ June. Richard Davenport turned
back from the huge venetian window that was the focal point of
his piano nobile, this his favourite eyrie for observing the comings
and goings at the Hall's grand portico below. He had noted with
a growing degree of fascination the now daily house calls being
paid upon one of his two recovering guests. One of those, now
announced and standing in the doorway from the marble landing
beyond, had made a gradual – if increasingly vociferous – recovery
since Richard Greene's providential intervention in what would
otherwise most certainly have been an agonising and lingering
death from strychnine poisoning.

The other guest, though, the demure, and wanly beautiful young
woman who was very obviously the prime concern of the young
doctor now returning to his waiting mount with a noticeable
spring to his step, also owed her life to that same man. "And,
that makes three of us," thought Davenport, unaware that he had
spoken the words aloud, only now beginning to register the fact
from the obvious puzzlement in the approaching Frenchman's
features.

"Ah, no, Richard; it is only we two."

Knowing better than to attempt an explanation, the squire waved Rousseau to a chair beside him. "Jean-Jacques, I bid you a very good day; you are regaining your colour as well as your vitality, I see. Are you and Thérèse still set upon leaving us, though?"

The Frenchman spread his hands expressively, "I fear," he said, "that we have little choice, Richard. For all your great kindness, your generosity, the fact that there is someone, perhaps among your own staff, who wants me dead, means that, as has so often been the case, we must flee once more. There has been little peace, little more than temporary refuge for me for so many years now, that I fear the planning of one's next escape has become the way of our lives."

"Then perhaps I can put your mind to rest, my friend. I have not wanted to burden you with the knowledge, but the name of your poisoner is known to me." He watched the wide-eyed expression of shock dawn in the saturnine face.

"You know, but have not said?"

"Let me explain, Jean-Jacques, for he is also known to you. You will recall the unwelcome sight of the creature de Rais, that first day in Ashbourne?"

"That piece of shit? It was him?"

"I now know that he must have been in the druggist's waiting room, unseen, when I first took Thérèse to the shop in Ashbourne. It was then that she mentioned your fondness for sugar cane, and then that I placed an order for it on your behalf and, thinking I would shortly be departing for Cheshire, leaving instructions that all of your wife's purchases were to be billed to Woollaton in my absence."

The Frenchman nodded pensively, as if such generosity was no more than their due.

"So, de Rais' presence hereabouts was all about his hatred of me. Now of course I understand. He must have gone to considerable trouble to follow me here."

"Forgive me, my friend," said Davenport, managing only with

difficulty to suppress a smile at his guest's vanity, "but in this instance, at least, you were not the primary objective. Discovering your presence, by nothing more than ill-chance, simply provided him with an unlooked-for opportunity for revenge. You said he hated you."

"That he wanted me dead, yes."

"Well, then we must be grateful that not only did his plan fail but also that he has now fled the county. He is already marked as a wanted felon, guilty of abduction and attempted murder, and I have made it my business to see that the local authorities are publishing his crimes abroad. He will not escape the noose a second time."

"But if not for hatred of me, why then was he here at all?" responded Rousseau petulantly.

"He was employed by a wealthy lunatic, himself with pretensions to diabolism; a deranged recluse by the name of de Langton. It is said that evil attracts evil to itself and this would certainly seem to have been the case here. At my request," – Davenport smiled bleakly at the memory of his furious harangue of 'the proper authorities' – "Ashbourne's constables were immediately dispatched to a godforsaken ruin named Malbecq Priory, up on the high moors, once the circumstances of the crimes committed against you and our young guest were known."

"But he had escaped, already," shrugged the Frenchman as if nothing less could have been expected.

What they found, Davenport went on to tell Jean-Jacques, was utterly grotesque. A large part of the Priory had been set on fire, probably accidentally, though none could say the same of the circumstances of de Langton's death. Even to approach the abandoned, still-smoking ruins, the constables were forced to shoot half a dozen mastiffs in their own defence. Providentially, all were armed and capable men. What they found amidst the wreckage was the body of Malbecq's erstwhile master reduced to gnawed bones and tattered robes of ceremony, scattered amidst a great pentacle laid out upon the ancient floor.

One of the Priory's servants, returning, it was believed, to collect more loot from the ruins, had identified the sorry rags as his late, unlamented master, and telling scarcely believable tales of the satanic rituals that were a regular occurrence behind supposedly closed doors; telling of local, whispered rumours of the disappearance of Romani children some years back, of how in living memory the place had been shunned by all who knew of its repute, of locked doors, missing keys and an open kennel on the day de Langton had met his end; of an empty cell and, on a moorland road, an empty coach abandoned to the winds.

Knowing now that he had little alternative but to unburden himself of the whole story to his fiercely attentive listener, Davenport related how the finding of a book – a black legend thought lost for half a thousand years – had brought obsession, death and ruin, had opened up a portal to a waking nightmare still not closed, and had tainted all and everything it touched.

"But you are saying it is here, now, in that little chapel over there, Richard?" the Frenchman gestured out into the sunlit day.

"Yes, for a few days more. Until it can be destroyed."

"And yet you say it can defend itself?" smirked Rousseau, a derisive curling of his full lips an eloquent expression of his disbelief. "So, will it not do so? Will it not summon up a demonic host to stop you?"

"That rather remains to be seen," replied Davenport stiffly, dismayed and affronted by the disbelief that had met his sombre account. "I shall, at least, not be alone in the task. I am being joined by our friends from Lichfield for the solstice fire."

"By me also, if you will permit, Richard. It is my experience that we all demonstrate our faith – or lack of such – in different ways; none, I believe, any better or worse than the other. I intend no offence when I say this, but I shall count it as an honour if you will permit me to deliver this 'oh-so-terrible' book to the flames. I shall much enjoy armouring myself with the power of doubt, the strength of disbelief. It shall be treated with the contempt it deserves, if you will allow it?"

Davenport found his eye drawn to the salt that lined his windowsill, his mind's eye to the darkness that had taken vile, voracious form within this very room, his memory quailing in the recollection of its stench and oily grace.

"Oh, I shall indeed 'permit', Jean-Jacques," replied Davenport, amazed at his own acquiescence to the jaunty proposition, "though you are making an offer greater than you can imagine in the here, the now. None of us who have encountered that thing out there will ever choose to renew the acquaintance, believe me. You will be doing a singular service. Although, please understand, it shall have to be done at my direction. I cannot agree otherwise."

An eloquent shrug of acceptance was his response.

(46)

On the right Hand the Shell Case. A great variety of Gun
Locks, which ſhew the gradual progreſſion of fire Arms, from
the firſt invention of Gunpowder, to the present time, viz. A
large Spaniſh Lock for a Wall piece, or small Cannon. An
Engliſh Match-lock. A single Wheel-lock, invented in the year
1568, the eleventh Year of the Reign of Queen Elizabeth.
Snaphanch, or first kind of Snaplock, invented in Germany. An
ancient Snaphanch from Barbary, A large English Dog-lock.

Lichfield and Woollaton Hall. Tuesday 23rd June. Saturday's
coach from York had brought nothing but disappointment. After
timing Margery's distraction elsewhere to a nicety, and snatching
a covert snack from a sideboard already laden in anticipation of
Henry Copeland's arrival, the Apothecary was met with no more
than a letter handed down from the postillion's mail trunk.

Opened amidst the frenetic bustle of the George's yard it
informed the crestfallen reader that a bad ankle-sprain and several
cracked ribs, taken from a bad fall out riding, were preventing
Copeland's return. Instead, it proposed that Richard and
Theodosia should agree to an autumnal holiday as his guest, and
insisting that any protestations involving pressures of business or
demands of curatorship would fall on resolutely deaf ears.

When the news was broken at Saddler Street, Margery was
outraged – not only at such cavalier thoughtlessness after all
her preparations for the soldier's arrival, but particularly at even

the prospect that her employers – both of her employers, if you please – might choose to absent themselves on holiday from shop, customers, patients, home, even that museum and all the myriad other responsibilities to which she could not quite put a name at that moment. 'All well and good for those as can pick and choose how to spend spare time and not give a jot for those as haven't got so much as a moment to spare', she was heard to murmur darkly, out of sight but addressing a strategically open door.

"We shall just have to invite Lionel, perhaps Erasmus and Tolly, too, if they can be persuaded at short notice," Theodosia said briskly to her glum husband on hearing the news, "now that your bachelor Supper is cancelled and my own evening of gossip and scandal with Elspeth, too."

"Couldn't Lionel and I just dine..?"

"Oh, by all means, Richard. You and Lionel go ahead and dine at The George, as if you can face the prospect of a domestic treasure scorned. I might well be forced to change my name and flee the country unless Margery's bounty can be consumed by more appreciative recipients than just the two of us, but don't let that colour your decision."

Her husband raised both hands in surrender. "You are of course, correct, my dear. Thank you for saving me – at least from myself."

"If only that were more often the case, husband," replied Theodosia, suddenly weary. "We have not discussed the actuality of this supposed jaunt to Woollaton, have we? Do you really suppose that I have failed to gather the significance of this particular bonfire to be held on this particular day?"

Before her abashed spouse could respond she added, "Just tell me that with this we shall truly be done with the wretched thing for once and for all, Richard. I simply cannot endure the prospect of forced jollity and social decorum otherwise."

"I hope and pray we shall, my dear," he replied with conviction. "In every sense we shall be putting ourselves in what I believe are Davenport's trustworthy hands. Now, forgive me, but, as you suggest, I shall see who can be summoned in short order to this evening's parade. Failing that, Apothecary and Mrs Smith shall, doubtless, be forced to flee the country together."

As Woollaton's coach neared its destination with the long shadows of its elegant team trotting before them on the dusty road, Lionel broke the companionable silence that had descended on its occupants as they gazed, appreciatively, at the mellowing glow of evening descending upon the passing landscape.

"Seward must have thought all this Midsummer solstice business smacked a little too much of paganism," he declared, to no-one in particular, adding, "He obviously feared exposing the ever-fragrant Anna to the wiles and lure of Nature Unrepentant."

"Without betraying medical confidences, Lionel, I think you will find that the Sewards' absence has more to do with the aches and pains of advancing age and a certain young lady's aversion to politics of a Radical nature."

"Oh, so the Rousseaux are still with us, so to speak? Damn' good thing Harry couldn't make it, in that case," said Lionel, adding, "Confronted by the great proponent of Noble Savagery no less? What a match that would have been," before falling into an abrupt silence following a look from his wife.

"Well, I think it will be altogether delightful, especially with the entire Darwin brood to bring a little youthful vitality to the proceedings," said Theodosia, hoping she was not over-emphasising the youth aspect.

Straight-faced, she continued, "Shall we be expected to jump through the Midsummer flames, too, do you think, Elspeth? Or is that daunting privilege reserved for these big, strong menfolk of ours?"

As one, three passengers turned on cue to watch the constern-ation grow in the Reverend Blomefield's long face.

When she had awakened, that first morning, in the softest bed she had ever known, in a bedroom much the size of her family home, to the sound of birdsong through the graceful windows – open to a perfect sunlit day, Emmy wondered for an instant whether she had died and gone to heaven.

Only the heavy bandaging about her slashed wrists – suddenly sore and throbbing as if attention had reopened the awful wounds – brought memory, shocking, terrifying memory, crashing back down upon her, so that she wriggled down beneath an eiderdown, light as the feathers it contained, whimpering with fear.

Then, though, with all the resilience of youth, day on day, her fears ebbed. Colour flowed back into pallid cheeks whose hollows filled out, tray by tray, from all the enticing morsels and delicacies sent up to tempt her back to life. The high spot of each day, though, was the visit of the doctor – the very young, attentive doctor – upon whose shoulder she had slept, upon whose coat she had bled, for what little she could recall of that jolting, galloping escape from the nightmare of the moors. She found herself counting the hours between his visits.

For what little it was worth, her tormentor's face had never been revealed to her, not once throughout those dreadful, solitary hours and days. A time beyond time, painted in the colours of delirium, peopled with the faces of a world beyond her ken, of sights and sounds outside of any senses she had ever known. She had known him, though, the skull-faced brute whose bloodless lips scarcely parted for the issue of a rasping, ruined voice, whose pin-prick eyes – like chancres sunk in bloodless skin – brought out cold sweat from those they fell upon. Now, though, for all her fears, the ones that sneaked into the smallest hours, he was no longer there. As if a shadow had been wiped away, she found the way to smile once more.

For all that she had grown up loved and cared for in a home-spun way, here in the grand house of the kind old man, Emmy Tillett had been nursed and cosseted to a degree she'd never known – and, being of a most practical disposition – suspected she never would be again once she was well. This was a process not to be hurried – a conclusion not to be unduly wished for – she decided, sinking with a little sigh back into bolsters that seemed as soft as clouds.

She was hardly surprised at all to wake, at some small hour of the night before the guests were due, to see the silhouette. A figure; slim and elegantly lithe, seated, sprawled at ease against the tawny blackness of the sky, beside a window opened to the breeze. For what seemed like weeks now, night nurses had come and gone, some snoring gently at her bedside, others seated just where this one was. Throughout the day, and – for all she knew – the night-time, too, servants had flitted, in and out, each with her comfort, her well-being apparently their sole concern. She sighed and settled down, perhaps not awake at all, perhaps just dreaming that he stood – for he it was – and stretched, cat-like in his grace before he moved away, back into the deeper shadows, black on black, now gone.

Nominally in deference to his children's bedtimes, though in reality far more to do with the opportunity for an extended lunch, Erasmus Darwin had contrived his family arrival at Woollaton shortly after mid-day. Disembarking from the already well-tested Improved Chassis Model that was its inventor's current pride and joy, the family were warmly welcomed by a Hall's master anxious to reciprocate the equally genial reception that he and his own house-guests had received at the fine house by the West Gate.

To the newcomers' surprise, expecting only the Hall's master himself, they were introduced to his young wards, newly arrived from Capesthorne Hall, Davenport's even grander house in Cheshire. In their mid-teens, the most personable youth and his sister – presented as Jasper and Phoebe – took immediate charge of the Darwin sons and whisked the delighted boys off on a mystery tour of the estate's nooks and crannies.

"They do love it here, a world apart from the cobwebs and

rambling antiquity of Capesthorne," their host explained as they waved off the departing youngsters. "I thought our bonfire and your gracious company too good an opportunity for them to miss, so summoned 'em at short notice."

"Delightful, alt...t...together d...delightful," declared Darwin as they were then led into lunch.

"When do our fellow 'Feldians arrive?"

"As early as business and nurture permit, I gather," replied Davenport.

"At that rate, p...probably scarcely before our dawn s... solstice," exclaimed Darwin, adding ambiguously: "They put professional d...dabblers such as us two to shame, don't you think, D...Davenport? Never an idle m...moment in our Apothecary's day – or that of his d...dear wife – what with c...cough-drops and c...curios to occupy every waking m...moment."

"Well, speaking as a surgeon-dabbler myself, Doctor, I do wonder that Richard has never chosen to adopt a title such as our own. I can attest that the evidence of its award hangs discreetly on the wall of his Consulting Room – as, of course, you'll surely know, given your long acquaintance – though it would suggest that an uncommon degree of professional humility is one of our good friend's many virtues."

"Indeed, ind...deed," agreed Darwin with finality, knowing quicksand when he met it; instead, unbuttoning his corset-like waistcoat in anticipation of what a laden sideboard had revealed.

The awaited party arrived shortly before seven, ushered through to join the rest of the company on a broad terrace whose flagstones gave back the amber-gold of the setting sun. They had heard the strains of music when they first alighted, and now, as their host hurried to meet them, saw its source as a string quartet busily at work despite the buzz of conversation that filled the soft, evening air.

As introductions were made and wine and cordials served by liveried staff discreetly circulating amongst the scattered groups of guests, Theodosia, glancing appreciatively up at the wisteria-clad walls, caught sight of a pale face set within a nimbus of flame-red hair, framed in an upstairs window. Emmy gave her a shy, hesitant wave before ducking back into the room. Following her gaze, Davenport came to Theodosia's side, "Our Miss Tillett is making a remarkable recovery from an unspeakable ordeal. Not yet well enough to join us, I regret, but most satisfactory, nonetheless. She would, no doubt, welcome a brief visit if you were prepared to do her that kindness. You know, of course, that she would not be here at all, had it not been for your husband's extraordinary courage."

"My husband has been his usual, infuriatingly reticent self, Mr Davenport. I have gleaned little more than the fact – to quote his own words – that he found himself 'in the right place at the right time'."

"If that be so, Mrs Greene, it was no less than his third such intervention within twenty-four hours. Both Rousseau and I have cause to thank him for much the same." Before he could be persuaded to elaborate, the slovenly bulk of Erasmus Darwin hove to alongside the pair, the social equivalent of a heavily armed boarding party. Theodosia gave him a warm smile before disengaging and going in search of a guide to the upper regions of the Hall.

She found Emmy Tillett sitting alone in the elegantly appointed bedroom, the empty tray at her side attesting eloquently to a regained appetite, her heavily bandaged wrists peeping from a long-sleeved peignoir.

"Hello, my dear, I hope you will forgive this intrusion, but I just wanted to see how you are. I hear you are making a wonderful recovery?"

"Yes, and thank you, Mrs Greene," came the quiet, self-composed reply. "I am being looked after with such kindness. The doctor comes every day. I would not be here, though, but for Mr Greene. He was so brave, so wonderful."

She thought: Indeed, but you would not be here at all, would not have been enchanted, seduced by that appalling thing; would not have been lost to us, abducted as a bargaining counter in a deadly game, brutalised and left to die, had it not been for my husband. He is brave, he is wonderful, but not one jot of this grim, wrong-headed adventure has been to his credit.

None of this escaped her lips, however. Instead, she said, "We are both so pleased that all is now well, my dear. He sends you all good wishes and, if permitted by your most attentive doctor, will pay his respects tomorrow before we leave."

"That will be most agreeable," said the young woman.

"Your Uncle James, too, sends all good wishes. He has been so frightfully concerned for you – as have we all – but has not wanted to intrude upon your recuperation. May I tell him you are now well enough to receive him? I know he has sent a small gift via Mr Greene, but will be so happy to see you himself."

"That, too, will be most agreeable. Thank you for coming, Mrs Greene. I am so happy to see you."

As she went to leave, Theodosia looked fondly upon the demure, seated figure, seeing now that the last of the unformed, girlish plumpness in her face had been burned away by her ordeal, leaving a milk-white, elfin delicacy to features framed by the red-gold miracle of her hair.

"My word, you are growing up, my girl, and no mistake," Theodosia thought, admiringly, beginning to understand what had been described as the unfailing attentions of Emmy Tillett's young doctor – to whom she had just been introduced, among the guests on the terrace below. Turning back at the bedroom door, she saw that the young woman's attention had already turned to something beyond her window, her small foot tapping to the rhythm of a lively piece that drifted in upon the evening air.

In what certain of this evening's guests recognised as a significant social concession, Jean-Jacques and Thérèse Rousseau had not only mingled with engaging courtesy on the terrace, but now seemed determined to add a sparkling and animated frisson to the opulent dinner party. By the time that the last of seemingly endless courses had been consumed by an increasingly jocular company, informality reigned as places were exchanged in order that Rousseau could demonstrate some counter-intuitive trick involving two water jugs and a precarious assemblage of glasses; this, watched in grim fascination by a host whose superb glassware, was now being stacked in an unsteady pyramid. At the other end of the long dining table, Thérèse's robust laughter could be distinguished amongst that of her equally engaged female companions now clustered in a conspiratorial huddle around her.

Much later, when the ladies had withdrawn, fine port had been consumed, and complete defeat finally acknowledged by all concerned, the plan for the morning's events had been announced by a noticeably sober host. The more able-bodied menfolk – Erasmus Darwin having happily excused himself from their number, with Lionel Blomefield failing to come up with a convincing reason for so doing – would be awoken before dawn and together make their way up to the chapel and the bonfire, built and standing ready, close by it. Offering no explanations for his decision, Davenport announced his agreement to Rousseau's proposal – his insistence, in fact – that he be the one to remove a certain object from its place of concealment and convey it, in their company – to the waiting pyre.

At this juncture the Frenchman stood, unsteadily, and gave a perfunctory bow, before falling back heavily into his chair, having apparently understood every word of what was being said.

With a smile of acknowledgement to his guest, Davenport continued that he had calculated the timing of sunrise as accurately as he was able, and so the pyre would be lit without further delay, coinciding – it was to be fervently hoped – with the first rays of the solstice falling upon it.

Shortly after that, he added, with the fire once seen from the Hall, the ladies, children and assembled staff would all make their way to join the menfolk for a hearty breakfast to be served in the large tented structure erected on the far side of the chapel and safe from the expected conflagration. Were there any questions?

Knowing full well that the question he so urgently needed to ask was not about to receive any answer he would wish to hear, Greene kept his counsel, and made ready to ascend the wide stairs to the rest he craved.

"Richard, a brief word if I may detain you for a moment longer?" Davenport laid a fineboned hand on his sleeve, nodding towards the open door of the Hall's library.

Once within, he closed the door behind them, turning back into the room and raising placatory hands to the Apothecary before his guest had time to speak.

"I am not unaware that I owe you an apology for what must seem cavalier behaviour, my friend, but please allow me to put your mind at rest."

Greene nodded impassively, waiting for him to continue.

"The more I have considered recent events and the more I have been able to research anything remotely similar to what we have endured, I have become increasingly convinced that such phenomena as we have experienced are essentially constrained – I can think of no better word – though by what or by whom I cannot begin to imagine. They appear to occur only when there are no other witnesses, only ever seeming to involve one – or occasionally, as with you and poor Lionel – two participants. It is as if by occurring within such limitations, by denying all opportunity for further witness, further evidence or testament, the indefinable power controlling them, the unguessable intelligence behind them, protects itself to an astonishingly effective degree. Any who are prepared to – who are foolish enough to – speak out concerning otherworldly experiences are universally subjected to disbelief and ridicule at best, confinement for outright lunacy at worst."

"You refer of course to 'safety in numbers'," said Greene, with weary resignation, "much as I thought when we received your invitation. Look, Richard, you have presented us, me, with a *fait accompli* here – and are honest enough to recognise that – but that does not mean that I must like it, or that I do not fear its consequences. You may well be right in your researches – I have neither your resources," – he gestured about the superbly stocked room – "nor the time to pursue them. We can only pray that the conclusion you have drawn is the right one. God alone knows the answer to that one, and He alone knows whether our French friend is even remotely aware of what he is taking on – but, frankly, I can say no more."

He held up a hand to forestall Davenport who had been about to respond.

"Yes, forgive me, I know that you will have recounted our story as fully as it can be told, but the cold fact remains that Jean-Jacques has experienced not one jot of it himself. What conceivable space can there be for that thing out there – for its vile potency – in his 'universe of reason?'" He shrugged in defeated resignation. "But now, if you will excuse me?"

"Before you go, and we part agreeing to differ," – once more the long-fingered hand rested on the Apothecary's sleeve – "I must tell you something that has greatly exercised my mind since we last met, Richard. It concerns the chapel, our destination before dawn."

Greene waited, newly attentive.

"You mentioned, in passing, your meeting with its verger, its caretaker if you will, waiting to lock up as you left?"

The Apothecary nodded, puzzled now.

"There is no verger, not in my time here at least, no-one of whom I have ever been aware; although the dear old place is always neat and swept, the sanctuary light always lit. When first we spoke of it, I told you that the door was never locked, that it was open to all who might seek it out, day or night?"

Another wordless nod.

"Each night since your departure, since your deposit was made, I have walked up there." The word 'Excalibur' sprang into Greene's mind.

"I have been drawn to assure myself of its security, its concealment, but have been denied entry."

"Denied? By whom?" The Apothecary could not contain himself.

"Not so much by whom, as by what, Richard. The door has always been locked, but..." – he seemed to hesitate – "...but stranger still, and you will think my senses are failing me, there is no visible keyhole in that ancient door. I have looked over and again to no avail. The sanctuary light burns bright, within. Its oil must be refilled, but how? When? By whom?"

"So, in the morning we are to expect a locked door with no other means of entry. Is that what you are saying, Richard?"

"Do you know, my friend, I no longer know what to say – or think," replied Davenport, suddenly looking like a very tired, very old man; lost, adrift, for all the grandeur of his surroundings.

"I do believe that the morrow will provide, trite though that may sound," said the Apothecary, quietly. "Just as you intended, we shall not be alone."

She awoke with lazy contentment, sensing, then knowing that she was not alone. The silhouette, his silhouette, stood, just as before, with pliant, cat-like grace stretching out both arms against the summer night. This time, though, he crossed the Turkey rug with silent tread and came to stand beside her. The face, the sculpted body, all revealed now in the moonlit glow seemed to steal her breath away; she had not known such beauty could exist.

Then he bent and with him came the scent of every wildflower that she'd known, the fragrances of hearth and home, of everything she'd ever known or loved.

He whispered in her ear and promised just what her heart desired before he turned and faded back into the night.

ITEM:

A Glafs Jarr, containing a full grown female Foetus in Spirits:
The Parietal Bones of the Head, and part of the Frontal
wanting; no appearance of Brain, but with two thin membranes,
much resembling the Ears of a Hare, proceed from the back
part of the Skull, evidently an expansion of the Dura mater:
The Face broad and flat, feems as if funk into the Thorax
or Chest, there being not the least appearance of Neck.

Woollaton Hall. Midsummer Morn. Unbecoming though it
might have looked, his carefully shaven jaw slack, his eyes wide
with astonishment, Richard Davenport stood and simply gaped
at the sight before him. At his shoulder, their host's late-night
words still in his ears, Greene followed the incredulous eyes. An
ancient, brass-rimmed keyhole set just where a keyhole ought to
be.

The patrician features, lined with incomprehension, seemed
somehow to have aged as the two men stood there in the shadowed
porch. Behind them, both with torches lit against the pre-dawn
gloom, Blomefield and young Parr, their flames casting an eldritch,
flickering shadow-dance into the shallow porch. Rousseau stood
between them, impassive in the ever-changing light.

"We may well encounter stranger before we're done," Greene
murmured *sotto voce* to the dumbstruck man. "I do not disbelieve
a word of what you told me. Shall we?" He indicated the heavy
oak door.

Without a word, Davenport pulled it open.

They were met by the reassuring smell of candle-wax and dusty age, the tiny ruby flame of the sanctuary lamp a beacon to eyes that darted left and right and saw nothing more than empty, bleached oak pews.

"Bring in the torches if you will, gentlemen," called Davenport, beckoning the Frenchman to their side. "That which we seek is behind the altar, protected and well-concealed. Jean Jacques. Richard and I will retrieve it and bring it to you here." He indicated the nearest pew. "You have brought the gloves?"

Rousseau nodded, though not without a sardonic flicker touching his full lips.

After climbing up from the darkened house, they had first inspected the great wigwam of timber and inflammable detritus collected from all around the grounds over the previous week. Providentially, there had been no rain during its building, though this morning – of all mornings – substantial clouds rolled high up in the east, grey against the false-dawn sky. On their master's instructions, a tunnel-like passage had been constructed by estate workers giving a crawl-space access to the void at the centre of the pyre. The watching Frenchman had at first gestured forlornly to his pristine breeches before glumly acceding to the proposition with a gallic shrug.

The smell met them as Davenport and Greene approached the reliquary niche concealed behind the great stone-slabbed table of the altar. The older man held the torch aloft as the Apothecary crouched down towards it, his round face a mask of distaste as the stench seemed to grow around them. Momentarily, the small man flinched back at what the torch revealed within, coming to his feet suddenly and drawing a large pocket-handkerchief from his coat. "Rats," he said disgustedly, shaking his head. "No, in fact more than rats, a Rat-King clustered all around the book. I have heard of this weirdness but hoped never to encounter one. I shall need a stick or something similar to remove it before I can lift the book."

Seeing the mystification on Davenport's face, Greene explained, "Look for yourself; I have no idea of how or why it occurs, but it is astonishingly rare. Some call it a cryptid, something existing only in the realms of imagination, but here it is! Formed when the tails of any number of rodents become inextricably knotted together. Not just a couple, it can be dozens, or so I've heard. There must be twenty in there, long dead; they appear to have become virtually mummified by the salt I spread."

A short branch was retrieved from outside and handed across the altar. Clutching the kerchief to his nose, Greene managed to hook it beneath the grey-green corpses and, with some effort and gasps of distaste, pry the disgusting garland away from the stone shelf. Extending it as far beyond himself as could be contrived the Apothecary came around the altar and passed between the waiting company, each turning away in revulsion as the ghastly thing was borne past them. With elaborate care, Greene carried it across to the waiting pyre and flicked it onto the heaped timbers.

Greene returned to the waiting group within the chapel, passing a Frenchman whose normally saturnine features had taken on a discernible pallor. "Are you ready, Jean-Jacques, I shall bring the book out now if you are?" He was rewarded with a hasty nod.

Returning to join Davenport behind the altar, the older man pointed down at what the light revealed. "You told me," he said, "that you had placed those horseshoes there to form an iron cross?" Greene nodded, absorbing what he saw.

"There seems to be little but rust-flakes left of them, if that's the case. It is as if the iron has been eaten away, eroded somehow. Though look at how the shape you made of them seems to have burned into the cover-stuff itself." Neither man wanted a reminder of what they knew that 'stuff' to be.

"Shall we take a moment?" said Greene, quietly, bowing his head without waiting for a reply.

"Though I shall walk through the shadows of the valley of death I shall fear no evil," he began. Davenport joined him.

Greene knew that it was time. He bent, slid gloved fingers beneath the book and lifted it out. Davenport stood back to let him pass. He came around the altar and laid the book, still with its front resolutely concealed, down onto the pew.

"You are ready, Sir?" he asked the Frenchman with studied formality. "It is vital that you be sure."

With a curt nod, though little of the sardonic reaction that might have been expected, Rousseau stepped forward and bent to lift the book.

In other circumstances, his reaction might have been amusing. Here, this morning, it was not. He straightened as if to stand with his burden but could not. He tried once more. "But this is not possible, Mr Greene! It is far too heavy to lift, although I have just seen you do so." A note of panic had entered his voice.

"Gently, my friend, gently," said Davenport, appearing at his side. "This is but one of its many tricks. Remember the power of disbelief of which you spoke. Now is the time to use that power if you truly possess it. The weight is a deceit. Please try once more."

Jean-Jacques nodded terse acknowledgment to his host, before grabbing down and heaving with all his might. He would have toppled backwards had hands not been there to arrest his helpless fall, book clasped in both hands, eyes wide with astonishment.

"But now it is like a..."

"A feather?" interposed Greene. "Yes. I know that trick all too well. If you are ready, we should take it outside now."

Fortunately, though by Davenport's design rather than by accident, the young doctor had been asked to remain outside the tiny chapel all this time, his host having explained apologetically that they would need 'room for manoeuvre' within.

The young man remained obviously perplexed by all that was occurring but was too polite to interfere. Davenport had depended on it, but now invited him to form up with them as they emerged from the porch.

Between the chapel and the waiting pyre stood the much-eroded stump of an ancient preaching-cross, and it was towards this that he led the way. Each of his companions became increasingly aware of the Frenchman's laboured breathing, his apparent agitation as they neared the weather-worn stone.

"Do you need to stop, Jean-Jacques? Say so if you do!" asked Davenport urgently. In response, the Frenchman broke past them towards the stump, barely reaching it before his burden seemed to become too much to hold. "Merde!" he shouted, free of it momentarily, as he slammed it down upon the lichened stone. Before anyone could approach, he had pushed his gloved hands deep into his armpits, grimacing with pain, his teeth chattering audibly. "It has turned into a block of ice. What is this game? Some trick you are all playing at my expense? Well, à l'Enfer, tous. Tous!"

As the furious figure made to turn away, just as Greene shouted out his frantic warning, the book slipped from its precarious resting-place, tipping as it went and fell to the stony ground with a dull thud.

For one awful moment it seemed as if the angry Frenchman was about to kick it where it lay, but as they reached him, they saw him pause, staring intently down at the symbol of the cover now revealed, its wrapping thongs now loosed and spread like wiry snakes about it on the ground.

Before anyone could stoop to retrieve the fallen book, a crawling shape, now two, then three and more then more began to emerge from between its flaccid folds, glistening, airborne, a mounting, buzzing nightmare erupting from the fallen thing. Corpse-flies again, Greene knew, a silent shriek trapped in his throat as all five men reeled away as one, twisting, arms flailing as they tried to bat away the swarming, stinking cloud that engulfed them where they stood. Blinded, sickened as they spat the crawling horrors from their mouths, clawed at ears, at eyes to drive the dreadful plague away.

Without thinking, squirming with disgust and terror, the Apothecary fell to his knees, followed by the ever-thickening fog of wings, scrambling, reaching out with strength borne of desperation towards the fallen book. Somehow, he dragged it towards him, scraping it across the broken ground to grab it, sightless, and by touch alone to twist and knot the thongs about it, to turn its face back to the ground and bellow out the words, three words, he'd once found deep within a dead man's pockets sometime in a distant, long-lost past. Gasping, sobbing, spent with effort, he lay face down, incapable of movement, before he heard the others gather round him in a silence, a stillness he'd thought never again to know.

"They went, they simply disappeared! What did you do? What did you shout?" He heard the voices, their confusion, their relief, but scarcely had the will to even listen, until a pair of steady hands, young Parr's, helped him to his feet.

All five stood there, swaying, ashen, like the sole survivors of some nameless war, incapable of dealing with the horrors that they'd seen. Rousseau turned away and was violently sick. Mathew Parr looked as if he had aged ten years, while Lionel Blomefield simply glared at him in mute anguish.

"That is why we have to do what we came here for," Greene croaked. "Can anyone doubt that now?"

"But what is all this?" began the young doctor, helplessly, the certainties of education, faith, and entitlement lying in ruins about him.

With uncharacteristic bitterness, Greene turned to Davenport before replying, "Perhaps you'll be good enough to explain that to our young friend, but only when we've finished what we have begun. It will not wait, Richard." He pointed to what lay at his feet: "That thing can be picked up again now. For this moment at least, it is constrained."

Davenport could not meet his eyes, but stooped to lift the book from the base of the broken cross. "My turn now, I believe."

As he stood, his eyes were drawn to movement in the lightening sky above the timber stack that was their goal. He paused, squinting up into the ebbing gloom. Greene followed his gaze, watching as the distant wheeling shapes began to coalesce.

No chorus had yet begun to greet the dawn, but high up there beneath the rolling clouds, dozens first, then scores of black-winged shapes became a flock, a spinning vortex darker yet against the rising light.

"Hurry now, we must be done with this," Greene called, a new urgency to his cracked voice as he watched the birds, nearer, lower now it seemed.

Without a word, Davenport set out towards the timber-stack, not pausing when he reached it, but, careless of his attire, bending low to fall upon his knees and scramble in, disappearing with his load into the narrow tunnel.

It was only as he clambered out, some moments later, that Greene realised he had been holding his breath, waiting for the elderly man's reappearance. As he regained his feet, brushing away young Parr's assistance, Davenport's grimy face broke into an artless grin, as he raised a broad-clothed arm to point triumphantly to the sky. As if on some operatic cue, the parting clouds revealed the rising sun, the drabness of the overcast dissolving in the lancing rays, the landscape springing out in clean-lit life around them, the cawing, circling multitude above their heads louder with each swooping pass.

"Now, light up! Light up!" shouted Greene, urgent, command-ing, above the aerial din, the flapping thunder of a thousand wings filling the morning sky. First one, then another flame sprang from the huge pyre, as the air seemed to blacken around them, the fire racing up the tinder-stack, as more flames leaped from the tower of wood.

"Back to the chapel, I think," called Davenport, gazing in

trepidation at the immense flock above them, "as quickly as you like!"

Once more, as one, they turned to hurry back to the shelter of the old stone walls and had almost reached the shelter of the porch, when young Parr slipped and almost sprawled, headlong, caught by Blomefield hurrying at his side. Regaining his footing, he glanced back, astonished by the speed with which the bonfire had caught. Lionel hurried on, stooping now, ducking, as if the countless crows had marked him out. Suddenly, Parr shouted out, a strident bellow that halted Greene and Davenport in their tracks.

They followed his pointing hand to where a white-clad shape was hurrying towards the roaring blaze. "Miss Tillett! Emmy, no!" they heard him shout, as he launched himself towards the fast-approaching girl. Helplessly, they watched, transfixed, as he tried to reach her across the shimmering ground beyond the blaze.

As he sprinted towards the night-clad figure, a blur of wings slashed down across his eyes, a foetid breeze gusted across his face, as a huge black bird dived past his head, its beak, its claws a sulphur yellow gash across the morning sky. Then another swooped, a talon ripping at his scalp as desperation drove him on. With a look of mindless rapture spread across her freckled face, the young woman who had captured his heart entire, hurried, arms spread now, to embrace the flames.

With a last despairing roar, half-blinded now by blood, the young man threw himself upon her as another swooping crow ripped at his neck and ears. He somehow broke his crushing fall, as pain knifed up from an elbow smashed against the stony ground, protecting her beneath him as more wings beat past in fury and the wall of heat seared both across their unprotected skin. Then, suddenly, Rousseau was there, his coat wrapped about his turbaned head, dragging at Parr's arms to bring him to his feet, then both heaving, shouting with effort, until all three were clear, collapsed, exhausted as the blaze beyond them roared and whistled, scorching up into the morning sky.

One moment, Greene, Blomefield and Davenport were rushing towards them, heedless of the swooping birds, bent only on reaching the spent survivors now spread beyond the fire; the next, they were sightless, smashed back, reeling from a blinding detonation deep within the incandescence of the pyre.

It was only then that Emmy seemed to jolt awake, eyes wide with shock, with total incomprehension as they tried to cope with what they saw: a writhing, tortured shape, all pliant grace burned back to blackened bone, clawing, for an instant as it tried and failed to climb the flames, gone then in tattered rags of soot and smoke, just torn away. Strong arms gathered her once more, a shoulder cradling her head, the red-gold nimbus that had stolen his heart, held softly by hands that would never willingly let go of her again.

His sight was coming back, a world of silent black and white was giving way to sights and sounds as the sunlit morning flooded back into their lives. Where countless birds had been were only some few blackened leaves, left fluttering to earth.

Richard Greene reached out shaking hands to grip his friends. That was enough.

(48)

A Nofe Flute, of hollow Cane perforated. A Fly brufher. A Bracelet for the Arm, compofed of Tufks of the Wild Boar, drilled, and faftened by a small twisted line. A Decoy for taking Fifh, being several Courie Shells faftened together by Strings, to a conic piece of Stalactite. Three four-footed Stools, of hard Wood, ufed for Pillows to fupport the Neck when they Sleep. Eafter Ifland. All the before-mentioned Articles were brought over by Captain Cook and other Circumnavigators, and prefented to the Museum by the Right Honourable the Earls of Uxbridge and Donegall.

The Museum, Saddler Street. 6ᵗʰ August. The heat had been stifling these last ten days, and even now, with every window open to what little early evening breeze there was, this uppermost floor of the tall house was as close to stifling as they could bear. Whilst the longed-for release of a thunder storm remained little more than a hint, a south-westerly smudge in the evening sky, the memory – a hastily contrived fiction – of a wildly errant strike of 'Summer Lightning' remained all too vividly in the minds of the four men who had staggered away from the solstice inferno in the company of the Apothecary. All faced the unenviable task of somehow finding the means to explain the inexplicable to the nearest and dearest fast approaching the scene. Looking back, a rueful Greene had to admit to himself that taller stories might have been swallowed, but not often.

Tonight, though, the reason for his – and Lionel Blomefield's – early departure from a supper served alfresco in the garden's blessed shade, now stood before them, wrapped, mysterious and wholly unexpected. Although delivered late that afternoon by a Derby carrier, it was only now that the object was being weighed tentatively in Greene's hands. He had valiantly resisted that childhood urge to shake it and see if it rattled, before picking up his scissors. With Blomefield craning over his shoulder he came across the letter first, tucked between the wrapping layers, and – congratulating himself on his patience and restraint – paused to break its seal before he continued. He read its contents aloud:

My dear Richard,

An infinity of unspoken words will always now lie between us, so now I shall be brief.

I leave for Capesthorne on the morrow, in company with the youngsters, but also with Miss Tillett, To my great pleasure Phoebe and that charming girl have become as close as peas in a pod over these summer weeks, and, for a time, Esmeralda returns with us as a companion to my own dear girl.

Though sharing a natural reluctance, both her Mother and a young Doctor of our acquaintance believe that a change of air, perhaps a removal from a place of more-than-mixed memories, will complete the healthful revival of a remarkable young woman.

She will, we can both be certain, return to more than one warm welcome before winter is upon us.

Our French friends have flown the coop, these two weeks past. Jean-Jacques – for all my reassurances – still pursued by the fears of malice and persecution that appear to be his inseparable companions.

Both he, and the ever-patient Thérèse asked that their felicitations be passed on to you and your dear wife – this I gladly do. To the matter in your hand: I have thought long and hard before parting with the treasure you now hold but give it now to say what words cannot.

I can think of no worthier recipient, nor of any better friend.
Richard Davenport.
August 5th at Woollaton Hall.

"Mmm. Most elegantly put. So, open it for pity's sake!" exclaimed the impatient cleric.

There was no stopping now; first a baize-backed frame came free of its many layers of waxed paper, and, when turned, revealed its contents to Greene in a single, heart-stopping moment of delight. "Oh, is that it?" came the deflated enquiry. It was ignored.

Behind the wafer-thin glass, three pieces were arranged: faint lines drawn out upon a fly-spotted sheet with corners chewed, a fold-line down its centre. A plan of Tutbury Castle, its title and a date of 1601 scrawled in an untidy hand. Next, a frayed and grubby scrap of needlework, its fleurs-de-lys deftly worked in wool and metal thread; then last – this was at the heart of all he held: a stained, part-ruined thing, its penmanship here smudged, there crossed through, its scratchings-out as lengthy as the text that still remained.

Greene drew a wondering breath, alone now in a world of utter absorption, then set the frame to stand where best the writing could be read. The fragment took him to a place devoid of hope, of sun, of all the things he knew and loved, the things that made his life worthwhile. It shook him to the core. He was holding in his hands Mary of Scotland's own account, written in her own hand, of the most reviled of her sixteen places of imprisonment. Quitting that gaunt, hilltop fortress, she had been led to Fotheringhay and her death.

Within the said enclosure there is a very old hunting lodge
built of timber and plaster cracked in all its parts, the plaster
adhering nowhere to the wood-work and broken in numberless
places; the said lodge – two lines were deleted, illegible from
angry strokes – *and situated so low that the rampart of earth*

which is behind the wall is on a level with the highest point of
the building, so that the sun can never shine upon it on that
side, nor any fresh air come to it for which reason it is so damp
that you cannot put any piece of furniture in that part without
its being in four days completely covered in mould. I leave you
to think how this must act upon a human body; and in short
the greater part of it is rather a dungeon for base and abject
criminals than a habitation fit for a person of my quality, or
even of a much lower... The only...

It ended there, the writer's name, the date of her misery barely legible beneath the furiously scrawled redaction.

A stage-yawn drew the Apothecary back to the museum room and bored companion. "Have you any idea who wrote this, Lionel?" he enquired quietly, his eyes drawn back to the grubby page.

"Someone most unhappy with their lot, I'd say. Hardly the thing for the interruption of a summer evening's supper though, if you'll forgive me for saying so, Richard. We've had more than our fair share of gloomy nonsense if you ask me."

"You're right, of course, old man," said Greene as brightly as he was able, recognising defeat when it stood beside him. "Why don't you go back down? I feel sure Elspeth will be missing you, and I believe a rather special dessert is in the offing." That was all it took, for his companion's rapid exit. "I'll join you shortly," Greene called to the departing back.

He sat then, as the sound of the hour struck from the Cathedral's Jesus Tower, the sonorous ring amplified as it tolled across the Minster Pool in the last of the evening light.

A great silence seemed to follow, as the curator of the Lichfield Museum sat, motionless and lost in thought, surrounded by the exhibits of a lifetime's passion; each piece, each fragment speaking of a long-lost past. A murmur here, a whisper there, a language spoken to the ear of faith; an imprint here, a faded image there, all signs and symbols to the eye of faith.

The voice that cried out from that inky sheet had chilled him through and through; its anguish and its desolate fury diminished not one jot by all the years since then. He saw her thoughts, her bid to marshal all she had endured set down, scratched out, then started over again in another bid to speak, to plead with ever-lessening pride, to distant, heedless power. An aching lament for seventeen stolen years. And yet where this cried out with all the vital strength remaining to a Queen betrayed, a plea from deep within a broken human heart, that thing that they had burned those weeks ago left nothing but a fading stench, a smear of rancid ash from what had held the arcane words, the honeyed lures and guileful traps that spoke of nothing that could live in light. It spoke to greed, to empty lust, of treasures promised but forever out of reach, of pacts that turned to smoke, and magic mirrors cracked beyond repair. And he had brought it here.

'No book should ever take the place of a living, breathing love'. Only now did the heartfelt profundity of his cousin's words take up their rightful place.

Now though, before introspection could begin to slip and slide down into despondency, footsteps sounded out beyond the landing door, footsteps loud upon the stairs, but advancing no further than the forbidden threshold.

"Mistress says as I've to tell you that she should've thought to tell you to be down in time to see what was made special for tonight's pudding. But seeing as it's there already now, brought out without you there, you're too late anyhow even though the reverend didn't spoil it all and got back in good time to see what was made so special, like, just for tonight. Don't know whether there'll be any left by now, that's if you even want to come and see what took a body most of a day to make."

It started as a grin, then spread to shoulders that began to shake, contained without success by a handkerchief pressed hard against his mouth and nose before exploding into helpless laughter, masked only by the sound of a slamming door and footsteps clumping emphatically down to floors below. He stood, quaking with laughter and made to follow.

"Endlessly caring," he murmured to himself as he returned with a new spring to his step, back to the land of the living.

finis

Artist, academic and sometimes bluesman, Michael Anson lives in Norfolk, England.

Acknowledgements

A particular thank you to Joanne Wilson, Museum and Heritage Officer at the Samuel Johnson Birthplace Museum, for her unstinting help in providing access to the prized copy of Greene's 1786 catalogue, items from which feature as chapter headings in each of the Apothecary Greene novels. In addition, the original catalogue frontis appears as an insert in the opening text.

The sole remaining trace of Jean-Jacque Rousseau's 'stranger than fiction' Staffordshire sojourn in 1766 is 'Rousseau's Grotto' at Ellastone. The now-roofless void formed in the natural rock was once enclosed by the terrace of Richard Davenport's grand house that stood above it, before being destroyed by fire a century later. It was in here that the great philosopher began work on his 'Confessions'.

Now described as the first genuine autobiography, it was first published, in Lichfield, in the 1780's.

Rousseau and his wife fled Davenport's hospitality when the Frenchman, notorious for his paranoia, became convinced that the Hall's servants were planning to poison him.

Although Bishop Walter de Langton was arraigned for 'Witchcraft and Conjuration' around the year 1300, as described in the text, the details of his two-year trial – if any survive – await rediscovery in some archival substrata of the Vatican. Pope Boniface, his judge on these and additional charges of Simony and Adultery was, himself, later charged with Witchcraft and the summoning of demons by the King of France. However unsavoury his reputation or his seemingly universal unpopularity, neither prevented de Langton's return to wealth and influence as Edward 1st's treasurer, and, subsequently, his appointment as the King's executor. He died at Eccleshall Castle in 1321 and is buried somewhere in Lichfield Cathedral, though all evidence of his tomb's location was destroyed along with most other monuments during the Civil War.

My thanks to both Bernadette Schmidt for her front cover photo of 'The Jaws of Hell', a remarkable carved medieval bench end from the church of St. Benedict, Horning, Norfolk, and to Bob Yeatman of Eastern Lightcraft for the back cover image.

My gratitude to Ralph James MBE. and to Nick Bundock for their invaluable pedantry, and, as ever, to Tom O'Reilly at Page d'Or, for his continued patience with a variety of authorial foibles.

ALSO IN THE APOTHECARY GREENE SERIES

The Burning Zone

Little knowing that the unearthing of a medieval grave slab will propel him into the realm of waking nightmare, Richard Greene, apothecary, antiquarian and museum-keeper extraordinaire, is the sole witness to a sadistic murder.

Badly injured in the doomed attempt to save the victim of a fire universally believed to be a tragic accident, Greene emerges from lengthy convalescence only to be drawn into the coils of a demented and murderous search for vengeance enacted from beyond the grave and across generations; a pitiless ritual of retribution inflicted upon all who had sat in judgement upon England's last heretic – the victim a crazed Anabaptist – sentenced to die a hideous death in the last judicial burning to stain English history.

Now, as the century of Enlightenment gathers pace around him, the terrors and obsessions of an earlier, darker time reach out to claim one final victim: the woman at the heart of Greene's own life.

A final offering to sate the ravening hunger of 'The Burning Zone'.

The Ashmole Box

Providential chance brings Apothecary Richard Greene to the aid of a terribly injured man – the victim of a mantrap on a nearby estate. An encounter that will ultimately reveal the survival of an astonishing Roman artefact – and with appalling symmetry – bring about not only the deaths of all who seek to gain from its discovery but also force Greene into questioning the passions and principles that have been the touchstones of his life.

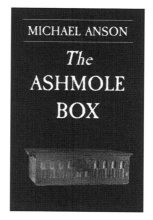

Beside that unravelling strand of sadistic cruelty, deprivation and corrosive greed, another narrative begins – a story close-on a century and a half in the making – when The Ashmole Box (and the deathless mystery it conceals) arrive at Greene's Museum door.

Somehow, then, as if the veil of time itself is pierced, a revenant, a memory so real in both its power to mystify, to terrify, is summoned by the opening of the long-forgotten bequest. A half-seen presence in a tower consigned to memory, a pointing figure glimpsed in a flag-draped aisle, a nightmare vision of a dance of death.

With every passing day the years that separate the long-dead Ashmole and the hapless inheritors of his legacy seem to dissolve and intertwine, as first one and then another of the cryptic pointers yield their secrets and point the way to a discovery beyond the Apothecary's wildest imagining.

To a place of ancient wonder whose guardian is Death.

The Ashmole Box
by Michael Anson

(4)

ITEM:

The following Medals in Sulphur, gilded. Oliver Cromwell,
Sir Isaac Newton, Pope Clement the 12th. Benedict the 13th.
Two Sons of the Chevalier de St. George.

Intrigued, though with wilting patience, the Apothecary sat across
from the clergyman he had known for so many years, knowing
that he was being played along. For several minutes, the gaunt
figure seated across from him craned this way and that, admiring,
quizzing and commenting on a variety of the exhibits; anything,
in fact, rather than admitting to the presence of the still-wrapped
object that sat between them on the polished tabletop.

Finally, he relented, and with a grin that stripped the years
away from his face, exclaimed: "Patience being the virtue that it
is, today you have excelled yourself, Richard. I'd wondered if you
could be persuaded to explode!"

Greene laughed, replying: "The fuse was lit, Lionel; great age
has withered none of your pyrotechnic skills. So now, unless your
package contains a collection of your briefer sermons, put me out
of my misery for pity's sake."

Suddenly earnest, though obviously relishing the moment,
Lionel Blomefield removed the covering with a flourish, revealing

a fine, scratch-carved box, much the size of a family bible; that being precisely, in fact, what Greene now expected it to contain.

"No, it is not," said Blomefield, intuitively, beating his old friend to the punch with another grin, reaching deep within a pocket as he did so, and continuing: "And if its contents are a mystery now, how much greater will they be when you read this, that accompanied it?"

As Greene reached out for the folded paper, he had time to glimpse a broken wax seal upon it before it was whisked away by his old, but more than usually trying, friend. Blomefield raised a mollifying hand to Greene's hiss of frustration: "The story of its delivery, first, followed then by its rediscovery." Greene groaned with resignation and sat back, bowing to the inevitable.

"According to our nicely painted signboard, one of my predecessors, Harrison by name, held the living of St Mary's from the early 1640s until well into the 1680s. – no small achievement in itself- though he was, by the few accounts still extant, a man of some standing and substance. It was to him this box was sent, in May of 1692. Therein, however, lies the first problem."

"That being?" enquired Greene, wearily; understanding his allotted role.

"That being that the Reverend Harrison had, by then, been the late Reverend Harrison for more than twelve years."

"Ah," said Greene, with no idea where this was leading.

"You should now, perhaps, become apprised of this," said Blomefield, handing the paper to Greene with no further prevarication; "The subsequent problems arising from it will then start to become apparent."

The Apothecary took the folds without apparent haste and pulled spectacles from a waistcoat pocket. He scanned the pages first: two narrow, grubby, ill-kempt sheets whose content – scrawled and blotty – promised little at first glance. He would realize within a dozen lines the extent of his misjudgment.

Brother Harrison,

Remiss in both my correspondence and felicitation
tho I have been these many months past,
I beg forgiveness of yr generous heart.
Accept now my greetings and a gift.
Gift indeed though it is meaned to be,
your tutored eye will plainly see
that which is concealed to be greater still,
though more as burden than as gift it could be descried
albeit by some lesser man.

I should have chanced on none of this,
had not the Source of your own gift led me to it.
For twas he that led me to an ancient place
whose key - though it lies now in yr hand -
was cannily contrived by old Row.Lee

For fear of peeping eyes and busy tongues I shall write no more
for you old friend shall read with ease my veiled import.
I have acted not without honour in this matter,
but much lacking in courage and firm judgement
though it shames me so to say.
Mayhap as free agent which I never was,
you may straightway
perceive a way where I saw none.

As above, so below.
Tis perception wherein fortune lies.

For him that you will doubtless meet
employ I pray your Best Offices
that he may be given the decent repose I could not bestow.

From him that I believe you will surely come upon
I pray you ask a similar benison,
and his intercession for your true friend.

Elias Ashmole.   at Lambeth.

Greene simply gaped. Ashmole: The historian of the Order of the Garter, Herald and genealogist, numismatist, epigraphist, connoisseur and lauded collector, one of the great names of Restoration England; the eponymous museum in Oxford one of the greatest ornaments of his troubled century. He read and reread the letter several more times before finally looking up at his visitor

Lionel Blomefield sat regarding the Apothecary with a mixture of amusement and intense expectation written across his bony features. "Well, did I exaggerate? Is it no more than the ramblings of a dying man, or is there something going on here that is passing me by in its entirety?"

"A dying man?" responded Greene.

"Indeed," said Blomefield, again fishing in his pocket. "Along with the letter, the counterfoil of a carter's receipt was inside the box when we happened upon it."

He finally retrieved what he sought and squinted at the crumpled note before passing it to the Apothecary.

"May 26. 1692." He read aloud. "St Mary – and some squiggle of a signature that is wholly illegible," said Greene.

"A churchwarden or some such, one imagines;" commented the cleric – "whoever took delivery of the thing. Its only address being St Mary, Lichfield. Where else could it have been taken; Harrison or no Harrison? And…" he grinned once more, "…by some strange chance it was delivered on precisely the same day as his own funeral, so I have learned. Writing that and sending this must have been among Ashmole's final acts. It would have taken a good week to arrive."

More than one cog strove to engage in Greene's head.

"So, you came across this where?" he enquired, an unworthy suspicion taking shape in his mind.

"In the lumber-room above the church porch. The priest's room, as was," replied Blomefield, looking away suddenly as if he had anticipated the Apothecary's next question.

"And you came across this when?" Greene continued, in a voice of sweet reason.

"Er… less than… no more than…"

"How long have you been trying to work this out, Lionel? How long have you been keeping this to yourself, Lionel?"

"Scarcely…" Blomefield began, a scarlet blush betraying his embarrassment.

"And when did you finally have to admit defeat, Lionel, and say 'I suppose the only thing left is to take the wretched thing to good old Richard and get him to crack the mystery for me,' Lionel?"

Blomefield capitulated, throwing grubby-cuffed hands up in mock surrender.

"My deceit has found me out! I've spent weeks poring over the damned thing without a glimmer of inspiration; and it's not as if the contents have helped one jot. Look for yourself. It is why I concluded that you would be the only man in Staffordshire who might perceive the slightest merit in them, Richard."

He shrugged and smiled disarmingly: "I had meant you to be a party to all this from the start, it's just that…" he tailed off, this time prompted by rather more than the theatrics of a moment past.

Greene continued where his old friend had left off: "…It is just that when we get so much as a sniff of the scent of the Secret, the Hidden, an inkling of something of value squirreled anciently away, our better judgment turns to putty, whilst our highly regarded propriety is all too often left at the door? Just as I number myself amongst the Fallen, I am heartily relieved that clergymen are as prone to frailty as we lesser mortals, Lionel."

"Look, then - for heaven's sake - at what all the fuss is about," Bloomfield said, diverting his obvious embarrassment by throwing open the lid and finally revealing the interior of the box.

"Oh, my word," responded Greene, peering in with rapt attention. "How very peculiar."

Praise for Michael Anson's *The Burning Zone*:

"...a well-crafted, well-constructed novel ... could do for Lichfield what Cadfael did for Shrewsbury."

— Ralph James MBE, *The Lichfield Mercury*

"The interesting balance of fact and fiction make this a great read and a real page turner."

— Alison Smith, *Express and Star*

Printed in Great Britain
by Amazon